Distortion

ANNE GRANGE

Published by Ramraid Press, Sheffield, UK, in 2016.

ISBN-13:
978-1541175891

ISBN-10:
1541175891

To everyone who lives to create.

If you play music, create art, craft, write, act or dance, you have a passion in life that should never be extinguished.

You may nurture and grow plants or cook wonderful meals. You may live a life full of compassion and caring for animals, nature and the future of our planet.

You may be creating an amazing new human being and bringing them up with the gifts of love and imagination.

There may be tough times ahead.

There will be barriers and blocks in our way; people and circumstances wanting to stop us.

The barriers may be within ourselves, forcing us to struggle daily towards the light.

If we help ourselves and each other, we will keep doing what we love.

There are choices that we make and things beyond our control.

It's up to us to make the best choices we can.

Anne Grange, December 2016

Thanks to Christopher Crewe for helping me to edit the book and putting up with me for almost twenty years!

A big thank you to Susie Morley for the wonderful artwork that really makes *Distortion* stand out from the crowd, and for the Ramraid Press logo.

Many thanks to all the people who beta-read the novel and persuaded me that it wasn't too long, including Kirsty Chamberlain, Sarah Peacock and Graham Matthews. The Sheffield Novelists Writers' Group read chapters of this novel for several years during the first draft and gave me great feedback.

Thanks to my parents for their support and their constant faith in me.

To everyone at Bearded Theory festival, which has inspired *Distortion,* with a special mention to John Gill, who encouraged me to pick up a guitar a very long time ago! Thanks to the Oxfam Festival Stewarding team and the whole Oxfamily.

Twitter: anne_grange

Facebook Page: Distortion and Outside Inside

Professional writing, editing, and teaching: wildrosemarywritingservices.wordpress.com

Also available by Anne Grange: ***Outside Inside***, a novel about love, betrayal and cider.

Chapter 1
September 2008
Something's Started

Jason

'Oi! Pikey!'

Bradley Smeed and his mates are lounging against the bus shelter on the opposite side of the road. I turn away, pretending they're not there. I feel like I'm acting my life and I have to be word perfect.

The guitar is still in the window of the charity shop. It looks dusty and unloved, but I want it.

'I'll look after the bikes,' Ben says. I lean my crappy bike up against the bench, and Ben gets his *NME* out.

I push the door of the shop open, ignoring Bradley. He can call me a pikey all he wants. He's not stopping me from getting the guitar.

Inside the shop, everything's muffled and peaceful. The air is smothered by the smell of mothballs and musty old books.

Mavis, the charity shop lady, looks up from sorting out a tangle of jewellery. She smiles at me and offers me a mint imperial from the crumpled paper bag on the counter. She used to give them to me when I was little, when Mum wasn't looking.

I shake my head.

'The guitar…' I cough, getting a whiff of her perfume stuck in my throat.

Mavis bustles over to the window and takes the guitar from where it's been leaning against the glass. Bradley Smeed must be watching the shop because I can hear his gang shouting and laughing in the background, mixed in with the noise of cars.

Mavis hands the guitar to me. I don't know what to do with it. I scrape my finger over the strings. The jangle sets my teeth on edge. Obviously it's out of tune but I don't know how to make it sound right. It's worse than it looked in the window. The varnish is scratched and there are dents in the wood.

'I thought you might like it.' Mavis gives me an indulgent wink. She fiddles with her plastic necklace. 'It's ten pounds, but just for you, it's a fiver. You're one of our best customers.'

I'm so glad I'm alone in the shop. What sort of thirteen year old goes into a charity shop every night after school?

I found a tape of Combat Rock by the Clash last week. Someone in Wirksworth must have had great taste in music once. You have to rummage through loads of rubbish and CDs someone's skated across the floor on, but sometimes it's worth it.

There's no brand name on this guitar. It's probably crap. If it's as bad as it looks, it can just go straight back to the shop. If I ask nicely, Mavis might let me swap it for some tapes.

Mavis feels sorry for me. Mum used to take me here all the time. I didn't mind wearing second hand clothes from head to toe. When I was little, Mum told me Mavis slept here, using lacy tablecloths as blankets. I actually believed her.

I put my hand in the pocket of my uniform trousers and take out a mixture of coins. I count out five pounds, going into silver and coppers, everything I've got, and put the money into Mavis' outstretched palm.

Ben's dad paid us for creosoting his garden fence in the summer. Not much left from my share now. I wonder if the neighbours need any odd jobs doing. I'd even shovel horse muck for money to buy records.

Mavis rings the sale through the till. Where else am I going to get a guitar for five pounds? What if I can't play it?

'Silly me, I forgot. It came with a case.'

Mavis disappears into the back of the shop, returning with a grey fake leather cover, like a cheap slip-on shoe. It's got a long strap, so I can sling it across my back when I'm on my bike. I zip the guitar into the bag.

I take a deep breath and push the door open. It should

be a relief to get into the fresh air, but Bradley Smeed and his henchmen are still at the bus stop.

'What's that you've got there, Kenny? Are you going to give us a tune?'

I don't dare to shout anything back. I cling onto the guitar, even though the case looks like dead elephant skin and makes my fingers sweaty.

Bradley Smeed has called me Kenny ever since my first day at primary school. I wore a coat with a big fake-fur lined hood. The hood felt soft. Mum walked me into the playground and kissed me goodbye. Bradley barged up to me when I was waiting with Ben. He looked really big and scary, like he owned the playground. Bradley shouted "Kenny" in my face. I told him my name was Jason.

He didn't stop calling me "Kenny". I didn't even know what he meant. We still don't have a TV at home – Mum refuses to. I watched an episode of South Park at Ben's house and saw the kid in the orange parka getting killed in a gruesome way. I deliberately lost my coat. It wasn't even orange.

It's not just about that coat. It's about my free school dinners and my cheap trainers – about everything I have and everything I do being a reason for him to hate me.

I keep my head down as I walk towards Ben.

'Great – you got the guitar.'

'Yeah, but it's crap,' I mumble.

'As long as you can get a tune out of it.'

'Not even sure about that.' I kick at the gravel on the pavement.

Ben pulls a thick stapled wodge of A4 paper out of his bag and hands it to me. The title says "Beginners' Guitar Manual", with a grainy drawing of an acoustic guitar on the cover. I flick through the pages – loads of numbers on horizontal lines, and diagrams with boxes and dots.

'It's what my guitar teacher uses. He wrote it himself – about a million years ago. I got Mum to photocopy it for you at work.'

'Thanks.' I shove it into the guitar case. I don't want to

look at it until I get home. What if I don't understand it?

'It'll get you started. I've learned most of the chords now.'

We get on our bikes. I arrange the guitar case and my school rucksack so they both balance on my back. Ben got a new mountain bike for his birthday last year. Mine's his cast-off. I've outgrown it already, the saddle screwed up as high as it'll go. The scratches are covered up with Mum's black acrylic paint.

'Pikey!'

'Kenny!'

'Scrounger!'

The insults blur into each other – shouted at my back. Sometimes I let myself believe them. I can't stop my cheeks from burning. It feels good to be out of town, cold wind rushing into my face, cruising downhill until the road starts to climb again. I can feel the guitar, bumping around on my back.

Before we get to the turn-off to Bolehill village, the bus rumbles past. A crushed Diet Coke can flies out of one of the little open windows, missing my face by millimetres. It bounces into the hedge. I nearly wobble over in the rush of wind behind the bus. Bradley Smeed shouts something and flicks his wrist at me through the back window. His mates flatten their faces against the glass as the bus squeezes under the bridge.

'Fucking scumbag!' I yell, not that Bradley Smeed can hear me now.

Ben brakes behind me.

'They can't do it for ever. Just wait until you've turned into a rock god.'

'Yeah, right.' I can always trust Ben to make me laugh.

Kaz

The sound of a guitar string being played, way too low, rattling against the frets, a boinging noise as the tuning peg is turned.

I freeze on the attic stairs, my right foot mid-air, carrying a pile of Jason's washing. Did I imagine the noise that just came from his room?

I listen. It sounds like he's trying to tune an acoustic guitar. I clutch the pile of t-shirts and Jason's ripped jeans to my chest in shock, remembering Daz; the way he guided my fingers onto the frets of that battered old classical guitar. I grab the banister for balance, so I don't tumble down the steep stairs and land in a pile of broken limbs.

My hand trembles as I knock at the door. I started knocking earlier this year, when he turned thirteen. It's not a good idea to barge in on him anymore. He needs his privacy.

'Mum?' he calls.

I push the door open and dump the washing on top of the chest of drawers. Jason's sitting cross-legged on the bed, hunched over a knackered-looking steel-string guitar. He stares up at me with a hopeful expression, pushing his fringe out of his eyes. I suddenly feel like someone punched me in the guts. There's a photocopied guitar tutorial in front of him. He's still wearing his school uniform. The trousers are too short, with a gap between the hems and his socks.

'I can't get it tuned right,' he moans.

'It looks like an old piece of shit. Did you get it from school?'

Jason gives me a wounded glance and I feel instantly guilty. For a second there, I almost thought Jason was Daz. I used to speak to Daz like that – but Daz was used to far worse.

Jason shrugs almost imperceptibly, fixing his attention back to the guitar. He's de-tuned the bottom string too low, making it wobble against the fingerboard, but he carries on turning the tuning pegs, his tongue sticking out.

He still has Harry Potter posters on his bedroom walls; his own drawings of Star Wars characters; a collection of snail shells, pebbles and bird skulls on his bookshelf. Band posters are tacked onto the sloping ceiling: My Chemical Romance from Jason's big emo phase that started when he was eleven. I suppose I shouldn't have been massively surprised he discovered Manic Street Preachers – and he's found a poster of them in their eyeliner heyday. Going even further back, he's got the classic Clash poster with Paul Simonon captured forever, about to smash his bass.

'Haven't you got anything better to be doing?'

'No.'

He throws the guitar on the bed. He stares at me with an expression full of thunder, dark eyebrows knotted. I recognise Daz's scowl combined with the look of frustration I often saw in the mirror when I was Jason's age. Maybe if I walk out of the room now, the guitar will never be picked up again, like the wooden model castle kit he wanted so badly for his tenth birthday. He stuck one of the turrets on the wrong corner with Superglue and then dumped it in the shed for kindling. I'd never burn a guitar, even a bashed-up one like this.

I sit on the bed. I pick up the guitar and put it on my knee.

'Don't make it worse,' he warns.

There's a charity shop price-tag on the side of the guitar.

'You bought it?'

He nods and stares at his faded duvet cover. I feel even guiltier for slagging off the guitar.

I wish I could buy him better, new things. He wanted an iPod for Christmas, but instead, I bought him a stereo I found in Oxfam. A bit old fashioned now – Jason calls it retro, but it's got a CD player, a tape deck and a turntable. It still works perfectly – and loudly. He's covered it with hand-graffitied stickers, like something Daz would have done.

The pile of tapes and CDs on the shelf next to his stereo is growing – and he's so proud of his slim stack of vinyl…

●

I'm back in my own bedroom, fourteen years old, that Joy Division bassline ripping through my head as I lie on the bed listening to the John Peel show. I'm standing outside the school music room, gathering the courage to investigate the guitar playing and drumming I've heard every lunch time for months...

I was half-hoping the musicians would be a band of sexy sixth-formers but they're two lads from my year. Lanky, awkward Darren Pratt – I mean, what a name – and his chunky ginger mate Pete Hollis. They were a permanent fixture in the library at lunch and break-times, reading sci-fi novels or 2000AD comics. So this is where they ended up.

I lurk in the gloom at the back of the classroom, next to a dog-eared poster of Beethoven on the brown hessian noticeboard.

Darren is thrashing out chords on a battered classical guitar. He's stuck a microphone in the sound-hole and there's a distorted noise coming through an amplifier. He's singing but I can't hear him over the noise of Pete enthusiastically bashing the drums. My friends laugh at Darren – his hands look too big – his hair is greasy, he has spots and he wears massive glasses.

Playing the guitar, he looks natural, relaxed. He's even throwing little poses.

Darren sees me and stops playing. He stares at me, frozen with alarm. Pete stands up and folds his arms. He's wearing an Iron Maiden t-shirt under his unbuttoned school shirt.

'What are you doing here? Get lost.' Pete still has a drumstick in each fist.

'I want to learn the guitar.' I say.

'What bands do you like, then?' Pete glares at me.

'Joy Division – and I like the Cure and the Cult...'

There's loads of cool stuff I've taped off the radio and I've bought a few albums by the bands I'm getting into but I feel tongue-tied. I walk nearer to the drum kit.

'I want to learn how to play 'Transmission' and 'Love Will Tear Us Apart'. Can you teach me?' I sound pathetic, desperate.

'You really mean it, don't you?' Darren laughs. He looks almost cute. I've never talked to him properly before.

'My friends don't understand. They like Rick Astley.'

'Daz – we don't want her messing things up!' Pete lurches towards him, nearly knocking one of the cymbal stands over.

'Actually the cool bits in Joy Division are mostly done on the bass.' Darren gives me a shy smile. 'But I can teach you what I know. There's another school guitar – it needs new strings but if you're nice to Mr Melton, he'll let you take it home.'

'I'd like that,' I say. Darren's eyes connect with mine briefly, before he stares down at his guitar.

I realise I'm tuning Jason's guitar, tightening up the E-string until it hits the right note, putting my finger on the fifth fret and tuning the A-string to the same tone. I carry on, surprised I can still tell the difference between musical notes. The tuning pegs turn smoothly between my fingers.

The guitar's actually not too bad. The strings are tarnished and buzz against the frets a bit; but it's got a nice sound and it feels good to play. It's obviously been bashed about, and there's nothing to say what make it is, but it seems like a good quality instrument, under the dust and dirt.

I've not held a guitar, or any musical instrument, since before Jason was born. My bass is wedged, in its case, at the back of the cupboard under the stairs. It feels so good to hold the guitar that, when I've finished, my fingers involuntarily run through the bassline of 'Rootless in Babylon'.

Jason stares at me, his slate-blue eyes wide – his father's eyes. I hand the guitar back to him.

'Mum!' he gasps. 'What the –?'

Jason

That riff she played was amazing. I had no idea she knew anything about guitars. I'd forgotten Mum was in a band before I was born. She told me about that when I asked about my dad. He played the guitar. His name was Darren. That's almost all she's ever told me. Their band didn't get anywhere. If they were any good, she'd talk about it, wouldn't she?

I work my way through the start of the guitar manual. There are six lines – one for each string, with numbers to show which frets to play. The manual says it's called tablature. Reading the music reminds me of the time I tried to learn the recorder. I soon got bored. No one ever looked cool playing the recorder. There are a few pages of little tunes, to let beginners get the hang of holding down the frets.

I play the notes for the *Batman* theme tune on one string. I recognise it! I try the riff from 'Smoke on the Water' next on the same thick e-string – I know it because Ben's dad listens to Planet Rock radio. I play both tunes until they get faster and smoother.

There's a red line across the tip of my left index finger. It's starting to feel sore but I keep playing. The manual says I should use the other fingers on my left hand too. I haven't felt this excited since Mum first let me loose with poster paints or when I first rode a bike without stabilisers, keeping myself upright by magic.

Ben's been having guitar lessons since the start of term. Some guy his dad knows. Last Saturday, Ben played me all the chords he's been learning. His guitar teacher taught him this old song called 'The House of the Rising Sun' but Ben was trying to play the chords in a different order and change the words. He wanted me to have a go at playing his guitar. I really wanted to try it but I was scared of being rubbish. A bit of me hated Ben for being able to do it already.

Then yesterday, I saw the guitar in the window of the charity shop.

I'm hungry for music. I can't do without it – food, water,

sleep, and music. I want to discover bands no one else at school has heard of. Ben wants us to form a band together.

Music was just something in the background until the end of Year 6. We had bikes, even though we weren't allowed to go very far on our own. We were obsessed with Star Wars and had only just grown out of making Lego space monsters. I was already a bit bored with playing on Ben's Xbox. Then Ben's sister Rachel went to Guide camp and wasn't allowed to bring her iPod. I borrowed it. She has quite good taste in music, even though Ben doesn't think so. I got into My Chemical Romance and Bullet for My Valentine that way.

Last year, in the summer holidays, I helped Mum with the vegetable patch. We had the portable radio on. They played this song, 'Motorcycle Emptiness' by the Manic Street Preachers. Mum said she didn't like it much, but I loved it. It was the first music I liked that was made before I was born. I wanted to listen to the guitar solo over and over again. I went over to Ben's house and his dad let me use his Amazon account to buy all of their CDs second hand. I like their early stuff best. I found out all about them. One of them – Richey –didn't play much guitar but wrote brilliant lyrics – he went missing years ago, and they never found him. James Dean Bradfield is a great guitarist, and I love the bass player, Nicky Wire.

Now I'm ransacking racks of vinyl and stacks of tapes in charity shops like a total music junkie. Ben's borrowing stuff from me. His dad's got a computer programme that turns tapes and records into MP3s.

I try to play 'Wipe-out'. I have to use more fingers; more strings. I play the notes slowly, trying to stretch, not like Mum – her fingers flew across the strings – but I'm starting to get the hang of it and I can recognise the tune. I can't understand why I was so afraid of learning the guitar – I'm not scared at all now.

'Jason! Jason!'

How long has she been calling my name? I don't want to put the guitar down. It's old and dusty, not new like Ben's –

but it feels like part of me already. An hour ago, I was so mad with it I felt like chucking it out of the window. Mum solved it, without making a fuss, like how she taught me to ride a bike when I was little; how she stuck plasters on my knees when I fell off.

I open my door. She looks guilty, as if she's been standing there, listening to me. There's a weird look on her face, like she's worried about something but pleased at the same time.

'What?' I really want to say *thanks for tuning the guitar*, but the words don't want to come out of my mouth.

'Tea's ready,' she says. 'Stuffed marrow. Fresh from the garden.'

I try not to pull a face. Stupid hippie food. I bet Ben's not eating stuffed marrow.

I'll start learning chords after tea.

Kaz

Everything's quiet upstairs. I think Jason's asleep now. I'm trying to get on with a painting. Jason played the guitar all evening, working his way through that manual. I imagined him, concentrating so hard his tongue was sticking out, contorting his fingers across the frets to form his first chords until they were sore with the effort.

He kept going so long, his fingertips must have been rubbed raw. I wanted to go in there to see how he was getting on but I know he'll lose his enthusiasm if I'm standing over him. If he's serious, I'll do everything I can, everything I can afford.

I have to tell him about Mission Control but I've spent so long pushing it away, denying my past. It was easy when Jason was little. He accepted it was just the two of us. When he was old enough to ask questions about his dad, I didn't tell him much. I didn't want to talk about Daz.

Jason needs to know about Daz and the band – especially now he's learning the guitar. I'm being selfish but

I'm just not ready to tell him yet.

I dip my brush into the dark green tone I mixed on my pallet for the shadow but my hand's shaking too much by the time it reaches the canvas. The paint looks too thick and black and I'm in danger of ruining the whole thing.

The photo I'm working from is one I took in the spring – a grove of ash trees with a path running through the middle. The painting will have menacing shapes coming out of the shadows in the background, but the rest of the painting needs to be light and innocent in contrast.

Maybe I can rescue it in the morning. I wipe the brush on a rag and clean it in the jam-jar of water. I shouldn't have started working in artificial light but I had to do something to keep myself occupied.

I need something to stare at now. Other people's problems to get occupied by. I'll never get a TV though. Jason got sick of asking me. It must make him a total freak at school. Elsa always said TV rots your brain. I can't afford the licence fee anyway.

There's an anxious tightness in my chest. I should go to bed but I can't face another sleepless night with that New Model Army song 'No Rest' getting stuck in my head, taunting me with the past I've tried to forget, with its lyrics reminding me there is no rest for the wicked. The only cure is to read myself to sleep – I used to read Jason's *Harry Potter* books, but he's going through a phase of Stephen King horrors. I picked up a pastel-pink chick-lit novel for 50p from a second-hand bargain bin. That'll have to do. Sometimes, I read until dawn. Sleep just doesn't come.

I fill the kettle and put it on the AGA. Rain trickles down the kitchen window. While I'm waiting, I tidy away the pots from the draining board. I feel a flash of anger. The plates are greasy and burned-on food is stuck to the casserole dish. Jason's washing up was slap-dash tonight. Then I remember how he couldn't wait to rush back upstairs and get on with playing the guitar. I smile and rinse the plates.

I make myself a cup of chamomile tea. It might help me to sleep. Or it might make me need a piss in the middle of the night, risking my neck on the stairs on the way down to the bathroom in a dopey semi-conscious state.

Shit. 'No Rest' is in my head already. If I ever see Justin Sullivan again, I swear I'll smack him. The song hovers around my head all the time, like my personal soundtrack, even though I haven't heard it in years. God, I loved New Model Army. I learned the tricky bass part to that song when I was still at school. It almost drove me mad, but it was worth it.

My heart thumps in time with the bassline in my head, which has somehow morphed into 'Rootless in Babylon'.

I stop in front of the cupboard under the stairs. I put my tea down and open the door. It's stacked with paintings. Some of them are waiting to be taken to local galleries and cafés, in the hope that they'll be accepted for sale.

Most of the paintings in the cupboard are ones that haven't sold – and pictures that went wrong, waiting to be covered in white gouache so I can start again. I stack the canvasses against the side of the stairs. Just a quick look. What harm can it do?

The back of the cupboard smells musty.

I need a torch but it's in the shed so I try to do everything by touch. The roughness of corrugated cardboard; metal clasps and sharp corners of old suitcases – full of things that belonged to Elsa. We packed the fragile ceramics away together when Jason was learning to walk, but I put Elsa's clothes, photographs and jewellery in here when she died.

That was nine years ago and, ever since then, I've been waiting. Someone might come to claim Wren Cottage and everything in it. Elsa told me to look after the house but I've got no right to be here, really. So I keep quiet.

Cobwebs brush my face as I reach to the back of the cupboard. Behind the boxes, I feel a slim rectangular shape with a fake leather texture. I grasp the handle and pull it away from the wall. Instantly, I remember the weight of the flight case.

I lay the case down on the living room floor, kneeling

over it. I snap open the metal clasps without thinking but take a deep breath before I force myself to open it. It's a shock to see the bass. It's still a beautiful thing, its angular shape like a piece of abstract sculpture.

The paint is black and shiny but the strings are tarnished and slack against the neck. I remember now, de-tuning it before I put it away. I did that automatically, having heard stories about the necks snapping when they were in storage, even though I was completely broken inside myself. Back then, this bass, my Gibson Thunderbird, was my baby. I bought it just before we recorded the first album.

Now my baby is a thirteen year-old boy who towers above me. I didn't even know I was pregnant when I moved into Wren cottage; when I hid my bass at the back of the cupboard, not wanting to get rid of it, but not ever wanting to look at it again.

It feels strange to be picking the bass up, holding it. My first instinct, like earlier, is to turn the tuning pegs. I start with the E-string, then I stop. Jason might hear me.

I pick up a crumpled piece of A4 paper lying in the case. I straighten it out. The set list from the final gig. Spiral Sun free festival. Staffordshire, May 1994.

The song titles, in Daz's spiky handwriting, have run so badly in the rain they're barely legible; the ink has separated into different colours. Not that I need to read it to remember.

●

We kick off with 'Twisted Skin', then one of our new ones – 'Forgotten Alien'. I'm playing the dub bassline, watching the stage lights reflecting off the wet faces and waterproofs in the audience – a sea of dancing cagoules. My sense of foreboding about tonight has disappeared and I feel warm for the first time today, under the bright glare of the lighting rig. We've almost made it. These people are dancing in the rain because of us.

The Spiral Sun festival booked us at the last minute –

couldn't believe their luck to get us, on the verge of the big time. Treated us right – a portacabin backstage; a proper rider with a slab of lager. Ash said it was a chance to try out the new songs on a loyal audience. It's working. People seem to love the new stuff, despite the weather.

Daz is on form too. He wasn't talking to me before we went on stage but now he's bending down to share the mic like old times to sing in harmony, grinning at me, pleased with the gig.

Pete's behind us, shaking the stage, he's hitting the drums with so much force. I glance over at Ash, eyes closed, lost in his own world of spiralling electronic noise and samples.

It's a gamble, playing new songs in front of an audience for the first time. In all the rain, the festival looks like a disaster, but the gig's going so well for us so far, after all those months of hard work and arguing in the studio.

It feels like we're saying goodbye to our old way of life: cheap cider and the backs of Transit vans. Time for the next chapter of Mission Control.

I start to sing the first verse.

●

I don't want to think about what happened after that...

Too late. I'm sobbing, holding onto the piece of paper. I stare at Daz's writing – apart from Jason, it's all I've got left of him. I shouldn't be doing this, I really shouldn't. What if Jason came downstairs and found me? I'd have to explain everything.

Something damp brushes against my legs. I let out a small scream and sit up. I laugh weakly with relief. It's just the cat. Her tortoiseshell fur is wet, flattened against her back. She's come in from a prowl in the rain for a nice sleep near the warm AGA, only to find a strange black shape in the middle of the living room and the woman who gives her food in a heap on the floor.

She lies down inside the flight case and rolls around on the purple plush lining to dry her fur.

'Patti – no!' She glares at me and slinks into the kitchen.

I pick the bass off the rug and put it carefully back in its case, drying the plush with my sleeve. I slip the set list under the strings.

The bass isn't going back into the cupboard, even if I don't dare to play it again. I stack the paintings back into the cupboard. I'm putting the bass under my bed. I don't care if I can't sleep.

I almost knock the mug of chamomile tea over as I carry the flight case upstairs. It's stone cold.

Chapter 2
Musical Differences

Jason

My Ultimate Burger wobbles as I carry it upstairs to Ben's room. My mouth waters at the thought of it. Mum made porridge for breakfast. That's what we eat when she's running out of money, with home-made jam in the middle of it.

This morning it went rubbery and got stuck to the bottom of the pan. The cat brought a dead vole into the kitchen and dumped it in front of the AGA. I bet most people's mums would scream, but Mum grabbed her camera, lay on the floor and started taking close-up shots of it. She made me look at it through a magnifying glass. Gross. But kind of fascinating. Its teeth were orange, and its front paws were sort of frozen in prayer as if it begged for mercy before Patti pounced on it. Then Mum scooped the vole up on a bit of old cardboard and buried it outside. Patti was disgusted with us for being so ungrateful.

I didn't really feel hungry after that, so I secretly scraped out most of my porridge under the blackcurrant bush in the garden. Cycling to Matlock Bath gave me my appetite back.

The Ultimate Burger is a tradition at Ben's house – we make burgers and pile on anything else we fancy from the kitchen. Today it's baked beans, crispy bacon, thick slices of cheese, brown sauce and tinned sweetcorn. Mum says tinned sweetcorn has no nutritional value. She grew some corn in the garden this year. We ate it at the end of the summer, roasted in tin-foil over an open fire.

Rachel, Ben's sister, squeezes past us on the landing, dangling her car keys from her fingers – she's just passed her driving test. She only turned seventeen a few months ago, but she was desperate to pass her test to get to gigs at Rock City in Nottingham.

'Why aren't you both enormous? Look at the amount of crap you eat. It's not fair.' She pulls a disgusted face.

'Have you noticed how much Jase has grown recently?' Ben says. 'He needs feeding constantly, around the clock – he only gets nuts and carrots and things at home.'

'Yeah and haven't you noticed he's not got a face like a pizza?'

'You've got a face like a horse –'

Rachel's eyes flash. She flounces past Ben and flicks his teetering burger with her long dark purple fingernail. The top layers tumble like a collapsing tower block, scattering sweetcorn all over the landing carpet.

Ben's face flushes red. He is a lot shorter than me now. I swear we were the same height in January. I had to roll these jeans up – they trailed on the floor. Now there's a gap where you can see my socks. If I grow much more, people are going to point and laugh at me in the street – not just Bradley Smeed and his Year Ten cronies – but little old ladies and the rambling groups that pass Wren cottage. At least Mum might make some money if she turns me into a performance art freak show.

I put my plate on the floor and help him to pick up the sweetcorn and the top of his burger bun. Ben puts it all right back on his plate.

'It's okay,' he says, blowing on the top half of the burger bun. 'Two second rule.'

I laugh. The bits of sweetcorn are covered in carpet fluff but Ben doesn't seem bothered.

'You're so lucky, not having a sister.' Ben sighs.

'She's not so bad.'

'She's always been nice to you.'

I open the door to Ben's room. The rest of the stairs are inside the room, which quite cool but his dad put banisters up so Ben didn't fall down them in the middle of the night. Ben's dad is the Health and Safety guy at a quarry. He tries to make everything safe. He won't let Ben out on his bike without his cycling helmet. I've had mine since I was ten, and my head has grown so much now it hurts to put it on. I haven't told Mum.

Ben's house is a tall Victorian terrace on the side of the

hill but it's all modern inside. Ben's attic is like the control room of a spaceship, with silver lights set into the ceiling. His desk is stuffed with gadgets. It's so warm, we're just in t-shirts, even though at my house we're already wearing jumpers, wrapping ourselves in blankets in the living room and going to bed with hot-water bottles.

I've been allowed to have a fire in the fireplace in my bedroom for a year now. It's so tiny, you have to sit right next to it to get warm. The sloping ceiling's great for posters but all the furniture's old. If I bounce around too much to music, the floorboards wobble and the CDs or records jump; and I've started banging my head on the ceiling. Ben's jealous I'm allowed to burn things, and he hasn't got a record player – but I'd love to have his room.

We met at playgroup. We were both playing in the sand-tray, pretending our toy cars were crossing a vast desert. Ben was wearing a stripy t-shirt. He was older than me, already three, but I was better at painting. One day, I got into trouble for getting both of us covered in poster paint. It was my idea. We were doing hand-prints and I thought it would be fun to do a full body print instead. Mum thought it was funny – and clever of me. When we got home, Aunt Elsa treated me like some kind of genius and took a photo which is still in a frame in the living room – one half of me is red and the other half is blue.

Ben's family has had to put up with me ever since. His parents can't really get their heads around my mum. They think her paintings are morbid but they bought one of them a few years ago, to save us from a really tough patch when our electricity got cut off. They must have felt sorry for us. It's a pretty good picture of a winter tree on a bleak hillside. They hung it at the end of a dark corridor near the spare bedroom.

I get a tape I bought in the charity shop out of my guitar case and hold it out for Ben. The grainy cover shows four people looking seriously at the camera. The man in front has gaunt cheekbones and veiny-looking hands. He's holding his right hand up, like he's pointing or beckoning.

'Wow…Television. Marquee Moon.' Ben stares at the tape like it's treasure from a lost civilisation. 'They mentioned it on this thing I was watching about punk.'

'It's sort of quieter than you'd expect punk to be.'

'Maybe it's not just about having spiky hair and a leather jacket and stuff.'

Ben touches the mouse-pad on his laptop. He goes to his favourites and finds a YouTube movie.

'You've got to see this.' He takes an enormous bite out of his burger.

The video starts playing and Ben makes it fill the whole screen. A skinny guy with teeth like tombstones, in ripped blue jeans, with an acoustic guitar plastered in stickers. He's talking incredibly fast about the history of punk rock, and it sort of rhymes. I eat my burger as the video plays. I miss what he's saying as I crunch through the bacon. He thrashes out chords on his guitar and sings, almost as fast as his talking. He plays the chords fast and heavy-handed.

Ben grins through a mouthful of food. He's finished his burger by the time the video ends. He has this glowing look, like he's just found a new religion and wants to convert me too.

'Anti-folk. My new musical direction. Like folk but punk at the same time.'

'He said something about Patti Smith. Mum named our cat after her. I didn't know she was famous. Mum just said she was a woman with a growly voice.'

'He said stupid on purpose became the new smart. That's so great. It doesn't matter that I can't do those boring guitar scales.'

'Any more of those worksheets from your guitar teacher?' I ask.

Ben pulls a face.

'I quit last night. Musical differences.'

'Are you nuts?'

'I couldn't stand it – all those scales. I asked him to teach me a few Ramones songs but he said punk ruined music. I had a big row with him.' Ben slaps his forehead in exasperation. 'According to him, Clapton is God. He says he likes the Blues – but he just wanted me to learn wanky guitar solos. Dad went mental. He's been mates with that guy for years.'

'If you don't have guitar lessons, how am I supposed to learn anything?'

How selfish do I sound? I know Ben's struggling, but those scales make sense to me, like ladders of musical notes.

'You seem to be doing pretty well by yourself,' Ben says. 'You're better than me already.'

'Learning on this crappy old thing?' I get my guitar out of its case and check the tuning. It looks knackered compared to the electro acoustic Ben's dad bought him for his birthday. But it's weird how my guitar hardly ever goes out of tune. One day, when I got back from school, it had been cleaned, and it had a new set of strings. Mum said it must be the guitar pixie. She had a stupid smirk on her face.

'Why don't you ask for an electric for Christmas?' Ben asks. Not even the guitar pixie could stretch to that.

'Oh, you think Santa will just look at his list and say Jason Knight's been a good boy – and put a Stratocaster in his sack for me?' It's my turn to sound bitter.

Sometimes Ben forgets. He's not spoilt, but his parents would buy him anything. Rachel's only just passed her driving test and they bought her a Ford Ka that's only a few years old – and a Satnav so she doesn't get lost.

'Your guitar's not so bad. You could use it as an advantage.'

I stare at him. I just don't get it.

'Like Seasick Steve.'

'Who?'

Ben's clicking away on YouTube again. Another man sitting down with a guitar on his knee. An old man with a long white beard, wearing a baseball cap and a plaid shirt. Other lads our age are looking at porn on the internet – at least they say they are. We must be totally sad. Even though Mum's art books are full of boobs.

The man says, in a deep American growl, that his guitar

has only got three strings. It's a battered old thing, much worse than mine. He says he's going to do "three string trance boogie" – suddenly there's an amazing noise coming out of it. I can't help tapping my foot, like Seasick Steve, who's kicking a wooden box in time with the music.

'Isn't it great?' Ben grins at me. 'I should be learning to play stuff like that, not boring shite –'

Suddenly I've got an idea that could help both of us.

Kaz

A freezing wind blows needles of rain into my face as I struggle down the hill towards the bus stop. I can't remember when I last went any further than Matlock or Wirksworth. The flight case pulls at my arm, catching the wind like a sail.

There are two musical instrument shops in Derby city centre – I checked the Yellow Pages. It takes all my determination and strength to fight against the wind without being blown into a lorry. The cold is numbing my brain and stopping me from thinking too much, which is good.

I walk towards the first music shop from the bus station. The rain's turning to sleet now. My scarf's pulled tightly around my neck so I feel half-strangled. There's a tight feeling in my chest too. Freezing drops of water dribble inside my coat but I can't let go of the flight case. My hand is frozen into position around the handle.

Derby feels like a big city to me now. A new shopping centre has been plonked on the edge of town since I was last here and there are people rushing around, running lunch-break errands under umbrellas. I stand on the corner, tugging at my scarf with one hand, trying to read the name of the street through the rain. I think this is the right place for the music shop.

'Watch where you're swinging that thing!' A woman in

high heels stands in front of me, rubbing her beige shin. 'Look at the state of my tights!'

'I'm sorry,' I mumble.

The woman stares at me, hard. Her hair is in one of those middle-aged styles like a helmet, solid with hairspray. It doesn't seem to be affected by the weather at all. Perhaps it's waterproof. Perhaps her make-up is tattooed on. Her pencilled-in eyebrows are raised, half-way up her forehead.

'Pay me for a new pair,' she demands.

In the old days, I would have told her where to get off but she's blocking my escape route towards the music shop. Reluctantly, I put the flight-case between my boots and fumble for change in my purse with my frozen fingers. I've only got my return ticket for the bus and a couple of quid. That's why I'm here in the first place. I stare at the coins in my hand.

'That'll do. Bloody nutter.' She snatches the money from me and walks off smartly.

I stand with my mouth wide open. I don't know whether to laugh or cry. Instead, I hurry up the street, head down against the wind and rain. This street is quiet; a dingy second-hand bookshop that looks like a front for something else, a couple of charity shops and a sex shop with a window display of rubber fetish gear.

I wore a basque like that at Reading '92 – for a joke – but it got us featured in *Kerrang!* It must have helped us to get that five "K" album review for the first album. I appeared in their 'Pandora Peroxide' cartoon strip for a few weeks, caricatured as Kaz K – Ecowarrior Princess, because we'd done a benefit gig for the Twyford Down road protest camp. They drew me swinging through trees in my rubber outfit, stopping bulldozers with sound waves from my bass. Hard to believe there was a cartoon version of me, now.

The music shop is on the left; gig posters stuck up in the window. I push the door open. A bell rings with a little jangle. I stand on the mat, my coat dripping. It's good to get indoors and I breathe in the long-forgotten smell – wood polish and warm plastic, combined with a faint mustiness and male sweat. The man behind the counter is selling a guitar lead to the only customer, a man in his mid-twenties with a ponytail, wearing a suit. They don't even glance at me. I look at the immaculate guitars hanging on the wall as I wait – I imagine the look on Jason's face as he tears off the wrapping paper on Christmas Day. What would he like best? A Fender or a Gibson? Daz bought guitars impulsively by the time we'd made *Losing Control*, but the Gibson Flying V was always his favourite…

'Can I help you, love?' the man behind the counter asks. I ignore his slightly patronising tone. The other customer has gone. I hadn't realised.

I put the flight case on the counter. I try to wipe off the rainwater with my coat sleeve but it's soaking wet.

'I want to sell this,' I say. I open the case. I put the set-list safely inside my bedside table this morning.

The man picks up my bass, turning it around in his hands. He's a big guy. His hands are too meaty for its slim neck. The Gibson guitar logo on his black t-shirt is stretched over a beer belly. He smells faintly greasy, as if he's eaten so many fried breakfasts they're coming out of his pores.

He makes a tutting sound as he looks at the crack in the lacquer on the top corner, drawing in his breath through his teeth, like the mechanic who used to service our van. I'd forgotten the bass was damaged. I threw it on the studio floor when we were recording the second album, after that huge row with Daz. Afterwards, I was gutted, but relieved the damage wasn't worse. Daz was the one who went in for instrument smashing, not me. He accused me of loving my bass more than him; that I wouldn't care so much if he was hurt. He was wrong – but he never knew, did he?

'This is a copy,' the man says. He shakes his head as he looks at the bass.

'What do you mean?' I stare at him.

'Quite well done but it's a cheap Chinese copy. You can tell by the wood they've used on the fingerboard. Where did you get it from?'

Bullshit. Well, if he can lie, I'll lie too. I put on a tragic face, in case my natural expression isn't genuinely sad enough.

'It belonged to my husband – he died – he bought it in America –' I make myself talk in a wispy voice.

I bought the bass from Chopper Music in Birmingham, with virtually my whole share of the advance for the first album. I spent a whole day trying out basses until I fell in love with this one, even though it weighed a ton. It was nine hundred and fifty quid. 1979 vintage. It seemed like total madness at the time. We were living in the loft above our studio, Mission Control HQ. I didn't let the bass out of my sight. I put it at the side of the mattress so I could put my hand on it while I was sleeping. Maybe Daz was right. I was obsessed with the Thunderbird.

'I'm afraid he was conned, love. And there's this damage to the lacquer.'

'Before he died, he told me it was worth at least a thousand pounds.' I get a tissue out of my coat pocket and dab at my eyes. The tears are genuine. I can't handle this.

'I can offer you a hundred –' He panics, seeing me cry. 'Okay – hundred and fifty.'

His flushed face and the way he's hanging onto the Thunderbird belie his words. His fingers leave greasy marks on the shiny black surface.

'Give it back to me.'

The man looks startled at the sudden change in my voice.

'You won't get a better offer.' He reluctantly hands the bass to me. I rub off his finger-prints with the duster I always kept in the case.

'Won't I?' I growl at him. He actually backs off, towards the till. I'm impressed: that almost sounded like the old me. If only I'd spoken like that to the lady with the tights.

I put the bass back in its case, gently, and clip it shut. I leave the shop and slam the door behind me, helped by a strong gust of wind. At least I'm blown downhill, towards music shop number two.

The second music shop looks like it's been here for a hundred years. It's in a really narrow old building. There are violins and clarinets displayed in the window. I push my way inside. All I can see is sheet music and classical instruments. The polish smell in here has a more expensive beeswax tang to it. Everything's really clean and bright. A lady with a gold chain dangling from her glasses peers up from a thick catalogue. She stares at me, taking in the looming oblong shape of the flight case.

'Electric guitars?' she asks, in a rich resonating voice like a cello. I wonder if that's what she plays. I nod.

'Third floor.' She wears a high-necked blouse and has greying hair pulled back into an untidy bun. I notice the carpeted staircase in the corner of the room.

'Thanks.' I force myself to smile, and wipe my boots on the doormat before trudging up the stairs.

The narrow third floor room is crammed with guitars and basses, hanging on the wall in rows. A man looks up at me, in the middle of re-stringing a guitar – a Fender Jaguar. He has wire-rimmed John Lennon glasses; his bony face seems to disappear behind them. He looks a bit like a bush-baby – one of those little marmoset things – all eyes and fingers.

'I want to sell this bass. I'm sorry. The case is a bit wet.' I haul it onto the counter.

The man smiles politely but his expression changes to one of guarded excitement as I open the case.

'Is it yours?' he asks.

I nod. There's no point lying now. It didn't get me anywhere.

'I don't play anymore. It's been sitting at the back of a cupboard for about fourteen years.'

'That's a shame.' He smiles at me sadly, as if he really wishes I was still playing.

'My son's learning the guitar now, though. I want to buy him something decent.'

The man picks the bass up gently, almost reverently.

'It's beautiful.' He examines it closely. 'The neck's in

original condition – that's good.' He runs his finger along the crack in the lacquer. 'This damage will bring the price down a bit – looks superficial – I could fix it. I bet there a good story behind it though?' His eyes sparkle with interest behind his glasses.

I shrug. 'Just a stupid argument. Holed up in the studio for too long – started to lose all sense of reality. It was either the bass that got damaged or someone's head.'

The man blinks. 'I can definitely make you a good offer. I'd like to take a better look at it first, road test it.' I can tell he can't wait to try it out. I think I can trust him.

'Okay. How long do you want? An hour?' I need to be at home before Jason gets back from school.

He nods, smiling. 'That should be fine. I'm Andy. I'll look after it.'

I hesitate. It's okay, I tell myself. No one cares about Mission Control any more.

'I'm Kaz.'

I'm out in the rain again. Now the bass case isn't weighing me down, I feel weird, as if I've left my right arm in the shop. I'm walking down a pedestrianised street with expensive-looking boutiques and coffee shops on both sides. I pass a charity shop, but since I only have a few coppers left, everything is out of my reach. For the next hour, anyway. I think the museum and art gallery is at the end of this street. I used to take Elsa there, before Jason was born.

The rain's bouncing off the pavement now. I'm soaked and one of my boots is leaking. I almost run through the museum doors and I'm suddenly blasted by warm air, enveloped in the hushed atmosphere.

I wander into the Joseph Wright gallery. The painted folds in the lace and velvet clothes look so real I want to reach out and touch them. I sit on a bench in front of one of the largest paintings and admire the dramatic use of darkness and light. Without the old fashioned clothes, the faces in the pictures could belong to people walking down the street. Elsa taught me to see things with her own startling clarity; to really understand shapes and perspective; the light and shade in everything. I learned to lose myself, just staring at things, making imaginary sketches, getting lost in the visual world. It saved me.

It's quite soothing being amongst the dark wood and grand portraits. I could fall asleep on the bench if I don't keep moving. I haven't been sleeping much lately.

I force myself to stand up and walk into the contemporary art gallery. The walls are white and the cork floor smells of polish. My mind drifts uneasily back to the music shop.

The paintings in here are abstract, by an artist I've vaguely heard of. The biggest canvas is circular, yellow in the centre, graduating to red on the outside. I stand in front of it, basking in its glow. It feels like months since I felt the warmth of the sun on my face. I can almost feel it for real. Then I'm shocked awake by the price tag on the painting. Two thousand pounds! That's probably cheap, too. I look at the painting more critically. The circular canvas idea is clever – but anyone capable of mixing different shades of paint could have painted this. Sour grapes. Just because I haven't sold a painting in months. If only somewhere like this would show my work. It's useless.

The tears come without warning. I dash to the toilets on the landing. The gallery attendant gives me a concerned glance as I rush past. At least he doesn't try to stop me. I barge into a cubicle and grab handfuls of toilet roll from the dispenser. My eyes still don't dry up. I need to get back to the music shop. There's a full-length mirror on the back of the door.

The warm gallery lights have made my wet hair spiral into curls. My face looks small, drowned by my oversized coat. My boots are worn, paint-flecked. My eyes are red-rimmed and heavy-lidded. My hand touches the door handle. A voice inside me says: *Don't sell the bass.*

I stare at myself. I need to sell the bass. I don't want the electricity to be cut off again and the council tax is overdue.

I could probably survive the winter on nothing but home-grown vegetables, but what about Jason? I could sign on, but I wouldn't get through the interrogation, the pages of questions, without crumbling. I want to stay independent. Under the radar.

I grab more toilet roll to dab my eyes and I leave the gallery.

The lady in the high-necked blouse smiles as I come into the shop again. I can already hear the rumble of my bass coming from several floors above. I almost break into a run up the stairs. Andy has strapped on my bass. The strings are new and shiny and he's plugged it into a decent-sounding amp. He's giving it some kind of funk jazz work-out, so wrapped up in what he's playing his eyes are closed. I could steal a guitar and he wouldn't notice. My fingers tingle as I watch him – as if the bass is calling to me.

'Can I have a go? For old time's sake?'

He stops playing suddenly, blinking.

'Sorry. I was getting carried away.' He hands me the bass. I take my coat off and lengthen the strap so it hangs on my hips. I stand and stare down at the bass, not sure what I'm going to do. My fingers touch the strings.

I don't even realise I'm doing it, but I'm playing the bassline from 'Transmission' by Joy Division – the first bassline that ever grabbed me. Just a few simple notes but they take me into a different world. Suddenly I feel like I've remembered everything. I stay with the Peter Hook theme and play the bassline from 'Regret' by New Order, making a few mistakes but I don't care. I play 'Twisted Skin' and 'Rootless in Babylon' until my fingers feel too sore to carry on. It took time to build up those calluses on my fingertips.

Andy stares at me, shocked but smiling. I unplug the bass and put it back on the counter.

'That was great. You said you hadn't played in years.'

'I haven't.'

He holds out a scrap of paper.

'I unscrewed the back plate – to check the electrics. I

29

found this.'

There's a picture on the piece of paper, drawn in fine marker pen. There's some writing scrawled on it too – Daz's handwriting. I snatch it out of the man's fingers. I catch a look of surprise on his face. The ink is still black and fresh. The drawing is a picture of me playing the bass, with my platform Doc Martens and wild dreads. I've never seen it before. The note says *To Kaz – the sexiest bass player in the world. I love you. Let's get married! Daz. Glasto '93'.*

Suddenly I'm shaking so much I can't even hold the note. Andy pushes the amp across the carpet and gently makes me sit down on it. Why would Daz hide a note under the back plate of my bass? Typical of him. He did weird things – expected me to be a mind reader at times. Daz seemed so excited and happy before that Glastonbury gig. I thought it was because it was our biggest gig to date – Saturday, mid-afternoon on the *NME* stage. He was grinning to himself, when I was a bag of nerves. Was he secretly hoping I would find the note? Why would I ever unscrew the back plate? Did he really mean it?

I look up at Andy but the room won't stop spinning.

'I'm sorry,' he says. 'I just wanted to clean it properly. I can offer you nine hundred for it. I'd love to offer more–'

'I'm not selling it.'

I can't, can I? Not now.

Jason

'I think I'm starting to get the hang of this blues thing,' Ben says. 'I sound just like Seasick Steve.'

I'm starting to wish we hadn't stayed on after school to practise. It's dark and chucking down with rain. Water's streaming down the road and my tyres are losing their grip.

'You're sounding good.'

'This Saturday?'

'Okay. If it's not raining.'

A four-by-four drives past. It splashes me but I'm so wet

anyway it doesn't make much difference. Mum told me to wear my cagoule and waterproof trousers this morning but I left them at home. I didn't want to look like a prat. But I could have put them on after school – no one would have seen me in the dark. Ben's all snug in his all-weather gear and his cycle helmet's keeping his head dry but he's got twice the distance to get home. He'll still be pedalling when I'm drying out in front of the fire.

The Land Rover pulls over a few metres further up the road. A man gets out. He's wearing a high-visibility jacket.

'Dad!' Ben brakes sharply.

'Why aren't you home yet?'

'I was practising with Jase.'

'Your guitars will be full of water at this rate. Come on, jump in the back, both of you.'

We sling our bikes in the boot. Even though I live just around the corner, I'm not going to say no to a free lift.

My wet clothes drip onto the leather seats. I hold my guitar case between my knees. I hope it's properly waterproof. Warm air blasts me and I start to feel drowsy. I'm only a few minutes away from changing into dry clothes and roasting myself in front of a log fire. I'm even looking forward to whatever Mum's made for tea.

Ben's dad drops me off outside our house. I bump my bike up the steep garden steps but it feels like something's wrong. The cottage is in complete darkness. I lift the back door latch. It's freezing. The AGA's gone out and nothing's cooking. I put my guitar down in the living room but my chest has a horrible empty feeling.

'Mum! Mum!' I yell. There's no reply. What if she's had an accident? She's been acting strangely recently. What if she's gone somewhere, abandoned me? The house feels spooky.

I try the light switch. At least the electricity's working. So far, anyway. I know things are starting to get a bit desperate. She stopped buying cheese weeks ago – about the same time those new guitar strings appeared. I'd rather have the guitar strings but I like cheese too. I don't want to do my homework by candle light again, having to explain why my books have melted wax on them.

'Mum!' It's so cold without a fire. I run up the stairs. They creak. I wish I'd put the radio on, to cover up the noises the empty house makes.

I push open her bedroom door. The old iron bedstead looms in the middle of the room. The ceiling is so low that if I grow a few more centimetres, I'll have to stoop in here.

There's a shape on the bed, under the covers. It's faintly silhouetted in the light from the landing. The shape looks weird and bulgy on top. My heart takes a dive. What if – what if she's done something to herself?

I gasp, and prod the shape. It's furry and it squirms under my hand. There's a yowl and a sudden sting on the back of my hand. A pathetic squeal comes out of my mouth.

The bedside light comes on. It's only the cat, staring at me in surprise. Mum is lying in bed under Elsa's old patchwork quilt. The cat's scratched me and drawn blood. Patti's a jumpy cat. She came to our doorstep as a stray. I lick my hand so I don't drip blood all over the quilt. Patti is purring now, obviously wanting some dinner.

I start to laugh with relief. Mum stares at me. She looks really ill. Her eyes are red-rimmed. She's shivering and her hair is damp, stuck to her forehead.

'What's wrong?' I ask.

'I'm sorry, Jason. I'm really sorry,' she says. She starts crying. Tissues are strewn all over the bed.

'I've let you down. There's no money left,' she sobs.

I don't know what to do. She's got herself into a total state. She's not been like this for ages. I realise I'm shivering too. I need to get the AGA burning.

Mum stares at my soaked clothes and bleeding hand with her eyes wide.

'It's okay, I'm fine. I'll make you a cup of tea. Some toast or something.'

She nods, silently.

Kaz

I open my eyes and there's a shaft of moonlight lying in a stripe across the bed. I'm completely awake, as if a switch has clicked inside me. I push the covers back and get out of bed. My legs feel shaky. I lean on the windowsill. The moon makes the garden look mysterious with unidentified shapes and long shadows.

In daylight, the garden is bare and drab. The shrubs are pruned back to bare twigs and the ground's soggy, but it's practical. There are carrots, potatoes, Brussels sprouts and parsnips to keep us going. We can swap them for eggs with the next door neighbours and I stock-piled flour, oats and pasta last time I sold a painting.

Elsa was so proud of this garden. I was determined to keep it going, even though I knew absolutely nothing about gardening at first. She taught me, and I learned. She taught me everything about art, the old-fashioned way. I want to capture the garden, right now. It would never come out in a photograph.

I grab my sketch pad – wedged at the side of the bed for moments when inspiration and insomnia collide – and a pencil from my bedside table. I balance the pad on the window sill and start sketching impressionistic patterns of pale light and shadow.

A fox runs across the lawn with something in its mouth. I pause with the pencil tip on the paper. Another creature jumps out of the bushes with an unearthly screech. It's Patti. She looks twice her usual size, ears back, hissing and spitting like a firework. The fox freezes, drops its meal and runs into the woods. Patti sniffs at the food. She eats it in several gulps, then starts washing herself, perfectly composed now. I have to paint it – the stand-off between two animals in the moonlit garden. I can see it in oils, on the big canvas I painted over when that painting of the hollow tree didn't turn out right.

I turn the page of the sketchbook and draw the cat and

the fox from memory, trying to capture the startled expression of the fox and the way Patti became a demonic ball of fur. I hear light footsteps on the stairs. Patti pushes the bedroom door open and curls up on the quilt, as if she hadn't moved since Jason came home.

When he brought me tea and toast, it felt like I was the child and he was the parent. He could look after himself now if he needed to. When he was little, I tried to keep going, for his sake. I love him too much to give up. Even though I'm skint, I've got Jason and my painting and the garden. We'll get by somehow.

My fingertips are still sore from playing my bass. Andy in the music shop let me keep the new strings. He just put the bass back into its case. He didn't ask me about the note. He was obviously embarrassed, but how was he to know what it would mean to me? If Andy had thrown the note away without showing it to me, I would have probably sold the Thunderbird after all.

It's a long time since I've spoken to a musician. It felt good. Andy understood why I'd changed my mind. I didn't tell him outright about Mission Control, but I told him more about my past in half an hour than I've ever told Jason, or anyone else. He seems like a good listener.

The Thunderbird is safely back under my bed. Daz's note and the set list are inside the pocket where I used to keep spare plectrums and strings. I can't believe I played it again. I can't believe I nearly sold it. For those few minutes, I was beyond everything. I was alive. I know that's how Daz felt when he played guitar, and Jason must feel like it too.

I have to buy Jason an electric guitar. Despite the state I was in earlier, I realised that for about two hundred and fifty quid, I could get him a Squier Stratocaster and a little practice amp. I think Andy could put together a nice starter kit. I feel I owe him, after today.

How am I going to get that sort of money in time for Christmas? I can't touch any of Elsa's things. If I sold them, it would be theft, although I don't know who I'd be stealing from. I'll look in the paper for a job – any job. I don't care if I end up as an elf in Santa's grotto. Jason needs a guitar and he's going to get one.

Chapter 3
Gainful Employment

Kaz

I press the doorbell. A tinkling tune – 'Edelweiss'? echoes, slightly off key, inside the house. It's at the end of a cul-de-sac in Wirksworth, overlooking the playing fields of Jason's school. If I'm not careful, he'll find out what I'm up to. I want the guitar to be a surprise for him.

This wasn't what I was expecting from the ad in the local paper – it's a semi-detached council house, on a respectable little estate. The privet hedge looks like it's been trimmed with a set square. I'm glad I chained my bike to a lamp post. It would look far too ramshackle in the spotless front garden.

The spotless square patio slabs look like they've been scrubbed with bleach. There are geometric gaps of raked earth, each with a cypress leylandii cut into a narrow cone; or a standard rose bush, pruned within an inch of its life. In the centre is a concrete statue of a lady dressed in Grecian robes.

I tried to find clothes without any paint stains but I look right out of place here.

The front door opens. It's a woman with grey hair, set in rigid curls. She's wearing beige slacks with sharp creases down the front. For a second, I want to turn and run.

I force myself to smile. I remind myself I'm doing this for Jason.

'Mrs Norton? I'm Karen – Karen Clarke. We spoke yesterday. About your advert for a cleaner?' I thought I'd better give an alias of some kind, even if it makes me feel like an imposter.

She gives me an uncertain smile.

'Yes – come in, love,' she says. Before she turns and shuffles back up the hallway, I notice she's wearing fluffy white slippers with button eyes and pink felt tongues. Her powder-blue sweatshirt has a picture of a Scottie-dog's face on it.

The hallway has floral wallpaper and the carpet has one of those see-through plastic runners. It looks immaculate so far. The house smells of cleaning fluid and washing powder, with a slight hint of that sweetish old-people smell. What does she need a cleaner for?

'I'm looking for someone to dust my collection. Two hours, twice a week. I can pay you five pounds an hour – cash. Is that alright?' That's not going to get me far. It'd be months before I could buy Jason a guitar, let alone anything else we might need. There was another cleaning job advertised in the paper. I'm going to have to try that too.

I nod. 'Your collection?'

Mrs Norton opens the living room door. My jaw drops. There are Scottie-dog ornaments on shelves, Scottie-dog plates, oil paintings in gold frames, cross-stitch tapestries...

She beams at me.

'Isn't it wonderful?'

I nod, biting my lip to stop myself from laughing.

'It's so much work, though. I'm forever dusting. I thought it would be nice to get someone to help.' Mrs Norton has a faint Brummie accent, disguised with gentility. My mum would be almost this age now. I try not to think about my parents. I was horrible to them when I was younger. They hated Daz.

I carefully pick up one of the ornaments. A tiny sitting porcelain dog, its mouth open and tongue lolling, as if it's laughing.

Mrs Norton smiles indulgently.

'He was one of my first figurines. Cheeky little chap, isn't he?' She suddenly looks alarmed. 'You're not clumsy are you? I wouldn't be able to cope if anything got broken.' Her voice wavers.

I put the ornament back down gently on its lace doily.

'I don't suppose you let your real dogs in here, then? Too many things they might knock over.'

Mrs Norton looks at me blankly.

'Oh no, dear. I haven't any real dogs. My husband doesn't

like them. He thinks they make too much mess. I've got a fur allergy. I love Westies – people buy them for me. I pick them up here and there.' She picks up another china model. 'My niece bought me this one.'

'They're lovely.'

'I'll get you a cup of tea,' she says.

'Thanks – milk – no sugar.'

I stand in the middle of the room, staring. Suddenly I have to stuff my fist in my mouth so Mrs Norton can't hear me laughing from the kitchen. I want to come back here with my camera. Barking. Absolutely barking. Mrs Norton is a normal person. Is there's lunacy like this behind every net curtain? I might enjoy this job if I can keep my face straight for long enough.

Jason

By the time I've parked my bike in Ben's shed, he's already waiting for me, grinning like an idiot, standing in the back garden with a greasy bacon sandwich in his hands. It makes me feel sick, so I look away. It's a crisp, cold day.

'Want some breakfast?' Ben asks.

'Not hungry.' We're really scraping the bottom of the barrel at home but Mum made a loaf of emergency scone bread. I had some earlier with blackberry jam she made in August. I didn't really feel like eating though.

I walk through the door into their fancy basement kitchen and take my guitar case off my shoulders.

Rachel's finishing her cereal with her Kerrang! magazine propped up on the fruit bowl. She takes a final slurp of black coffee before loading her breakfast things noisily into the dishwasher.

'Ben's been boring us solid with the same songs over and over,' she says.

'I've got to be word perfect.' Ben scowls at her. 'How else do you think I get to learn anything?'

I sit on a breakfast bar stool and tune my guitar; start

running through our songs. My mouth feels dry.

'There's a Salvation Army band outside the Pavilion,' I say. 'Playing 'Silent Night' already.'

'It's not even December yet,' Rachel groans. 'I bet the place is crawling with tourists.'

'Coachloads. And hundreds of cars trying to park.'

Rachel slings her bulging *Nightmare Before Christmas* rucksack over her shoulder.

'I'm off to Jen's house, anyway. Tell Mum I'm staying over. Otherwise she'll freak.' She smiles at me over her shoulder as she leaves. 'Good luck, Jase.'

'You're nervous,' Ben says with a grin.

'Aren't you?'

Ben shrugs. He doesn't seem bothered. On the way here, my hands were slipping on the handlebars. My palms feel sweaty. I feel okay as long as I concentrate on playing the guitar. It's only two months since I started playing. Maybe it was a mistake to think people would actually want to listen to me. Ben's bouncing around the kitchen as if he can't wait to get started. I should have asked Mum for advice. She used to be in a band. She must have performed in public. I haven't even told her I'm doing this.

'Coffee?'

'Just some water.'

Ben pours a glass of water from the filter jug in the fridge. My hand shakes as I pick it up and gulp it down. What if someone from school sees us? Maybe the embarrassment would cancel itself out, like last Sunday when I was in the woods and Bradley Smeed walked past me. I almost dropped the logs I'd collected and hid behind a tree but then I noticed he was with two old people, and Bradley was walking a poodle on a pink lead with its own little pink raincoat. We just stared at each other without saying anything, in a sort of truce.

'Or maybe something stronger?'

Ben runs upstairs to the living room and comes back with two tiny glasses full of something from his parents' drinks cabinet.

'Whisky,' he says. 'One shot can't hurt.'

'Then we go out and do it?'

Ben nods. I look at the whisky dubiously and down it. Ben does the same. The taste makes me shudder but my nerves sort of feel numb at the edges now.

Ben laughs.

'Jason Knight's descent into addiction started with one shot of whisky before his first public performance,' he says, in a bad American accent. 'By the time his band headlined Glastonbury in 2020, he had to drink a bottle of vodka and snort ten lines of coke before he set foot on the stage.'

'As if.' I poke him in the ribs with the headstock of my guitar. I'm laughing too. We need to get on with it. Otherwise I'll never do it.

We launch into one of the songs we've been writing in the school music room. It worked quite well if we tried to write a song in the style of someone else and made up Christmassy lyrics.

I've eaten my oats and now I'm full.
I got fifteen billion toys to pull.
Around the world in a single night.
We make sure Santa gets it right.'

Ben sings in a gravelly American accent – pretending to be Seasick Steve. His guitar playing has really improved since we thought of the idea of writing Christmas songs. He's only playing the chords, but he seems way more confident. I know the lyrics are silly but Ben manages to make them work. I play a heavy blues riff.

'*I got the reindeer blues,*' Ben sings.

People laugh as they pass us – but in a good way. We've picked a great spot between the Rose Cottage pub and the aquarium. There are no shops to distract people in this gap. They need something to throw money at. There's a regular chink of coins falling into the top hat. Ben's dad wore it when he was the best man at a wedding. He doesn't know we've borrowed it. He's on a Health and Safety training course so he's not going to find out.

Ben grins at me. He's loving this. I'm starting to have fun too, even though my fingers are getting a bit numb with the cold. When Ben sings, people seem to take notice of him, leaving me free to enjoy playing the fancier guitar parts. People don't usually look at Ben like that. He's quite normal looking. Brown hair. A bit freckly. Maybe his mouth's a bit wide for his face. So what's different now?

A youngish guy with red hair almost walks past us, then stops and listens. His hands are deep inside his fleece pockets. He laughs out loud. He's wearing baggy black and white checked trousers. He watches us until we finish the song. He pulls a wallet out of his pocket and throws a handful of coins into the hat along with a white rectangle of card. He gives us a grin and hurries on.

Ben peers into the hat.

'It's a business card. It says he's a guitar teacher. Sam Baxter. He lives at the Fishpond pub.'

'He might be better than your last one.'

'Does he think we need lessons that badly?' Ben's joking, but the anxiety on his face gives him away.

'How much money did he give us?'

Ben rakes around in the pile of coins.

'I dunno.' He grins. 'Hey – there's about a tenner in here already.'

'We can't be that bad, then. Put most of it in your pocket – someone might nick it while we're playing.'

Ben straps his guitar back on.

'Want to do the one about the sledge?' he asks. I take a deep breath.

'Yeah okay.' I've got to sing now. I wrote most of the lyrics for 'Little Red Sledge from Sainsbury's'. I based it slightly on 'Small Black Flowers That Grow to the Sky' by the Manics. It's way too ambitious and my voice is nowhere as good as Ben's, but having earned a tenner gives me confidence to try.

Kaz

I scrub at a sticky mess on the kitchen worktop. It looks like someone knocked over a glass of orangeade, and then the fluff from someone's socks and clumps of cat hair have got stuck in it. I was only here two days ago but the place already looks like it hasn't been cleaned for months.

Jennifer's daughter Fiona barges into the kitchen through the back door, letting the Labrador in. They both walk mud all over the quarry tiles I mopped half an hour ago. Jennifer pays well but I'm lucky if I break even, cleaning-wise, by the time I leave. Her family has a special talent for creating dirt and mess.

'Hi,' Fiona says. 'Mum's not back, is she?'

'Not yet.'

She dumps her sports bag on the kitchen table with a loud thump. Jason is tall for his age but Jennifer's family are built on a much larger scale – blonde and hearty like Vikings. Fiona's still wearing her hockey kit. Her legs are mud-stained and muscular. She makes me feel like a midget, although my thighs are turning rock hard from cycling up this hill three times a week, as well as my normal slog up Cromford Hill.

Fiona opens the overstocked fridge. She hacks off lumps of cheese and ham, slathers best butter onto thick-sliced bread, leaving more mess on the work surface. She stomps into the living room. Crumbs fall off her plate, instantly hoovered up by the dog. I grab the dog's collar and steer him into the hallway. The coconut matting might absorb some of the mud. I use a bit of extra antibacterial spray on the work surface before I re-mop the floor.

It'll be good to come back to a reasonably clean house. I felt bad at first, turning Jason into a latch-key kid. When I was a teenager, I loved having the house to myself. Daz liked coming round after school, before Mum and Dad came back from work. Jason doesn't seem to mind being home alone either. He's usually got Ben for company. Sometimes Jason even gets the tea ready. He makes great scrambled eggs and he's mastered my emergency soda bread recipe.

I told Jason I've signed up to a yoga course. I think my air of exhausted calm convinces him. This job keeps me so busy I've not got time to dwell on anything else. It is quite like meditation really – I can empty my mind.

There are mysterious dribbles on the front of the fridge. I become absorbed in restoring its pearly blue shine.

I'm startled by a clatter of shopping being dropped on the floor behind me, followed by a loud sigh. It's Jennifer. I move away from the fridge.

Jennifer is surrounded by reusable supermarket bags straining at the seams – where do they put all this food? The fridge is already full to bursting but Jennifer's family seem to have boundless appetites.

'Tough day?' I ask. Jennifer's a doctor at the Whitworth hospital, a few miles up the A6. I don't like hospitals but it's small and cosy; a cottage hospital, really. I went there when Jason was born – and Elsa died there a few years later.

'God, you've done wonders in here, Karen' she says.

It still looks like chaos to me. I fill the kettle and set it to boil. It's a globe of clear glass that changes colour as it boils but it's chipped and covered in greasy finger marks. I rinse a j-cloth and wipe it, before the kettle gets too hot.

Jennifer gets heavy earthenware mugs from the cupboard and puts Earl Grey teabags into them. There's a crack running down one of the mugs. Jennifer eyes her daughter's sports bag and puts it on the floor.

'Is Fiona doing her homework?'

Of course she's not doing her homework. She's sitting in front of the TV, or she's on the internet, or doing both things at the same time.

'She's in the living room.'

'What about Toby?' Jennifer's son is the same age as Jason but he goes to a private school.

'He went upstairs.'

Jennifer sighs again.

'If only I could keep them on track. They have to motivate themselves, really.' She sits down heavily on one of the kitchen stools. 'You've got a teenager – what's your secret?'

I don't even know if Jason's doing his homework. He could be bunking off school for all I know. Until a few months ago, he chatted to me about everything.

'Don't ask me. I'm a terrible mother,' I say.

Jennifer raises her eyebrows. I've probably made her think Jason's hanging around on street corners. How do I dig myself out of this hole without revealing too much about myself?

'I worry too much, I think.' I force myself to smile. 'Jason's a great kid. He spends all his time practising the guitar.'

Jennifer smiles, relieved. 'How do you get him to tear himself away from the TV? Toby's addicted to that bloody X-box.'

'We don't have a TV.'

Jennifer looks baffled. I pour boiling water into the mugs, to make myself look busy.

'One of my friends asked if I could recommend a cleaner. Could you squeeze her in?'

'Maybe…' I mentally calculate. Three weeks until Christmas – depending on how much work she needs. I might just be able to get Jason's electric guitar on time.

'She lives at the top of this road.'

Jennifer scribbles a name, address and a phone number on the back of an envelope. It's true what they say about doctors' handwriting being terrible. I manage to decipher it.

'Barbara Fleming?' My mouth suddenly feels dry. The wildlife artist. She's good. Her paintings are very precise and perfect. Incredibly detailed. The originals go for thousands.

'You've heard of her?'

'I've seen her greetings cards.' They sell by the rack-full. Jennifer doesn't know I'm an artist. I didn't think it sounded compatible with being a cleaner. When I get home, I'll work on the painting of the fox and the cat in the moonlit garden. I'm tired, but I think having a more relaxed mind helps my painting. Maybe I'll take up a yoga class for real, once Jason's got his guitar.

I want to see the inside of Barbara Fleming's house. I want to find out what kind of books she has on her shelves and what brand of washing up liquid she buys. If she likes my cleaning, I might tell her I'm an artist.

'Her daughter plays hockey with Fiona.'

'I'll call her.' I smile.

Jason

'So what do you think she's doing?' Ben asks. He puts his guitar down, picks up the poker and jabs at the fire, making sparks shoot up the chimney.

Mum says she's doing yoga, but when she gets home, her clothes smell of bleach. Whatever she's doing, I think it must be a good thing. There are no more crumpled up tissues scattered all over her bed and down the sides of the sofa.

'I reckon she's got a job. She's buying food – we've got cheese in the fridge again.'

'I couldn't live without cheese. I'd buy her paintings – we should use them on our album covers…'

'Who says we'll get that far?'

'We've made forty pounds each – it's a pretty good start.' Ben laughs.

For the last couple of weeks, Ben's dad's been collecting him from our house on his way back from work. He decided it was too dangerous for Ben to be cycling all the way home in the dark. He picks him up just before Mum gets home.

It gives us time to practise. The Christmas songs are sounding really good and I've worked out some cover versions: a few Beatles songs; the Ramones songs that made Ben fall out with his old guitar teacher – crowd-pleasers, mostly.

'How about another busking session on Saturday?' I ask.

Ben grimaces.

'I've got to go Christmas shopping in Nottingham with my mum and Rachel. I'm going to slip off for a bit and look in the record shops.'

'We could go busking on Sunday though. There might be some bikers around. They might be generous – especially if we learn 'Smoke on the Water' properly.'

'Yeah, okay.'

Ben picks up his guitar and strums a chord progression. It sounds quite good, even though he's just brushing the strings, as if he's sketching with a faint outline he might rub out later. I pick out a few notes and join in for a minute or two but then Ben trails off. He picks at the rag rug.

'I wrote a song – a proper one. Do you want to hear it?'

I nod. Ben pulls a crumpled piece of paper out of his trouser pocket. He was scribbling something in science today, staring into space, long after we'd all finished copying what Mr Sturgess had written on the whiteboard.

He picks his guitar up and starts playing his new chord progression again: E-minor, G and C.

'I tried to talk to you today,' he sings. *'But you just looked away. So busy all the time – I'll never make you mine.'* He's singing in his own voice, rather than doing an impression of another singer.

I bite my lip and stare into the fire. His voice is good, but I feel hot with embarrassment.

'So I just stand and stare – at the way you do your hair. It shines in the sun, but I wish I'd not begun.'

The chords change and his strumming is more upbeat.

'To love you from afar – I'm invisible to you.
To love you like I do – I'm just the boy with the guitar.'

There are two more verses and he repeats the chorus for ages before he finishes. My hands are curled stiffly around my knees. I sigh – and Ben stares at me sharply. I realise I was holding my breath while he was singing.

'You didn't like it, did you?'

'Your singing's quite good – and I liked the tune, but…'

'It's the lyrics, isn't it?'

I nod slowly. I don't want to rain on his parade but the

46

words were terrible.

'Is it real? I mean, you haven't told me there's anyone you really fancy. Who are you singing about?'

'Hayley Green.'

'She's way out of your league. You know that girls never go out with anyone in the year below them. She wouldn't be seen dead with you.'

Ben stares at me. The firelight is reflected in his eyes, making him look slightly demonic.

'I don't want to go out with her. I just fancy her a bit. She has got nice hair. That bit was true.'

'You're pretending you're in love someone just so you could write a song about it?'

'I noticed her laughing with her friends when we were queuing for dinner. Her hair caught the light – that gave me the idea.' Ben puts his guitar away, roughly.

'You could be a bit more honest. A song about someone you fancy a bit in the dinner queue...'

Ben slides his guitar out of its case again.

'Yeah – maybe,' he smiles slowly. 'Perhaps you should have a go too, if you think you're so clever.' He's joking but I know when he's challenging me.

'Okay, then.' I grin at him. How hard can it be?

Kaz

I've seen Barbara Fleming before. She was the special guest at an art show in Bakewell a few years ago. I had some paintings in the exhibition and I managed to sell one of them.

Her house is a grand Victorian villa, set back from the road.

She's left me waiting in a large room overlooking the front garden while she takes a phone call. It's lined with her pictures – tastefully, but a bit overwhelming. This room must be where she meets gallery owners and the people who buy her paintings. I stare at a larger than life-size painting of a badger's head in profile, against a background of bracken. Every hair is defined, painted with the finest brush. Did she borrow a stuffed badger? Did she get a tame one to pose for her? She's managed to capture its expression – brave and inquisitive but almost comically short-sighted. I could ask her how she did it but I'm not supposed to be an artist, I'm just a cleaner.

Barbara Fleming returns with an apologetic smile. She's delicately made, with long silver-blonde hair in a loose half-ponytail, elegantly dressed in black, with glasses too big for her face. Maybe she wears them so she can see all the details she puts in her paintings.

'Let me show you around,' she says. 'So you're available on Monday, Wednesday and Friday afternoons?'

'I can come to yours before I clean Jennifer's house. I may as well make it the same days.'

She walks me briskly down the high-ceilinged hallway. I try to look at the framed pencil sketches of Peak District as I follow her. They're good – I recognise most of the views. There's a smudginess about them that suggests sweeping rainstorms and dark clouds.

The pictures change dramatically as she takes me up the stairs, reflecting her travels to Africa, Australia, and the Middle East – bright, earthy colours. The carpet has a thick pile. I'm not sure if I was expected to take my boots off but she didn't say anything when I wiped my feet on the mat.

Barbara Fleming opens the bathroom door.

'I'm afraid it gets rather grubby. My schedule's so busy, but the house needs to look good – for work, you know – always entertaining people.'

The bathroom is a little dusty but it's wonderful. I have to stop myself from gasping in amazement. The bath is round, big enough to fit about four people. The shower has curved glass doors and an enormous shower-head, set into the ceiling. One wall of the bathroom has a mural of a tropical beach-scene. It could be cheesy but the painting's so real, you could lie in the bath and imagine you were on an exotic island. It's like something from the most luxurious hotel rooms I've ever been in – not that there were many of those. Most of the time on tour, if our rooms had en-suites, they were mean little things with plastic sinks and cramped shower cubicles.

She pushes open the door of a suspiciously tidy teenage bedroom. There's a large painting of a chestnut horse and posters of clean-cut male film stars.

'Doesn't look like much needs doing in here,' I say.

'I know. Just push the Hoover around and flick the duster about occasionally. Charlotte's such a neat-freak. I'm worried she takes after her father.' I stare at the wallpaper and give a flicker of a nod. There's no sign that a man lives here. I heard somewhere that she used to be married to a local businessman but he left her for another woman and Barbara Fleming got to keep the house.

Back downstairs, she shows me an enormous kitchen which looks like it belongs in a magazine advert. She shows me the cupboard where she keeps the Hoover and the cleaning stuff.

She peers at me through her glasses, rather searchingly, standing in front of the only door I don't think I've been through yet.

'This is where I can relax – where I keep the art I really like.' She opens the door. It's a comfortable living room, facing the vast back garden, its white-painted walls crammed with contemporary art: a huge abstract painting with rectangular blocks of solid colour; a pink neon sign in scrawled handwriting, the slogan reading "Take me home to love". I've seen a photo of it somewhere before, while I was flicking through the art section in Cromford Books.

I stare at the painting above the mantelpiece and blink in amazement. It's my painting – the one I sold at that art show. It was bought anonymously, paid for in cash. It's large: a triptych, made from the panels of a shattered dressing table mirror I found in a skip. I sanded the wood down and painted it with acrylics. I painted a woodland scene, fading in each panel from spring, to summer and autumn. It's only when you look closer that you see the skeleton lying in the undergrowth; brambles twining around the leg bones, a wren's nest in its eye-sockets and bluebells growing through its ribs. As I stare at the painting, I almost stumble. Barbara Fleming gives me a strange look.

'Good, isn't it? It's just something I picked up locally. No idea who the artist is –Amazing talent though…' Her eyes flick up and down at me. 'Perhaps it's not your thing.'

I just stare, tongue-tied.

'Jennifer thinks you're wonderful, so I don't think I need another reference. You can start today if you like. I'll be in my studio if you need anything.' She points through the sash window, at a large wooden shed with huge windows at the bottom of her garden.

She whisks me out of the room and back into the kitchen, leaving me on my own. Now I've blown my chance. I should chase her across the lawn; tell her I painted the picture in her living room. She wouldn't believe me.

I open the cleaning cupboard. I might find a good way of telling her about the painting eventually.

Chapter 4
The Giant Robin

Jason

My notepad is covered in scribbled words, crossed out. I never realised this would be so hard. I've tried a few different chord progressions; I've picked out tunes but nothing seems to stick. Ben's song is sounding really good now. He changed the lyrics. It's simple but it's saying something real.

I don't want to write a love song. Most girls just talk to each other all the time about who's going out with who. All those songs about love mean nothing to me, really.

A sudden gust of wind slaps rain against the window. We were supposed to be busking today – just over a week before Christmas but Ben called an hour ago to cancel. It would be hopeless in this weather. He's been roped into helping his mum bake mince pies for their family party. We'll go busking tomorrow instead, if it's dry.

I've got lists of words I've written as possible rhymes: bane, chain, drain, feign, drain, pain, lane – but I can't think of anything to say with any of them. I screw the sheet of paper up into a ball and throw it into the fire. This is so frustrating. Harder than any English homework I've ever had.

Generation Terrorists will help me. I slide the CD into my stereo. I press play and turn it up loud. I know the words pretty much by heart but it feels good to hold the booklet in my hands. I sit on the bed, staring at the rain droplets running down the window, turning the outside world into a blur of grey and green.

I pick up my guitar. I've been learning to play the songs by listening to them over and over again until I find the right notes for the guitar parts and work out the chords, even though they don't sound too great on my guitar. I've done it with other songs too but this is my favourite album. Ben's tried learning stuff from CDs but he mostly gives up and gets the chords off the internet, which are usually wrong anyway.

I'm half way through playing along to 'Little Baby Nothing' when I hear knocking on my bedroom door. I press pause and throw my guitar onto the bed before I open the door.

Mum's standing there. Her clothes are dusty and the Christmas decorations box is beside her feet on the landing. The tiny door to the loft space is open.

'What are you doing?' she asks.

'Writing a song.'

She gives me a twisted smile, as if she's forcing herself to look cheerful.

'Do you want to help me with the Christmas decorations?'

'Not particularly.' I didn't mean to sound nasty but she looks disappointed. She opens her mouth as if she was going to say something but then she closes it again.

I'm not even sure why she bothers with those tatty old decorations. Every year, she gets out the Santa Claus I made from red tissue paper, and she glues new cotton wool onto the fake snowman.

'Maybe later. I'm just a bit busy now.'

'Sounded more like you were playing along to the Manics.' She peers into my room. 'Are you up to date with your homework?'

'Don't nag me. I'll do it before I have to…'

She comes into the room and sits on the bed; strums my guitar strings with her thumb. She hands the guitar over to me.

'Want to play me your song?'

'It's not ready yet. The words won't come out right.'

'What's the song about?'

'I dunno. Nothing works.'

'It doesn't matter what you write. Just keep going. Maybe you've been cooped up in your room too long. It'll come to you when you're doing something else. '

'That's why I was listening to the Manics…'

'I always thought Richey was trying too hard to prove he was clever in his lyrics. The meaning gets lost – there were sometimes too many words.' She talks quietly, staring at my posters.

'That's why I like them. You have to work things out.'

'James couldn't fit them to the music properly. He had to spit the words out.'

'You said they sounded like cheesy metal and then just got boring.'

'Richey had an amazing presence. Pity he couldn't actually play the guitar…'

'Did you see them? Before he went missing?' It almost sounds like she knew them.

'I came up with song ideas when I let my mind wander. Most of 'Rootless in Babylon' came to me in the shower – the melody, the bassline – everything. I just wrapped myself in a towel and ran into my room to write it down – left the shower running…'

'You wrote the songs in your band?'

Mum stares at me as if she didn't even realise she was talking out loud. She stands up and brushes the dust from her jeans. She picks up the box of decorations and runs down the stairs.

'I might actually be interested!' I shout – but it just echoes down the stairs. I follow her, but she's disappeared. She's not in the living room or the kitchen and the Christmas decorations box has been dumped at the bottom of the stairs.

I open the box of decorations. It's like this job, or whatever she's doing now. She hasn't told me anything about it. She layers up little secrets like the papier-mâché robin we made together, gluing strips of newspaper onto a balloon with wallpaper paste.

I get the robin out of the box. Its beak is wonky and its poster-paint colours have gone all dull. Why did I want to make a giant robin? I made it when I was ten.

I throw the robin against the wall. Its head comes off. Then I stamp on the head and body until the robin is totally flattened. The surge of rage suddenly subsides and I feel numb. I stand back and look at the pieces on the floor. A bit pathetic, really.

I put my jacket and trainers on and slam the back door as hard as I can behind me. Mum's near the compost heap, wrestling with the overgrown Christmas tree in its pot. If she thinks she's going to be able to drag it inside, she must be nuts. I turn towards her. She stares straight through me. She's biting her lip and her eyes are shining. I want to help her. I want to be that little kid making decorations again.

I barge into the shed, grab my bike and bump it down the steps, turning my face into the rain. I cycle downhill toward Black Rocks as fast as I can go.

Kaz

There's an amazing view of the whole valley from the top of Barbara Fleming's lane and a dim winter afternoon light silhouetting the shell of Riber castle against the washed-out sky. The dry-stone wall is freezing and poking into my thighs as I sketch furiously.

The pictures in Barbara Fleming's hallway made me want to look at landscapes in a new way – to give reality a hint of sinister glamour, like the dark shadow of the cursed castle, floating above Matlock.

A cold wind gusts across the field and threatens to rip the sketchbook out of my hands. Rain is looming and there are dark smudgy clouds on the skyline. I glance at my watch. I should have been at Barbara Fleming's house five minutes ago. Why did I lose track of time? I should have done this another day but I had my sketchbook in my bag. I put it back in my bag, and take a panoramic sweep of photos I can stick together later as a reference for my painting.

My camera pre-dates Mission Control. A present from my dad on my sixteenth birthday. It hangs around my neck heavily and makes satisfying clunks and clicks. I used it at college. Later I took endless rolls of film on tour, to stop myself from getting bored. I took the photos on the inside cover of the first album. *Select* magazine printed some of them when we did a European tour diary, back in '92. I wish I still had a copy of it – photos of Daz and the others posing on top of the Berlin wall; grim soviet-era architecture; the interiors of some truly awful hotel rooms.

I wrestle my bike free from the tangle of dead grass and brambles in the hedgerow and sling my bag into its basket. I jump on the bike and free-wheel down the hill. At least it won't take me long to get to Barbara Fleming's house.

I feel more comfortable at Mrs Norton's house. She let me take some photographs of her this morning, with her collection. She was really proud – she wants framed copies. She would never understand why I'm fascinated by all her Scottie-dog memorabilia. I've persuaded her to let me do some of the normal cleaning; she needs the help after all. Her husband just sits in his chair in the conservatory, watching TV. Occasionally I see him moving slowly around in the garden, pulling out any weeds daring to appear, and putting down slug pellets on the soil around his prize plants.

I steer around the corner. The road gets steeper, with a few large houses – Barbara Fleming's is one of them. I'm so late, I turn the pedals, trying to give myself a bit of extra speed. The bike hurtles down the hill – my hair streams behind me and cold air rushes at my face. I relish the feeling of freedom, even though in a few minutes, I'm going to be pushing a Hoover around.

My hands squeeze the brakes. I don't slow down. I'm still flying down the hill. I try again, palms drenched with panic. A car is coming up the lane towards me – no room to get past – parked cars on the other side. I've missed Barbara Fleming's house now. I put my feet down. The toes of my boots scrape the ground.

The car is very close now. Blaring its horn. The man's face behind the steering wheel is frozen with horror. He knows I can't stop. I keep squeezing the brakes. I think about Daz. Maybe this was meant to happen.

I see Jason's pale, anxious face, flicking his fringe out of his eyes as someone tells him I'm dead. We've hardly spoken to each other since Saturday. I could have told him about Mission Control. I could have told him about Daz.

If I don't do something now, I'll crash onto the car's bonnet and through the windscreen. What would Jason do without me?

I turn the handlebars sharply to the left. My right arm and my knee scrape along the tarmac. My head hits the ground. Everything's black and muffled.

Daz gives me a lazy, devilish grin. He's lying in a tangle of sheets. Sun streams through the window. I hear rushing water in the background. For a second I don't know where I am. The Watermill studio. It's going to be another busy day recording, so we'd better make the most of the early morning. I feel Daz's hand on my leg. I try to move towards him but I'm stuck. I feel paralysed. I try to reach him but I can't. He shakes me gently.

'Karen. Karen. Can you hear me?'

Why is he calling me Karen, like my mum? Daz never calls me that. We're always Kaz and Daz – a stupid in-joke that stuck.

'Daz!' I try to shout. I open my eyes. The bed in the studio was a dream. I've woken into another dream. White walls and an antiseptic smell. I'm in a dream about Daz being in the hospital. I try to move but I'm in bed, propped up on pillows. There's a nurse with a concerned face staring at me – and Jennifer, standing near me.

'I wasn't expecting to see you until I got back from work,' she says, smiling, but her eyes are wide with concern.

I'm suddenly back in the present. My right arm hurts – a stinging, throbbing pain. It's bandaged, strapped to my chest. My leg hurts too but it's covered with a sheet. I'm wearing a hospital gown. Where are my clothes?

'Where am I?' I blurt out. Before they can answer, the logical part of my mind reassures me. Jennifer's here. I'm in the Whitworth hospital. I fell off my bike; the brakes weren't working. My head throbs and everything spins again.

I feel sick. The dream, when I was with Daz, felt so real.

'It's okay. You're safe,' Jennifer says. 'You hit your head. A man brought you here in his car. We're going to transfer you to Derby for some scans.'

'What about Jason?'

'Your son? He's at Anthony Gell school, isn't he?'

I try to nod but my head hurts so much. This is like the worst hangover I've ever had, even though I haven't been drunk for fourteen years.

'Jason Knight – he's in 9RB…'

'But you're Karen Clarke?' She sounds confused.

'I lied. I'm Karen Kenning – No! Keziah Knight. I changed my name by deed poll.' I feel myself slipping. The corners of the room dissolve into a fog.

'What about any other relatives? Someone who can look after Jason?'

'Jason's friend Ben Braddon. His parents…' My voice echoes around my head. It sounds like someone else is speaking, not me. 'Where's my stuff? My bike – bag – camera – boots?'

My head hurts so badly I have to close my eyes again.

'I'll call Barbara. She'll look for your things…' Jennifer's voice fades.

The next time I open my eyes, Daz is there, waiting for me, on that bed in the Watermill studio.

Jason

Mr Young's portacabin classroom feels airless. The windows are steamed up and the electric radiators are whirring, making the mathematically designed Santa hats and Christmas stars spin round on their cotton threads. I wish I could go back to Year 7 maths, making a shape template and then spending most of the lesson colouring it in.

I'm struggling through equations that we're not allowed to use calculators for. Sometimes I'm okay at maths, but once they start throwing in algebra and long division, my brain sort of freezes. I can't even compare my answers with Ben, because Mr Young makes us sit boy/girl. Vicky Pearson is sitting at my desk but she's put her fluffy pencil case between us like a barrier and she's shielding her work from me with her left arm. It wouldn't hurt her just to let me glance at her exercise book.

'Your time's up,' Mr Young says. 'Everyone who gives me a correct answer gets a fun size Mars Bar.'

Ben catches my eye from the opposite side of the classroom. He mimes clapping like a performing seal while Mr Young's back is turned. Bribing us with sweets is the only way Mr Young tries to make our lessons bearable.

'Right, question one – what's 342 divided by 6?' Mr Young always tries to sound jolly but there are probably a thousand places he would rather be than teaching us maths the week before Christmas.

Vicky Pearson's hand shoots straight up.

'Fifty Seven, sir,' she beams at him.

Mr Young throws the Mars Bar in a graceful arc but Vicky fumbles the catch and it lands on my desk. I hand it over to her and she gives me a brief smile. I got the answer right too. Maybe I'm not so hopeless at this after all. I put my hand up tentatively when he asks the next question.

There's a knock on the classroom door. Mr Young opens it. Mrs O'Connor, the school secretary, stands in the doorway. Vicky gives me a puzzled look as she unwraps her Mars Bar and shoves it in her mouth. Mrs O'Connor never comes out from behind her glass window. She always sends the reception duty kid. She comes into the classroom, whispering something to Mr Young, who stares straight at me. My heart begins to thump.

'Jason, you need to go with Mrs O'Connor,' Mr Young says. He looks really serious. 'Bring your bag and coat.'

'What's happened?' I ask. 'Am I in trouble?'

He doesn't tell me. I put my pencil case and maths book in my bag and grab my jacket from the back of the chair. I can't remember when my form was this quiet. It's like someone's turned the sound off. Ben looks at me, worried.

Mrs O'Connor walks as fast as she can across the playground but she's quite fat and short. I almost stumble over my feet trying to walk at her slow pace.

'What's going on?'

'Your mum's had an accident on her bike.'

Something in my head starts buzzing, like my ears have popped. Suddenly, I'm rooted to the spot, but Mrs O'Connor walks ahead and holds the door to the main building open for me, smiling sympathetically. She smells of vanilla. Is it perfume or custard creams?

'They've taken her to the hospital in Derby. She's not fully conscious. I'm sorry, love, that's all they told me.'

I nod. I'm not really taking it in.

'But what do I –' What if she dies? How long would it take me to cycle to the hospital? She's been upset again. I should have helped her with the Christmas decorations. I was angry with her because she started telling me about her band – she got me interested – and then she ran off. Maybe I should have been more patient.

What if it's too late now? I might never find out. I put my hand in my jacket pocket and find a handful of busking money from Sunday.

'Can I get a taxi to the hospital?'

'I'm just phoning someone for you now. Wait here.'

She sits me down in one of the woolly blue chairs visitors use and brings me a plastic cup of water too cold to drink. I put it down on the Formica coffee table.

The bell goes for the end of the lesson and suddenly there's shouting; the sound of feet running down the corridor. Everyone can see me sitting here as they walk past reception. I keep my eyes on the cup of water.

The tremors from everyone thumping around makes the surface of the water vibrate like that scene in *Jurassic Park* when the dinosaurs are coming towards the car.

'In trouble, Kenny?' I glance up. Bradley Smeed. I refuse to look at him.

'What you doing here then? Ill or something?'

I shake my head and hug my knees.

Bradley Smeed sits in one of the chairs next to me, splayed out with his legs stretching out into the corridor.

'You're in trouble, aren't you? What did you do?'

'Nothing. Just go away.'

'Not nice of you, is it? Were you rude to a teacher? Did you tell them to "go away"?' Bradley sits up in the chair, leering at me.

'No.'

'Maybe your house burned down. Mind you, I heard you lived in a field. Maybe your mum died or something.'

I stare at him in alarm with my eyes wide. My heart stabs with fear. I can't help it. Does he know about the accident? How does he know? It must be a coincidence – he was only saying random horrible things – but my eyes are filling with tears. Bradley Smeed suddenly looks scared, as if he knows he's gone too far.

'She's not dead!' I shout.

Mrs O'Connor looms in the reception window. Bradley Smeed grabs his bag and runs off. I carry on waiting, with my hands in front of my face.

Kaz

I put Daz's mug of tea down on my bedside cabinet with a plate of home-made biscuits.

'Thanks,' he says. He takes a ginger snap and crunches it. He's buried deep in his scuffed school copy of *1984*, making notes in his exercise book. I promised I'd help him with his essay but he's really getting into it.

'The bit with the cage of rats on his head would make a great idea for a song,' he says. 'Imagine them all nibbling at your face…'

'I'd quite like a pet rat. I could train it.'

I plug my bass into my practice amp. We only have one amp so we have to take turns. I run through the bassline of our new song 'Sherbet Lemon'. We wrote it together but the lyrics are mostly mine. I know they still need some work. It's about sweets or sex or both.

'I'm your sherbet lemon, baby – sweet and sour crazy – whatever you want me to be – just wait and see...'

I sing the words quietly because I don't want to disturb Daz's concentration. His guitar is lying on my bed, a battered white Flying V. He bought it second-hand with the money from his paper round, saving up for months. He covered the guitar with marker-pen doodles of aliens. He's scared his dad might sell it so he takes it everywhere with him, even at school, or gets me to look after it.

'Sounds good,' he says. 'Why don't you use the open E string instead of the seventh fret? It sounds heavier.'

I run through it the way he suggested. He's right. We work well together. Strange, how I gravitated naturally towards the bass. I got it for Christmas. It's a cheap one but it plays well. Mum doesn't think it's feminine – she's mystified by my change in attitude and appearance. She thinks I should have kept my old friends. She gets cross when I tell her they're a bunch of bitches. They completely ignore me now but the feeling's mutual. It's just me and Daz – and Pete – against the world.

Daz comes here every day after school now. This is our time. I tried going round to his flat but it was horrible, to be honest. The place was a tip: his dad slumped on the sofa; the coffee table was crowded with empty lager cans and an overflowing ash-tray. His dad called me 'darling' in a way that freaked me out. He was creepy with me but he swore at Daz and told him I was too good for him. He said 'I don't know what she sees in you, you lanky piece of shit' and wouldn't listen when Daz told him we were just friends. When I was alone with Daz, in his little bedroom plastered with posters, he was trying not to cry. He said things used to be alright, before his mum left. Daz can't wait to finish school and leave home.

Daz lifts his mug to his lips and takes a sip of tea. The lenses of his glasses steam up. He takes them off and wipes the lenses on the bottom of his school shirt. He stares blankly, deep in thought, like he's forgotten I'm here. His eyes are dark blue, like thunder clouds. I haven't really seen him, unselfconscious like this, without his glasses distorting his face. His skin has really cleared up, pale against his dark hair, which he's growing long. I bought him a bottle of Head and Shoulders and now his hair is shiny, clean-smelling.

Pete says I'm bossy but I don't care. If I didn't wait for Daz to finish his paper round with a carton of orange juice and two slices of toast, he wouldn't have any breakfast. If I don't look after him, no one will. No one understands him like I do, not even Pete.

He puts his glasses back on and carries on reading. I look down at my bass, noodling around with a blues scale to cover my confusion. I'm in love with Daz. I realise I've been in love with him for months – there was even a spark of something that first day in the music room. I just had it in my head he was ugly. Maybe it's wrong to feel this way about him. It could ruin everything. My cheeks are burning hot.

'Do you like me?' I blurt. I can't believe I said that.

I sit next to him on the bed, feeling the warmth from his leg through his school trousers and my tights. He doesn't move his leg away from mine. That must be a good sign but he's still reading. I need to get his attention.

I make a grab for his glasses and snatch them off his face.

'Kaz – I need them,' he pleads. I throw them onto the carpet. What am I doing? This is stupid. 'Don't break them!'

He blinks, looking lost and hurt. His eyes are fringed with long black lashes.

'What are you doing?' he asks.

I'm still playing my bass, my fingers running up and down the frets randomly. I stop playing and put my hands in my lap. I take a deep breath.

'Look, I know we're already friends, Daz but will you go out with me?'

'Seriously?'

Daz's face flickers with doubt. He's had girls, well, everyone, really, taking the piss out of him ever since he started secondary school, probably before. His dad tells him he's worthless every day. Surely Daz can tell I mean it?

His face comes closer to mine and suddenly, we're snogging. His mouth tastes of sweet tea and ginger biscuits. My arms are wrapped tightly around Daz's back, feeling his shoulder-blades through his shirt. My bass bumps between us and gets in the way...

Jason

The hospital floor has coloured lines on it so people don't lose their way. I follow Ben's mum. She told me to call her Brenda years ago but it still feels weird. She left work and came to pick me up; brought me straight here, breaking the speed limit in her Fiesta.

We get to the head injuries ward and a nurse leads the way. There are people in the other beds. I don't recognise Mum, until the nurse walks right up to the bed. I still wouldn't have recognised her. Mum's head is covered in bandages and her eyes are closed. That's all I can see of her. I can't even tell she's breathing, but her pale lips are curled into a slight smile.

I find myself grabbing hold of Brenda's sleeve.

'Is she going to die?' I whisper.

The nurse looks at me.

'She's had her scan. No fractures or internal bleeding. She's lucky.'

I nod, swallowing a sob.

'Is she in a coma?'

The nurse smiles.

'She's just sleeping. We have to keep an eye on her though.'

'You can talk to her,' Brenda says.

I sit on the plastic chair next to the bed. Mum's face is so pale, it looks like light could shine through her skin. There's a small graze on her right cheek. The bandages cover her eyebrows. I reach out to touch her face.

'Please be okay. I'm sorry.'

Her eyelashes flutter and her eyes open. Her green eyes are the only bit of colour on the bed. She focuses on my face.

'Daz…' she murmurs.

Who? She stares but doesn't seem to recognise me.

'Mum – it's me.'

Her eyelids are drooping shut. The smile is back on her face. I just want her to wake up. Instead, Mum's locked in her own dream world and she doesn't even know I'm here.

'She's confused,' Brenda says. She pats me on the shoulder. 'Don't worry.'

My dad's name was Darren. Is Daz the same person? I wish I knew more about him. All I know is that his name was Darren, he played the guitar and he died before I was born.

'Mum – wake up, please,' I say. She's just lying there, still and silent – as if she's having a good time in her dreams and doesn't want to wake up. As if she'd rather be asleep than alive.

I'm on the sofa bed in Ben's room. I've stayed here hundreds of time before, listening to music, playing computer games and talking for hours before we finally fall asleep. Now I just want to be home, in my own creaky bed, under the softness of my washed-out duvet cover. I want Mum to bring me a hot water bottle and to sit in the white wooden chair, reading a book to me, even though I told her to stop reading to me when I was eight. I remember telling her I was too grown up, that I could read my own books now. The last book she ever read to me was *Charlie and the Chocolate Factory*.

I throw off the duvet and find the book on Ben's shelf. We were both nuts on Roald Dahl when we were younger, especially when we were in Year Four. Ben's copy still looks new, its spine barely creased. Not the same as my copy, which has yellow pages worn soft at the edges, a faded cover and a comforting musty smell.

I wrap myself in the washing-powder scented duvet and start reading, trying to remember Mum reading it, doing funny voices; showing me the pictures. These are the wrong pictures anyway. My copy of the book is so old it doesn't even have the scribbly Quentin Blake drawings; the pictures in my book are neat and detailed. This is better than nothing. I can almost convince myself. I wish they had let me stay at home on my own, even though the cottage felt empty earlier when we went to feed the cat and get my stuff.

'I made you hot chocolate,' Ben says, coming up the stairs inside the room. He's carrying two mugs. He hands me one of them. There are drips down the side of the mug and it looks like he's spilt quite a lot of it on his way up from the kitchen.

'Thanks.' I take a sip. It's gritty with sugar and lukewarm. Ben sees what book I'm reading and he smiles.

'Look – do you want anything? Are you okay?' he asks.

'I'm fine.' I hope it didn't sound like I was snapping at him but I'm tired of the way they've been fussing over me all night. 'Thanks, though.'

Ben sits on his bed, staring at me, as if he's waiting for me to say something.

'Put some music on,' I say.

'What do you want?'

'Anything. I don't care.'

Ben puts on *Elephant* by the White Stripes – something we both like. Right now it's just something to block out the silence. I lie down and carry on reading. As long as I concentrate on the words, I don't need to think about anything else.

'Can I turn the light off?' Ben asks. I'm not sure how long I've been reading. 'Are you sure you don't want to talk?' He looks at me as if he's scared I might burst into tears at any moment. Well, actually, I might. I just don't want him to know.

'Yes. Sorry.' I feel like I've been transformed from just being Jason to some tragic little orphan who everyone has to treat kindly. What if Mum died? It would be like this all the time. Maybe even Bradley Smeed would start being nice to me. Yeah, right.

Even though they told me Mum won't die, there's a part of me that doesn't believe it.

Ben pulls the cord for the light from his bed and I put the book down. I wish I had a torch so I could go on reading. In the dark, I can't stop imagining how much worse the accident could have been. I pull the duvet over my face and shut my eyes. Tears escape out of my eyes and I can't stop them.

Chapter 5
Fairy Lights

Kaz

'You're coming to our Boxing Day party, I hope?' Brenda asks, as she turns up Cromford Hill. She's the world's most careful driver, but every bump in the road makes my head throb. I feel a bit sick. It must be a side-effect of the pain-killers.

'Thanks – it depends on how I'm feeling.' I'll be a bundle of laughs, stuck in a chair, with Ben's nan for company. I caught my reflection in the car window earlier. I'd fit in at a Halloween party, maybe, but not one of Brenda's tame family gatherings.

'Are you sure you'll be alright at home?'

'My head looks worse than it is. I'd rather be at home than clogging up a hospital bed.'

'Jason was so upset. He seemed to be blaming himself –'

'How can he blame himself?'

Brenda gives me a worried glance, before fixing her eyes back on the road.

'I'm sorry. I shouldn't have worried you.'

'I needed to know. He keeps too much inside these days.'

'Were you angry with him about anything?'

I can't remember. There are weird gaps in my memory. Brenda takes the left turn to Bolehill village. The journey seems to be taking hours. The dull throb in my head gets worse; presses down on the back of my eyes. I'm home.

Brenda parks the car. She walks round and opens the passenger door. I try to put my weight on my right leg but my knee buckles and I grab onto the car door.

'Fuck – sorry. I forgot…'

Brenda blinks, then holds my arm steady.

It's taken Brenda years to get used to me. She disapproved of me at first. At the playgroup, she was years older than me, primly dressed. I wore draggled jumble sale clothes with paint stains, hair hacked short. Just Brenda's luck that her son and my scruffy child were drawn together like magnets. She thought I was a bad parent, an anarchist on the loose in her neat Derbyshire village. She wouldn't let Ben come to play here at first.

I suppose I was prejudiced too. I've always felt on my guard with Brenda, poised between being over polite and wanting to shock her. She's been so kind this week, taking time off work. What would have happened to Jason if she hadn't helped?

The pain in my leg makes my eyes smart. I feel so weak. My head swims with the effort of staying upright.

'Mum!' Jason hurtles down the garden steps, joy and shock in his eyes, which he quickly masks with a smile.

'How am I going to get up the steps?'

'We'll hold you up…' he stares at me. He's probably wishing I could have stayed in hospital. I'll be almost helpless for the next few days. 'Wait there.'

He bounds back up the steps. It's something I took for granted, rushing about on my bike; taking long walks in the woods with my camera. Now I can't even limp. I stare at my scuffed, unlaced boots, blinking back tears of frustration.

'He's so pleased to have you back at home,' Brenda says.

Jason comes back with Elsa's old walking stick. He puts it in my good hand and I lean on it heavily. With Jason supporting my arm, I make it up the steps, one-by-one. By the time I've got to the top, it's almost dark.

Brenda puts the bag with my overnight things in it – Jason's old school bag – down by the back door.

'Thanks,' I tell Brenda. 'You didn't have to do this for me.'

'It's alright, Keziah. What are friends for?'

I nod. It's the first time she's called me a friend. She's almost old enough to be my mother – and that's the way she acts most of the time, like I'm a wayward teenager, not really capable of looking after myself. I watch as Brenda walks briskly back down the steps. She waves as she gets into her car. I can't wave back. My good hand is leaning on the walking stick.

Jason opens the back door and helps me inside. The house is warm. There's a baking smell coming from the AGA.

'They gave me the rest of the week off school.' He smiles.

'Crap way to spend it though, looking after me.'

He helps me to shuffle towards the living room. Then he stops. Jason slips behind the door. I lean on Elsa's stick, still out of breath from my climb up the steps.

'Shut your eyes,' he says. I close them, trying to keep my balance. I feel Jason's hand on my arm and he gently leads me forward.

'You can look now.'

Jason has managed to drag the overgrown Christmas tree into the living room. It's glittering with twinkling blue lights and covered with silver tinsel, as well as all the old decorations: the salt dough silver stars we baked rock-hard in the AGA; the gold-sprayed pine cones; the fairy I made for him when he was five – underneath the sparkling dress, she's a jumble sale Barbie doll with a broken leg. There's a fire glowing in the grate and he's made the sofa into a bed with pillows and Elsa's old patchwork quilt.

'Wow.'

'I'm sorry,' Jason says.

'What for?'

'For the robin. I'm sorry I broke it.'

'Oh, that.' I'd forgotten about the squashed remains I found on Saturday afternoon.

I lower myself slowly onto the sofa. The room smells of pine resin and wood smoke. It's a world away from the antiseptic and strip lights of the hospital. It feels so good to be home. The tree branches stretch into the room, casting strange shadows in the firelight. The tree shakes. It's the cat, climbing through the branches.

'It's like living in a forest. I love it,' I say.

'The lights do different patterns – look!' Jason presses a control pad, making the lights twinkle, shimmer and then flash manically. I have to shut my eyes again. My head's pounding.

'Not that one!' I laugh. 'It's not doing my head much good.'

Jason

The needle makes a swishing noise as the record runs out of grooves, and the arm of the record player swings back into place with a clunk. Mum wakes up with a start. She wanted to hear some of Elsa's old classical records. I chose the Bartók string quartets. I grew up with this music. There's a whole stack of records; they must be about fifty years old. The old records were the only music Mum had, until I started collecting stuff. There's something a bit weird about someone who says she used to be in a band not having any records of her own. She listens to the classical records while she paints.

There's a pile of tinny old jazz records too, brittle 78s, that I remember bouncing around to when I was really small. It's one of my first memories, whirling around on the living room rug. Ben says his first memory is watching Oasis on Top of the Pops.

I remember breaking one of the 78s when I was little – I was trying to get it out of the cupboard and it rolled out of its paper sleeve, smashing into shards on the floor. Mum was cross and said it could never be replaced but Aunt Elsa just laughed.

I turn the record over carefully, put the needle on the record again and the ancient string quartet crackles into life again. I like the old things in this house, really. I've lived with this stuff all my life. It's like a museum to Great-Aunt Elsa. The record player is in a massive wooden cupboard with built-in speakers – Mum calls it a radiogram. It's got a radio too, with a dial that lights up with a soft glow. It's probably the newest piece of furniture here, bang up to date in the 1950s. Funny that everything this can do, and more, can now fit onto a piece of plastic in the palm of my hand.

I bet the radiogram will outlast Ben's iPod though.

I sit on the floor, next to the sofa. Mum puts her good arm around my shoulders.

'I thought you'd gone off Christmas,' she says.

'It just seems really fake.'

'That's the whole point. People need to brighten things up this time of year. Otherwise, they'd just top themselves.'

I laugh.

'Did you borrow the lights from Ben's house?'

'We've been busking. I've been saving for an electric guitar – but…'

'Jason – I need to tell you. I got a couple of cleaning jobs.'

'I kind of guessed that.'

'The thing is, I was trying to…'

There's a knock on the front door. Mum twitches on the sofa. Her eyes are wide with panic.

'Who's that?' she asks.

'How should I know?'

The front door's blocked by the Christmas tree. It was the only place I could put it. We don't use that door anyway. The knock comes again.

I slip on my trainers and open the back door. A blast of icy wind hits me in the face. My heart beats faster. I don't even know why I'm so nervous. It's probably just someone collecting for charity. I don't know why they bother with us.

I walk around the corner of the house. A small figure is standing by the front door, lit by the moonlight and the glow from the window. A woman, carrying something bulky.

'Hello?' My voice comes out scared-sounding, between a growl and a squeak.

'I'm looking for Karen.'

'My mum?'

'I've got her bike. And her bag.'

I take the bike and put it in the porch. It's wrecked. The handlebars are twisted and the front wheel is buckled.

'Come round the back,' I tell the woman. She follows me through the kitchen and into the living room. She's a lot older than Mum. She has lines at the corners of her mouth. Her eyes widen behind her big glasses, making her look like a goldfish.

It's not exactly a normal room. Apart from the Christmas tree, Mum's easel stands near the window, with the painting of the fox and the cat. It looks finished. That's her working corner, with a big noticeboard covered in photos, odd scraps and sketches. A few of Mum's paintings are hanging on the walls, but the rest of the room hasn't changed since Elsa was alive. The woman stands in the doorway, taking everything in: the string quartet record; Mum lying on the sofa.

'Barbara.' Mum shifts herself into a sitting position, the pain obvious on her face. 'I'm sorry if…'

'Your bike's outside. I don't think you'll be able to repair it.' The woman's not looking at Mum. She's staring at the painting on the easel.

'Thanks for bringing it back. I might turn it into a sculpture and grow climbing roses up it.'

'I found your bag when Jennifer called. It was wedged under a parked car. I suppose it got missed in the rush to get you to hospital.'

Mum nods. The woman – Barbara – gives her the scruffy black rucksack. Mum clasps the material tightly in her good hand. The woman stands over by the easel.

'You painted this?'

Mum nods, biting her lip. She looks ashamed. I don't know why. It's a great picture. She stares at the rug. Barbara peers at the signature on the painting.

'Keziah Knight. So you painted that picture in my living room?'

Mum's bottom lip trembles and she looks like she's about to cry. This is too much for her, whatever's happening.

'Why didn't you say anything?' Barbara laughs.

'You were looking for a cleaner, not a failed artist.'

'Failed?' The woman looks sharply at her. 'I adore that painting. You've no idea…'

Mum unzips her bag. She takes out her sketchbook and

puts it on the sofa. She examines her camera, shakes it gently.

'I think it's broken,' she says. 'Something's rattling inside it.' She looks devastated.

'You looked at my pictures properly,' Barbara says. 'And you had paint on your shoes. When I saw this sketchbook, I recognised the style and I wondered – but all this?' She indicates the room.

I'm standing in the doorway.

'This is Aunt Elsa's house,' I say. 'We live here. Can I get you a cup of tea? Mum? Are you okay?' She looks very pale.

'She wasn't our real aunt.' Mum laughs, nervously.

That's news to me. I stare at Mum.

'She was very frail. She died when Jason was four. I looked after her – she taught me everything about art –' Mum trails off, examining her camera, avoiding my eye.

'What are you going on about?' I ask. 'She was your Great Aunt.'

'I know I told you that.' Mum looks guilty. 'We were so close, it felt like we were related – but it was just one of those things – like calling Mavis in the charity shop Aunty.'

'Right,' I mutter. What else is Mum hiding? Like the stuff she said about writing songs in her band, and calling out for someone called Daz when she was in the hospital?

The light in the room goes weird. The blonde woman – Barbara – is holding the table lamp upside-down, examining its base.

'This is Wren Cottage – Elsa Day's house?' She puts the lamp back on the radiogram.

Mum struggles to stand up. She looks terrified.

'Please don't tell anyone. Elsa told me to look after the house – especially the garden. But there's nothing official. If she had real relatives who realised we were here and wanted to sell Wren Cottage, we'd have nowhere to go.'

'Her interpretation of surrealism is fascinating. I studied her as part of my Fine Art degree. Have you got any idea how much her pieces like this are worth?'

The table lamp is shaped like a miniature lighthouse, blue

and white striped on its own rocky island. These things have just always been here. The lamp looks a bit naff, like a present from the seaside.

Mum shakes her head.

'There are more ceramics but they're not mine to sell. They're all stored away. Jason was a toddler – he could have knocked things over…'

Barbara nods.

'I'd like to see more of her work.'

'The garden's the most important thing, really, but it's down to its bare bones at the moment. It's beautiful in spring – May's the best month. I can open the storage boxes any time. It would be nice to look at her things…'

'Not until you're feeling better.'

'Do you still want me to work for you? When I can walk properly again. Nothing's broken. I was lucky. Just sprains – bad grazes. My head'll be okay…'

'I think I can find another cleaner.' Barbara says. Mum opens her mouth in shock.

'Please – I need the money. I can't sell any of Elsa's stuff.'

'What about the painting on the easel? Is it for sale?'

'I've only just finished it.' Mum says.

'How much do you want for it?' Barbara asks. Mum looks blank. 'Okay. Fifteen hundred. I know I'm selling you short but…'

'Really?'

Barbara smiles mysteriously, as if she's had a wonderful idea she doesn't want to share with anyone yet.

'Can you pay in cash?' Mum sounds desperate.

'Of course,' Barbara says, laughing.

Mum uses Elsa's stick to lever herself off the sofa. She hobbles towards Barbara and gives her an awkward, one-armed hug, almost falling over. Who is this woman? Mum's smiling and crying at the same time.

I duck into the kitchen and fill the kettle. I was going to start cooking tea soon. Mum's talking about her camera now and Barbara is giving her advice on getting it repaired or going digital. It could be hours before we get rid of her. I open a tin of beans and cut slices off the new loaf of bread. I'll eat mine now. Mum's tea can wait if she's going to chat to this woman for hours.

It's great that we'll have some money. At the same time, my head's whirling. Why did Mum lie to me about Elsa being our aunt when she wasn't? How did Mum end up here? If Elsa was a famous artist, why didn't Mum ever tell me? All this time we've been struggling for money while everything in the house is worth a fortune.

Barbara's going nuts over everything now – Elsa Day's table lamp; Elsa Day's radiogram; Elsa Day's washing up bowl; Elsa Day's saucepan with baked beans in it. Surely we could get away with selling something?

I'm going round to Ben's tomorrow to look Elsa Day up on the internet. I never thought of doing that before. I thought she was just my Great-Aunt; a crazy old lady who used to make sculptures and things. It's not unusual, round here. Half the people in Wirksworth call themselves artists. It doesn't mean they're famous or make any money at it.

The door is suddenly pushed shut. I try to listen, but they're talking in quiet voices and I can't make out what they're saying. Fine. I'll eat my tea in the kitchen.

I turn the portable radio up loud, to drown out my thoughts, even though it's tuned to Radio Two, with stupid Christmas songs on heavy rotation.

Kaz

I have to dial the number for the music shop with my left hand and then snatch up the phone receiver again when it starts ringing.

'Guitar department.'

'Is that Andy?' I feel breathless. I've grabbed my chance to do this. I sent Jason round to Mrs Norton's house with a Christmas card, a picture of a Scottie dog in a basket I drew for her before I fell off my bike, and some surplus vegetables from the garden. I feel guilty about not coming back to dust her collection. I asked Jason to explain about my accident.

'You might not remember me. I came into your shop last month. I wanted to sell my bass…'

'Kaz? Are you okay? I was worried.'

'I had a bike accident and I can hardly get off the sofa – but apart from that…'

'Are you playing the bass again?'

'My arm's in a sling. I managed to get the money for my son's electric guitar though.'

'Excellent. About the money, I mean. I'm sorry about the accident.'

'There's a lady coming into the shop today to buy a guitar for Jason. Her name's Barbara and she'll be paying in cash.' I glance up at the empty easel. I miss the moonlit garden painting. I wish I could start something else. Maybe I'll try in a few days when I'm allowed to take the sling off my right arm. Lucky I'm left-handed. I always played bass the right-hand way but it felt like my left hand was doing more work, holding down the frets, finding the notes.

'I'll put a starter kit together – you know – decent budget guitar, a good little amp, leads…'

'He'd love an effects pedal. And one of those padded guitar cases he can strap on his back.'

Part of me wants to blow all the money from selling the painting to buy Jason something really amazing but he's still learning. I don't want to buy him an instrument that intimidates him. He needs to be able to take it everywhere with him on the back of his bike – a guitar that won't mind getting a few knocks and scrapes – something he can cover with stickers if he likes.

It would be stupid to spend all the money. After lugging Jason's Christmas present around this afternoon, Barbara might change her mind about helping me. I might need to carry on with my cleaning work and it'll be weeks before I'm properly mobile again. I'll need a replacement bike too.

'He's a lucky kid,' Andy laughs. 'You'll be able to play

together then, won't you?'

'Maybe.' What would Jason think if I wandered into his bedroom with the Thunderbird hanging on my hip, playing the bassline from one of his favourite songs?

Chapter 6

Christmas Day

Jason

I can see the sky from my bed, through the gable-end window. It's dark grey. I almost wish I hadn't opened my eyes. I stretch an arm experimentally out from under the duvet. It's freezing. It's warm in bed and, if I put my hands inside the fluffy hot water bottle cover, I can still feel some heat.

Even last year, I was still jumping out of bed at dawn on Christmas day to open my stocking. Mum always hung one of my PE socks on the back of my bedroom door, stuffed with sweets and little toys. I twigged it was Mum pretty early on but I still came downstairs and said 'look what Santa's got me' until it was a bit of a joke. Pretty unlikely to be anything this year. Still worth checking, though.

Reluctantly, I slide out of bed. I've put rugs down so my feet don't touch the floor on the way from the bed to the door but it's cold enough. Not a crisp Christmassy sort of cold, just foggy and damp.

I turn the door handle. Instant disappointment. I can't feel the stuffed sock banging against the door. Maybe it's fallen off. I check. Nothing on the other side of the door. I don't know what I was getting so excited about anyway. The sweets would have been okay but I think I've grown out of being thrilled by a miniature tractor or an Action Man from the charity shop bargain bin. She usually gives me a couple of decent books, too, but I'm not holding out much hope this year.

We were so skint before that artist woman Barbara bought the painting – and since then, Mum hasn't left the house. I had to stop her from trying to go out into the garden yesterday. I've been looking after the vegetable patch since her accident but if I didn't keep an eye on her, she would be trying to prune the shrubbery or lug heavy plant pots about.

I get back into bed, switch on my bedside light and try to get warm again. I open the book I'm reading – Ben found it on his dad's bookshelf – *Hammer of the Gods*. It's about Led Zeppelin. They're not my favourite band but the book's great. I've only started it, really, but Ben says it gets really crazy once they start to get famous – trashing hotel rooms, drugs and groupies. Jimmy Page didn't start playing guitar until he was fifteen. So I've had a head start, even though it sounds like he learned pretty quickly.

Mum's bedroom door opens and the stairs creak as she walks down them really slowly. Last night she decided she was sick of sleeping on the sofa. I had to help her up the stairs. It's going to take her ages to use the bathroom. I try to get into the book again but I need a pee. She won't be able to have a proper bath though, not while she's covered in dressings.

I pick up my guitar, stretching so I don't have to get out of bed again. The whole thing is cold to the touch. I run through some scales to get my fingers warmed up, the duvet wrapped around my shoulders. I get absorbed in making up a new riff. It's sort of jagged, like something from *The Holy Bible* – the bleakest Manics album: the one just before Richey went missing. I've been listening to it a lot since Mum's accident. The new riff would sound good as a hook for a song, if I could think of any words.

It's gone nine now. I put my guitar down, put my old black hoodie on over my t-shirt and walk downstairs with the second-hand art book I bought Mum for Christmas. In the living room, there's a fire in the grate and the Christmas tree lights are twinkling. I wedge the book behind the sofa cushions.

Mum's in the kitchen. The AGA's hot and she's laid out the croissants I bought yesterday on a baking tray. There's a pan of milk on the hob, coming to a boil. Mum smiles at me. We always have proper hot chocolate and something nice for breakfast on Christmas morning but I didn't expect her to make it. She must be feeling a bit better.

There's a scabby graze in the middle of her forehead,

surrounded by a purple bruise, turning green around the edges. She looks tired. She's leaning against the work surface, standing on her good leg. At least her arm's out of the sling now. I went back to the Whitworth hospital with her when they changed the dressings yesterday. It was a shock to see how the gravel on the road had cut her skin to ribbons, shredding through her fleece and her jeans. I don't know why I'm disappointed that I haven't got any presents. I could have been waking up at Ben's house, or in care. She could have died.

'I was about to shout for you,' she says. She pours milk into a saucer and starts stiffly bending down. I take the saucer from her hands and put it on the floor, next to the cat. Patti is crunching biscuits from her bowl but when she sees the milk she laps at it greedily. We don't normally give her milk but it's Christmas Day. I used to make cat toys out of cotton reels and feathers as presents but she usually ignored them.

I feel much better with a belly full of hot chocolate and warm pastry. Mum carefully tears the wrapping paper off the book I bought her. She reads the cover and beams at me.

'Photos of Paris in the 1930s. This is amazing, Jason. Elsa might even be in here somewhere. You know she lived in Paris. Her husband was French, but when the Nazis invaded, they had to escape to England. She had a really mad life out there.'

She flicks through the book, staring at photos of circus performers, artists and exotic dancers.

'You shouldn't have bought me a present. You bought the tree lights with your own money.'

The book was only a few quid from Cromford Books. It's not a big deal.

'There's something for you in the cupboard under the stairs,' she says. 'Sorry, I couldn't wrap it.'

It seems a weird place to hide a few books. The cupboard's stuffed with paintings but there's a tall object leaning against the door frame with an old curtain thrown over the top. I pull off the curtain. It's a padded guitar case. Next to it is a small practice amp. I unzip the guitar case. My hands are shaking and my mouth has dried up. I take out the guitar. A Squier Stratocaster, fire-engine red. Brand-new. I hold it in my hands, overwhelmed.

'Oh my god,' I gasp. I carry the guitar back to the sofa and sound the strings. It's perfectly in tune. I play a barre chord. The guitar sounds like it can't wait to be amplified.

'Andy – in the shop – he set it up properly. It should be really good to play,' Mum says.

'This is amazing. I never thought…'

She laughs and hugs me with her good arm, kisses me on the cheek.

'Go on, then,' she says. 'Plug in the amp. Turn it up loud.'

I get everything else out of the cupboard. A proper Fender amp. It's pretty small though. How loud will it go? In the pocket on the front of the guitar case, there's a red strap with lightning bolts on it, a guitar lead, a packet of spare strings, a little box full of plectrums and an electronic effects pedal.

I want to get straight on with playing the guitar but the effects pedal looks amazing. I open the packaging and flick through the instructions.

'I hope it's not too complicated to set up,' Mum says.

'It looks easy.'

I plug the amp into the socket and plug the lead into the guitar with a satisfying clunk. I've messed around with a knackered old electric guitar in the music room at school so I know what I'm doing.

Everything smells so new. I can't believe the guitar – and everything else – belongs to me. I can't look at Mum without breaking into a massive grin. I switch on the amp and turn up the volume knob on my new guitar. I strum an E-chord. It sounds good, nice and clean. I try different chords, riffs from different songs. I fiddle around with the amp, turning the gain control all the way up. It makes a great dirty rock sound. The guitar feels amazing to hold in my hands. I attach the strap so I can play standing up. I try the guitar solo from 'Motorcycle Emptiness'. The amp does go pretty loud.

The cat comes into the living room and tries to settle in her favourite place on the windowsill but I can tell by the way her fur sticks up and the stiff way she's positioned herself that she's not impressed by the noise. She'll get used to it.

'Try the effects pedal,' Mum says, when I've finally stopped. She perches on the edge of her sofa watching me, eyes shining. Mum seems to love the noise.

I plug in the effects pedal and switch it on. I strum chords and try out riffs while I change the effects. The distortion effect sounds brilliant. I can make the guitar sound really weird and wobbly; like a human voice, or like I'm playing in a gigantic cave.

I realise the phone is ringing. It's not just another weird effect. I pick it up.

'Hello?'

'Hi, Jase.' It's Ben. It sounds noisy in the background. I can hear kids shrieking. His little cousins, uncle and aunt and his nan are staying for Christmas.

'You'll never guess what I've got,' I say. Before Ben's got chance to say anything, I put the phone receiver down and rest it on the arm of the sofa. I let rip with a barrage of chords and distorted guitar. Then I change to the effect that makes a sound like a spaceship taking off when I strum a chord.

'You got an electric guitar!'

'I'll bring it round tomorrow. There's an amazing effects pedal too. That's what I was using just now.'

'I got a Boss loop pedal and a microphone, so I can sample myself singing too. It's brilliant. *Listen to this,*' he sings, and it repeats over and over again, getting deeper and deeper until it becomes an indecipherable growl.

'That's really cool,' I say. Even though I'm still not sure why Ben wants to sample himself singing.

'My mum wants to know if your mum's coming

tomorrow. Is she okay now?'

'Getting better.'

'Bring your old guitar too – we could do some busking at the raft race. But now you've got your electric guitar –' He sounds disappointed.

'Course I will – it'll be fun.'

'Dad's picking you up about half nine – we need time to get down to the river before the rafts come through.' Someone yells at Ben. 'I'd better go. I've got to set the table for Christmas dinner.'

'Cool. See you tomorrow.'

I put the phone down and I look at the time. It's nearly twelve already and I'm still in the old jogging bottoms and t-shirt I wear in bed. How did so much time go by so quickly?

Kaz

Jason doesn't let me help him with the cooking. I sit on the sofa with the book of Parisian photographs. The photographer has written about the people he's captured, bringing them to life. A vanished world where poverty mixed with glamour and the artistic set expressed themselves with a freedom that would be shocking today. All the nudity. Elsa belonged to that world. It seems strange that, in the end, she wanted to escape to Wren cottage. But I ended up here too, didn't I? Maybe I recognised something of myself in Elsa.

Jason darts back into the room. He's tied a tea-towel around his waist. He changes the record; the Ramones, *Rocket to Russia*. It's crackly and worn. It sounds good on the radiogram.

'You've got impeccable taste, Jason,' I tell him.

'Ben bought it in Nottingham. He already had it on CD so I swapped a Velvet Underground tape for it.'

He's brought down my favourite records from his limited vinyl collection – old punk records, ancient history as far as his classmates would be concerned, but he loves it. Just like

Daz. I'm glad Jason's musical taste is expanding.

'I think the nut roast's nearly ready,' he says. 'It's gone brown on the top, anyway.'

He sets the table. He's dug Elsa's old linen tablecloth and proper napkins out of the tea-towel drawer. He puts out wine glasses. We never use them – we never have wine. They've been gathering dust for years at the back of the kitchen cupboard. Jason catches me staring at them.

'That Barbara woman gave you a bottle of wine. We should drink it.'

'Since when have you been drinking wine?'

'At Ben's house sometime when I have tea there. His dad's in the Sunday Times wine club. His mum says they're drowning in the stuff.'

'Go on, then.'

Jason stares longingly at his new guitar, leaning against the amp in the corner of the living room. I can't believe he managed to stop playing it for long enough to cook Christmas dinner. There's a weird burning smell coming from the kitchen and Jason races back.

'Shit,' he yells. 'I let the carrots boil dry.'

I try to get up, to run into the kitchen. I put my weight on my right leg, not thinking, but I'm in so much pain I have to collapse onto the sofa again. I remind myself it'll take time; that I'm already feeling much better. It's so frustrating being an invalid.

The carrots have been rescued, sort of. The burned bits have been picked out and Jason's mashed them with butter and some chives from the garden. The nut roast got a bit stuck when he was taking it out of the baking tin, so it's gone a bit crumbly but it looks perfectly edible and he's poured plenty of gravy over everything.

There are tall green candles burning in the ceramic candle holders that look like the petals of a poinsettia. Elsa must have made them, and they look very pretty.

Jason pours me a glass of wine and one for himself. It's not like a few glasses of red wine are going to turn him into an alcoholic. How am I supposed to know what he's getting up to with Ben? I'm sure they're fine. I just don't want Jason going off the rails. He's too sensible for a thirteen year old. He's been so grown-up since my accident. Sometimes I think he's more mature than me.

'What do you think, then? Mark me out of ten.' He digs into his own plate of food with gusto, slurping the wine like Ribena.

I take a sip of the wine. It's rich and fruity. I don't know the first thing about wine but it's from Marks and Spencer, so it must be posh.

Jason watches me as I taste everything on my plate. It's good. I probably couldn't do much better.

'Eleven out of ten for effort – nine for the finished result. You lose a mark for the carrots.'

'Cool. That's better than I get in food technology.'

'I know you'd rather be playing your new guitar.'

'It's alright. I quite like cooking.' He takes another gulp of wine and a fork-full of nut roast.

I take a few more sips of wine. My head starts to swim a bit. I'm not used to alcohol any more. I was never a serious wine drinker but this is nice. It numbs the aches in my arm and leg. It's a pity there's only one bottle...or maybe it's just as well.

'I'm going busking with Ben tomorrow at the raft race,' Jason says.

'I wish I could watch but I wouldn't be able to walk back up that hill. Could you dig up some potatoes tomorrow morning? I want to say thank you to Brenda properly.'

Jason laughs.

'Is that the proper way of saying thank you? With potatoes?'

'The best way of saying 'I love you' is with a bunch of carrots.' I think the wine's having an effect.

'We'll play for you later – do our Christmas songs, if you like.'

'It'll do me good to leave the house. I'm going a bit stir-crazy.'

'I'm going to save up enough money to buy a new bike. And then you can have my old one.'

'Thanks.' I catch his eye and he grins at me.

'You'd better have my cycle helmet too, though.'

'I notice you've not been wearing it.' I make a token effort to sound like a mother. Jason's nagging me – but he's right to – I nearly died because I didn't notice my brake blocks had worn out.

'It's too small for me now. It might fit you though. I'll get a new one for myself. I promise.'

'If Barbara Fleming carries on buying my paintings, I'll be able to buy you a bike.'

'Don't bank on it, Mum,' Jason says, staring at me, his eyes dead serious.

'Why not?'

'You just go on about her all the time, like she's going to solve all our problems.'

'Well, hasn't it? You've got your guitar – she even picked it up from the shop.'

'I just don't want her to let you down, that's all.'

'It sounds like you don't trust her.'

Jason saws through a roast potato with his knife and fork. He takes a slurp of wine.

'Why did you tell her Aunt Elsa wasn't our real Aunt? I didn't even know that. I didn't know we've got no right to live here.'

'It was the painkillers. I was drugged up. I wasn't expecting Barbara to be an expert on Elsa. I'm sorry. You know Elsa wanted us to stay here after she died. You were so little. I didn't know what else to do and no one came to claim Wren Cottage, did they?'

I hold my breath, hoping he's not going to ask any more questions. I wish I'd told Jason everything as soon as he was old enough to understand.

'If she really wanted us to have this house, she would have left us a will, wouldn't she?' he said.

'I was expecting one, at first. Maybe she changed her mind. Maybe she just ran out of time.'

'She was pretty weird at times.'

'You remember her?'

'She thought every picture I drew was a work of genius. I could tell the nursery teachers were only saying nice things because they had to but Aunt Elsa used to really go wild over them.'

'Like your fish picture,' I say.

Jason grins.

His fish picture is still hanging on the landing. Jason was at nursery school. When he got back from a trip to the aquarium in Matlock Bath, he drew multi-coloured shoals of fish in crayon on a long roll of blue sugar paper. He was completely absorbed in it for days. I paid to get it framed. It was our present to Elsa on her eighty-third birthday – only a few months before she died.

'She wouldn't have wanted us to be turfed out, would she? She must have left some kind of clue.'

'No one's going to turf us out. We've been here too long. No one knows it's not our house.'

'Apart from Barbara Fleming,' Jason says. 'But she seems nice enough.'

He finishes off his Christmas dinner and goes back into the kitchen, coming back with his plate piled high with roast potatoes covered in gravy.

Jason

After dinner, I go straight back to playing my Stratocaster, trying out all the riffs I've been learning but they sound so much better on an electric guitar with an effects pedal. It's really exciting. Once I get together with Ben tomorrow, we'll be able to try out some new songs.

Mum settles back down on the sofa. She's been soaking the dishes in the kitchen, even though I told her not to bother. She picks up the book I gave her again.

I practise making up guitar solos, improvising using the scales I've learned by heart. Ben can't seem to get his head round playing solos, even though I've tried to teach him. He just gets frustrated and goes back to playing chords.

Things that sounded clumsy on my old acoustic guitar now sound great, especially with loads of distortion on it. My fingers glide smoothly across the neck. The frets don't buzz at all.

But there's so much more to learn. Shredding. Pinch harmonics. The intro to 'Hand of Blood' by Bullet for My Valentine. Techniques you can't learn from books or copying records. I've still got that guitar teacher's business card. Maybe I should check him out. He's spoken to me and Ben a few more times when we've been busking. He seems genuinely interested in our playing.

Mum's scribbling something in her sketchbook. She keeps glancing up at me. I get closer to the sofa to see what she's doing.

'You're drawing me!'

She's made sketches of me playing the guitar. She looks up at me, startled and guilty.

'Can I have a proper look?' Mum hands the book over.

She's caught me with my head bent over the guitar, my fringe flopping over my eyes, concentrating. She's using fast, loose pencil strokes. She's shown the tension in my left arm as I hold down a barre chord. In the drawings, I don't look like a kid any more. With the Stratocaster, I look confident.

'I like them.'

Mum did loads of drawings of me when I was a baby and when I was just learning to walk. Elsa encouraged her to spend hours drawing every day. That's why she's so good. She often does quick sketches of me when I'm not looking – when I'm up to my elbows in washing up or trying to do my homework. This is the first time she's drawn anything since her accident.

When I pass the sketchbook back to her, she gives me a twisted smile. She keeps blinking. It must be the wine.

'What's up?' I ask.

'You look so much like your dad…' she blurts out.

'How should I know? You've never even shown me a

photo of him.'

She bursts into tears. I wish I hadn't sounded so angry, but I know next to nothing about my dad. Is she holding back another big secret? After the Aunt Elsa revelation, I don't want to think about what she might say. He could still be alive for all I know.

I want to shout at her and storm out of the room. Why does she throw information at me and keep me in the dark at the same time? I turn away from Mum, thrashing angry chords. She needs treating carefully at the moment. She must still be feeling like crap, barely able to move when she's used to bombing around everywhere on her bike and digging in the garden. How can I be angry with her when she's been working so hard, cleaning people's houses to buy me an electric guitar?

'I wish you'd tell me about my dad.' I deliberately drown myself out with a barrage of distortion on my effects pedal. It actually sounds quite good. I try the new riff I invented this morning. It gives me an idea for a song.

Kaz

I shouldn't have mentioned Daz. Jason has taken his guitar upstairs now but I can hear the distorted chords he's playing, the sound coming through his bedroom floor. The cat seems relieved anyway. She's licking her paws, sitting on the windowsill. I limp over to her. I scratch her behind the ears and she starts purring. Tears gather in my eyes. Patti pushes her small damp nose into my cheeks. She can be a very understanding cat.

The wine made me too emotional. I should be happy. I've managed to buy Jason a guitar and he's over the moon.

If Daz had lived, what would he be like? Would the band still be going? Would we still be together – a happy family? Unlikely. Maybe Jason wouldn't even exist. I imagine myself doing a pregnancy test in a hotel bathroom. Maybe I would have had an abortion; concentrating on promoting the second album, thinking about my lost child in lonely moments on long-haul flights.

Perhaps Daz and I would have split up long ago, living bitter separate lives, ploughing on with unsuccessful solo careers, both long past our sell-by dates. Daz was moody and selfish, even though I loved him. He probably would have been a crap dad. But then again...

It's useless wondering, because he's not here.

I should be happy with what I've got – a talented son – and my art, which is finally showing signs of taking off. Things could be a lot worse.

I listen to the noise from upstairs, above the drone of Patti's purr in my ear. Jason is playing variations on the same chord progression. It sounds like he's working something out, or writing something. Jason's changing. Sometimes there's a flash of Daz's anger in his eyes but he nearly always stops himself from lashing out.

I damp down the fire, switch the lights off and start to drag myself up the stairs. I clutch my book of Parisian photos to my chest while I grasp the banister with my left hand. It's really early but what's the point of sitting down here on my own? Jason sounds so wrapped up in his guitar playing that he's not going to bother coming downstairs again.

The cat runs up ahead of me and, when I reach my bedroom door, she's already curled up on the patchwork quilt. It takes me a few minutes to get my breath back – it takes so much effort to move around. The sound of Jason's guitar comes straight through the ceiling. I can hear him singing but I can't make out the words.

I reach under the bed and slide out the Thunderbird's case. I undo the clasp and take out the bass. I tune it, straining to hear the notes. I start to improvise a bassline to Jason's chord progression. My right wrist aches, even though I'm just striking the strings gently with my fingers, not using a plectrum, but it feels good to be doing this.

This is the perfect way of practising in secret; Jason's never going to hear me over the noise he's making. If I could remember how to play all the Mission Control songs, I'd be able to show Jason what we were like. I think he'd understand.

Chapter 7

Eggs

Jason

There's a massive crowd by the river. It's sunny but freezing. I'm keeping my hands deep in my fleece pockets. There's a raft decorated like a pirate ship, with a guy at the back firing smoke out of a cardboard cannon. It looks pretty good but another team dressed as convicts with arrows all over their soaked overalls ram their raft and try to capsize it. People lean over the railings and cheer. On the footbridge, there's a group of kids throwing flour-bombs at the rafts. It's an old tradition but they seem to be doing it with more malice than normal. When the clouds of flour clear, I realise one of them is Bradley Smeed. He's shouting, not at me for once though.

'He's such a dick –' I mutter.

Ben nods.

'Let's get playing,' he says.

'I'm bored of the Christmas ones though.'

We stand by the wishing well, strategically close to the public toilets and the car park, put Ben's guitar case on the floor in front of us and launch into 'Should I Stay or Should I Go?'

We're taking it in turns to pick the songs from our limited non-Christmas repertoire. Plenty of people are smiling at us and dropping coins into Ben's guitar case as they pass by on the way back to their cars. The crowd is starting to drift away from the river now; they're looking forward to a pub lunch or turkey leftovers. I'm feeling a bit peckish, thinking of the buffet lunch at Ben's house.

Ben's chosen 'Don't Look Back in Anger'. He loves Oasis. I think they're boring but we've agreed to disagree. It works well on acoustic guitars though and Ben does a brilliant nasal Liam Gallagher impression. I think people appreciate we aren't taking it seriously. The frets of my old guitar feel clumsy and I have to concentrate to hit the right notes in the guitar solo.

Suddenly something hits the body of my guitar, the force of it making the strings jangle against the neck. It was something hard but there's a yellow mess splattered all over the guitar and running down my legs. I look up, into the laughing face of Bradley Smeed. He launches another egg. It hits me in the chest. One of his mates throws a white bag which explodes all over me. I can't see anything.

'Did your mum die, Kenny? Is that why you're having to beg for a living?' Bradley Smeed says. I open my mouth, shocked, but I breathe in a big lump of flour and double up over my guitar, coughing. There's a knot of anger in my chest. But I can't do anything. I wish I was anywhere but here.

'Stupid pikey –' one of them laughs.

'Leave him alone!' Ben shouts. I wipe my face with my sleeve.

'Make us, gay boy,' Bradley says.

Ben charges towards them but they laugh and run across the road. Ben chases them, dodging cars. His guitar is still strapped over his shoulder. Ben always protects me, as if I'm too weak to defend myself.

I sit on the edge of the wishing well, keeping my head down. If I cry, it'll probably turn the flour on my face into glue. I unstrap my guitar and try to wipe it but it just seems to make it worse. I collect the money from Ben's guitar case into my pocket. About a fiver. Not bad for half an hour, really. But all the happiness got knocked out of me when that egg hit my guitar. I was excited about playing Ben the song I wrote last night but now I might as well forget it.

'Are you alright?' a man's voice asks. I want to tell him to fuck off and leave me alone.

I look up. It's Sam Baxter, the guitar teacher from the Fishpond. Weird. I only dug his card out yesterday.

'You were doing really well. I was about to give you some money.'

He's pushing a buggy with a toddler in it, a little girl with

93

a striped bobble hat, staring at me with wide eyes. The blonde woman standing next to him must be his wife or girlfriend.

'I'll get some hand towels, get the worst of it off for you,' she says, rushing towards the toilets. I'm embarrassed she's making a fuss over me.

Sam rummages in his pocket and pulls out a handful of change. I shake my head. It feels like he's just giving me money to make me feel better.

'Sorry,' he says.

'I was going to ask you if I could have a few lessons. I mean, I can work out how to play stuff but I don't know if I'm doing it right. I can pay. I need a new bike though but Ben's dad says he knows someone at work who might be selling one cheap…' I stop myself from gibbering on.

'That would be great.' Sam gets a new-looking mobile phone out of his pocket. 'What's your name?'

'Jason – Jason Knight if you need my full name for lessons and stuff.'

'Good name – you sound like a guitarist already.' Sam smiles at me. I give him my phone number. I start to feel better now I'm doing something normal.

The little girl seems scared of me. She puts her hands over her face and stares at me through the gaps in her fingers, like I did when I watched *Alien* at Ben's house.

His wife comes back with an armful of wet green paper towels. I'm grateful to be able to wipe my face and clothes, even though I still look like a walking cake. I hope I can get the egg and flour mixture off my old guitar.

Sam looks apologetic.

'The pub's going to be busy until after the New Year…'

'We'd better get back now, Sam,' his wife says. 'The place is going to be rammed. Mum can't hold the fort forever.' Sam seems oblivious, checking his phone.

'How about the eleventh of January – it's a Sunday. Three o'clock? Come round the back.'

'That'd be great.'

'Will you be okay?' Sam's wife asks. I nod.

I watch as they walk up the promenade, back to the pub. At least I can cling onto the hope of the guitar lesson, and my Stratocaster, waiting for me in Ben's house.

Ben comes back, panting, red in the face.

'I lost them,' he says. 'Tossers.' He slides his guitar into its case.

'I've got the money,' I tell him.

Ben takes one of the paper towels and tries to wipe the worst of the egg off my guitar.

I'm going to have to walk up to Ben's house looking like this. Everyone's going to see me. They'll fuss and feel sorry for me and I'll have to take a shower and change into Ben's clothes. His trousers will be massively short for me. The worst thing is that Mum will find out I'm a pathetic bullied loser. The last thing she needs is to be worried about me all the time.

Next time, I'll stand up to Bradley Smeed, whatever the consequences. I imagine smashing his grinning face into a pulp. The unlikeliness of this makes me laugh.

Ben stares at me as if I've gone mad.

'What's up with you?'

'That guy from the Fishpond saw me just now. I've booked a guitar lesson.'

'As if you need lessons,' Ben scowls.

Kaz

The blackbird watches me from his perch on the cherry tree as I put a crust of bread on the bird table. I scatter peanuts and seeds. I haven't been able to put out much bird food for the last couple of months but they haven't deserted our garden, despite the cat prowling around. The birds have been eating the holly and rowan berries but now they're mostly gone and they need some extra help.

My gardening gloves don't give much warmth to my hands. It's grey and raw today, fog still hanging in the valley. It's good to be out in the garden again, without Jason hovering over me. He's trying out his new bike with Ben on the High Peak trail. It'll do him good. I'm not well enough for cycling yet – maybe in a couple of weeks, and I need to get over my fear. Jason's old bike is just the right size for me though.

I put Elsa's old kneeling pad down in front of the rows of Brussels sprouts. They need TLC. Some of the taller stems are leaning over and need tying with stakes. A bumper crop this year. I've run out of exciting ways to cook them but as long as there's plenty of gravy, Jason doesn't mind eating them. I lower myself down gently – my leg still hurts – my trowel and everything I need is in the old garden basket so I don't have to stand up again. I feel like I'm turning into Elsa but at least my bones are made of tougher stuff. When I had my dressings changed yesterday, Jennifer said gentle exercise would do me good. My arm and leg are very scabby and sore but at least I can walk now.

I've learned from experience that the plants go mouldy if the yellow leaves aren't picked off quickly. Jason did his best but he hasn't got my eye for detail when it comes to gardening.

I didn't know he was being bullied – not like that. When he came back covered in eggs and flour, Jason seemed calm, determined, almost detached. He's been like that ever since. He's like Daz. If he's too quiet, I can tell he's upset about something, as if there's a cloud hovering over his head.

I'm surrounded by cheeping, as a crowd of greenfinches flies over my head onto the bird table. I watch them, entranced. They add flashes of green and yellow to the drab garden as they squabble over the seeds. I suppose they all came from the woods. How did they know I'd put food out? They flock into the naked rowan tree as if something's startled them. I look around for the cat but it's Barbara, standing on the front lawn, wearing green wellies and a smart fleece. She's staring at the finches too, with a large camera in her hands, taking a photo. My leg's seized up with kneeling but I manage to stand and slowly walk towards her.

'That's a great picture – finches in the tree – maybe a

Christmas card,' she says. Barbara shows me the photo on her camera screen. She's zoomed in so the birds are in close-up, in incredible detail.

'Before I came here, I didn't know anything about birds. We get so many of them coming to the garden.'

'I was walking in the woods, taking some photos,' Barbara says.

I feel a territorial twinge. These are my woods; my garden – my artistic territory.

'I thought I'd show you my camera, in case you're tempted to go digital.' She stares at me. 'You're looking much better.'

I feel awkward in front of her, in my baggy patched jeans and woolly hat.

'Is your son enjoying his guitar?'

'He spends hours on it every day. He's getting really good.' I realise Barbara is looking around the garden as if it's fairyland, distracted by the sculptures and statues appearing out of the flowerbeds. 'I'll show you around the garden.'

'I'd love that,' she said. 'So how did you meet Elsa Day? No one knew she was here.'

I laugh suddenly. Barbara looks startled. No one knew I was here either. That was the whole point.

'I helped her with her shopping and she asked me to stay. I was in a bit of a mess – living out of a van at the time.' I don't want to say any more. I don't want Barbara to know everything.

●

No one will know who I am, here in this small Derbyshire village; shops and pubs nestled at the bottom of a steep hill, like they've slid down it. There should be plenty of woods; deserted quarries near here, where I can hide away.

I've got to keep moving. I don't want anyone to find me. I park the van at the side of the road and walk back down towards the grocery shop, keeping my eyes to the pavement.

Don't need much. Can't seem to stomach much food. Keep feeling sick.

The shop has narrow, crammed aisles. Bit like Singh News. Everyone probably knows each other in here. Shit. I don't look like a tourist. They might remember me. Ripped leggings I've been wearing for weeks, one of Daz's old t-shirts: black, tie-dyed with bleach. I hacked my hair off unevenly in a half-hearted attempt at a disguise.

I grab a basket. A jar of jam, white bread, biscuits, tins of baked beans. I queue behind an old woman with a Zimmer frame. I'll buy fags, and vodka too. Something to force back and knock me out for the night. I keep my head down. Get out of here as soon as I can. Then what? I can't go back. I can't face them, can I? Can't face anyone. Going to have to decide what to do soon.

The old woman is taking ages. She keeps ordering things, as if she's never got her head around self-service. A young girl stands behind the counter, in a white overall; blonde hair and red cheeks. The old woman asks for marmalade and the girl runs around the shop to find it. Then it's the wrong sort: she wants Robertson's Golden Shred and not the Happy Shopper stuff. Then she has the girl chasing around for the right sort of crumpets; a bottle of Domestos; tinned sardines. All the time, the metal shelves, the smell of sliced bacon, the low strip light ceiling, are pressing down on me, closer and closer, until I can't breathe. I didn't want anyone in here to notice me, but now I've got to escape.

'Fuck this!' I drop the basket.

I'm frozen, mesmerised. I stare at the tins of beans rolling out of the basket and across the floor; the exploded red star shape of smashed glass and strawberry jam.

The old woman turns around – stares at me with ice-blue eyes glittering with amusement.

'You must be the angel of anarchy, my dear.'

I run – out of the shop, back to the van. Can't even get as far as turning the key in the ignition before a tidal wave of grief hits me. Just hug the steering wheel. Cry for what seems like hours.

My tears dry. Juddering breaths. A growing sense of calm and certainty. My plan seems clear. Drive up the hill. Find a quiet lane overhung by trees.

I start the engine, ease off the handbrake, and find I can only go up the hill in first gear. So steep. A line of angry cars behind me.

The old lady hasn't got very far. She's still at the edge of the village, carrier bags swinging around on the Zimmer frame handles; making painfully slow progress.

I don't know what makes me stop. I feel bad now, about what happened in the shop. She couldn't help taking so long and needing so much help. I pull up a couple of metres ahead of her. Get out of the van and walk around to the pavement.

She stops shuffling forward. She stares at me as if she knows everything about me.

'I'm sorry,' I say. 'I didn't mean...'

The old woman laughs, but there's warmth in her smile now.

'Quite an interesting thing to do with a jar of jam, I thought.'

'I could give you a lift home. The van's a mess, but...'

'Delightful. I'll show you my garden.' She looks straight into my red, puffed up eyes. Somehow, I feel I can trust her. 'I think you'll find it restful, particularly this time of year.'

She grasps my hand for balance as she slowly climbs into the passenger seat.

●

Barbara studies a rusted iron sculpture intently. The figure of a woman, welded together from bits of scrap metal. Elsa made her in the sixties. The sculpture is very fragile now so I wrapped chicken wire around her for extra support. Elsa grew white flowering clematis up her so in early spring she looks like a bride.

'This is magical. I never realised…'

Barbara trains her camera on the sculpture. A screen shows the shot before she takes it. Barbara clicks the shutter and shows me the image on the screen.

'You need a computer though, don't you? To do things with the pictures?' I ask.

Barbara smiles.

'They don't bite. You can do wonderful things with Photoshop.'

'I mostly just use photos to help me with paintings.'

Barbara takes more photographs as she wanders around the garden. She gives me a curious look.

'You were a total stranger – and Elsa Day trusted you?'

'Everyone in the village thought she was just a crazy old woman but I fell in love with her garden – and her art. Elsa was fiercely independent but she couldn't cope on her own any more. She needed someone to do everyday things for her. Shopping – cleaning.'

We've reached the shed at the back of the garden. It's covered with wisteria, a sculpture in itself. I push open the door.

'Then I found out I was pregnant.'

My mangled bike is leaning against the old chest of drawers we use for tools and odds and ends. Elsa worked on all her sculptures in here. I must get around to germinating some seeds on the windowsill. I push my finger into the rotting window frame. That'll need replacing soon, before it falls apart. I try my best to look after everything. I've even climbed onto the roof of the house a few times, fixing slates back into place after storms.

'Elsa's old potter's wheel is in here. Her kiln too. This was her ceramics studio.'

'Can I see?'

The potter's wheel is covered by a sack of seed potatoes. I lift them up for Barbara's benefit and she gives an excited gasp. She tries to move the wheel but it's completely rusted up.

'I had a go at restoring it once,' I say. 'Scraped at it for hours and used a whole can of WD40 but it still didn't go round. The kiln's really rusty too.'

'I've decided to open my own studio,' Barbara says. 'I think I've made enough money from badgers and tea towels. You inspired me. I want to support young, contemporary artists. That's why I came to see you.'

'You can hardly call me young.'

'Young enough. And with your unique pedigree…'

'I'm not a dog.'

'You were trained by a lost genius. You're mainlining pre-war surrealism. I've got a vision, Keziah. The Elsa Day Gallery.'

I grab onto the workbench. Barbara laughs at my panic-stricken face.

'Why are you so scared?' she asks.

Because it would ruin everything, I want to say. Because this has been a safe place for me and Jason. Elsa liked it that way too. It would be like smashing a bird's nest open.

I wish I'd never met Barbara Fleming. She's stirring everything up and I can't stop her. Elsa never mentioned any living relatives but what if some grand-niece or nephew of Elsa's finds out about our house and decides it would make a great holiday cottage? I push my way out of the claustrophobic shed. I limp towards the vegetable patch, my eyes filling with tears.

Barbara grabs me by the shoulders and shakes me gently.

'We've got nothing,' I say. 'If anyone finds out we've got no right to be living in Elsa's house, we'll be out on the street…'

'It's more of a lane – and anyway…'

'What if they take Jason away from me?'

Barbara pulls a cloth hankie out of her pocket and hands it to me. It has red polka dots and smells of lavender. I wipe my eyes.

'If you can make a living – a proper living – from your art, you'll be in control of your own life. You've got the talent. I've done it. Now I'm giving you the chance.'

'To do what?'

'Your own exhibition. Your own gallery space, even.'

'I'm happy here. I don't want to go to London...'

'I've found a great space in Cromford. An old garage. An absolute barn of a place, and it's going for a song.'

'I'm skint. I can't help you there.'

Barbara laughs, throwing her head back.

'I want you to view it with me on Monday. You'll see the potential. I'll show you my plans. I want you to make some commissions for me. Sculptures like these.'

I nod, reluctantly, to get her off my back more than anything. Jason was right. I should be more cautious about Barbara. A voice in my head shouts: *yeah, if you want to clean other people's houses and hide in the garden for the rest of your life.*

'I'll pick you up at two, then we can discuss it over lunch,' Barbara says, smiling.

Barbara is just using me because I knew Elsa Day, but she seems to actually like my paintings. It was stupid to blurt everything out about Elsa before Christmas but, because of that, Jason got his guitar.

I've got a queasy feeling Barbara's scheme is going to cost me dear but I've got no choice – she's making me come along for the ride.

Chapter 8
Puncture

Jason

I lean on a scuffed Year 7 display of designs for clocks, my arms wrapped tightly around my new guitar case. I'm not letting it out of my sight. I needed it to persuade Mrs Lyons I'm good enough to take GCSE music. Me and Ben went to see her together. We've spent most of our lunchtimes since September lurking around in the practise rooms but we were a bit afraid of her at first. She kicks you out if she thinks you're dossing about. We played her some of our covers and Ben's song about Hayley Green, and Mrs Lyons said we definitely had potential, particularly when I told her I'm starting guitar lessons on Sunday.

Ben's at the dentists now. His mum picked him up at lunchtime. I wish I'd asked her to take my guitar but I would have worried about it getting stolen from the boot of her car.

Kevin Watson and Danny Taylor kick a brand-new football across the corridor while we're queuing to get into the classroom. Everyone's showing off the new stuff they got for Christmas and for once, I've got new things as well. I've got my guitar, and just the thought of it sitting inside the case makes me feel more confident, even without Ben.

Since the egg incident, I've had an image change. I bought a pair of men's suit trousers from a charity shop – much too long – and used safety pins to make them the right length. Mum offered to hem them but next time I wake up and realise I've grown several inches overnight, I can adjust the length straight away. I've used some Shockwaves gel on my hair. I cut it myself a bit. Mum didn't say anything. I don't know if she noticed. I customised my black denim jacket too.

Mr Lord's class is still having afternoon registration. They're making a load of noise and Mr Lord is struggling to read out the announcement about the jumble sale. Some of the kids call him Mr Lard. I'm not looking forward to Design and Technology. We only get one term of it a year. Last time, we spent the whole time making a wooden spatula.

'What's your new guitar like, then?' Josh Robin asks. He's into some decent music. He lent me his Muse CDs last year. Josh used to go mountain biking with me and Ben, before he got addicted to windsurfing. He's in a club at the reservoir with his dad.

'It's brilliant. Come and listen to us in the music room next time I bring it in.'

'I daren't – I can't play anything,' Josh laughs.

'We're well in with Mrs Lyons now. She knows you're okay.'

'Is it just you and Ben in the band, then?'

'We're starting to write our own songs.' I'm still perfecting my new song. I didn't sing it to Ben after all; I just played him the chords, and he thought it was pretty good.

'Don't you need a drummer? And a bass player?' Josh is even shorter than Ben. Did I grow again over Christmas? Everyone else in my form looks like a little kid.

'I don't even know anyone who plays the drums, so…'

'I'd like to learn the drums but I've probably not got time. I spent most of the holidays windsurfing on Carsington.'

'You must be nuts.' Freezing them off, more like. Even in a wetsuit, you wouldn't get me on that reservoir in the middle of winter.

Josh shakes his mop of surfer dude blond hair. 'It was great. That feeling when you catch the wind…They have taster sessions if you want a go.'

Mr Lord's form tumble out of the classroom. Shit – it's Bradley Smeed's form. Most of them hurry away to lessons – but he's homing in on me.

'It's emo-Kenny,' Bradley sniggers. I try to ignore him but I tighten my grip on my guitar case, turning my back on him.

'I might give it a try one day,' I tell Josh, even though I've got no intention of getting on a windsurfer. 'Maybe in the summer. How much does it cost to hire a wetsuit?' Josh's eyes flicker uncomfortably between the floor and Bradley.

'Hey, Kenny, why have you written things on your jacket?'

I turn slowly to face him.

'You wouldn't understand.' I mutter.

'What does 'Art Riot Revolution' mean, then? Sounds fucking gay to me.'

I look him straight in the eyes, even though I can feel myself shaking. Bradley Smeed acts like some kind of gangsta with a gold chain hanging out of the collar of his school shirt.

'It's a Situationist statement,' I say, as witheringly as I can manage but I stammer a bit. I just sound like a pretentious twat. It's a Manics thing – they used to spray-paint their clothes when they were starting out. The Clash did it too. I stencilled it on the sleeve of my jacket with white acrylic paint. I should write something more original like 'Bradley Smeed is a dick'. That might work.

'Show us your new guitar, then.'

'No.'

Bradley Smeed breaks away from his friends and looms close to me.

'You still stink of egg.'

'Fuck off,' I mutter. The rest of my class has gone into the design and technology room. Just me and Josh left.

'Ooh,' he mocks, leering right into my face. 'Kenny's getting brave. Even without little gay Ben Ten to stick up for you.'

'My name's not Kenny.' I keep my gaze steady. I'm not going to lower my eyes and run away. I'm so close to Bradley Smeed that I can see he's just a person. There's a cluster of blackheads around his nose. Maybe I'm a tiny bit taller than him. He's not really some hard nut: I know he lives in a barn conversion on the other side of Cromford. He has a step-sister in my year called Mary who plays the cello. His granny has a poodle with a pink lead. His dad's an architect.

'Go on, show us your guitar.'

Bradley tries to snatch my guitar case. I pull it out of his grasp and stick the guitar into Josh's hands. I shove Bradley Smeed, hard. Bradley reels backwards, almost falling over; a surprised look on his face. His mate, the one who threw the flour at me, laughs nastily, but at Bradley, not me.

Bradley tries to look like he never stumbled. His eyes look angry. Now he looks scary; like a charging bull. He slams me into the wall with his meaty hands. There's a bang as I hit the display board.

The breath's knocked out of me and the back of my head hurts. Everything goes a bit fuzzy for a second.

Bradley stands in front of me, his breathing quick and shallow, as if he's waiting for me to do something.

'Hit him, Jase,' Josh says.

Bradley's friends cluster around the back of him, chanting "fight", "fight", "fight", but quietly, glancing at the classroom door.

I could throw a punch but where would that get me? Instead, I stare at him. His eyes are a washed-out pale blue. His eyelashes are almost see-through. I stand up straight.

'You can't hurt me, I'll only get stronger,' I say. I try to sound cool, like someone in a film.

'Wanna bet?' Bradley growls.

I make myself smile at him, like I'm not bothered at all. I feel weirdly calm. Concussed, maybe. Bradley looks confused. I'm not following the rules. I'm not just a little kid being pushed around by a bully any more. Bradley's lost face because of me. Dangerous.

'Bradley!' Mr Lord appears in the doorway of the classroom. But Bradley Smeed and his mates are already legging it down the corridor.

Josh hands my guitar back to me. I sling my bag over my shoulder.

'Thanks,' I tell him.

'Nice one,' he whispers.

Mr Lord stares at the end of the corridor, his hands on his hips. The rolls of fat under his jumper wobble around. He turns to me.

'What happened?' he asks. As if it isn't obvious.

'Nothing, sir,' I say. I don't want to grass on Bradley. This is between me and him.

Kaz

Barbara parks her four-wheel-drive in the forecourt of a large building. I suddenly remember. This is the garage where I took the van, until it failed its MOT and had to be scrapped. It's only a short walk from Cromford Books. It looks ugly and derelict.

'Isn't the location perfect?' Barbara says. She leans across me and fishes in the glove compartment. 'I've been toying with the idea for ages, but it's time to finally take the plunge.' She finds a set of keys with a brown cardboard label.

'Won't it be a lot of work?' I ask. I open the passenger door and step down, gingerly, clinging onto the bodywork.

It just looks like an old garage, with rusty signs advertising MOTs. There are still old bits of car bumper lying around and the carcass of a Nissan Micra in the corner of the yard, with last year's growth of bindweed creeping up its wheel arches. That would make a good painting.

'I've been talking to a local architect. He'll be able to get things moving pretty quickly. With the economy the way it is, builders are desperate for work. We can get involved too. I really can't wait to get my hands dirty.'

Barbara rushes ahead. She's wearing a fitted camel-coloured trouser suit, very chic, but unsuitable for poking around in an oily old garage.

'There's plenty of room for parking – and this bit at the side could be a sculpture garden café.' It's just a bit of concrete hard-standing with the desiccated remains of last year's weeds growing through the cracks. I want to rain on her parade but, despite myself, I can see it in the summer, transformed into a courtyard full of plants; tables with arty-looking families drinking tea.

'Won't people steal the sculptures?' I've heard news stories about people stealing Henry Moore bronzes and selling them to scrapyards.

'I'll commission you to make them out of scrap metal,' Barbara says. 'If people steal them, I'll pay you to make more.' She seems to have it all worked out already. I haven't told her that I've never welded anything in my life before.

Barbara unlocks the door of a lean-to extension at the side of the garage and we walk in.

'The estate agent was so kind, letting me have the keys. It's the third time I've viewed it. I just want to be sure.'

This room was the office. It's empty now, apart from a broken desk, a pile of dirty rags and a topless calendar, advertising engine parts. The girl in the calendar is flashing a white-toothed smile, her hair in a very eighties blonde perm. I don't suppose it was the hair the mechanics were looking at. Maybe the girl in the photo has now got grown-up children of her own and her magnificent bosom is stretch-marked and saggy. The actual calendar dates from March last year, when the garage must have gone out of business. The paper is spotted with mildew. There's a smell of damp and engine oil.

'We'll knock this down and build the café. And just look at the gallery space.'

I follow Barbara into the cavernous old garage. I flinch, startled at the sound of fluttering wings. There are pigeons perching among the metal roof struts. The air is filled with contented low cooing, but the concrete floor is splattered white with pigeon poo. The far reaches of the garage are too dark to see.

'Isn't it wonderful?' Barbara says, almost disappearing into the gloom. 'We'll put skylights in – keep it simple and white. This village needs something fresh.'

I look at the breezeblock walls, streaked with green damp. It's taking all my imagination and all I can see is the bloke who used to run the garage, smoking a fag and reeling off a list of things wrong with the van. This garage was always grotty-looking, but they didn't ask many questions. If I'd bunged them a few quid, they probably would have given me the MOT, but Jason was a baby and I didn't want to drive around in a death-trap linking me too strongly to the past.

'I'm thinking of a mezzanine floor – that's why we need the architect. It'll be very light and airy.'

A shaft of winter sunlight breaks through a hole in the roof, illuminating the vast space. Suddenly I can see it. If Barbara can pull this off, it would be amazing.

'Are you sure you want to call it the Elsa Day gallery?' I ask.

Barbara's expression hardens. The smile's still on her face, but her eyes glint like sapphires in the dim light.

'Her art shouldn't be hidden away, out of fear. Neither should yours. You could be a major talent, Keziah. Take the risk. What's the worst that could happen?'

I stare at Barbara. There's so much she doesn't know.

'What if we got kicked out of the house? We'd have nowhere to go…'

'Don't you want to see Elsa's art displayed here? To get it out of those boxes and cupboards? We could be business partners. That little cottage isn't the boundary of your world.'

I'm suddenly afraid of her.

'What if I said no?'

Barbara stares at me, her lips pursed.

'Your loss. If you want to go back to scrubbing people's toilets…'

If I refused to work with Barbara, what would stop her from going ahead with the Elsa Day gallery anyway?

'I can't really take it in.'

I walk out of the building and sit on the low wall surrounding the yard she wants to make into a garden. I take deep sniffs of air, trying to eradicate the smell of pigeon shit. I can hear the fast-flowing water of an old mill-race. The air smells of earth and water, with a tinge of iron.

Barbara comes out of the office door and locks it. She rubs the cuff of her camel coat with her hand, noticing an oily streak. I stare at the sleeve of my fake leather jacket, which is coming apart at the seams, with the weird foamy lining escaping from inside it.

Barbara sits next to me on the wall. She takes an elegant cigarette case out of her handbag and offers me one. I don't refuse. Her gold Zippo lighter is engraved with her initials. I light the cigarette, and for a couple of minutes we sit, side-by-side, not talking, listening to the traffic and the birdsong, staring at the building that could mean everything to us. The smoke feels harsh in my lungs. I've not smoked at all since I found out I was pregnant with Jason.

'The back wall of the building is a lot older. I think it's part of an old mill,' Barbara says.

'It could be beautiful here,' I say, growing lightheaded.

'Come for lunch at my place. You haven't seen my studio properly yet. We need to talk properly. I'll show you the plans I've drawn up.'

I nod.

Jason

Josh's dad is waiting outside the school in his camper van. He waves at us. It's quite a cool VW bus but slightly ruined by the slogan "Alan Robin Plumbing Solutions" on the side of it.

'Thanks for backing me up earlier,' I tell him.

'No worries,' Josh says. 'Do you really want to try windsurfing?'

'God, no!'

Josh laughs. 'Thought so. I might come in and have a bash on the drums, though, in the music room. I mean, if you don't mind.'

'No, it'd be great. We're going to need a drummer.'

I put on my new cycling helmet and get on my bike as

the camper van disappears down the road. Before I get to the end of the road, I realise there's something wrong with the back wheel. It's really spongy. I didn't notice while I was wheeling it out of the school gates. Typical. Josh's dad would have given me a lift. I get off and feel the wheel. Totally flat. I've not even got a pump or a puncture repair kit with me. When anything goes wrong, I usually rely on Ben. I've got to push my bike all the way home now, with my guitar pressing on my back. The back of my head still throbs a bit. Now it's raining too: icy drops of water.

I should have checked this new bike more thoroughly but it seemed fine when I took it out on the High Peak trail with Ben. I thought it was pretty cool – apart from the pastel blue colour. A proper mountain bike for thirty quid from a guy who works with Ben's dad. He was quite fat.

Maybe the inner tyre was put in wrong – the rubber could be perished. I push the bike down the street, until I lose the crowd of other school kids and I'm on my own, pushing the bike towards Bolehill village in the dark. I switch on my bike lights and sling my cycle helmet around the handlebars.

My heart sinks as I realise the house is dark. I remember Mum saying she had some kind of appointment with Barbara Fleming. She didn't seem to be looking forward to it. I wonder how long she's going to be, whether I should get the tea ready.

I wheel my bike into the kitchen and turn it upside down on the floor. Dirty water drips off the wheels. At least Mum can't tell me off for making a mess.

My guitar case is sopping wet but my Stratocaster is okay. I take it out and lay it carefully on the sofa.

I shove a load of wood in the AGA and I put my guitar case near it to dry out.

I kneel down next to the bike and turn the tyre around. There's something shiny stuck in it. I get the torch from the kitchen drawer and run to the shed. I take the pump from Mum's old bike. I rummage around in the tool drawer until

I find pliers and a puncture repair kit. When I get back to the kitchen, at least there's some warmth coming from the AGA. I take off my wet jacket and hang it on the back of the kitchen door.

I manage to work the thing in the tyre loose. It's a nail – a new, shiny nail. Someone must have put it there deliberately. Bradley Smeed. It must have been him. I want to kick the bike across the kitchen. What if he punctures my tyres every day? I was an idiot to think I could just stand up to Bradley Smeed. What did I think he was going to do? Give up? He probably thinks it's more fun to have a victim who fights back. It's hopeless. I'm shivering and the gel has run out of my hair into my eyes. I sit on the floor, in front of the AGA.

The sound of the cat flap makes me look up. Patti winds herself around my legs. Her fur's wet. She opens her mouth in a silent miaow. Her food bowl's empty. I get up stiffly. The kitchen floor tiles are freezing. What was I thinking? My face is quite warm but my bum's frozen. I pour out Go-Cat for Patti, fill the kettle and put it on the AGA.

I was in danger of giving Bradley Smeed what he wants. I used to wonder what was wrong with me, to make him pick on me more than anyone else. I was easy to bully, that's why. At least I started changing things today. I've got strong with cycling and all the firewood I chop. Mum says I'm getting guitarist's arms from all the practising I'm doing. I'm getting muscles. But it's mental strength that counts against Bradley Smeed.

Kaz

It's gone eight o' clock. Barbara insisted on driving me home. She's had a few glasses of wine. I wanted to call a cab, but she promised me she was okay. Her driving seems fine, anyway, as she forces the car up the steep incline of Cromford Hill, negotiating the curves in the road with ease. When I cleaned her house, there were always several bottles of white wine in the fridge; a staple, like milk; a wine-rack fully stacked with bottles of red.

I didn't want Jason to worry. I tried to call home several times but no reply. Barbara insisted he would be alright, that at his age he could look after himself for a few hours. At Barbara's house, we ate picnic food that didn't need cooking: olives, exotic cheeses and bread; Barbara had smoked salmon. She showed me the designs of the new gallery she's sketched herself, and talked about her vision for the business and how she wants me to be involved. I felt dizzy, and it wasn't just the wine. My head is still spinning from the possibilities and implications.

As soon as I get out of Barbara's four-by-four, I can hear Jason playing the guitar; angry, thrashing chords. His shadow looms in his bedroom window. If we weren't detached, the neighbours would be complaining. His little amp is powerful. That explains why he didn't answer the phone.

I push open the back door. The kitchen's a mess – more like Jennifer's kitchen: muddy footprints, crumbs on the worktop; Jason's new bike upside-down in the middle of the floor. I run upstairs, getting to the top before I realise my leg isn't hurting me so badly. Maybe it's the painkilling effect of the wine.

I'm about to barge through the door when I remember my no-knocking rule. I knock gently at first but I'm banging on it so hard I'm almost grazing my knuckles by the time he stops playing and opens the door. The fire's burning in the grate in his room and he's only got his desk lamp lit, so the walls are flickering.

'Where were you?' he asks. He's still got the guitar strapped over his shoulder.

'I tried to call you about five times.'

'Sorry.'

'What's wrong with your bike?'

His face is suddenly distorted with anger.

'It's war.'

'What do you mean?'

'Me and Bradley Smeed. Look what he fucking did.' Jason unstraps his guitar and puts it down, almost tenderly, on his bed. Without his guitar, his hands are shaking. He thunders down the stairs in his socks. I follow him.

In the kitchen, he shows me a galvanised nail.

'He put this in my tyre.'

'How do you know it was him? You could have just run over it.'

'His form tutor's a design and technology teacher. Bradley could get handfuls of nails if he wanted to. It was pushed right in.'

'You haven't fixed the puncture?'

'Couldn't be bothered.' He scowls, folding his arms. Translation: too angry; couldn't face it: wanted me to help him.

'Let me see.' I kneel down stiffly on the dirty kitchen tiles. He's got the puncture repair kit from his old bike. I squeeze the tyres. The back tyre is very squashy.

'How do you get the wheel off?' I ask, looking for the axle nuts.

'Quick release,' Jason mumbles, managing to get the wheel off in one easy move.

'Get the kettle on, will you? I'm parched.'

I use the levers to ease off the tyre. When I remove the inner tube, I pump it up. There's a neat, round hole where the air escapes.

'I see what you mean,' I say. The floor's hurting my knee and I wince. Jason brings me one of the living room cushions to kneel on. I get up and put a carrier bag on the floor underneath it. We'll have to start looking after Elsa's things more now. God knows what's going to happen.

I use the sandpaper around the hole and squirt the glue onto the tube. The kettle boils while I'm waiting for the glue to dry off a bit. I love the smell of tyre glue. It's good to focus on something practical.

'What are you going to do about it?'

Jason puts the tea down on the floor next to me.

'He tried to snatch my guitar – Ben wasn't there – so I

114

ended up pushing him – and he shoved me back – so then I said something I thought was clever. Now I'm really screwed.'

'Did you tell anyone? A teacher, I mean.'

Jason flicks his fringe out of his eyes. The rest of his hair looks shorter than normal but his fringe is still flopping into his face.

'You think I'm a complete loser?'

'This is serious. Attacking you with eggs and deliberately damaging your property.' I stick the patch on the tube, pressing it down really hard. I imagine I'm squashing the delightful Bradley Smeed like a slug.

'It felt good when I pushed him. I've got to stop him.' He sounds determined.

I peel the back off the patch. Neat job, nicely mended. I pump the inner tube up a little bit and then pop it back onto the wheel. I start to gently press the tyre back into the rim.

'Ben's got this stuff called tyre slime. You put all this gloopy stuff in your inner tubes and it just goes round and round – when you get a puncture, it instantly fixes it. None of this messing around…'

'Very futuristic. Not sure it would work on nails.'

'So what's happening with Barbara Fleming? Is she going to buy more of your paintings?' Jason seems more relaxed now, his hands in his pockets.

My heart does a strange flip.

'She wants to open a gallery in Cromford. The Elsa Day gallery. She wants to put Elsa's stuff on display. My paintings. She wants me to be her business partner.'

'That sounds brilliant,' Jason grins. 'You'd almost be famous.'

'But the house doesn't belong to us, and I don't want anyone finding out.'

'I don't mind where we live. I'd like to have a bedroom where my head doesn't touch the ceiling.'

'Everything's changing.'

'Maybe it has to.' Jason leans against the work surface.

I turn my attention back to Jason's bike. I fit the wheel

back and start pumping it up, keeping my head down.

'I'm scared.' I try to stop my voice from breaking into sobs.

'Mum – this is what you wanted.' Jason squeezes the bike wheel. 'You always wanted people to buy your paintings. If you were a famous artist, like Barbara Fleming, you wouldn't be worried about money any more. You could just paint.'

'I promised Elsa I'd look after everything for her.'

'She'd love all of this. Everything will be alright, Mum. Stop worrying.'

'What if I don't want to be famous? What if I was happy the way things were before?'

'I want to be famous,' he says. 'I'll work really hard at my guitar playing, and Ben's got a great voice. I'm sure we can make it. We just need to put in the effort.' His voice is quietly confident.

'What if you're one of those people who can't handle fame?'

'What, like Richey Manic or Kurt Cobain or…?' He stares at me. 'What makes you think I can't handle it anyway?'

I can't say anything. I blink away tears.

'Did your band get anywhere? What was the biggest gig you played?'

I turn Jason's bike the right way up.

'Your dad died before we got anywhere,' I mumble into the handlebars. I open the back door and wheel his bike out of kitchen.

'Mum – I wish you'd just…' he shouts. But he doesn't follow me.

I lean the bike against the chest of drawers in the shed and stand in the dark, squeezing my eyes tight shut. Why did I lie to Jason? I've been lying to him for so long I don't know how to tell him what really happened. Once I start getting involved with Barbara's gallery, people are going to start asking questions – making connections – finding out who I really am.

Chapter 9
Mission Control

Jason

I park my bike in the yard behind the pub. There's a pile of old ashtrays from before the smoking ban came in, some knackered tables and a row of silver beer kegs. The back door is half open. I knock and wait. My breath is shallow and nervous, making clouds in the cold air.

Maybe they haven't heard me. I open the door a bit wider and brush aside the curtain made of silver links. I walk inside, feeling like I shouldn't be here. I'm in a room with a big sink and what looks like an enormous dishwasher.

'Hello?' Maybe Sam isn't here. Did I make a mistake about the date? It's dead on three o'clock.

An oldish woman bustles into the room. She almost drops the pile of dirty plates she's carrying when she sees me by the door. Then she notices the guitar case strapped to my back, and sighs.

'Come into the kitchen. Sam's doing the last order.'

She stacks the plates into the dishwasher, then I follow her into the next room. Sam is standing over a deep-fat fryer. He turns round.

'Sorry – I'm running a bit late. Some idiots always turn up right at the last minute.'

The woman glares at him and leaves the kitchen. Sam lifts up the basket of the fryer, shaking the chips violently.

'Jason – whatever you do, don't ever live with your in-laws, let alone go into business with them.'

I shrug.

'Can you do me a favour?'

'Yeah, okay.'

'Wash your hands and get the salad garnish ready.' It wasn't exactly what I had in mind but I lean my guitar case against the work surface and rinse my hands at the sink.

There's half a lettuce, a cucumber and a couple of tomatoes on a chopping board. Sam gets two clean plates and I start cutting the salad into artistic shapes.

'How come you work here when you're a guitar teacher?' I ask.

Sam laughs.

'I've been in loads of bands. But nothing really happened. Even my last band.'

'What were they called?'

'Trampoline Nightmares.'

'Right.'

See? He told me the name of the band straight away.

'We had great songs. Hundreds of plays on Myspace. We got a good following locally – supported Supergrass on tour once. Still didn't get anywhere.'

Sam takes the chips and a couple of burgers out of the fryer. The chips look crisp and golden. My mouth waters. Sam arranges everything on the plates and his mother-in-law collects them and takes them into the pub.

'Thanks for the help. You're good at this.'

'I quite like cooking.'

'Have some chips.' Sam puts the rest of the chips in a bowl. I felt really nervous before I came here so I didn't have much lunch. I taste a chip. It's lovely. I keep eating.

'Not really filling you with confidence, am I?' Sam washes up the chopping board and turns off the deep-fat fryer. 'I was doing sound engineering – session musician work too – the money's quite good. Had my own flat. I met Jenny and we got married. Then she got pregnant and wanted to move back up here. I'm going to run the function room as a music venue.'

'Have you got many other students?'

'A few. I'm going to have a proper studio as well. I've just got a back room at the moment, but…' Sam takes his apron off. 'Come on, I'll show you.'

I pick up my guitar and Sam takes me into the bar and through a door marked "Staff Only". The flat upstairs has flowery wallpaper and beige carpets. The lounge door is open and Sam's wife waves at me. She's sitting on the carpet with the baby, surrounded by toys.

Sam opens a door, smiling proudly. His studio is smaller than I'd expected – not much bigger than my bedroom, but the ceiling's higher. The room is plastered with posters – really mixed up – Blur with Bob Dylan, Metallica; The Strokes. There are guitars hanging on the wall – two electrics and one acoustic. One wall is totally packed with CDs and shelves of music magazines, neatly arranged and organised. There are a couple of amps and a long crowded desk with a computer, effects pedals and recording equipment.

'I wish my room was like this.'

Sam takes a black Stratocaster off the wall and slings the strap around his shoulders. He noodles around a bit, stretching his shoulders and taking deep breaths. Even without being plugged in, I can tell he's a much better guitarist than me.

I get my guitar out of my case.

'Snap! – almost.'

Sam smiles. 'Very nice. Christmas present?'

I nod. Sam plugs a lead into an amp and gives me the other end. I plug it into my guitar. I tune up.

'A bit more distortion?' Sam asks. I nod.

Sam perches on a stool.

'Just play for a bit – show off.'

I stare at my guitar, feeling self-conscious. Then my fingers launch themselves into 'Motorcycle Emptiness'. I follow it with the solo from 'Death to Rock 'n' Roll'. Sam smiles, like he's enjoying it. I should play him something more up to date and I don't want him to think I only play Manics stuff, so I play him a bit of 'Knights of Cydonia' by Muse. I haven't finished working it out properly yet though – there's a bit in the middle I keep getting stuck on, so I switch to playing my new – and only – song. Sam looks at me keenly. I feel a bit embarrassed so I turn away from him, facing the opposite wall.

Something makes me glance at a poster in the middle of the wall – a woman and the slogan *"I'd Rather Go Naked than Wear Fur"*.

She's naked but you can't see anything. She smiles over her tattooed shoulder, clutching a black bass guitar to her chest, so there's only a small curve of boob showing. Her wild black hair has a bright green streak, matching her eyes.

Her green eyes are as familiar to me as my own reflection, despite her smudged eyeliner.

I stop playing and just stand there, staring at the poster. I can feel my heart thumping. I've seen the tattoo of the bird with outstretched wings thousands of times before. It matches the symbol on the bass guitar in the picture.

'What's up?' Sam asks. 'You were doing really well.'

I open my mouth but it's so dry, I only manage to croak.

'My mum.' I force out the words.

'That's Kaz K from Mission Control. She's…'

My mum. Naked – and really young.

'She never told me the name of the band.'

Sam's mouth hangs open. 'How old are you?'

'Fourteen next month.'

'Shit.' Sam stares at me as if I'm not real. I don't feel real any more. 'Oh my god. Is she alive?'

'She was about an hour ago.' Mum was in the shed, doing something to make the seed potatoes sprout. Nothing makes sense. I've seen those anti-fur posters before – you have to be someone to be in one of them. 'She said her band were crap.'

'Mission Control? They were the best band of the nineties.'

Sam has the same shining look in his eyes Ben gets when he's wildly enthusiastic about something.

'What happened?' I ask.

'Jason, what do you know about your dad?'

'He was some guy called Darren. She told me he was dead.'

'Your dad's Daz Lightning?'

'Daz?' I think of Mum in that hospital bed when she thought I was him; the times when she gets upset for no reason and just stares at me. Now Sam is giving me the same kind of look. A bit creepy to think I look so much like my dad and I never knew him. Now it turns out he was famous.

'I should have known. Look at you. After all, one of the last sightings of her was at that petrol station on the A6...'

'What are you going on about?'

'What's she told you?'

I can't stop staring at the poster of my mum. It feels like she's laughing at me. I don't know anything about her. I knew she had secrets – but...

'I don't know anything, do I?' I unplug my guitar and put it back in its case. I can't stop shaking.

'Shit. I'm sorry.'

'It's not your fault.'

'I thought your mum was still missing. It was a big shock, the band breaking up like that. The true fans never forgot her though. After your dad...'

Sam turns away from me. He takes two CDs down from the shelf.

'Just tell me. Please. What happened?'

'I shouldn't be the person who tells you.'

'You've already told me more than...'

'You need to hear their music.' He holds out two CDs. I take them. Mission Control, written in a space-age font.

'How many albums did they sell?'

'They got a gold disc for *Calling Earth* by the end of '92. Not bad for an independent release. *Losing Control* sold well at first because of...everything – but then people lost interest.'

I look at the CD covers. *Calling Earth* has cartoon aliens at the controls of a spaceship, with planet Earth trained in the sights of a ray-gun. *Losing Control* is different: fragmented reflections of four people in a broken mirror. I recognise Mum's face. Two of the men don't look anything like me – one is Asian: handsome with a hawk-like nose. The other guy has a round, good-natured face. The third guy in the photograph has long dark hair and a scowl, or maybe he's just been told to look like that for the camera.

'Is that him?'

Sam nods.

'Criminally underrated guitarist. You'll see what I mean. I'll make copies for you. I'd lend you the originals but if anything happened to them, they're difficult to find. Even on eBay. Have you got an iPod?'

I shake my head. Sam slides a blank CD into the computer.

'I ripped the tracks onto my hard drive. I'll copy you the Peel Session from '91 and the Radio One recording from Glastonbury '93 too. I had them on tape but I converted them into MP3s.'

'Sounds like they're your favourite band.'

Sam writes the track-list on the sleeve of the CD. I open the cover of *Calling Earth* and flick through the lyrics, stare at the photo of the band on the inner cover. It says the front cover was designed by Daz Lightning – my dad. I can't take it in. Sam slides another CD into the computer.

'You should read this. But not until you've spoken to your mum.' He pulls out a magazine. *Select*, July 1994. The headline: *"Death and Disintegration: the end of Mission Control"*. The photo on the cover shows the band looking moody in a field.

Sam hands me the copied CDs. I put them into my guitar case with the magazine.

'I wish it hadn't happened like this. You're going to be a great guitarist. I always believed she was still alive – but –'

'Why didn't she tell me?' Especially with my Manics obsession, with a missing person on a poster staring her in the face every time she comes into my bedroom. Why is she so afraid of being found? If she was so famous, why hasn't anyone recognised her?

'Promise me you'll go straight home?' Sam says.

I wheel my bike across the road and into the Pavilion gardens. It's getting dark. Across the river, there's a grotto with a bench inside, lit by a streetlight. The park is deserted. The only thing I can hear is the rushing of the river.

I sit on the bench. It smells of stale fags and piss in here and there's an empty bottle of White Lightning in the corner of the grotto.

My hands already feel numb as I take the magazine out of my guitar case. I stare at the photo of the band on the cover; then I turn the pages until I find the article. At first, I just look at the photos: their first gig in a youth centre; backstage at Glastonbury; a publicity shot with the band posing with toy ray-guns; the anti-fur poster; their last gig...

Mission Control – The Final Countdown

This summer should have been Mission Control's bid for success. Their second album, released on a major label. A busy schedule of festival dates. The start of their first world tour. We should have been covering Daz Lightning's latest on-stage outburst or interviewing Kaz K about the joys of Japanese food.

But in May, in a wet field in the Midlands, it was all about to go tragically wrong.

Story by Marilyn Richards.

December 1987: Stoke Park Comprehensive School.

In a classroom in Coventry, three fifteen year olds run through their first songs. In their heads, they are already a world away from suburban boredom. They all have visions of the rock 'n' roll dream. Darren Pratt has christened himself Daz Lightning. He's been playing guitar for a year, escaping into music from the harsh reality of his life.

Karen Kenning is learning the bass. Her librarian parents are bemused but supportive. Her head buzzes with riffs and lyrics. She can't wait until the band is on stage.

Pete Hollis loves playing drums. He's been Darren's friend for years. One day, he knows Darren's talents will be recognised.

Ashok Singh, the son of the newsagent where

Darren has his paper round, is at sixth form college, dreaming of big city university life. By the time he joins Mission Control in two years' time, he will have discovered the Hacienda, house music, Ibiza and Ecstasy.

Fast forward: Saturday 20th May 1994:

Early evening, a derelict WWII airfield in Staffordshire. I've been stuck in traffic, got lost, and the photographer's train was late. It's been raining all day. Battered trucks and buses are huddled together on the tarmac alongside rain-lashed tents and Portaloos. One stage and a dance marquee. A sorry collection of burger vans and clothes stalls under dripping tarpaulins. Anti-Criminal Justice Bill campaigners wander around with clipboards.

A handful of ravers dance in front of the stage as local hopefuls try to convince the audience they're the next Stone Roses. The dance tent blasts out house and jungle, steam rising from the doorway. Despite the downpour, there's anticipation in the air for Mission Control's headline slot, their first live outing since last autumn.

Mission Control are already waiting. Ash Singh welcomes me, spliff in hand. Affable drummer Pete Hollis greets me warmly, offering me a can of lager. Daz Lightning sits on the edge of a table, hunched over his guitar. Kaz K perches on a plastic chair with her bass on her lap. She shoots me a nervous look as she shuts her spiral-bound notebook.

'Just making sure I've memorised the new lyrics,' she confesses.

I ask if the band is confident about playing the new songs. It's less than a week before the release of their hotly-anticipated second album, *Losing Control*, recorded in Watermill Studios in the Brecon Beacons. The album is slicker than their début, but there are rumours of arguments; of a near split between Kaz and Daz while the band were in residence in the studio.

'The new songs speak for themselves,' Kaz K tells me. 'We've matured.'

'People think that because we've signed to a major, our songs aren't going to be about anything important. But we're still angry. There's so much to be angry about...' Daz doesn't look up from his guitar.

'The BNP. I mean – they're sick, aren't they?' Pete says. 'What do they think they're going on about?'

'The Tories haven't got a clue,' Kaz agrees. 'Everything's fucked up. People are turning to the politics of hate in desperation. That's why we're playing at the ANL carnival next week.'

Mission Control are synonymous with benefit gigs, the 90s equivalent of Hawkwind; like a British Rage Against the Machine, champions of the dispossessed, oppressed and the pissed off. Spiral Sun festival is a return to their roots.

'The government are scared of people organising themselves.' Ash rifles through his record box and grins. 'At raves like Castlemorton, people started creating their own society. It was a spontaneous act of humanity. They want to stop ordinary people thinking they can do this.'

I ask if they feel accused of trashing their DIY cred by signing to Futurediscs.

'We're not selling out. We want to reach more people. What's the point of being in a band no one's heard of?' Kaz K rests her bass on the table. She opens a can and takes a sip, grimacing.

So are they ready for the punishing schedule awaiting them? Does touring strain band relationships?

An uneasy look passes between There's silence in the room.

'I've been working out a bit. You've got to pace

yourself on tour,' Pete says.

'He's turning into a fucking lightweight,' laughs Daz. 'But you can't cane it too much before a gig. Afterwards, though!'

'It'll be good to get back into touring.' Kaz K smiles wryly. 'I love it. The adrenaline, the audience – I can't wait to go out there tonight. Going to Asia and America for the first time's going to be amazing.'

'We always have a laugh,' Pete says. 'It's like being on holiday.'

'I felt a bit trapped in the studio,' Kaz says.

'It's the whole travelling vibe. Wandering musicians. Like Kaz said, we've always been on a mission to reach people.' Ash has a faraway look in his eyes. 'We'll have a tour bus. Proper driver, road-crew. Hotel rooms.'

'Maybe we won't be able to handle the luxury.' Kaz K laughs.

Night falls and Mission Control take to the stage. The crowd gives them a heroes' welcome. The rain is now a special effect. Despite ignoring each other backstage, the chemistry between Kaz K and Daz Lightning has a new intensity. Kaz's basslines and Pete's drumming send hypnotic vibrations into the crowd. Ash Singh's samples, loops and aural weirdness add the spacey dimension.

Kaz K's voice, the raw power of the songs, is what makes Mission Control special. The fans go crazy to the songs from *Calling Earth* – thousands singing the chorus of 'Rootless in Babylon'. The songs from *Losing Control* go down well – there's an immediacy and urgency to them.

When Mission Control leave the stage, they're waving, smiling. They've conquered the rain. They look like they're ready to conquer the world.

Two hours later, the rave is in full swing in the

dance tent as Ash Singh plays one of his rare DJ sets with Kaz playing live bass.

Someone climbs onto the stage, shouting, pointing frantically Ash rips off his headphones and Kaz leaves her bass on stage. They run out of the marquee. The dub white label is left spinning on the decks. The crowd are bombed out of their minds. They don't care as long as the beats keep thumping.

I grab the bass and follow Ash and Kaz as they race towards the runway, where a group of travellers have been racing scrambler bikes all evening. The motors are silent now.

Daz Lightning is unconscious, lying next to a floored motorbike. Kaz throws herself on the ground, sobbing. Daz is everything to her: best friend, musical collaborator, first love.

Paramedics strap Daz to a body board. Kaz K gets into the ambulance. There's a streak of blood on her face.

Pete and Ash are still standing on the runway, soaked and shivering. Ash takes the bass from me, protecting it from the rain with his jacket.

There have been rumours about Daz and drugs. Had he taken anything? Ash and Pete exchange wary glances. Pete admits that Daz had an argument with Kaz.

'He just ran off. I followed him,' Pete says.

Daz wandered over to the lads on their motorbikes. Pete tried to stop him but Daz got onto a bike. He got careless. He skidded on the wet tarmac. He wasn't wearing a crash helmet.

'He couldn't even drive,' Pete says. 'What the fuck was he doing?'

Two days after Spiral Sun, Daz Lightning died from severe head injuries. Kaz K never left his side. While she kept her vigil, the media gathered outside the hospital: in the wake of Kurt Cobain's suicide, they

wanted their own rock star death story. When Kaz
K finally left the hospital, she was mobbed by the
press.

Kaz returned to the band's Birmingham HQ with
Ash Singh. In the early hours of the next morning,
she withdrew her share of cash from Mission
Control's account and drove off in the band's van.
She's been missing ever since, apart from an
unconfirmed sighting reported at a Derbyshire
petrol station. The police are concerned about her
safety, and Kaz's parents have made an appeal:

'The media attention may have weakened Karen's
already fragile state,' said her father in a press
conference on May 31st. 'If you hear this, Karen,
please get in touch.'

I read the article again, trying to take it in. My hands are so
cold, they're frozen in position holding the magazine. My
brain feels like it's bulging, totally overloaded. My face is
freezing and I can't think properly. I try to make some sense
of things:

My parents were both famous. My dad died in a stupid,
pointless accident. Mum has been missing for nearly fifteen
years. My name isn't really Jason Knight – it should be Jason
Kenning. Bradley Smeed would love that – Kenny Kenning
– or worse – Jason Pratt. No wonder Daz Lightning
changed his name.

I thought Mum was just an ex-art student who'd had a
rubbish band for a while and was a bit mental. But before I
was born, she was a brilliant musician.

My dad was Daz Lightning. Real name Darren Pratt. Sam
thinks he was a genius, but he sounds really fucked up.

So this is why she gets weepy and depressed. Why didn't
she tell me anything?

My whole life is a lie. Mum told me we had no family;
just each other.

I have grandparents, but maybe they're dead by now.

Chapter 10
The Train

Jason

I put the magazine back into my guitar case and rub my hands together until some feeling comes back into them. I strap on my cycling helmet, get back on my bike and cycle unsteadily out of the park.

Ben's house is dark. I ring the doorbell anyway. Feet thunder down the stairs. Ben answers the door. He's wearing the stripy slipper socks he got for Christmas.

'How was your guitar lesson?'

I shrug.

'You look weird.'

'Is anyone else in?'

'Mum and Dad went to see my nan and Rachel's gone to the cinema with her mates.' I'm relieved that we're alone. The last thing I need is Ben's family fussing over me.

'Can I dump my bike here?'

Ben nods and I wheel my bike into the hallway. I take off my helmet and put it on the table.

'What's up with you?'

'I need to tell you something.'

I follow Ben up upstairs to his room, my guitar case still on my back. My heart's thumping as I run up the stairs but I try to look calm. The warmth of Ben's house starts to thaw my face and hands.

I open my guitar case and hand the *Select* magazine to Ben. He glances at the cover.

'Mission Control?' Ben asks, puzzled. Then he looks at the photo more closely. 'Shit. That's your mum.'

I nod.

'Read the article. It starts on page forty three.'

Ben sits on his computer chair. He reads the article intently. I watch the movement of his eyes as he scans the page. I sit on the floor, leaning against the radiator.

'Sam had that poster of her in his room. That's how I

found out,' I say.

'Your mum was fit.'

'Shut up. Why didn't she tell me any of this?'

'I dunno. It explains everything.'

'Like what?' He's right. It's why I've had nothing all my life, because my mum's been hiding from reality.

'She knew what guitar to get you. She's helped you loads.'

'She lied to me.'

Ben stares at the magazine again.

'That Daz guy –he's your dad?'

'Yeah – I always wondered…'

'You look just like him – like both of them. Don't you want to hear what they sounded like?'

'Sam copied their albums for me.'

'Let's listen to them.' Ben doesn't get it.

'Not yet.'

'Mission Control must have been massive, back in the nineties.'

I wish I hadn't told him anything. I snatch the magazine out of his hands and clutch it to my chest. I need more time for it to sink in. I'm not ready to share it.

'Aren't you excited?'

'I knew my dad died before I was born. At least that was true. I've got grandparents. They don't even know Mum's alive.'

One thing never really sunk in when I read about Richey Manic disappearing. It's not just about the missing person, is it? It's about their parents, family and friends not knowing what happened, wondering if they could have stopped it.

I feel like a ghost.

'What's your mum going to say?' Ben asks.

'How should I know? Probably carry on refusing to talk about anything.'

'Her real name's Karen Kenning? And she's from Coventry?'

'Yeah.'

Ben spins around on his chair and wakes up his laptop. I watch as Ben finds a Directory Enquiries web page, then searches for "Kenning" and "Coventry". There are three results, with addresses and phone numbers. Ben presses "print". I take the page from the printer.

'Shall I call them? It's going to sound a bit weird –'

'Yeah. Let's call them.' Ben picks up his mobile. He starts dialling a number.

I grab Ben's arm and wrestle the phone out of his hand. Ben stares at me, shocked. I grasp the phone tightly, realising my fingernails have left red scratch marks on Ben's wrist.

'What the fuck?'

'Sorry.'

Ben rubs his wrist. 'It's just a phone call. What's the problem?'

'Let me do it myself. I want to find my grandparents, but...'

'I'm just trying to help.'

The list of names has fallen on the carpet. I pick it up. My hands are shaking.

The first address is for M Kenning, 32 Cross Road, Edgewick, Coventry. I close my eyes and rehearse what I want to say. Ben's right. I just need to do it. I sit on the edge of Ben's bed and I dial the number slowly and deliberately. The phone rings at the other end. My palms are sweaty. Part of me hopes no one answers.

'Hello?' A man's voice; picked up on the fifth ring.

'Are you Mr Kenning?'

'Who's that?' He sounds bad-tempered.

'Have you got a daughter called Karen who was in a band called Mission Control?'

'No.'

'Sorry. Wrong number.' I feel desperate, even though I'm sure this man isn't my grandfather. He might be related to me somehow. 'Are you sure you don't know Karen Kenning?'

'Yes! Bugger off. Bloody kids,' he mutters and slams the phone down.

I stare at Ben, losing hope.

'That didn't go too well.'

'Keep trying.'

I dial the next number: M and P Kenning, 538 Woodway Lane, Potters Green, Coventry. There's an engaged tone. I try the number again, just to be sure I've dialled it right, but it's still beeping.

I might as well try the last number: B and S Kenning, The Old Farmhouse, Church Lane, Ryton-on-Dunsmore, Coventry. The phone rings but then there's a click and an answerphone message starts: a woman's voice – it sounds warm but a bit unsure of what to say:

'Hello. This is Brian and Sheila Kenning. I'm sorry we can't come to the phone at the moment but please leave your name and telephone number and we'll call you back...'

The answer machine bleeps but I can't think of anything to say. The lady on the message sounds fairly old but not too doddery.

'Hi...my name's Jason. I'm looking for my grandparents,' I manage to say but then it bleeps again, like it's stopped recording. I end the call and put the phone down on the bed.

Ben smiles.

'At least you tried. What are you going to do now? Are you going to tell your mum?'

'I'm not going home.'

'You could stay here. As long as you don't attack me again,' Ben says.

I'm not really paying much attention to him anymore. In my imagination, I'm standing outside The Old Farmhouse. There's a warm orange glow coming through the windows. A lady opens the door. She's wearing a cardigan and has a pair of glasses dangling on a chain. She puts them on and smiles at me. 'You must be Jason,' she says. She hugs me. 'You look so much like Karen.' She invites me in.

I blink and force myself back into Ben's bedroom. I know what to do now.

'I'm going to Coventry.'

'Now?'

I nod. I know it could just be a fantasy, but I want to go there, to see if Brian and Sheila Kenning are my grandparents. I've missed them for my whole life – all my birthdays, Christmases, holidays. Stuff Ben takes for granted.

Surely they'll be really pleased to find out they've got a grandson and their daughter is alive? It might be a bit of a shock for them, but they might take it better if I'm there in person, standing on their doorstep.

'When's the next train?'

Ben clicks onto Google and starts searching for the train times from Matlock Bath.

'Have you still got your Discman?' I ask.

'My mum uses it to listen to audio books. It's probably in her bedside cabinet.'

'I really need to borrow it – to listen to the Mission Control CDs.'

'I'll go and fetch it.' Ben leaves the room and goes downstairs.

I jump into Ben's chair. I check the train times and prices to Coventry and note them down. The next train goes in twenty minutes and I'll need to change trains twice. All I've got is the money for my guitar lesson and I'll have less than a tenner left if I buy a return ticket. If I don't find my grandparents, I'm stuffed. I'll be stuck in Coventry until Monday morning with nowhere to stay.

Ben's drawstring swimming bag is hanging on the handle of his wardrobe. I put the CDs and the magazine in it. I haven't got any other stuff with me. I push my guitar under Ben's bed.

I pick up Ben's guitar and strum a few chords, to calm the rising panic in my chest.

What if I never go home? I'll need an acoustic guitar. I could busk for a living. What would happen to me? I picture myself on my own in a big city, sitting in an underpass with a guitar with missing strings. Being hungry and lost.

I put the guitar back down and wake myself up. Reality check. I'm not running away.

Even if I don't find my grandparents; if I can't face going home tomorrow, I can stay here with Ben.

Mum isn't a bad person, even if she is a massive liar. I've never really suffered. If I went home now, there would be something hot to eat, and she'd want to know all about my guitar lesson.

I can't face her yet. I've got to do this.

I hear Ben's footsteps on the stairs. He hands me the Discman and some AA batteries.

'It eats batteries. It took me ages to find these in the kitchen drawer.'

'Thanks. I'm borrowing your bag. My guitar's under your bed.' I sling the swimming bag over my shoulders.

'What about food and stuff?'

'The train goes in ten minutes.'

Ben runs downstairs again and I follow him into the kitchen. He grabs three cans of coke from the fridge and raids the kitchen cupboards, shoving a packet of cookies and several bags of crisps at me. The swimming bag's pretty full now.

'I've got to go. Can you hide my bike?'

Ben nods. I open the back door.

'You'll be alright, won't you?'

'Don't tell anyone I was here – don't tell them I know about Mum.'

'Okay, but –'

I look at my watch. I'll miss the train. I run down the passage, down the steep street and straight across the main road, into the railway station car park. I sprint onto the far platform, for the trains going to Derby. A bunch of older teenagers in hiking gear are waiting for the train. They're messing about, eating chips. In the shadow of the platform, getting my breath back, I feel so alone. Stupid, I know, because I could just go home – or go back to Ben's. But the rails are already singing with the vibration of the train through the tunnel.

Kaz

I watch the margarine melt in the pan and put in a couple of spoonfuls of flour, beating it smooth.

I gradually add goats' milk, from the neighbours down the hill, and sprinkle in a pinch of mustard and grated cheese. Jason loves cheap rubbery cheddar. I pour it on the pasta and vegetable mixture, sprinkle on breadcrumbs, grate more cheese on the top and put it in the AGA.

Jason should be back from his guitar lesson soon. He was really excited about it. He's been practising hard, which seems a bit mad, when he's going for lessons. Like Mrs Norton asking me to clean her already spotless house. Jason doesn't realise how talented he is: how quickly he picks things up.

I go back to my painting. I asked Jason to play his guitar in front of my easel while I sketched him out on a new canvas. I haven't done portraits on a large scale like this before, and it's changing my style. Everything's more fluid, with a sense of movement. I like the strong contrast of colours: the red Stratocaster against his black t-shirt; his pale arm, the muscles taut. I get so absorbed in the painting, I forget the time. When I finally glance up at the clock, it's five pm.

Jason should be home by now. I rush into the kitchen and take the pasta bake out of the AGA. Luckily it's not burned. The breadcrumbs are golden brown and the cheese is bubbling on the top. The delicious smell of food brings the cat into the kitchen and she winds herself around my legs, purring. She loves cheese. Sod it. I take a spoonful of sauce from the corner and put it in her bowl, along with a sprinkling of Go-cat. She gulps it down in seconds flat, even though it's still hot. It's not like Patti's going to get obese: she's the most fearsome hunter in the village.

Jason probably just got carried away. I cover the casserole dish with foil and go back to my painting but I keep glancing at the window. I haven't drawn the curtains yet. Half past five. My chest tightens with anxiety. I pick up the phone, then put it down again. What's the panic? It doesn't matter if Jason's a bit late. I pull a book about Renoir from the shelf and leaf through it. I can't concentrate.

I wait in the window, feeling pathetic, leaning with my elbows on the windowsill. The cat jumps up and presses her nose against the glass.

It's so quiet. It's just an old person's house without Jason playing the guitar, listening to music or leaping up two stairs at a time. I switch on the radiogram and tune it to Radio Four, just for background noise. I go back to the kitchen. The casserole dish is almost cold. Jason didn't say anything about staying out late. Not that it's late yet. I thought he was coming straight home for his tea. He's probably gone to Ben's house.

I pick up the phone again and dial Ben's number.

'Hello?' It's Brenda.

'It's Keziah. Is Jason there?' I try not to sound worried.

'We've only just got in. I'll ask Ben.' There's a clunk as she puts the phone down on the table.

'Ben!' she yells. She can shout when she wants to. 'Is Jason here?'

I hear a faint shout in the background. Brenda comes back to the phone.

'He says he's not seen Jason all day.'

'Shit.' I have visions of Jason's mangled body lying on the roadside.

'Is everything okay?' Brenda asks.

'He didn't come home. I'll have to look for him.'

'Oh.' Brenda says. 'I'm sure he's fine.'

'What if something's happened?'

'Don't worry. We'll let you know if he turns up here. I wish you had a mobile sometimes. Call me in an hour.'

I switch off the radiogram. I tear a strip off my sketchbook and write a note for Jason. It would be awful for him if he came home and thought I was missing:

Where are you? I've gone to find you. Next time, call!!!! There's a pasta bake if you want it. Love Mum. xxx

I put on my boots and jacket and take the torch from the

kitchen drawer. I leave the kitchen light on. I lock the back door and put the key in its hiding place. I've not ridden a bike since the accident. My right leg feels stiff and painful again. I wheel Jason's old bike out of the shed and bump it down the steps. The dynamo bike light flickers as I set off down the hill, making me feel as if I'm in an old black and white horror film.

Jason

As the train pulls out of Matlock Bath station, I take the Discman out of the bag and find the *Calling Earth* CD. I don't know what to expect. I stare at the tracklist Sam wrote. It's frustrating not being able to look at the artwork and read the lyrics. I stare out of the window instead, as the dark countryside rattles past.

I press "Play". The first track kicks in. Mum's voice is really powerful. The song's called 'Rootless in Babylon'. I remember. It's what she played on my acoustic guitar, back in September. It's a killer riff. It drives the song. The lyrics are about feeling like you don't belong anywhere, feeling different from your family and friends.

I think 'Twisted Skin' might be about racism: *'Deep within your twisted skin / You don't know where to begin / You can't see the lies they've been telling all your life.'* The vocals are angry but it's got a bouncy bassline. I can't believe my mum played this music and didn't tell me anything about it.

The guitar plays grungy riffs and jagged lines weaving around the vocals and bass. It's really difficult to describe: somewhere between Kurt Cobain and Johnny Marr, but totally unique. Daz doesn't go into rock overdrive just for the sake of it. I can't picture him like Slash, standing on a clifftop with his hair billowing in the wind. Daz always seems to put the song first. I understand his guitar playing, a connection with him through music. I listen to the songs and I try to imagine what Daz was like; what Mum was like when she was young.

The conductor comes down the train. I buy a return to Coventry. For a moment, the reality of what I'm doing hits me, but I just put the tickets in the pocket of my jeans with my change. I think about Daz instead. It sounds like he was moody and unpredictable, and he took drugs.

The train reaches the outskirts of Derby and pretty soon, the hikers are putting their rucksacks back on. *Calling Earth* is only half way through but I stop the CD as the train slows down into the station. I have to concentrate. I get out the sheet of paper with the addresses and the train times on. I feel jittery. I've been to Derby a couple of times on my own, record shopping. Anywhere else is uncharted territory.

I've got to find a train that goes to Birmingham and then change for Coventry. I feel a stab of panic. I've hardly been anywhere in my life, especially without Mum. The furthest away home I've ever been was to Devon with Ben and his family when I was eight, staying in a caravan park. I pick up the bag and get off the train.

The Birmingham train leaves in fifteen minutes. I hurry across the bridge to the main station building and stare at the big departure board. The train to Birmingham's going from Platform Five. I run up the steps and over the bridge again. There's a train already waiting on the platform. There's a digital display in the window that says "Birmingham New Street" but I still feel nervous.

I get on the train and force my way through the automatic doors into the carriage. There's an old lady sitting at a seat with a table. She's knitting something with a ball of fluffy orange wool which is unravelling on the table next to a bag of sweets.

'Is this is the train for Birmingham?' I ask.

'Yes, it is.'

'Is this seat free?' I might feel a bit safer, sitting near her. She looks a bit like the way I imagined my grandmother.

She nods but she gives me a wary look and moves her possessions a bit closer to herself.

I glance at my reflection in the darkened window. I don't think I look threatening, but then again, I am dressed all in black with a slogan painted on the sleeve of my jacket. I smile at her but she ignores me. What if I find my grandparents but they're scared of me and don't believe me when I tell them about Mum? They're Kaz K's parents. They'll be used to people wearing black and looking a bit weird.

I sit down anyway, in the seat closest to the window. I get the CD player out again and press play, skipping back to the start of the last song I was listening to: 'Smash and Grab'. It's spikier and more sinister than the other songs so far. I wonder if Daz wrote the lyrics, although Mum's pretty dark at times in her paintings. I always wondered why she sees the world like that. It sounds like it's written from a man's point of view but Kaz is singing, which makes it seem really twisted, and the melody sounds almost like an innocent pop song: *'I'd do anything for your pretty hair / Watching life behind blacked-out windows / You can't escape from me / No escape from my stare'*. I'm getting cold shivers down the back of my neck and I'm sure it's not the draught from the sliding doors, which are now stuck open as a few last people struggle onto the train.

The train moves off and gathers speed. I can't see anything out of the windows, just black nothingness and a reflection of my face. I try to keep my breathing steady. Just concentrate on getting to Birmingham; then Coventry; then to the last address on the list from Directory Enquiries. If I find my grandparents, then what?

Chapter 11
The Fishpond

Kaz

The road to Matlock Bath is quiet and dark. There's no sign of Jason. I stop outside the Fishpond. Jason told me his guitar teacher lives here. I get off Jason's old bike and chain it to the railings at the front of the pub. I walk into the bar. The pub is almost deserted. The barman is a guy in his late twenties with ginger hair, leaning with his elbows on the bar, reading a book. He glances up casually. Then he blinks and stares at me.

'I'm looking for my…'

'Oh my god!' he gasps. 'It really is you!'

'My son, Jason. He had a guitar lesson. He hasn't…'

'Kaz K! Oh my god.'

He's recognised me. The first person to recognise me as Kaz K in over fourteen years – not since that kid in the petrol station. I almost bolt for the door. The barman looks very pale.

'Have you seen my son?'

The man comes out from behind the bar. He takes a deep breath.

'I'm sorry but I had to tell him. I mean, what was I supposed to say? He saw the poster.'

'What poster?'

'Your anti-fur poster.'

It's so weird, I laugh. The drinkers in the bar stare at us.

'You must have had that poster since you were Jason's age.'

'I saw you at Brixton Academy. October '93. I managed to talk to you all at the stage door. I've still got the plectrum Daz Lightning gave me.'

'You're Sam, right?' I remember Jason telling me his guitar teacher's name. 'Jason hasn't been home. I need to know what happened.'

'He didn't have a clue who he was. He was upset.' Sam is

almost shouting at me. I stare at him, and he stares back.

'I was trying to protect Jason. You don't know…'

'You've been here all this time. And no one knew.'

I stare down at the pattern on the pub carpet. It seems to be moving around. My leg hurts so much from cycling that my whole body throbs.

Sam catches me before I collapse. He steers me onto a bar stool. I burst into tears.

A serviette is thrust into my hands, then a shot glass swirling with golden liquid.

'Brandy. You'll feel better.'

I neck the drink. The alcohol numbs my lips but makes me feel warmer – numbs the pain in my leg.

A plump woman in her fifties squeezes behind the bar and fixes Sam with a stare.

'Giving drinks away, Sam?'

'This is Kaz K. From Mission Control. She lives near here! Jason – the kid who was here for a guitar lesson – she's his mum.'

'Well I've never heard of her.' The woman looks at me critically. I realise I'm still wearing my gardening jeans and I've got red paint on my hands.

'Jason's gone missing. It's only been a couple of hours since he should have been back, but I'm worried.'

'He'd never seen that poster before, Judith. He didn't know his mum was famous.'

Judith gives me a disapproving stare. She starts pulling a pint of bitter for the old man who's sitting next to me at the bar.

'You're the woman in that poster?' she says, accusingly. Surely I don't look anything like I did in the poster?

'Can I use your phone?' I ask. I need to call Brenda again. Ben must know something.

'There's a pay phone in the corridor.' Judith scowls.

I feel my pockets but I've forgotten to bring any money.

'Use my mobile.' Sam slides a sleek silver phone across the bar. I fumble with it, until Sam shows me how to dial the number and make it ring.

'Hello?' Brenda's voice again.

'It's Kaz – Keziah.'

'I've been trying to ring you. We've found Jason's cycling helmet in the hall.'

'What?'

'Ben didn't want to tell us but we got the story from him eventually.' Brenda sighs. 'Jason did come here. Ben says he got on a train to Coventry.'

My heart plummets.

'I'm coming.'

I give the phone back to Sam, trembling. I get down from the bar stool and run to the exit but Sam catches up with me, grabbing the sleeve of my jacket.

'Kaz!'

I shrug myself free.

'What are you doing? My son's gone missing. What do you want? An autograph?'

'Let me help look for him. I've got a car. I sort of feel responsible.'

'Come with me then, if you want.'

'Wait outside,' he tells me. 'I'll be five minutes.'

Sam disappears through a door by the bar marked 'Private'. Judith glares at me from behind the bar. I walk out of the pub to unchain my bike. The railings have a coating of frost. Jason wasn't even wearing his fleece.

An old estate car pulls out of the drive at the side of the pub. Sam gets out and loads my bike into the boot. I tell him Ben's address and we drive there in silence. Sam's driving is jerky and the car almost stalls as he drives up the steep incline to Ben's house.

'I'll wait in the car,' Sam says. 'I don't really trust my handbrake.'

My hand shakes as I ring the front door bell.

Brenda answers the front door. Uncharacteristically, she hugs me.

'I'm so sorry,' she says, pulling away from me. I follow her into the hallway. 'What did you expect? Keeping a secret like that from him? You lied to all of us.'

'Please – I just want to know where Jason is.'

Ben thunders down the stairs.

'He didn't even know his grandparents existed until tonight. You told him your parents were dead.' He stares at me as if he's never seen me before.

'You never told us why you turned up in the village,' Brenda says. I never thought you were famous. Why didn't I recognise you?'

'I wasn't that famous.'

Ben hands me a piece of paper.

'We looked on the internet. We tried calling but...' It's a print-out of names and addresses in Coventry. The first two don't mean anything to me but the last one does. Uncle Brian and Aunty Sheila's house. My parents aren't on the list. A horrible thought hits me. What if they're dead? What if I've killed them by causing them endless grief and worry? Ben's right. I told Jason we were on our own, after Elsa died. He really believed she was his Great-Aunt. Now everything's unravelling.

'None of these people are your parents?' Suddenly Ben looks less sure of himself.

'No. My aunt and uncle live at the last address.'

'He's going straight to that house. He was sure they were his grandparents.'

'You thought he'd be fine going off all by himself?'

'I couldn't stop him,' he mumbles.

'How could you let him do something so stupid?' Brenda says. 'Anything could happen to him.'

'Sorry,' Ben says, looking down at his socks.

'I said you should have got him a mobile phone,' Brenda says.

I stare at the piece of paper. The only way I can find Jason is to phone my aunt and uncle – and explain everything. I need to find out why my parents aren't in the directory. My head spins. I sit down on the stairs.

'I need to call them.' I take a deep breath as Ben hands me the cordless phone. I hold it but I can't stop my hands from shaking. I dial Brian and Sheila's number first. It rings but then a voicemail message clicks in. It feels strange to hear Sheila's voice. I can't leave a message, not yet. There's something else I've got to do.

I dial the number. It's etched in my brain. It starts ringing. I feel my chest tighten so I have to gasp for breath. Brenda and Ben are staring at me but I'm glad they're here.

'Hello?' Mum. Her posh telephone voice.

I've got this far before but I haven't been able to speak. This time has to be different.

'It's me. Karen.' I force the words out, sounding like someone who's been chain-smoking for the last twenty years. At least I spoke.

I hear a sharp intake of breath.

'Who is this?' She sounds scared and shaky.

'It's me. I'm sorry...'

'Jim! Jim!' she shouts – for my dad. They're both still alive. I smile with relief. Mum's voice sounds muffled, as if she's put her hand over the receiver. 'It's one of those prank calls.'

I gasp with a sudden cold shock.

'I'm not a prank!'

'What if it's real, Jim?'

A rustling noise comes from the receiver.

'Look, I don't know who you are but this is an utterly despicable thing to do.' It's a relief to hear his voice, even though he's angry.

'It was a mistake that time. I couldn't speak, I'm sorry.'

'If you don't put the phone down, I'll call the police.'

'Please. It's really me. I've lost my son.'

The phone goes dead. I stare at it in my hand. If I phone back, would it make things worse?

'They didn't believe me,' I say. I pass the receiver back to Brenda.

'That was your parents?' she asks.

I nod. I stand up and stagger down the hall.

'I'm going to Coventry.' I struggle with the Yale lock.

Ben opens the door for me. His eyes are wide with worry.

'Will you call? When you've found him?'

'What if I don't find him, Ben?'

I run to Sam's car. It seems even colder outside now.

'It's definitely Kaz K…' He's talking to someone on the phone. 'Pretty good actually. Maybe a bit rough around the edges, but…' He stares up at me. 'Shit. Got to go.'

I open the passenger door and he hastily pockets the phone. I don't know who Sam's been talking to, but he's looking guilty.

'Do you know where he is?' Sam asks.

I sit down in the passenger seat.

'He's gone to Coventry. He's trying to find his grandparents. I spoke to them, Sam. For the first time in fifteen years.'

'I've spent years wondering what happened to you.' He stares at me, as if he can't believe I'm real.

'I've got to go there, now. They didn't believe it was me.'

'I told Jason to go home. I thought you would sort things out with him. I didn't think he'd do anything drastic.'

Sam knows I heard him talking about me on the phone. He had no right. My son is out there – lost, confused.

'I need you to drive me to Coventry now.'

'Seriously?' Sam gasps, but I can tell he's secretly thrilled. 'My in-laws will kill me.' Sam starts the car and drives down the hill, his brakes squealing as he stops at the junction with the main road. 'Let me stop at the pub first. Won't be long. Do you need anything from your house?'

'I've fed the cat. I just need Jason.'

The car's suspension makes a grinding noise as Sam turns right. It's a musician's car, battered from constantly being stuffed with drums, instruments, amplifiers and people; kept going with hope and crossed fingers.

Jason

I drain the can of Coke. I felt so thirsty after I finished the crisps. I can't see a bin in the carriage, so I crumple the can and put it back in my bag. I felt too nervous to eat before I got on this final train, desperate to find the right platform at Birmingham New Street. It was so big: stark and draughty – and I felt like I was miles underground. I check my watch. The train is nearly in Coventry already. I look out of the window and the patch of dark countryside between here and Birmingham is already turning into houses and lampposts.

I keep my headphones on as I stand up to leave the train. Since I left Birmingham, I've been listening to *Losing Control*. It's different from *Calling Earth* – it's got more of a big rock sound but with an unsettling undercurrent of electronic noise and samples. You can tell it was recorded in a big studio and the producer has spent hours deciding exactly how each instrument needs to sound. They obviously thought it was going to sell millions. The drums have got a huge echoey sound. Daz's guitar cuts through everything at the right moments. The rumble from Mum's bass almost makes me lose my balance as the train grinds to a halt at the station. I press "Stop", wind the headphones up and put the Discman in my bag.

As soon as I get off the train, the cold hits me and my breath comes out in white clouds. I walk along the platform to the station building. Coventry station is a lot smaller than Birmingham New Street. It's made of concrete, with big glass windows. I get the piece of paper out of my pocket. I need to get to Church Lane, Ryton on Dunsmore.

The station is quiet but there's a row of taxis waiting outside the entrance. There are a few people standing near the entrance with bags and suitcases, looking bored. They must be waiting for someone to pick them up. There's a man with short greying hair and a black overcoat, reading a folded up newspaper.

'Excuse me?' I ask. The man takes a step backwards, one hand firmly gripping the handle of his case. The other people waiting here are giving me sidelong stares. I've never had this effect on anyone before. Perhaps I've inherited Daz Lightning's moody expression.

'Sorry, but where does the bus to Ryton on Dunsmore go from?'

The man visibly relaxes and he smiles.

'There aren't any buses to Ryton on Sundays, I'm afraid.'

'Really? How long would it take me to walk there?' I thought this was a city, not some crappy village in the middle of nowhere.

'It's about six miles away. It'll take you a couple of hours to walk there at least.'

'I'd get a taxi if I were you, love,' a woman buts in, loading her case into the boot of a red hatchback. 'He's right. The bus service out there is non-existent on Sunday these days.'

'Oh. Thanks.' I take the change out of my pocket and count it. I wander over to the taxi rank, the money in my hand. The taxi rank isn't very busy. The drivers of the first two taxis are chatting in a foreign language: an old Asian guy with a round white hat and a beard behind the wheel of a taxi and a young guy in a leather jacket, leaning in through the window.

'Is eight pounds fifty enough to get to Ryton-on-Dunsmore?' I ask. Both men stare at me. The old man scowls but the young guy smiles.

'It'll do.'

'Thanks. I'm going to visit my grandparents. I didn't realise there wasn't a bus.'

The young man gets into his silver taxi. There's an advert for an airline on its side. I sit in the back, on the vinyl seat.

'Couldn't you get anyone to pick you up?'

The taxi sets off, so fast I almost slide off the seat. I buckle the seat belt.

'It's a surprise.'

'That's nice.'

Will it be a nice surprise or just a massive shock? I wonder what I'm going to say to them. My heart flutters as the taxi speeds along. It's the can of Coke I drank earlier on. I got into this taxi under the influence of a massive caffeine and sugar rush. Maybe I should have thought this through a bit more. It's too late to change my mind.

Kaz

Sam parks outside the pub, mounting the pavement on the wrong side of the road. While I wait for him, I rummage through the glove compartment. There's a small stack of CDs, including copied versions of *Calling Earth* and *Losing Control.*

I'm so out of touch with music. Some bands I've only heard of through Jason. I stare at the cover of the first Foo Fighters album. Until last year, I didn't know Dave Grohl had formed Foo Fighters soon after Kurt Cobain's suicide. This album came out the year Jason was born. One year after Kurt Cobain shot himself. One year after Daz died. What would have happened if I'd carried on as a musician? Instead, I carried on hiding.

Sam gets back into the car and starts the engine.

'What did you tell your wife? Does she know what you're doing?'

I screw my eyes shut as the car swerves across the road. When I open my eyes again, we're heading south on the A6, driving past the old cotton mill.

'She's sick of my Mission Control obsession and thinks I've finally flipped. But she wants me to find Jason. Says it's my fault he's run away. My mother-in-law wants my head on a spike.'

'She didn't warm to me very much.'

Sam drives on in silence. If Jason managed to change trains; if the trains were all on time, he'll be in Coventry by now. He'll be on his way to Uncle Brian and Aunty Sheila's house. Please let him be okay. Jason is sensible. Even though he's done something completely ridiculous, he seems to have done it for the right reasons. I can't even begin to imagine what must be going through his mind right now. What will Uncle Brian think?

'You're driving too slowly,' I tell Sam.

I slide *No Remorse* by Motorhead into the car stereo and crank it up. When I drove the band's van and we were running late, I put on Motorhead tapes. It always worked.

Sam is soon nudging the car above the speed limit. We whiz past Cromford. Sam switches on the full beam of his headlights as we plunge into the dark countryside.

'I thought maybe you'd escaped into drink and drugs and lost your mind.'

'Cheers.'

'So what have you been doing?'

'Painting. Gardening. Being Jason's mum. That's about it. Why does everyone think I'm on drugs?'

Sam laughs.

'I'm sure Barbara Fleming thinks so too.'

'Barbara Fleming? The artist who paints those animal pictures? My mother in-law collects her tea towels.'

'Barbara doesn't just do cute animals. She's going to set up a gallery in Cromford. She wants to work with me. Turn me into a successful artist.'

'Someone would be bound to recognise you,' Sam says.

'It's not like anyone still cares. Apart from you, anyway.'

'Are you kidding? We haven't forgotten you. There's a Facebook group for Mission Control fans. There are about four thousand people on it. Not bad for a band from fifteen years ago.'

'Who were you on the phone to? When you said I was rough around the edges?'

'You heard that?'

'I know I look a state, but my son's missing. What do you expect?'

'It was Marilyn Richards.'

I freeze.

'She's writing a book about Mission Control. I've known her for ages. I was in a band she interviewed, way back. She's alright.'

'What the fuck?'

'She's got an arts column in the *Guardian* now, but she still loves Mission Control. She was there. She saw...'

'I know what she saw.' I shiver, trying to block out that image of Daz, blood pooling around his head.

'I gave Jason the *Select* magazine with the article,' Sam says. 'The last interview. I told him not to read it until he talked to you.'

'He's thirteen. If you tell him not to do something…'

'The *Select* article is okay. Not like those tabloid rubberneckers. Don't you think Marilyn Richards has the right to find out what happened to you?'

I think about that last interview at the Spiral Sun festival. The photographer made us stand in that field. It was freezing. Daz wasn't talking to me all day. He thought I'd slept with Ash.

'This is too weird.' I need to find Jason. My parents need to know I'm still alive.

'So why did you stay missing? What were you so afraid of?'

Sam is driving fast around the bends, headlights eerily illuminating trees in each turn in the road.

We reach Ambergate and turn onto the road leading to the motorway. I lean back on the seat. Every minute of this journey is taking me closer to Jason. That's what I need to focus on, to take away the feeling of helplessness.

'You could have ended up anywhere. Why somewhere that's a two hour drive from Coventry?'

'I wanted to be alone. I drove into the countryside. I didn't really know where I was. I thought I wanted to kill myself.'

'I always believed you were alive, somewhere.'

'I didn't want to think about Mission Control, but when Jason started learning the guitar, it brought it all back.'

'What about your parents? What about Ash and Pete? Didn't you want to tell them you were safe?'

The last night in our studio, the night Daz died, I made the decision to take the van and run away from what was left of my life.

We were at his bedside when his heartbeat stopped after two days in the hospital, his head covered in white bandages and gauze. Daz had really died the moment his head had hit the ground. I couldn't take anything in. I remember Ash saying he'd take me home. Back to the studio, not to my parents' house. They wouldn't understand. They hated Daz.

I was blinded by photographers' flash-lights as I left the hospital: a crowd of people shouting at me, asking questions. I closed my eyes and let Ash and Pete lead me out of there. I wanted to be on my own, in darkness.

When I got back to the studio; into our room, it was too much of a shock. The records we'd bought together, Daz's guitars, the teetering pile of music magazines in the corner; his clothes strewn on the mattress, as if he was going to come back any minute. He would never make music again. He was lying in a hospital morgue.

I put one of Daz's t-shirts on and lay on the bed. I hugged his old leather jacket. I thought I was never going to stop crying. I remember Ash coming into the room, covering me up with the duvet, talking to me softly. He told me he had always loved me and he'd look after me whatever happened. I pretended to be asleep.

I blamed myself for Daz's death. I should have made him see sense. The last time I saw Daz alive was when we had that blazing argument at Spiral Sun, when Daz stalked off into the rain, Pete struggling to keep up with him. Daz was drunk, angry; paranoid. He accused me of getting up to all kinds of stuff with Ash, even though it had been just one kiss when we were off our heads at the Watermill studio.

I thought we'd got over that. Me and Daz had been pretty good for weeks. But Daz wanted Ash to leave the band. He wanted Mission Control to go back to being a three-piece. I wasn't going to let Daz have his own way. He'd been friends with Ash since he was sixteen. They'd set up the studio together. I was close to Ash. It was undeniable, there was a spark between us, but it was just part of our friendship. Sometimes there was a bit of flirting, but I loved Daz.

If Ash really did love me, it changed everything.

I had been a fool not to see what was happening.

'It was all my fault, anyway.'

'How wrong can you be?' Sam says. The anger in his voice surprises me. 'How can you blame yourself for Daz's death?'

'You weren't there.'

Chapter 12
Lost

Jason

After a few minutes, we get onto a dual carriageway. The driver really picks up speed, g-force sticking my head to the back of the seat.

'You don't live round here, then?' The taxi driver sounds friendly. I don't think I've ever travelled this fast in a car before. I feel like I'm on a race-track.

'It's the first time I've been to see my grandparents.'

The houses thin out and it starts to look more like countryside, trees lining the road. We pass a long row of railings. There's just a black stretch of nothingness behind them, where I would have expected buildings.

'That's the old Peugeot factory. My dad worked there most of his life. It's all gone. Just piles of bricks. It's dead quiet out here now.'

The taxi finally slows down and turns left up a quiet road with a pub at the end.

'What number do they live at?'

'The Old Farmhouse. I don't think it's got a number.'

'You can find it yourself, can't you? It's a dead end, anyway. Can't be too difficult.'

My head's spinning a bit from the speed of the taxi ride. I give the driver my money – all of it. The taxi meter says £12.57, so he really is being kinder than he needs to be.

'Thanks.'

'I bet they can't wait to see you.'

I slam the taxi door shut and stand on the pavement, as the driver turns around and speeds off again. The cold makes me fold my arms against my chest. The houses at this end of the street are semi-detached, red brick, set back from the road with neat front gardens.

Under the street lights, the hedges glitter with frost. I walk down the lane, checking the number of every house, looking for a name plate. After about five minutes, the lane gets darker and narrower, with bigger houses and taller trees.

On the left hand side of the road is a large white house with a porch sticking out onto the pavement. The painted wooden sign by the side of the door says "The Old Farmhouse". A soft light glows through the windows.

Are my grandparents inside, sitting on floral armchairs, with blankets and cats on their knees, watching TV? I can't hear the telly but they've got double-glazing. The porch door has an old brass door-knocker in the shape of a dolphin. I grasp it. It's freezing to touch but smooth, worn by people using it for years.

I knock on the door, hoping I'm not too loud. I don't want to upset my grandparents. I can't hear anything. I wait. Maybe they're deaf. Ben's nan has a hearing aid and you have to shout or she can't make out anything you say to her. I hammer on the door, making myself jump, but no one answers the door. Perhaps they're scared. I can't hear anything from inside the house. I bend down.

'Hello?' I shout through the letterbox. I can't see anything, just black bristles for keeping out draughts. Maybe they've gone out for the evening. I should have realised no one would be in when they didn't answer their phone but I told myself they were just busy.

I look around the side of the house. There's a narrow lane next to it, and the garden is bordered with a tall wooden fence. There's a gate, but it's locked. On the other side of the house is an empty parking place. I think about climbing over the fence but that would just look like I'm trying to break in. I'm so cold, the idea is quite tempting. What would my grandparents think if they came back from a posh restaurant and found that I'd broken into their house? Anyway, there's a burglar alarm box under the roof.

What am I thinking? I need to wait for them. There's nothing else I can do. I sit in the porch. The stone flags are really cold. I take the *Select* magazine out of my bag and sit on it for insulation. I zip up my hoodie as far as it can go and pull the hood over my head. I put the Discman in my pocket, plug the headphones into my ears and press "Play".

I carry on listening to *Losing Control*, trying to lose myself in the music and forget the cold. I quickly eat another packet of crisps and a few biscuits, then I tuck my hands into my sleeves and squeeze my eyes shut.

Something cold and wet is touching my face. I open my eyes in shock. It's a dog, sniffing at me. A big dog. I gasp. A low growl comes from deep inside its body and I jump up, pressing my back to the door.

'What's up, Toby?' a man's voice asks. A large shape fills the entrance to the porch. The man freezes. He's seen me. The dog drops back and waits by the man's side.

'I know you're there. You can't hide,' the man shouts.

'I'm waiting for Mr Kenning,' I squeak. Could this man be my grandfather? I take the headphones out of my ears and push my hood off my head.

'You'll be lucky.' The man gives a short humourless laugh.

'I thought Brian and Sheila Kenning lived here. I'm looking for my grandparents.' My teeth chatter together as I try to speak.

'Who are you?'

'Do they have a daughter called Karen? They haven't seen her for a long time…'

'Not that I know of.' A jangling sound comes from the man's pocket, as if he's fumbling for keys.

'When are they coming back?'

The dog comes up to me again, nosing my leg. Now I'm a bit more alert, I realise it's an overweight Labrador.

'The Neighbourhood Watch committee are watching this house like hawks. So if you're scoping the place out, forget it.'

'I'm not…'

'Clear off. We don't want your sort round here.'

I grab my bag and bolt out of the porch. I stumble against the man, almost losing my balance on the frosty flagstones. I run down the road on my stiff legs as fast as I can go. I hear the dog bark behind me but soon I'm at the

155

end of the road. I stop and stare at the pub. It looks quiet but the door's open. I really need to pee. Maybe I could ask if I could use their phone – call home. Tell Mum I've made a massive mistake.

The *Select* magazine is still in the porch. I can't go back for it: that man will be there. He wouldn't help me in a million years. I can't believe I lost the magazine. So stupid. My eyes start stinging and suddenly I'm crying. I blink, trying to stop myself but holding in the tears makes my nose run. I wipe my face with my sleeve and I start walking on the narrow pavement next to the dual carriageway, past the railings in front of the old demolished factory. I wish I was at home, in bed, with a hot water bottle, and the covers over my head.

I put my hands into the pockets of my jeans as I walk and I feel the list of addresses crumple under my fingers. One of the other Kennings on the list might still be my grandparents. I should try to see them before I give up and go home. I've got nothing to lose, have I? There's no train back tonight now. I pull the list of addresses out of my pocket and read it under a street light. I've got to get to Potters Green. I don't know which direction to walk in but this place seems miles away from anywhere so it's probably a good idea to get back to the city centre.

There's still a steady stream of cars in each direction. I check my watch. It's nearly nine o'clock. I could cross the road and stick my thumb out for a lift but I'm too scared. At least walking is helping to warm me up a bit.

Kaz

The digital display on the dashboard of Sam's car says 21:07. We've reached the small row of shops at the end of Mum and Dad's street. The hair salon is still called "British Hairways", with the same sign it's had since the Seventies. The bakery has become a branch of Subway.

'Singh News,' Sam gasps. 'Is that where Ash grew up?'

'Yeah.' It looks the same, with its faded orange Happy Shopper sign. Only the Subway and a mobile phone advert on the bus shelter prove we've not disappeared into a time-warp.

'Turn right here.' I tell Sam. He drives slowly down the street. Everything feels a bit dream-like. 'It's number forty two.'

I stare at the house. It's in shadow, but I picture the pale yellow pebble-dash and black mock-Tudor beams. Is Jason inside? I wonder if he turned up at Uncle Brian and Aunt Sheila's.

'I can't believe I'm actually outside your house,' Sam says. He squeezes into a parking space.

The silence in the car is unbearable, after the loud music and the rattle of the engine.

'Everything will be okay, I'm sure.'

'Come with me – please?'

My heart hammers in my chest. It feels like all the air's getting squashed out of me. I nervously unclip my seatbelt, and my leg almost gives way when I get out of the car. Sam takes my arm. I can feel him trembling. I think I can trust him, despite him selling me out to Marilyn Richards.

Before I've even had the chance to ring the doorbell, the curtains in the bay window move and I hear running footsteps. The front door opens. Mum's standing there. She looks tiny. I'd forgotten that she's even shorter than me. Her face is lined and there's grey in her hair.

'It really is you,' she gasps. She wraps her arms around me. I start crying with relief.

'What have you done to your face?' She touches the fading bruise on my forehead.

'It doesn't matter.'

Mum stares suspiciously at Sam.

'I'm Jason's guitar teacher,' he says. 'I just drove her here.'

'Jason?'

'My son.'

The living room door opens. Dad stands in the hall. His mouth is open with shock. He's almost bald, his remaining hair white and sticking out from behind his ears, giving him an Einstein look. He looks much older and slightly lost. I rush forward and hug him, resting my head on his chest. He feels bony, under his shirt. He hugs me so hard, I think he'll leave bruises.

'Karen…?' He sounds stunned, as if someone's hit him over the head.

'Is Jason here?' I ask.

Mum and Dad both look confused and they stare at me, then at Sam.

'We wrote down the number you rang from.' Mum says. 'Is it a Matlock phone code?' She shows me where she's written Brenda's number, on a Barbara Fleming notepad with robins in the corners.

'Is that where you live?' Dad asks.

'I live in a village near there. Jason's gone missing. He's almost fourteen.'

'Is he –?' Mum gasps.

'Did Uncle Brian call? Jason came to find you but he didn't have the right address.' I show them the piece of paper.

'We're ex-directory,' Dad says.

'He didn't even know he had any grandparents until this afternoon.'

'He didn't know he had a family?' Mum says. 'Karen, how could you?'

I stare at my boots, my face hot with shame.

'He found Uncle Brian's address and caught a train. Jason was convinced that Brian and Aunty Sheila were his grandparents. He might be there now.'

'Brian's not there,' Dad says. A jolt of panic goes through me.

'He booked himself on a six-week SAGA cruise in the Caribbean,' Mum explains. 'When Sheila was in the hospice, she told Brian he had to enjoy himself. Do something he'd always wanted to do.'

'Aunty Sheila died?'

'It was very peaceful in the end. There was nothing more

158

they could do for her.'

'I'm sorry.' I try to swallow but my throat feels blocked.

'I'll drive you to your uncle's house,' Sam says. 'Is it far?'

I shake my head.

'I'll come with you,' Dad says. 'We've got a spare key. Brian gave the Neighbourhood Watch our number in case there was a problem.'

I can't speak as we drive to Ryton on Dunsmore. I just want to find Jason.

'The old car factory's gone. Demolished. Closed a couple of years ago. Of course, Brian had already retired.' Dad points out the dark, empty space that used to be the car factory. I shiver as I realise we're almost there. Dad's just nervous. His running commentary on the changes in the city and buildings that have been demolished is his way of filling up the silence. As a teenager, I would have yawned and moaned at him. I stay quiet, my hands clamped between my knees.

We drive down a side road. I recognise Uncle Brian's house. I bolt out of the car as soon as Sam parks it. There's a light on. I can't see Jason. I step inside the porch. I push against the front door but of course it's locked. There's something under my feet. It's a *Select* magazine, July 1994. The one Sam gave to Jason.

'Jason!' I shout. He might still be here somewhere, inside, or in the garden. I rattle the door handle and hammer on the door. 'Jason!' I scream. I run out of the porch and stare desperately, up and down the empty street.

'Kaz, calm down.' Sam says. I show him the magazine. Dad stands on the pavement, looking at me nervously, as if he's not sure of my sanity.

'He was here.' I show Sam the magazine. He nods.

'Where is he? What are we going to do?' I'm sobbing onto Sam's chest. He puts his arms around me. Dad watches me like I'm a stranger.

'What's going on?' A stranger's voice, quite posh. A middle aged man is standing on the opposite side of the

159

pavement with a large black dog on a lead.

'I'm Jim Kenning. Are you Mr Berry? Neighbourhood Watch?'

'I was going to call you. Some youth turned up here. Claimed he was looking for his grandparents. He was asleep in the porch. I thought he was a burglar. He scarpered pretty quickly…'

'You idiot!' I shout. I could have found Jason by now. All it would have taken was for this guy to listen to what Jason was saying; to make a phone call to my dad. I pull away from Sam and plant myself in front of the Neighbourhood Watch man, who looks slightly less sure of himself now.

'He was telling the truth. Where did he go?'

'He ran off. Look, how was I to know he wasn't a burglar? They get up to some pretty clever tricks. Claiming to be from the gas board and stealing people's life savings. He looked very suspicious.'

'He's thirteen! He's never even been away from home on his own before!'

'Karen.' Dad puts his hand on my shoulder. 'It's a misunderstanding. It's not Mr Berry's fault.'

'He looked older,' the Neighbourhood Watch man says. 'We've had a lot of trouble lately with undesirables.' My skin prickles uncomfortably.

'He's my son!'

'If he comes back, please call me. Here's my mobile number.' Dad gets a business card out of his coat pocket. I sneak a look at it. It has an outline of the cathedral spire and it reads 'Jim Kenning. Local Historian'. There's an email and a website address. He's moved more with the times than I have.

'He ran down the road, towards the dual carriageway,' the man says. 'It was about an hour ago. I tried to chase him but I've got a heart condition.'

'Thanks for letting us know.' Dad nods.

We get back into the car.

'Maybe we should try calling the other numbers first,' Dad says. 'He might be on his way there.'

I stare at the piece of paper. Both addresses are miles away, north of the city centre. Sam hands me his phone. I phone the first number but it just rings and rings without an answer phone. I dial the second number, the one in Potters Green. It picks up on the third ring.

'Hello?' A woman's voice

'I know this sounds crazy but my son's gone missing and there's a chance he might turn up at your house,' I gabble.

'Who are you?' She sounds scared. I can't blame her. I take a deep breath and try to speak calmly.

'I'm Karen Kenning. My son's looking for his grandparents and he found your address by mistake. It's a long story. You've not seen him, have you? He's thirteen but he's tall. Short dark hair. His name's Jason. It's such a cold night…'

'If he comes here, I'll call you.' She has a warm, reassuring voice. I give her Mum and Dad's number. I read out the mobile number from Dad's business card too.

'Don't turn him away. He's a nice kid,' I blurt out.

'It's okay, I won't. I hope you find him. My name's Pauline Kenning – but I guess you know my second name already. You could be related to my husband.'

'Thanks so much.'

I pass the phone back to Sam. He starts the engine and drives slowly down the street.

'So what do we do now?' he asks.

'Keep looking. Anywhere between here and Woodway Lane,' I say.

'I'll call the police,' Dad says. 'We know Jason's out there now. But we should search for him ourselves.'

'Did you drive round looking for me?'

'We tried everything.'

Now I know how it feels. I imagine this feeling going on for days; weeks; months and years – until Jason is nothing but a clutch of hopes and memories and fading photos. I did this to my own parents. Sam drives slowly along the quiet dual carriageway. I scour the side of the road looking for Jason, swallowing back tears.

Jason

I check the A-Z of Coventry, I'm only a few streets away from the second address on my list. Woodway Lane. I shouldn't have stolen the A-Z. I've never really stolen anything before, apart from a bag of sweets when I was eight and I felt guilty about them for ages.

This time it was different. I would have asked the man behind the counter in the shop for directions but he was on his mobile phone, shouting in a foreign language and waving his arms around. I waited for ages but he didn't stop talking. The A-Z was on a shelf of shabby stationary and I just sort of slipped it into my jacket pocket. The man didn't even seem to notice when I left the shop again, even though it made the bell jingle. Then I ran like hell, luckily in the right direction. Maybe I could put the A-Z back, or post it through the door. I suppose it doesn't even matter really. It's not like anyone's going to die because I stole it. I probably couldn't find that convenience store again if I tried, even with the map.

I've been walking for hours. It's almost midnight. I think I'm going a bit mad. I've only got a few biscuits left. I drank the last can of Coke about half an hour ago. I listened to both Mission Control albums again and they helped to keep me going. Mum got me these boots in the Christmas holidays with the money from her painting and they haven't worn in properly. I've got blisters on both heels and they rub with every step but I feel weirdly light-headed. I've had the streets to myself for ages. There are only a few cars driving round now. I don't even know what I'm going to do when I get there. It's just somewhere to go. I don't even think the people on Woodway Lane will be my grandparents. The only other thing I can do is to wait at the railway station until the first train to Derby appears. I don't want to admit I've screwed this up bigtime. I just want to stop walking. I don't even care if the people in the house call the police. If they find out the A-Z's stolen, I could get arrested but at least I could sit down in a police cell. Maybe they'd call Mum.

I turn left, following the A-Z, and I'm actually on Woodway Lane. I'd do a little dance, if my feet weren't so sore. It looks like a massively long avenue and I'm looking for house number 542. The numbers are in single digits at the moment and most of the houses are quite big too. At least it's flat. I walk as fast as I can, counting the numbers, trying to ignore the blisters.

Number 542 is a bungalow, with a door in the middle and two bay windows either side. The house looks sleepy, as if its eyes are drooping shut. I stand on the pavement. There are lights on in the right-hand window and there's a flicker of a TV.

I open the little garden gate, walk up to the front door and ring the bell. A lady answers the door, wearing a Mickey Mouse nightshirt and spotty pyjama bottoms, with a dressing gown. She's about Mum's age, maybe a bit younger, and she's big; curvy, Mum would say, with dark brown skin.

This whole idea was really stupid. Everything I've done since I left Sam has been more and more stupid. I should have just gone home and had a massive argument with Mum.

'Sorry for disturbing you,' I say. My voice comes out as a pathetic squeak. I turn away. I can't stop my eyes from filling up with tears. So embarrassing.

'Wait. You're Jason, aren't you?'

'How do you know?' I blink and try to look like I'm not crying.

'Your mum said you might turn up here.'

'She's looking for me?'

'She's absolutely frantic. Come in. It's freezing.'

The lady notices me limping into the hallway. It's so warm in here. My nose starts to run. I must look a total mess.

'How long have you been walking?' she asks. She has a large bosom that wobbles when she moves and I stare down

163

at the leaf patterns on the carpet.

'Dunno. Hours.'

She opens a door into a living room with a large cream sofa. The TV's on and the gas fire is glowing.

'Sit down. I'll make you a sandwich.'

'Thanks.'

As soon as my bum hits the sofa, my eyelids begin to droop, just like the windows of the house. I'm only half-aware of the lady picking the phone up.

Chapter 13
Found

Kaz

The phone's ringing. The phone in the hallway of my mum and dad's house. Am I dreaming? I open my eyes. Somehow, I'm on my parents' sofa, covered with a duvet. Mum answers the phone. I stumble out to the hall. She hands me the phone.

'Is that Karen?'

'Yes.'

'He's here,' the voice says, kindly. I feel the knot in my chest loosen.

'Is he okay?'

'Shattered, poor thing.'

'Thank you so much. We'll come and get him now.'

I put the phone down. The same phone, faded to off-white, that I spoke to Daz on for hours, the cord overstretched from trying to sit on the landing with my feet against the radiator, writing song lyrics together.

Mum, Dad and Sam are all staring at me.

'He's safe.' I smile with relief.

'Let's go,' Sam says.

I put on my jacket and pull my boots on without tying the laces, and run to the car. Sam sets off with a screech of tyres. I put the Motorhead CD in the stereo again and turn it up loud, to make Sam drive faster. I take out the piece of paper.

'Take a left here,' I tell Sam. 'I had driving lessons around Potters Green. I used to practise parking on Woodway Lane.'

Sam breaks the speed limit on the quiet roads. In fifteen minutes we're driving down the long, leafy road. Most of the houses are in darkness. I make him slow down so I can read the house numbers. We find it – a cosy double-fronted bungalow. I get out of the car, open the gate and ring the doorbell.

A lady answers the door. She must be Pauline. A proud, firm bump pulls the material of her pyjamas tightly across her stomach. Our eyes make contact and we smile.

'Karen?' she asks. I nod.

'Thank you for keeping him safe.'

'He's in here,' she whispers.

Jason is asleep, a plate strewn with crumbs on his lap. His long fringe has flopped to one side of his forehead. There are shadows like bruises under his eyes. His mouth's slightly open, with a few crumbs and a smear of mayonnaise around his lips. My beautiful baby. I put the plate on the coffee table.

'Jason, wake up. I'm here.' I bend down and gently take his hand.

He opens his eyes. He looks confused.

'Mum?'

I sit next to him on the sofa and put my arms around his shoulders. It's such a short time since I was able to pick him up; kiss him better. His jacket is still freezing to touch.

'I should have explained everything years ago.'

'How did you find me?'

'You left your cycle helmet in Ben's house. Sam drove me here.'

'I thought I could find them on my own. I was stupid.' His eyes fill with tears. 'You lied to me.'

'They can't wait to meet you, anyway.'

Jason blinks.

'Who?'

'Your nan and grandad. Whatever you want to call them.'

'They're not dead!' Jason stands up, grinning. He glares at me. 'You said we were on our own.'

I don't want to argue here. I stare at the carpet. There's a scattering of leaves on the carpet near Jason's feet. I pick them up off the carpet and put them in the waste paper basket.

'You don't need to do that,' Pauline says.

'Sorry we disturbed you,' I say.

'I'm glad you found him.'

Jason picks up a blue swimming bag from the sofa. We walk into the hall and Pauline opens the front door.

'Sam copied me the Mission Control albums,' Jason suddenly beams. 'I've listened to them over and over again. They're amazing.'

Pauline smiles at me shyly.

'You're Kaz K from Mission Control!' she says. 'I thought I recognised you.'

The draft through the door is freezing cold, but Pauline just stands and stares at me.

'We saw you a few times at the Kasbah, back in the day. You haven't even changed that much. I can't wait to tell my husband.'

'See?' Jason glares at me. 'Everyone's obsessed with Mission Control.'

'He died, didn't he? That other guy...' Pauline falters, as she looks from me to Jason.

'We really need to go.' I put my arm around Jason. 'Thanks for everything though.'

'Of course. I'm sorry.'

We walk to the car. Jason limps slightly.

'Are you okay?'

'Yeah.'

Sam looks up at us, his phone in his hand. Marilyn Richards must be having an exciting night, with up-to-the-minute updates about my reappearance.

'So how did...?' Jason asks.

'I was worried when you didn't come back for tea. I went to the Fish Pond. Sam told me what happened. He should have driven you home. I would have told you everything.'

'I was too angry to go home.'

Jason opens the front door of the car and sits down next to Sam. I get in the back seat, as if I'm the lost child.

'Jason! You alright?' Sam starts the engine and moves off. Music blasts out of the stereo.

'Cool. Motorhead!' Jason says.

I sigh with relief. He's safe. He doesn't seem too badly damaged by his adventure.

Jason

Sam drives fast. When we reach the junction at the end of Woodway Lane, his brakes squeal.

'You drove all the way here to look for me?'

'Your mum made me.' Sam laughs.

I turn round to look at her. She's staring out of the window. I'll never be able to look at her again and just see Mum. I'll always be thinking of the poster; of her face on the cover of magazines. The lady in that house changed completely when she realised who Mum was – all embarrassed and flustered. Sam's the same. I can see why Mum wanted to escape from all of that when Daz died.

'Turn left here,' she says. Sam indicates and steers the car. It's weird to think she knows this city so well, when she's been away for my whole lifetime. We drive past a small row of shops and down another road. Sam parks the car. The houses are semi-detached.

'We're here, Jason,' Mum says. 'This is where I grew up.'

I'm afraid to get out of the car but I unclip my seatbelt and open the door. It feels like I'm moving in slow motion. I follow Mum. Sam lags behind. He must feel even weirder than I do.

The front door opens before Mum can press the bell. My grandparents stand there, waiting. My granddad is tall, white-haired. He stares at me like he can't believe what he's seeing.

'He looks just like Darren…'

'Shut the door, Jim,' my gran says. 'He's been out all night. He needs to get warm.' She looks at me with wonder; the way Mum sometimes looks at the plants in the garden. She has the same green eyes. Her hair's short and peppered with grey. She takes my hands.

'You're still frozen, aren't you? Karen's old bed is ready for you. I hope you don't mind wearing your grandad's pyjamas.'

This is like a really weird dream.

'We didn't know you existed, a few hours ago,' Grandad says. 'Nearly fourteen? I was tall at your age too. Mind you, so was Darren – like a beanpole.'

'Your face is like Karen's too,' Gran says.

I glance at Mum.

'I've got school tomorrow,' I say, like a stupid kid.

'It's one in the morning. You're exhausted,' Mum says. 'I'll call them, say you're ill.'

'Karen's right. Now go and get warm in the living room. Hot chocolate?'

Mum takes my arm, like I'm a little boy who can't cross the road on his own, and tugs me into a big living room full of bookshelves. My legs are so tired they don't seem to work properly anymore. The gas fire gives out a cosy glow and I sit down right in front of it on a little stool. My hands are still freezing.

Grandad sits in an armchair and Mum and Sam perch on the sofa. No one says anything. They're all staring at me, like they're expecting me to do something. I turn towards the fire and stretch my hands out. I feel really shivery and I can't feel my fingertips properly. Maybe I've got frostbite. What if I couldn't play the guitar anymore?

Gran comes into the room with a tray of empty glasses and a large mug of hot chocolate. She hands it to me and I grip the handle, wrapping my fingers around the mug and feeling them defrost.

'I don't know about anyone else, but I need something to steady my nerves,' she says. It sounds like she's forcing herself to be cheerful, which is something Mum does a lot. Gran opens a small cupboard with a few bottles inside. It's not as impressive as Ben's mum and dad's drinks cabinet.

'We've still got that big bottle of sherry from Christmas,' Gran says, pouring herself a large measure. 'And of course, Jim has his gin and tonic.'

'I should be getting back,' Sam says.

'You can't go driving around all night. Could be black ice out on the country roads.' Grandad looks worried.

'I'm used to long drives, with gigs and stuff,' Sam says.

'Nonsense! There's a folding bed in my study. One of those futon things. You can sleep on that.'

'Thanks. I'll be in big trouble if I miss the deliveries,' Sam says. 'I can drive you and Jason home early tomorrow.'

Gran pours Sam a glass of sherry. She pauses and stares hard at Mum before pouring her a glass, as if she thinks Mum will go loopy if she drinks it.

'You've been amazing, Sam,' Mum says. 'I'll give you some petrol money when we get back home.'

'I wouldn't take it, Kaz.'

I sip my hot chocolate. It's even better than the stuff Mum makes.

'So you play the guitar, just like Darren?' Gran asks me.

'I've been listening to Mission Control tonight. I've only been learning for a few months.'

'He's already really good,' Mum says.

'What else do you like doing?'

'Mountain biking,' I mumble.

'He likes reading too,' Mum says. Gran's face lights up. The magazine article said Gran and Grandad were both librarians. Perhaps Mum is trying to impress them with my literacy skills. 'He used to be nuts about *Harry Potter*.'

I hope Mum doesn't start telling Gran and Grandad that I used to have wizard duels in the garden with Ben, acting out terrible curses and trying to make potions.

'Couldn't get through the *Lord of the Rings* though. Got bored of all the details,' I mumble. I want to stay awake, even though it's really embarrassing to be the centre of attention like this. My eyelids are flickering. I yawn.

'Here we are, asking you silly questions when you're dropping asleep,' Gran says. 'We can talk in the morning.' Gran waits for me to finish my hot chocolate, then bustles me up the stairs. I'm being treated like a little kid, but I don't mind right now.

'Luckily we had a few spare toothbrushes. Jim seems to buy them in bulk these days.' Gran shows me the bathroom. 'I'll put a blue towel out for you.'

She opens a bedroom door. The walls are lined with books and there's an armchair by the window that looks just right for curling up and reading in.

'This is Karen's old room. I'll get those pyjamas.' She goes into another room. I sit on the bed and unlace my boots. I still feel cold and my hands shake as I fumble with the laces. When I peel my socks off, my feet are red and sore.

Gran comes back with a pair of old-fashioned striped pyjamas and puts them on the bed. They smell of washing powder; freshly ironed. Mum says ironing's a waste of time. I know I should think it's gross to be wearing my grandad's pyjamas but I've grown up with second-hand things and Great Aunt Elsa's old furniture so it's okay.

This room looks like a bookshop with a bed in it. There are shelves of old paperbacks. Children's books too. Gran sees me staring at them and smiles.

'Darren liked reading. He liked sci-fi, fantasy. Pretty dark stuff.' She turns back to the books. 'There are lots of things here you might like. I was a school librarian. I could never bear to throw away books when they got worn out, so I took them home. Started my own library.'

'Have you got *Charlie and the Chocolate Factory*? I grew out of it years ago, but…'

'You never grow out of a good book.'

She finds a copy instantly, takes it off the shelf and gives it to me. It's the old version that Mum used to read to me. I open the cover. There's a label inside with a picture of a rainbow and a cartoon cloud. It says "Property of Karen Kenning" in faded felt-tip.

'It's Mum's book!'

'Of course. It's still her room. I kept all her books. We didn't get rid of her bed – in case she ever needed to stay here. Even though we didn't know where she was.'

'I'm here now.'

'I forgot the hot water bottle.' Gran says. 'Get ready for bed. I'll bring it up to you in a minute.'

She leaves the room and closes the door behind her. I get

undressed, put on the pyjamas and get under the covers. The duvet cover is faded black with white polka-dots. The bed is a bit cold in the middle but it's soft and smells lovely. My head's still spinning. How can any of this be real?

Kaz

I let Jason go upstairs with Mum. Jason needs time on his own with his grandparents. He needs to get to know them. I down my sherry. My brain's still buzzing uselessly.

'It's great we've found Jason,' Sam seems desperate to break the silence. 'He seems okay.'

'Why didn't you tell him about us, Karen?' Dad says. 'We could have helped you.'

'I thought it would be better if he didn't know about Mission Control.'

'We don't know anything about you now.'

'I'm an artist. Nothing exciting. I was hardly making any money but things are picking up now. I grow vegetables. Paint pictures.'

'We always hoped you weren't dead,' Dad says. I stare at the painting of Coventry cathedral on the wall above the mantelpiece.

Mum comes downstairs, and I follow her into the kitchen. She's filling the kettle. My old hot water bottle cover lies on the work surface. Mum made it for my fifth birthday, a dog made from blue fur fabric with floppy ears, complete with legs and a tail.

'Jason's lovely,' Mum says. 'But we've missed his whole childhood.'

'I tried to call you when Jason was a baby. I wanted to tell you about him. I was in a phone booth. You answered the phone but I couldn't speak. You were angry. You slammed the phone down. I tried again a few times but for years I've been too scared to even dial your number.'

Mum gasps.

'I remember feeling guilty. The breathing sounded like

172

you, but that seemed so stupid. Karen, if only I'd…'

'I should have called months earlier.'

'We had some problems. People phoned us, pretending to be you, or pretending to know where you were.'

'But that's sick! How could they?'

'We told the police. We got our hopes up at first, when the police told us someone had seen you at a petrol station in Derbyshire.'

The kettle boils and Mum fills the hot water bottle. She screws the stopper on tightly and pulls the cover on. Mum gives it to me, and I hug it.

'Do you remember his name?'

'Mr Muddles.' I look into its mismatched button eyes and feel its warmth against my chest.

'Let's take this up to Jason.'

Mum pushes open the bedroom door; my old bedroom. When I moved out, she lined the walls with books. At least I don't have to be confronted with my old posters of Ian Curtis and Robert Smith.

Jason is already asleep, flaked out on his back with a book still in his hands. I slip the hot water bottle under my old duvet cover. Jason stirs but doesn't wake up.

The book drops from his fingers. At first I think he's brought it from home. There's a label inside the front cover. My copy of *Charlie and the Chocolate Factory*. I smile, but I can feel my eyes welling up. I put the book on the bedside table, bend down, and kiss Jason's forehead.

'I think I'll lend him a copy of *Tales of the Unexpected*. Unless he's read it already?'

'I don't think so.'

We leave the room and shut the door gently. 'He's mostly been reading music books since he started to learn the guitar.'

'He really takes after Daz, doesn't he?'

'Sometimes I look at Jason and wonder if Daz would have been like him, if he'd had a bit more love. I've tried…'

'At least we can get to know him now. And you. That's the worst part – not knowing.'

'I'm sorry,' I whisper. We leave Jason in peace, switching the bedroom light off.

On the landing, Sam is wrestling a sleeping bag out of its cover. There's barely room for the fold-out bed in the box room Dad uses as his study. He gives me an awkward smile.

I didn't even know Sam before tonight, even though he seems to be Mission Control's biggest fan. Now he's standing on my parents' landing. It almost seems funny now: that frantic chase down to Coventry in Sam's rickety car; me having to be restrained from assaulting that Neighbourhood Watch guy. It was worth it.

'Jason's safe. That's the main thing.' I think of him fast asleep and tucked up in his grandad's pyjamas with my old hot water bottle.

'And so are you,' Mum says. 'You're home now.'

My eyes fill with tears. I stare at the carpet, which hasn't changed, unless they've replaced it with an identical beige one.

Chapter 14
Mission Accomplished

Kaz

For a few seconds, I don't know where I am at all. The streetlight outside casts a faint glow. I'm in Mum and Dad's living room, curled up on the sofa. I really need the loo. I kick off the duvet and find my way through the room in the dark. The furniture is exactly the same, and there's an indelible map of this house in my brain.

I switch on the light in the hallway. The clock above the front door tells me it's three in the morning. Am I sleep-walking? I've had so many dreams about being at home with my parents. I feel the pile of the stair-carpet under my feet, tracing the pattern of the wallpaper with my fingertips. They're supposed to be flowers and plants but Daz always said they looked like staring eyes and that whenever you walked up the stairs, you were being watched constantly, like *1984*. We wrote one of our first songs about it, 'Eyes of Ivy'. It was a B-side to 'Twisted Skin'. There are memories everywhere.

I wrote 'Rootless in Babylon' in the bathroom, standing in the shower. I heard the bassline and the chorus in my head and had to get the song written straight away. Mum wasn't impressed with the shower left running, the soaked bathroom floor and trail of wet footprints on the landing carpet. I was already grounded anyway, but I was elated. It sounded like an anthem – a hit single. Four years later, it was.

I wash my hands and splash water on my face. I stare into the mirror, and dry myself with a threadbare yellow towel that might have once been mine.

Out on the landing, I hesitate outside my old room. I turn the door handle quietly and slip inside. By the landing light, I can see Jason, curled up under the covers. I can just make out his head on the pillow. I listen to him breathing, steady and peaceful.

Last night, he went to bed excited about his guitar lesson. So much has happened since then that I can't take it in.

When Jason was small, I used to watch him sleeping all the time, but as he got older, I realised he might think it was a bit weird if he woke up with me looming over him.

As I walk out of the room, I crash into a bookcase, banging my arm. Several books fall off the shelf. I bite my lip to stop myself from crying out.

Jason sits up in bed.

'Mum?' he croaks. I hope he's not coming down with a cold after traipsing the freezing streets for hours.

'It's okay. Go back to sleep.'

I pick up the books and put them back on the shelves. I recognise the stark black and white title of a paperback book. The stylised photograph of a figure with a red megaphone sends shivers through me. I take the book downstairs with me, turn on the standard lamp next to the sofa and wrap the duvet around me again.

I open the book. I was right. It's Daz's copy of *1984*, with notes in his own handwriting and tiny illustrations in the margins. The first page has the school stamp. He never gave it back after he handed in his essay. He loved it too much. I don't know how it's ended up here. I was sure it was in the studio. Tears start rolling down my face but I wipe them away with the duvet cover and carry on reading. The words of the novel are as vivid as the memories of Daz that surface as I turn the pages.

That first time my parents went on holiday on their own and trusted me with the house. They'd planned the itinerary of their two-week holiday to Greece with a ridiculous amount of visits to ruins. I was sixteen, in the long summer holidays after my GCSEs.

The hot weather broke on the first day of Mum and Dad's holiday. I met Daz at Singh News. He was working behind the counter, having upgraded from his paper-round. He quite enjoyed it there. He was allowed to read all the music magazines and work on his song lyrics and artwork between customers. Mr Singh always seemed a bit formal and distracted, as if he was constantly surprised he was running a newsagents in Coventry, but he was kind to Daz and pleased he could rely on him, with Ash at uni in Manchester and his sister Kavita, who was in our year, so busy with her athletics.

That afternoon, though, I could hear a noisy argument from the maisonette upstairs. At first I thought it was something on the TV but I recognised their voices.

○

'Ash is back,' Daz says, rolling his eyes up to the ceiling. 'He's in trouble. They thought he was at uni but he dropped out. He went abroad and didn't tell them.'

'Have you seen him?'

'Just for a minute. He's got three earrings in one ear and a tattoo on his arm. His mum went ballistic.'

'Coming round tonight? I've got the house to myself, remember?'

'I've got an amazing riff for the new song. I need to work on the solo.'

'Do it at my house.'

'I need to concentrate.' I'm offering myself to him but he's blocked out everything apart from the music. At times like this, I may as well just be Pete. It's so frustrating.

'I might just stay in, then.' I fix my eyes on the shelf of rental videos.

Daz comes out from behind the counter. He moves my damp hair aside and kisses the back of my neck, making me shiver. I turn around and we kiss. His breath smells of mint imperials because he nicks them from the pick 'n' mix. He pulls away when the shop door jangles. Old Mrs Kenneth from the end of my road, buying her daily supplies of cat food and condensed milk.

'So what video do you want to get out, then?' Daz asks, in a loud, false voice, even though Mrs Kenneth doesn't seem to have noticed we were snogging. She's too busy shaking her umbrella on the doormat.

'I haven't seen *Beetlejuice* yet.'

Daz pulls a face.

'Me neither, but what's the point of a comedy horror film? Sounds like a kids' thing. I've heard Winona Ryder looks cute in it, though.'

I elbow him sharply in the ribs. I take the video off the shelf. Daz goes back behind the counter and I pay two pounds for the rental, as if I'm just an ordinary customer.

It was great to be watching the film by myself, but now it feels weird to be alone in the house all night, with bucketing rain and loud rumbles of thunder outside, like being stuck on an island. *Beetlejuice* is brilliant. I think Daz would love it too.

I help myself to another whisky and coke from Mum and Dad's drinks cabinet and put *Sonic Temple* by the Cult on the stereo. I lounge on the sofa and consider getting my bass out and playing along, but I'm mentally planning a new hairstyle, inspired by Lydia, the character Winona Ryder plays in the film. I could easily give myself a jagged elfin fringe and experiment with back-combing. While Mum and Dad are away, I could get some jet black hair dye. Dark brown isn't quite gothic enough. It has to be black.

There's a loud bang on the front door. I spill my drink all over myself. It's past midnight. Someone's hammering on it, like they're trying to break the door down. Maybe burglars have noticed the car missing from the drive and think no one's home. I grab the heavy wooden giraffe from the mantelpiece to use as a weapon. I tiptoe into the hall. A flash of lightning illuminates the figure standing outside. There's a pale hand pressed against the frosted glass. Blood drips from the hand. I scream.

'Kaz! Let me in!'

'Daz!' I drop the giraffe and open the door. Daz stumbles inside. He's holding the neck of his guitar but the body has been smashed into pieces bundled up in a plastic bag. He's soaking wet, shivering. His mouth is swollen and bloody and he's not wearing his glasses. I'm surprised he managed to find his way here. I make him sit on the stairs. I fetch a large towel and wrap it around him.

'I'm going to kill him,' he says.

'What happened?'

'I was practising. He came back from the pub and yelled at me to stop making a racket. I ignored him – I'd nearly finished the song. It was brilliant. He came into my room and tried to snatch the guitar off me. I fought back but…'

Daz starts crying. I've never actually seen him cry before. He wipes the tears away angrily with his fists. His knuckles are grazed and the cut to the palm of his hand is oozing blood. I run into the kitchen for the first aid kit and some kitchen roll. Daz sits still, wincing a bit while I dab at his cuts and grazes with TCP. I put a plaster on his hand but I'm not sure what to do with his mouth. I try to kiss him but he shrugs me off.

'I'm never going back home.'

'You'll need to fetch your stuff.'

'Pete can get it for me.'

'Where will you go?'

Daz fiddles with the broken pieces of his guitar.

'I need a guitar. If I don't have a guitar, I think I'll go mad.'

Daz has been saving his paper round wages for months to buy his own amp. He's only had it for a few weeks, so it would be impossible for him to buy another guitar unless he sells the amp and then he'd be back where he started.

'Mum and Dad gave me money for food and stuff while they're away. And there's my savings account.'

'I can't take your money. You'll need to eat while your parents are away.'

'There's enough food in the cupboards for a siege.'

'Can I stay here?'

I put my arms around him. He's shaking. His hair is still dripping. This time he responds to my touch, holding me tightly.

'My glasses got smashed.'

'They never suited you anyway.'

'I'm free of that bastard now. I'll show him. I'll be famous. Then he'll be sorry.'

●

It's still dark outside but I know there's no chance of any more sleep. It's six in the morning. This room hasn't changed much. Some of the pictures have been replaced and there are more bookshelves than I remember. They have a new flat-screen TV.

I drift into the kitchen and switch on the kettle. I open a cupboard without thinking about it. It's still the tea and coffee cupboard. I find a mug. I even think I remember it. It says Coventry Civic Society in faded blue letters. While I'm waiting for the kettle to boil, I play a game, opening all the cupboards to see if anything's changed: tins of beans; tinned fruit; flour and cake ingredients. It's all in the same places. Only the packaging has changed.

'What are you looking for?' Mum stands in the doorway, wrapped in a dressing gown. I must have been making more noise than I thought.

'I'm just making coffee. Did I wake you up?'

'How could I sleep?'

I reach behind the flour containers and bring out the biscuit tin: an old Quality Street tin, decorated with ladies in Crinolines. I shake it.

'It's empty.'

'There's not much point in baking when it's just me and your dad.' Mum smiles. 'Now we've got a grandson to spoil.'

'He's always moaning that I make him eat healthy food all the time.'

Mum sits down at the kitchen table. I bring over two strong black coffees and sit down.

'Darren could demolish a whole batch of biscuits in one sitting. I don't know where he put it. He was so skinny.'

'There wasn't a lot for him to eat at home.'

'At the time I thought he took this place for granted. Took advantage of you.'

'He wasn't like that! We were in love!' I feel like my sixteen-year-old self, arguing across the kitchen table about Daz. Nothing's changed. Except that the person we're arguing about died fifteen years ago.

'I don't mean it like that,' Mum says. She did at the time. All those arguments about how I should be careful and make sure I didn't get pregnant and throw my life away. She thought I was wasting my time with Daz and Mission Control.

'I thought you hated Daz.'

Mum puts her hands on mine. Her hands have aged more than her face – papery skin and her knuckles look swollen; arthritic. They're still beautiful compared to my hands with their mixture of red paint and garden soil stuck in my cuticles and under my nails; skin dry and flaky from spending too long in the garden.

'I worried you were losing your independence. You'd stick up for Darren, whatever he'd done.'

'You knew what his dad was like! No one else cared for Daz the way I did. That's why I took him breakfast every morning and brought him home with me after school – long before we went out with each other.'

'We wanted the best for you.'

'You thought he wasn't good enough, didn't you?'

'Everything you did was because of Darren – being obsessed with music – not wanting to go to university…'

'They were my songs. We wrote them together. You didn't even seem proud we'd got on the cover of the *NME* or played in front of thousands of people.'

'I was proud, love. But I worried. I read those music papers you showed me. I knew there were drugs and things.'

'That wasn't why Daz died…'

I look up. Jason is standing in the kitchen, looking more lost than ever in his grandad's pyjamas.

He looks at me warily, as if he isn't sure who I am.

'You were talking about my dad?' he asks.

'Yeah –' I croak, fighting tears.

'Good morning, love,' Mum says. 'You're up early. I

181

thought you'd sleep for hours yet. Do you want some breakfast?'

Jason grins. 'Thanks, I'm starving!'

Mum stands up and opens the fridge.

'How about a nice bacon sandwich?' she asks.

'We're vegetarian,' I frown.

'You might be, but I'm not. I eat what I like at Ben's house.' Jason shoots me a look of total disdain. 'I'd love a bacon sandwich please, Gran.' Jason beams at her.

Jason's growing up and making his own decisions. I might not always agree with them but I've got to live with it. Last night, he decided to do something that changed everything.

Mum gets a packet of bacon out of the fridge.

'Tea and bacon sandwich coming right up,' Mum says, smiling indulgently.

'Can I have a shower?' Jason asks.

'Use the blue towel, remember? When you come down, I'll show you some photos of your mum growing up.'

'I'd like that,' he says. 'She's never shown me anything like that before.'

He runs back upstairs. I know he's still angry with me but I can tell he's happy and excited from his footsteps; jumping up several stairs at a time. I grab a piece of kitchen roll in time to stop the tears from spilling down my cheeks. Mum puts her arms around me.

'When I went off, I thought you'd be glad Daz was dead.'

'You weren't thinking straight, Karen. We only ever wanted you to be happy. Darren had his faults but we never hated him.'

She lets me go and turns on the cooker; gets a frying pan out of the cupboard.

'I'll always love him, Mum.'

She puts the bacon in the pan. It starts to sizzle. She was never a cooked breakfast sort of mum when I was young; it was all wholemeal toast and muesli. I remember arguing with her for ages because she wouldn't let me have anything chocolaty or covered in sugar. I've become my mother, haven't I? I open the breadbin and pull out the loaf. I'm relieved it's good old thick-sliced wholemeal. I find the plates. I spread margarine on two slices of bread for Jason's sandwich.

'Darren's been gone for a long time,' Mum says. 'You need to start living again. For Jason's sake too.'

'I'm helping another artist to set up an art gallery. Barbara Fleming. She likes my paintings.'

Mum's eyes widen. 'Barbara Fleming?'

She puts on a pair of oven gloves and holds them up so I can see the design. They've got Barbara Fleming paintings of otters all over them. The glove part is slightly singed.

'Your Aunty Sheila bought these for me, Christmas before last. There's a matching tea towel.'

I realise that everyone in the country – apart from me – has one of her tea towels, or perhaps a breadbin, or a chopping board. Barbara must be seriously rich. It seems like she can afford to take a chance on me. This is a big deal.

Mum hugs me, still wearing the oven gloves.

'You've always had so much talent. I'm glad you're not wasting it.' She laughs. 'When you first walked through the door – that red paint on your hands, I thought…'

Jason
Sam's car is covered with a thick layer of frost. He shakes an empty-sounding can of de-icer which runs out when he's only halfway through spraying the windscreen. He tries to use a broken CD case as an ice-scraper.

'You could have been out in this all night,' Mum says. She puts her arms around me, trying to scoop me up in her arms like she did when I was a kid but it just seems a bit silly now. She's too small to hug me properly.

'I would have been alright,' I mumble, escaping from her. I'm not sure though. It's so cold the ice has made patterns all over the car.

'They're going to bloody kill me if I don't get back

before lunchtime!' Sam groans. He came downstairs about half an hour ago in a panic, with someone shouting at him down his phone. It's still early. I don't want to go but Grandad says the weather forecast is for snow and we might not get home at all if we don't leave now. Mum's worried about the cat. Grandad is standing on the doorstep in his dressing gown.

Grandad unlocks his own car, which looks old but quite posh. He gets out a large can of de-icer and a proper scraper. He shuffles towards Sam's car in his slippers but I'm worried about him slipping over. He looks ancient. Not as old as Great Aunt Elsa though.

'It's alright, I'll do it,' I say.

I spray all the windows and get them clear in a few minutes.

'I don't want to leave,' I tell Grandad. 'You still hardly know me. Can't I stay here? I could come back on the train later.'

Grandad smiles.

'We're coming to see you on Saturday, if the snow clears up. I think you and your mum have got some talking to do first.'

Mum glances anxiously at me. She's got no choice now. She's got to start talking. She looks exhausted and she's clutching a carrier bag with a large notebook inside it.

'My scrapbook of cuttings about the band,' she says. 'Old photos too.' I feel a shiver of excitement. Photos of my dad.

Gran comes out of the house with a blanket and the hot water bottle.

'You need to keep warm. You were out in the cold for hours.'

'Thanks,' I say. I tuck the hot water bottle inside my jacket.

'You are happy at home though, aren't you?' Gran whispers. 'Last night was such an upsetting time for Karen…your mum.'

I don't know what she's getting at.

'Mum's not mental, if that's what you're asking,' I say, loudly. I feel some loyalty to her kicking back in.

Mum stares at us, her mouth open.

'She is a bit crazy. But she's always been a great mum. When you come at the weekend, you'll see what it's like at home. I want you to hear me playing the guitar.' I could learn something specially for my grandparents. They only had classical CDs in their living room. I could learn something from one of Elsa's old records. I have a sudden jolt of worry thinking about my Stratocaster. It couldn't be safer, tucked under Ben's bed. But if it snows really badly, I might not get it back for days.

Gran smiles.

'We're looking forward to it. I hope the weather thaws out a bit.'

'We live up a very steel hill,' Mum says. 'If the weather's bad, you could get a train. We could get a pub lunch. We'll work something out.' Mum makes it sound like Gran and Grandad have been visiting us for my whole life. It's like she's trying her hardest not to sound mental.

'Talking of pub lunches, we need to be off,' Sam says.

I hug Gran and Grandad and get into Sam's car. Sam starts the engine after a few coughs and splutters. My grandparents stand in the porch, their arms around each other like china ornaments, both waving. As the car pulls away, I wave like crazy from the back seat, even after I can't see them anymore. Sam's car is freezing. Maybe Gran was right about the hot water bottle.

'It took fifteen years to do that,' Mum says. 'I was mental. Completely mental.' She seems to be laughing and crying at the same time. I see Sam's knuckles whiten, tightening his grip on the steering wheel as we pull onto the dual carriageway. I feel sorry for him. We've dragged him into all this.

'Can I still have guitar lessons?' I ask Sam.

'Yeah, of course.'

'I've been teaching myself but I don't know if I'm doing it right.'

'You've done quite well so far.'

'I feel like I don't know anything. I can't play like Daz.'

'You're getting there. You've got potential, Jason,' Sam says.

'He's really good at working things out from CDs and records,' Mum says. She sounds more normal again. She blows her nose.

'Are you going to pay for the lessons then, Mum?'

'The money from that painting's running out already.'

'You'll soon have the gallery with Barbara Fleming. Everything's all sorted isn't it? Come on, you're famous!'

'We're still skint.'

'Bollocks, Mum. I'm sure Barbara could get someone to buy another painting if we need the money. She thinks you're amazing. I could busk for my guitar lessons, but that would be kind of ironic.'

Sam laughs. 'You don't need to pay! You're the son of Kaz K and Daz Lightning. It would be an honour to give you guitar lessons.'

'No,' Mum says. 'We should pay.'

'Then why don't you help me out in the kitchen on Sunday lunchtimes before your lesson? You were really good yesterday.'

'What would that scary lady say – your mother-in-law?'

'I think she'd be pleased. It's not like we'd actually be paying you. We could listen to music. It can be part of your lesson, really.'

'Cool.'

'There must be a lot of bands you haven't heard of. We can start with the biggest influences on Daz. Have you heard of the Buzzcocks, the Cardiacs?'

'I've heard of them. I'm sure I'd like them.'

'He was the first person I knew who played the guitar,' Mum says, in the dreamy tone of voice she always uses when she lets stuff slip. I will her not to shut up. 'I didn't know how talented he was at first. It wasn't until we started going to gigs – and putting on our first gigs at the youth club – that I realised. He was head and shoulders above any other guitar player I ever met.'

'He was brilliant,' I say.

'He'd hear something on the radio and work it out in five minutes. He said it was easy. It used to make me really jealous. He wasn't being arrogant. I used to get frustrated. I was just an ordinary bass-player.'

'That's not true, Mum. You were amazing.'

'Maybe you've forgotten how good you were,' Sam says.

'We didn't have much money when we were kids so we used to tape the John Peel show,' Mum says.

Sam laughs. 'I think we all did. Everyone who was into music listened to John Peel. Nowhere to download music in those days. We just had to swap tapes.'

'I still swap stuff with Ben. We don't have a computer at home. We're still stuck in the fifties or something. We need one, Mum. You need to type essays and things in Year Ten. I'll need the internet.'

'We'll see,' Mum says.

Sam's driving on the motorway now. His car rattles when it's going fast. Mum's gone quiet again. I shouldn't have interrupted her flow. I could pester her about computers any time.

'I wonder what happened to our record collection,' Mum says. 'I left everything in our studio.'

'I'm sorry, Kaz. Ash burned the studio down.'

'What?'

'Marilyn Richards followed the story when she started writing the book. Ash seems to have started the fire deliberately. He'd turned reclusive – said he was working on a solo project. He'd locked himself into the studio for months. Then he set fire to it and ran off to Goa.'

'Shit.'

'That's why you need to talk to her. She's done lots of research but she can't write the book without you.'

'No one's going to read a book about Mission Control. Why would anyone be interested?' she asks.

'You were the best band of the nineties,' Sam says. 'And what a story – especially now you've turned up, alive and…'

He starts concentrating fiercely on the road, overtaking a slow lorry.

Mum rummages in the glove compartment. She slides a CD into the car stereo. 'Rootless in Babylon' rumbles through the car and drowns out the rattle. She doesn't say anything.

Marilyn Richards? The lady who wrote the *Select* article? Writing a book about my mum? My head spins. I can't believe Mum had me fooled for so long. I've set the whole story spinning into motion again, like an old funfair ride covered in cobwebs. What else am I going to find out?

Chapter 15
Home Truths

Jason

Mum hasn't said anything since we got onto the motorway. As Sam drives up our lane, we're halfway through *Losing Control*. It's starting to snow, just a few flakes, but the sky is dark grey. It's not even lunchtime yet, but today seems to have gone on forever already, staring through the car window, worrying about Mum.

'Looks like I got you back just in time,' Sam says. He pulls up by the steps to the cottage. The CD cuts out as he stops the engine. It feels weird to be home again, even though it's only been one day since I set off for my guitar lesson.

'Thanks, Sam.' Mum leans over and kisses him on the cheek. Sam looks amazed. 'He might still be lost without you.'

I climb out of the back seat of the car and get Mum's bike – my old bike – out of the boot.

'I wasn't lost. I had a return ticket,' I mutter. They're not listening.

Sam gets out of the car and walks round to the passenger door to help Mum to get out, which is a bit over the top. Her accident was weeks ago and she can manage to get out of a car on her own now, surely? Mum smiles gratefully.

'I'm sorry I've put you through this.'

Sam just smiles. 'Kaz, if you need anything – if you need driving anywhere again…'

'I'm not sure I'm ready to talk to Marilyn Richards.'

'I shouldn't have called her. I was overexcited.'

Mum hugs the carrier bag with the scrapbook closely to her chest. I can't wait to see what's inside it. Her smile is so sad, it's like a crack in an icy puddle.

'Guitar lesson on Sunday, then?' Sam asks me.

'Awesome.'

'Come for twelve then. It'll be nice to have company and some good tunes in the kitchen.' Sam glances at his watch. 'Christ, is that the time? See you later. Call me, Kaz.' He gets back in his car and turns it around carefully, his tyres starting to make tracks in the thin layer of snow.

I bump the bike up the steps and put it in the shed. The snow is falling thicker and faster now, landing on my jacket and covering everything in the garden. My boots leave footprints. I can't resist sticking my tongue out to catch snowflakes. I screw my eyes shut so I don't get snow in them. When I open my eyes, Mum is watching me.

'I'll get some firewood,' I say, to cover up my embarrassment. 'I bet the house is freezing.'

'I hope Patti's okay. She must have worried, when we didn't come back.' Mum says. She gets the key from under the flowerpot and unlocks the back door in a hurry. I gather an armful of wood from the shed.

When I get through the back door, Mum is laughing.

'Patti ate the pasta bake!'

The cat is sitting on the top of the AGA, next to the casserole dish. All that's left in it are pieces of pasta and vegetables, licked clean of the cheese sauce. Patti mews loudly, demanding food. Mum scoops up the cat as I stoke the AGA with wood and kindling to get it going.

'I was going to heat that up for lunch.'

'She still looks hungry.' I pour out a bowl of Go-Cat and top up her water. Patti leaps off Mum's shoulder and crunches through the cat food as if she's been starving for days.

'You're soft,' Mum says. 'She's probably eaten a couple of shrews and raided next door's bin already this morning.'

For a minute, it's like nothing's happened. Everything's how it was before I set off from home yesterday. But everything's changed.

'Can I look at the scrap book?' I start to take it out of the carrier bag.

'Not yet!' she shouts, as if the scrap book is red-hot.

'Why the fuck not?'

She hunches her shoulders, scoops bits of pasta into the bin and puts the casserole dish in the sink, not looking me in the eye. I feel terrible. I hope she's not going to start crying. I didn't want to start an argument.

'Because I've not opened it for years either. Not since…you know. Let me make some lunch and then we can look at it together. Get the living room warm and go and play your guitar or something. Do some homework.'

I sigh, but there's nothing I can do, is there? I've got to tread carefully again. I want her to tell me everything, so I can't scare her off before she's ready.

The living room is freezing. My breath comes in clouds. It's snowing fast outside now, already settling in the window frames as if it's Christmas again. I build a fire in the grate and light the kindling. I'm good at lighting fires. That's why it's one of my jobs.

I sit and watch the flames, pulling one of Aunt Elsa's old crocheted blankets off the sofa and pulling it around myself. I must look a right state. Mum phoned school before we left Gran and Grandad's. She said I had a temperature. Maybe she wasn't lying on my behalf after all. I feel really funny and shivery. It feels like there's something stuck in my chest, making my breathing feel tight. I hope I'm not getting asthma or I'm suddenly allergic to cat hair.

My acoustic guitar's in my bedroom. I climb the stairs, wrapping the blanket around my shoulders. My bedroom is even colder than the living room, with a thin dusting of ice on the inside of the windows. I scrape the ice with my fingernails. It feels sad and empty in here, like I left home years ago, like the house thought we weren't coming back.

I grab my guitar and run back downstairs. The fire's burning nicely now and the cat's curled up in front of it. I tune my guitar and practise scales, cross-legged in front of the rug. As my fingers start to loosen up, I start to improvise.

I realise I'm playing the guitar part for 'Rootless in Babylon'; Daz's guitar part. I must have heard it about five times now. At first, there are power chords that follow the bassline but then it turns spikier, a more unpredictable counterpoint to Mum's melody. I didn't have to work it out, like it went straight from my brain hearing it to my fingers moving on their own. Weird. It would sound miles better on my electric guitar but I practise it, singing the words under my breath.

The kitchen door moves and I look up. I stop playing and hold my breath. Mum is standing there, watching me, tears shining in her eyes.

'Lunch won't take too long,' she says. 'Soup and emergency scone bread.'

She disappears upstairs. The tight feeling in my chest gets worse and I feel like smashing my guitar on the floor for a second. I force myself to breathe calmly. So much has happened and all Mum can talk about is fucking soup.

She comes back downstairs, carrying a slim black flight case. It looks slightly battered, with a strip of silver gaffer tape on one edge of it. She puts it down on the rag rug in the middle of the living room, unclips the catches and opens the lid.

There it is. The black Thunderbird bass she was holding in that poster. The one she played on *Calling Earth* and *Losing Control*. She kneels down and takes the bass out of its plush lining. She balances it on her knees and turns the tuning pegs but it seems to be in tune already. She starts playing 'Rootless in Babylon', unamplified. I join in, making a few mistakes but I don't want to break the spell.

She starts singing, shakily. She stops after the chorus. At first I think she's going to give up but she stands up slowly. She slings the strap around her shoulders.

'Let's start again,' she says. She launches into the bassline, moving around as if she was on stage. I stand up too, playing along as well as I can but I'm totally mesmerised by Mum. She performs the whole song as if she's playing in front of a crowd. She's more alive than I've ever seen her before. When the song ends, she puts the bass gently back in its case. She's smiling, but she wipes her eyes with her sleeve.

'You've still got it, Mum,' I grin.

'Thanks, Jason.' She blushes and shoots into the kitchen, muttering something about checking the bread in the oven.

Storytime: it almost feels like I'm five again. Sitting on the sofa next to Mum with a big book spread out on her knees and she's showing me the details in the pictures and explaining things to me. Except these aren't exactly children's stories.

'These photos are from '91. Shit, I'd forgotten how many gigs we did. Good job I kept a note of them all here. That was the really crazy year. Playing any venue Ash could book. By Christmas we thought we'd made it. We got some support slots with the Levellers. Started playing bigger places.' She traces the photos wistfully with her finger.

There are other things stuck in here too: Plectrums, backstage passes, labels torn from beer bottles with scrawled signatures. She lingers over a photo of the band in front of a battered Transit van. It looks like they're at a motorway service station. Mum isn't in the photo – she's taken it. The guys look scruffy but happy; they've all got cans of lager. Pete's leaning on the bonnet and Ash has his arm around my dad's shoulders. Daz is laughing. He's wearing a stripy t-shirt and his hair is shaved at the sides but long on top.

'We lived in that van for months on end. Look at the state of me!' Mum is in the next photo: wearing cut-off jeans and a torn Cure t-shirt, her hair in dreads. She's holding a cigarette. The photo's obviously been taken by someone much taller than her, which could have been any of the guys in the band, really, but she's smiling at the camera as if she's sharing a secret joke, so maybe Daz took the photo.

'You look fine.' She looks very young, but confident, as if she knows where her life is going. There are smudges of makeup around her eyes.

'I used the showers in motorway service stations. We converted the van into a sort of campervan with a sort of deck we could all sleep on – all our gear was piled up underneath.'

'It looks like fun.'

'If you want to be a musician, that's the sort of thing you're going to have to put up with.'

'Who had the worst B.O.?' I think about that camping trip with Ben. He didn't have a shower for the entire time.

'Pete. Sweaty drummers.'

'Gross.'

'Living in a van is brilliant at a sunny festival but not too great in January. God, I was eighteen in that photo. Thought I knew it all.'

She turns the page. There are live reviews on yellowed newsprint: the band performing on stages that look barely big enough to fit the four of them, Mum screaming into the microphone, wearing a lacy nightie. She hasn't got her Thunderbird bass: the one in the photos is covered in stickers. I scan the reviews. They're mostly ridiculously enthusiastic. One of the reviews says "Kaz K is the pin-up of choice for the red-blooded grebo male", making me think uncomfortably of the anti-fur poster in Sam's music room. What's a grebo, anyway? Another review says Daz Lightning "throws cartoon-perfect mean and moody shapes but invents mesmerising and truly original lines soaring above the pounding, hypnotic rhythm-section."

'You were brilliant, Mum. I wish you'd told me earlier.'

'It never seemed like the right time.' She gives me one of her sad smiles. 'It's not such a bad time now, is it? I mean, you really love music. You got into playing the guitar all by yourself. I didn't want you to feel like you were pushed into it, or that you'd heard so much about me and my stupid band you were sick of it and wanted to grow up to be an accountant or something.'

'I'd never do that. I'm not good enough at maths anyway.'

'Mr Young said you just lacked confidence in your abilities. He wants you to go into a top set next year.'

'Can we stop talking about school?'

With a sudden squeal, Mum points at a serviette with an

autograph scrawled in black marker pen.

'That was when I met Robert Smith backstage at Reading. I was such a massive fan. I had to get his autograph even though we should have been acting cool. He was really nice.'

'Mum –' It's great to hear her talking about the past and all the exciting things she did. She seems to be really enjoying herself. But there's something I need to know.

'That Reading gig was brilliant for us – the first one I did with the Thunderbird.'

'What was my dad like? I know he was amazing at playing the guitar but I want to know what he was really like.'

Mum's smile fades.

'You're right,' she says. 'I was getting carried away.'

'It doesn't sound like he was very happy.'

'Daz didn't have the best start in life. He had no confidence in himself. He never fitted in. You know what school's like. Kids are cruel to anyone who's different.'

'Don't I know it,' I mutter.

'I'm sorry, Jason. I haven't helped much. But at least I try. After Daz's mum left, he just came home to a pile of empty beer cans and his dad passed out on the sofa.'

'Oh.' Everything I've been through with Bradley Smeed and my charity shop clothes sounds like nothing at all.

'His dad hit him too. He had a horrible time at home and at school. For the first three years in secondary school, I was one of those people. Hanging around with my bitchy mates, laughing at Darren because he wore an anorak and had massive glasses, thinking it was hilarious when he tripped over his own feet in the corridor. I didn't change until I started to get into music. That's when I really got to know Daz.'

'Was he really like me?'

'You do look a lot like him – with much better eyesight. You're into some of the same things too. He was brilliant at drawing as well as the guitar. He was funny and clever, but not many people got to see that side of him. He came

195

across as being moody. He put up barriers to stop people from getting close to him. I suppose Mission Control were the closest thing he had to a family.'

'It was stupid, wasn't it? The way he died…' I say. I wonder if I've pushed it too far. Mum looks panicked. 'Why did he have that argument with you?'

'He had a terrible temper. We'd been having arguments about all sorts of things. Things weren't perfect between us. I loved him though. I've never stopped loving him.'

'Did he know about me?'

'No. Neither did I, at the time.' Mum sniffs loudly. She's crying. She wipes her eyes with her sleeve. She shuts the scrapbook and hugs me, like she used to do when I was little. 'When I found out I was pregnant, I told Elsa – and she understood. I didn't tell her much about the band but she knew Daz had died. You were the most precious thing in the world. It was like a tiny bit of Daz was still alive.'

She really starts crying now; she tries to talk again but she's sobbing too hard, her breath coming in choking gulps. I get off the sofa and fetch a whole toilet roll from the bathroom. I feel terrible. A few minutes ago, she was happy, remembering life on the road and meeting her idols. I remember her crying like this when I was little and I didn't understand why. Now I know. Sort of.

I return with the toilet roll and she blows her nose noisily, dabbing at her face, which has turned all red and blotchy. I feel really bad. I didn't need to bring up Daz's death, did I? She tries to smile at me but she can't seem to stop crying. I don't know if this is a good thing or a bad thing.

I don't know what to do, so I go into the kitchen and make her a cup of tea. I put loads of sugar in it, even though she doesn't normally take sugar in her tea. I take it into the living room and Mum tries to smile but then her face collapses into tears again.

'Are you alright? I'm sorry.'

She nods.

'What…have…you got to apologise for?' she splutters.

She takes a deep breath and wipes her eyes.

'I just wanted to know about my dad. I didn't want you to go into meltdown.'

She coughs and dabs at her eyes with the tissue again. But she seems a bit better. She takes a sip of tea and pulls a face.

'Jesus, what did you put in this?'

'I thought you needed it – for the shock.'

'I had the shock fifteen years ago!'

'It's not like you're over it or anything, are you?'

'Sorry.'

I sigh and wander over to the window. Everything's gone white now, with more flakes falling in a dark grey sky.

I sit on the sofa again and open the scrapbook. I wish I'd seen it years ago, but Mum's right in some ways. It wouldn't have meant so much. I start reading a review of *Calling Earth*: a 5 "K" review in Kerrang! magazine by a journalist who obviously fancied Kaz K something rotten.

'Mission Control were brilliant,' I say. 'You should have carried on making music.'

'It wouldn't have been the same. Not without Daz.'

'Why did you run away? I don't get it.'

'I couldn't cope with people. I wanted to be alone – if I hadn't met Elsa, I think I might have killed myself.'

'And then I wouldn't have existed.' I feel really weird now. My head feels too light and my ears are buzzing. I'm glad I'm alive though. I mean, what would be worse? Mum killing herself on her own in that van, without even knowing she was going to have me, or having a nice quiet life and being in denial for years?

The phone rings. I jump up from the sofa and pick up the receiver.

'Hello?' I say. Maybe it's Gran and Grandad.

'You're back home and you didn't call me. You promised.' It's Ben and it sounds like I've pissed him off.

'Sorry.' That seems to be my favourite word this afternoon. 'We only got back this morning.'

'So what happened?'

'Everything went to plan. I was lost for a bit but I found my grandparents and they're coming over on Saturday – if it stops snowing.'

'Brilliant!'

'I'm going to start working at the Fishpond on Sunday lunchtimes to pay for my guitar lessons.'

'I'm getting guitar lessons with Sam Baxter too. My dad's finally relented.'

'That'll be cool.'

I check the time. It's only half past two.

'Are you ringing me from school?'

'They sent us home when they realised how bad the snow was getting. We've got tomorrow off too.'

'Nice one.'

'Can I come over tomorrow?' He sounds really enthusiastic. 'Dad's got to go into work. He could drop me off – and I could bring your guitar and your bike.'

'Yeah. I'll check.' I glance at Mum on the sofa. She's staring at something in the scrapbook, tears shining in her eyes again. 'Can Ben come round tomorrow? We're off school.'

'Of course he can,' Mum says. 'It's the first time it's ever snowed and you've not rushed out in it straight away to make a snowman.'

'It's fine. We can muck around in the snow if you want,' I tell Ben.

'There's some Mission Control stuff on YouTube. Your mum and dad really rocked.'

I'm jealous that Ben's finding out about Mum on his own. But her past was waiting there, all along, for me to Google. I feel so stupid. She managed to fool me. I had no reason to doubt her, until I picked up that guitar and she started letting things slip.

'I've listened to their albums loads of times now,' I say. 'I'm already learning my dad's guitar solos.' I hate myself for showing off. It's only natural that Ben is curious.

'See you tomorrow. It'll be early so you'd better be ready for me.'

'It'll be nice not to have to go to school though. I've got lots of stuff to tell you.'

'Cool.'

I put the phone down.

'I'm impressed that you've learned the guitar part to 'Rootless in Babylon'. It's not easy at all,' Mum says.

'Thanks.' I can't stop myself from grinning. Suddenly, I've got an idea for my song. 'Do you mind if I go up to my room? I'm working on something.' I grab my guitar.

'You'll go far, Jason Knight,' she smiles.

'Don't you mean Jason Pratt?'

Mum shakes her head. 'Daz got rid of that name as soon as he left home. If anything, you should be Jason Lightning.'

'I'll work hard until I'm as good at playing the guitar as my dad.'

Kaz

The cat curls up next to me as I flick through the pages of the scrapbook. I bury my fingers in her warm fur and she purrs. She must have been lonely without us, even though she ate well. Patti doesn't do snow. She just stands and miaows at it from the warmth of the kitchen until I push her out of the cat-flap.

I stare at the first photo that I stuck into the book; taken with my trusty camera, almost brand new then. All four of us are in the photo. It's the very first photo of us all together: the night we formed Mission Control for real. I used the timer function and balanced the camera on the living room windowsill. It's the night after Daz left home. His face is battered, but he's smiling, despite his bloody, swollen mouth. I'm kissing him on the cheek. Pete is grinning insanely. Ash looks calm and collected, one eyebrow raised and an amused look on his face. He was nineteen after all, three years older than us. He'd been to uni, been to exciting clubs like the Hacienda and then had his escapade in Ibiza. We were just kids with a dream of being in a band.

Daz was determined to never see his dad again. But there were so many problems to sort out. The night he left home was the first night we spent together, commandeering my parents' bed, which was great, if a bit weird, but Daz was just exhausted and angry. He needed to sleep. At least he could stay safely at my house for two weeks while he worked things out.

We called Pete in the morning. He was happy to fetch Daz's stuff from his room and said he'd come round with it later. Daz had run out of the flat without his key, but Pete told us it wouldn't be a problem. Daz's biggest problem was his smashed guitar. There was nothing we could do about that but Daz was getting restless without being able to play. Everything was blurred without his glasses. He was due to start a shift at the newsagents, but it would be useless if he couldn't even read the titles of the videos.

We held hands as we set off for Singh News. The rain had stopped but there were big puddles everywhere. Daz seemed to know where he was going, even though I had to stop him from crossing the road in front of a car. His hand enveloped mine. When we opened the door of the newsagents, Ash was behind the counter on his own. He gasped when he saw Daz.

◉

'Shit. What happened to you?' he exclaims. He flicks his hair back as he stares at Daz's mangled face. His hair is in curtains and he's wearing a Stone Roses t-shirt. I haven't seen Ash since he went to uni. I'd forgotten how good looking he is. Out of my league. Anyway, Daz is my soul-mate. To Daz, without his glasses, Ash probably looks like a vaguely human-shaped blob.

'I can't work today. I've got to get new glasses.'

'Did you get into a fight?'

'Yeah. With my dad. I've left home. I'm staying with Kaz.'

'Wow. Well done, mate! As you can see, I'm stuck here again. If I hadn't run out of cash I'd still be out there in the sun. Everything in Ibiza is amazing.'

'I'll start work again as soon as I can. My dad smashed my guitar so I need the money. And I like working here...' The cut in Daz's lip opens up and starts bleeding again but he just dabs off the blood with the back of his hand.

'Please don't let them sack him,' I plead. 'He can't help it. He can't see.'

'I think they'll understand, Daz. Mum and Dad trust you – more than they trust me, anyway!' Ash laughs. 'Go and get some new glasses – without them, you'll be mixing *Twinkle* up with *Playboy.*'

He opens the till and looks furtively towards the door at the back of the shop where his parents might burst through at any moment. He pulls out a £20 note and gives it to Daz. 'Take this, in case you need anything.'

'Is that coming out of my wages?' Daz asks.

'No. I'll explain everything to my folks. They'll be okay.'

'Thanks, Ash,' Daz says. We turn to leave the shop.

'Hey? I've got an electric guitar somewhere. Do you remember my metal phase?' Ash says.

'No, but –' Daz says.

'I got quite good for a while but when I was in Ibiza it was all about Acid House. I've got some top ideas. Really weird electronic noise combined with heavy guitars.'

'Sounds interesting,' I say.

'Can I come round tonight? I'll bring the guitar.' He sounds really keen. He's not treating us like we're kids who have only just left school.

'Really?' Daz sounds shy and uncertain.

'I know your address anyway, Kaz.' Ash gives me a cheeky grin. 'I remember from my paper round – *Just Seventeen* for you and *The Guardian* for your parents.'

I feel myself blush. 'It's *Melody Maker* now.'

'I'll come round about eight, then.'

'Yeah, great.'

Daz squeezes my hand as we leave the shop.

'He's going to lend me his guitar. How cool is that?' Daz whispers.

Pete comes round first, effortlessly carrying two bin-bags and Daz's amplifier; everything Daz owns.

'I waited until I was sure your dad was out and I broke the door down.'

Daz laughs. It's handy to have a friend who's built like a barn door. He sorts frantically through the bin bags: tapes, black t-shirts and records spilling out of them like a jumble-sale in the middle of the hall.

'Sorry, Daz. I think he's already taken some of your records,' Pete says.

Daz holds a Megadeth album up to his face so he can see it properly. We went to the opticians but his new glasses won't be ready for a few days.

'That's the last time he takes anything from me,' Daz says, quietly.

Pete and I exchange glances. Daz has taken control of his life for the first time. Ever since I've known Daz, he's been trying to maintain some semblance of a normal life; doing his best to tidy the flat, buying food with his paper round money, stealing money from his dad's wallet to pay the electric bill. Daz is braver than anyone will ever know. He loved his dad once.

We drift into the living room. My bass is plugged into the amp in there. I pick it up and start playing one of our riffs but it's not the same without Daz playing his guitar too. Daz slumps on the sofa next to Pete. It's difficult to read his expression behind the bruises on his face. I put my bass down, go into the kitchen and make tea. While I'm waiting for the kettle to boil, I can hear Daz playing my bass. By the time I bring the tray through, Pete has got his drumsticks out and is bashing the hell out of the lacy cushions.

The doorbell rings. Daz and Pete barely notice it but my heart thumps like mad. I open the door. It's Ash, holding a guitar case.

'Hi!' I say, hardly daring to look him in the eye. 'Come

in.' Ash has always seemed a world away from us. At the same time Daz started his paper round every morning, Ash always left the Singhs' flat for sixth-form college, wearing cool band t-shirts. I always wanted to know what tapes he was listening to on his Walkman.

'Thanks.' He stops and listens to Daz playing the bass and the muffled thump of Pete. 'Your parents are out?'

'They're on holiday.'

Ash smiles with relief. 'Thank fuck for that. Mum and Dad haven't got off my case since yesterday.'

Daz stops playing and opens the living room door.

'You brought the guitar!' He tries to grin, but his mouth's gone scabby and he winces.

'It's only a Marlin.' Ash unzips the case. 'Looks cool though.' He takes out a generic-looking black electric guitar but Daz's eyes shine as if he's just been given a vintage Les Paul.

'I haven't played it for about two years.'

Daz takes the guitar and strokes it as if it's alive. He sits cross-legged on the floor and dusts the strings with his sleeve, then tunes it. We all stand there, watching him. I hold my breath. Daz plays a few chords.

'It's cool.' Daz says. 'Thanks for lending it to me.'

'You can have it, mate.'

'Really? No way!'

'It's not like I need it. I'm going to make electronic music. Samples, sound effects...'

'The guitar needs new strings though. Did you find any in my room, Pete?'

We follow Daz into the living room. He unplugs my bass and plugs the lead into his new guitar, cranks up the distortion and starts playing, improvising solos, perfectly contented, in a world of his own.

'We're a band,' I explain, loudly. 'We're called Omission Control, with a slash in the middle.'

Ash laughs. 'I think you've already got a Slash! Daz is brilliant!'

'Not Slash like in Guns 'n' Roses,' I say, although I'm

impressed that Ash likes Daz's guitar playing. 'It's a statement about censorship and freedom.'

'I'm not sure about band names with punctuation. Too confusing.'

'I told you.' Pete folds his arms. 'It looks okay on the posters Daz designs but people keep thinking we're two bands.'

'What about Mission Control?' Ash suggests.

'That changes the meaning,' I say.

'Sounds good though,' Pete says.

'So have you guys had many gigs?'

'Only in the youth club. Got a few people to come. Kaz is a good singer.'

'I could get you some gigs,' Ash says, casually. 'I know a bit about the music biz. It's just a matter of talking to the right people.'

'You really think you could get us a gig in a proper venue?' I ask. 'We're underage, remember?'

'That won't matter. I'll sort it.'

'Daz!' I shout. 'Ash thinks he can get us some gigs.'

'What?' He stops playing.

'I could manage you – get you gigs.'

'You haven't even heard any of our songs yet.' Daz sounds suspicious.

'I could come to one of your rehearsals. I could bring my synth.' Ash sounds slightly desperate to get involved. Daz stares at him. I think he feels indebted to Ash because of the guitar. At the same time, it feels a bit like Ash is trying to charm his way in, change our band. The way Ash looks back at Daz reminds me of an over-enthusiastic puppy, eager to please.

Daz smiles, flattered.

'Yeah, okay. Why not?'

'That's great.' Ash sits back on the sofa and pulls a Rizla packet out of his pocket. 'Mind if I skin up?' he asks. 'I can't do it at home. Smuggled the weed back inside a tape case.'

I take a sip of lukewarm tea.

'Yeah, that's cool,' I say. We've never tried drugs before, unless you count the time we tried to smoke oregano. Suddenly, with Daz leaving home and Ash hanging out with us, things are getting more exciting and grown-up. Maybe Ash can get us the gigs he's promised. There was something missing from Omission/Control. Perhaps a name change and some weird electronic noises are exactly what we need.

○

The phone rings. I flinch and the cat leaps off the sofa, her eyes wide with alarm. It's almost dark outside but there's a phosphorescent glow from the snow, shining through the window. I pick up the receiver automatically.

'Is that Kaz?' It's a woman's voice. I don't recognise it. I shiver.

'Who's this?'

'Marilyn Richards.' Shit. It's started. 'It is you, isn't it?' she says. 'I can't tell you how excited I am.'

'I told Sam I needed time to think.'

'I need to talk to you,' she says.

'Sam told me about your book. I bet you can't believe your luck.'

'You need to tell your story to the world. I want to help you,' she coos.

'Because you were at the Spiral Sun festival? Because you saw Daz after the accident?' I'm about to slam the phone down but Jason's standing at the foot of the stairs, staring at me.

'Who are you shouting at?' he asks. I put my hand over the receiver.

'Marilyn Richards.'

'That's amazing! Does she want to do an interview?'

'I don't want people to know my story.'

'What about Pete and Ash? Don't you think you should find them and tell them you're alive?' Jason says.

'A Mission Control Reunion!' Marilyn Richards gasps, her voice loud and enthusiastic, audible through my hand over the receiver. I hold it to my mouth again.

'How can we have a reunion without Daz?'

Jason runs over and snatches the phone out of my hand.

'Hi! Look, Mum needs some time to think things over. We need to talk to Pete and Ash first. It's just all been a bit sudden for her, but she'll be okay.' Jason stands there for what feels like ages. I can't move or talk. Marilyn Richards is obviously talking to Jason about me. He smiles. 'Yeah, I'm Daz's son. Thanks. Well, I'm learning the guitar, anyway.' He stretches the telephone cord across the room and picks up a stub of pencil from my desk. He scrawls a number on the front of my sketchpad. 'We'll call you soon, when Mum's ready for the interview. It'll be worth it. See you later.' Jason puts the phone down with a satisfied smile on his face.

'What did you do that for?' I ask.

'We have to find Ash and Pete. You need to tell them everything.'

'What if I don't want to?' I blurt out.

Jason gives me a withering look, his dark eyebrows pulled together into a frown.

'Then you're a selfish, self-pitying bitch.' He turns and runs up the stairs. He slams his bedroom door so hard the whole house shakes. I follow him, slowly, my dodgy knee creaking. I knock on his door but he doesn't open it.

'Jason, I'm sorry!' There's no answer. I really regret my door-knocking rule. But if I barged in, we'd have a massive argument. I sit at the top of the stairs outside his room, not daring to move. After a while, I hear Jason playing his acoustic guitar. I expect him to be thrashing around angrily but he's playing chord progressions and a riff I don't recognise, singing softly. I can't make out the words but it sounds good.

Chapter 16
Igloo

Jason

The alarm clock starts beeping. I reach out to the bedside table and I'm sitting up, shivering in my freezing bedroom, before I remember school's been cancelled today. I snuggle down into the pillow again and pull the duvet over my head. I try to get back to the dream I was having where I was on stage with Metallica in the middle of a desert...

There's a giant woodpecker trying to destroy the stage. It hammers on the roof. 'Jason! Jason!' it shouts. How is it managing to peck and shout at the same time? The rest of Metallica give me dirty looks and walk off stage. There's a muffled thump too. Sounds like a snowball hitting a pane of glass.

Shit. I forgot Ben was coming. I sit up and wipe some frost off the window. The garden's disappeared under a white blanket. Ben's standing on the bit where the lawn should be. He pelts another one at the window. He's a good shot. It's still dark outside. He's got two guitar cases with him, and my bike, lying in the snow.

I open the top bit of the window.

'I'll let you in. Wait there!' I yell down to him and run down the stairs as quickly as I can without slipping in my socks. I unlock the back door and Ben's standing there, looking like he's ready for an Arctic expedition.

'You were asleep, weren't you? You forgot I was coming.'

'Your dad drove up the hill okay then?'

'He loves it. Showing off in his Land Rover.' Ben puts the guitar cases inside the kitchen and wheels my bike into the shed. I should put my wellies on and help, really, but I just stand there like a Muppet, watching him. I tuck my hands inside the sleeves of my hoodie.

I stoke the AGA with logs from the basket. The glowing embers at the bottom of the stove burst into life again and start licking around the new logs. We're running low on wood. It'll be easy if Ben helps me later. Good job I'm off school today.

Ben comes into the house, stamping his feet on the mat. He gives me a really weird look as he unlaces his boots; as if he expects me to be different since I last saw him. It was only Sunday, but it feels like ages.

'So, go on,' Ben says. 'Tell me all about it. It must be brilliant to find out your parents were rock stars.'

I grab my guitar case.

'Let's go to my room. I've got something to show you.'

Ben follows me up the stairs. I feel a bit ashamed of my room. It's a mess. I kick a pair of boxer shorts under the bed.

'It's freezing in here,' Ben says, even though he's still wearing his coat. He sits down on the edge of the bed and puts my duvet around his shoulders. Not that I mind, really.

I unzip my guitar case. My Stratocaster's in there. It's so amazing to see it again, I kiss the lacquer. I hope Ben doesn't notice me doing that. I take it out of the case. It's gone out of tune slightly. I turn the pegs until it's perfect. I plug the guitar into my amp and start to play the song I was working on last night. I sing the words too but they're a bit drowned out by the guitar.

'Will anything work out right? It's a fight to the end. It's a fight for my life…' I tried to imagine what Daz felt like when he was my age. *'Just trying the best I can. It's never enough for my old man.'*

I finish the song, a bit uncertain at the end. I feel too nervous to look at Ben properly. Now I know how he felt when he played his first song – and I just slagged it off. I feel terrible. Ben grins.

'That was awesome,' he says.

'It's my new song. It finally all came together.'

Mum knocks on my bedroom door. I've been avoiding her since yesterday afternoon. I open the door. She looks knackered, wearing her oldest pyjama bottoms and a baggy jumper with a hole unravelling in it.

'That's one way of waking me up,' she says, peering into the room. 'Sorry, Ben, I should have got up earlier. You must think we're complete slobs.'

Ben's staring at her.

'I saw you on YouTube. You were amazing.'

Mum rubs her eyes. She looks blank.

'What's YouTube?'

'I lit the AGA,' I say.

She smiles.

'I'll rustle something up for breakfast. I'm sure you won't mind a second breakfast, Ben.'

'Thanks.'

Mum almost closes my bedroom door – and then she opens it again.

'That was your own song, wasn't it?'

I nod. She wrote so many songs. She's not going to think too much of my first effort.

'It was great.'

'It's about Daz.'

She freezes, hanging onto the doorknob.

'Sing it to me later. I want to hear the lyrics.'

Mum retreats down the stairs. I can't tell if she's upset or pleased or both.

'How can you put up with this in winter?' Ben complains, blowing on his fingers. 'There's frost on the inside of the windows.'

'We're used to it,' I say. I make a pyramid of kindling from the pile in the bin next to the fireplace and scrunch sheets of newspaper. Flames are soon licking the twigs. I can tell that Ben still thinks my fire-starting abilities are quite cool. I'd miss it if I had to move to a house where you just pushed a button for instant heat.

'So when are you going to start living in the twenty-first century? Central heating? Double-glazing?'

I throw a couple of small logs on the fire. Ben sits next to me with his guitar on his lap.

'I found out loads about my dad yesterday. Mum's got a scrapbook of cuttings about the band. Daz was just like me. He had a hard time growing up.'

'Were you really lost, when you got to Coventry?'

'I walked a long way. Got loads of blisters. Gran and Grandad are really nice. They're coming on Saturday.'

'So it all worked out?'

'Mostly.'

Ben starts playing his song and I work out a solo for it while he's strumming the chords for the verse. Then I get a bit bored and start playing my song.

'It's not fair. You're so much better than me. How am I supposed to play along with that? You know I can only do chords really.'

'Stop being a mardy-arse.' I study my guitar for a few seconds. 'Look, you can do this. It needs a solid rhythm guitar part.'

Ben stares at the shapes my fingers are forming on the neck of my guitar and he slowly works out what to play.

'See. You're actually pretty good. And you can sing and make stuff up far better than me.'

'Hmm.' Ben is concentrating hard on the rhythm guitar part. He doesn't sound convinced.

'I'm going to find the other members of Mission Control.'

'Then I bet your mum will be famous again and you'll have a guitar-shaped swimming pool and hang out backstage at gigs and stuff.' Ben sounds almost resentful. I don't know what's up with him.

'Ash trashed the studio and went mad. He thinks Mum's dead. That's why I want to find them. They need to know. Mum doesn't even want to be famous, not even as an artist.'

Mum knocks on my door. She's made tea and fresh emergency scone bread with jam. I wonder how much of the conversation she heard. She's dressed in her painting clothes now.

'Thanks, Kaz.' Ben says, using her Mission Control name. I'm not sure I like him doing that.

'I'd get out in the snow if I were you. It looks lovely out there,' she says.

It's light outside now. The sun is dazzling on the pure white landscape. We munch the bread in silence. It's still hot, and the margarine has melted into it, just right.

'Maybe she's right. Fancy building a snowman?' I ask. 'Or is that a bit lame, at our age?'

Ben smiles slowly.

'I made a massive snowball yesterday lunchtime with Josh, before they cancelled school. Bradley Smeed kicked it but he just hurt his foot – it was that big.'

'Awesome.'

We race downstairs and I pull my old coat on, over the top of my pyjamas and put on my wellies, gloves and a woolly hat. I don't care what I look like. Suddenly, I'm really excited about getting out in the snow, as if I was five again. Mum's already working on a painting; the snowy view out of the window under a pale blue sky. She looks at me and laughs.

Ben beats me out into the garden. The air is so cold and still, it almost takes my breath away. The snow almost reaches the tops of my wellies. Ben makes a massive snowball and chucks it, hitting me square in the chest.

'Git!' I shout, trying to put a snowball together before Ben has a chance to make another one, but he catches me by surprise on the ear. It's freezing and I can't hear anything until I wiggle my finger around in my ear and shake out the snow. I charge into Ben and push him over. I lose my footing and crumple in a heap next to him.

'Snow angels!' Ben shouts, fanning his arms in the snow. I do the same. We stand up, encrusted in white. I hope we're not trampling any precious plants – the snow is too deep to tell.

'Let's make an igloo!'

'Cool.' We race together towards the shed to get spades and something we can use as a mould for the bricks.

Suddenly it's how it used to be between us, before we started competing over everything.

Kaz

I didn't think the living room rugs were dirty but now I can see patterns that weren't there before, obscured by dust and cat hair. They seemed clean until Barbara gave me her old Dyson. She went into raptures over the ancient Hoover Elsa had painted to look like a frog to entertain Jason. It must have been the last thing she ever painted. I hadn't realised it might be worth a fortune. Not my fortune though. And its suction power has dwindled to almost nothing.

The wooden surfaces are polished and shining and books have been returned neatly to shelves. Before Jason left for school today, he complained our house looked too tidy – like a museum where he wasn't allowed to touch anything. I woke up at dawn this morning and cleaned out all the kitchen cupboards, terrified that Mum's going to inspect everything tomorrow; scour the place for signs that I'm a mad, bad mother. She shouldn't have spoken to Jason like that on the driveway: it made him worry, and watch me. It makes me feel like I'm not allowed to be left on my own with scissors.

Only my painting corner still looks scruffy but what can I do about that? It's where I work; my own space. I've looked after Wren Cottage, just like Elsa told me to. Now I feel like I've got to hang on tight to everything, before it slips out of my fingers.

I've not touched the cupboard under the stairs yet. Barbara wants me to catalogue everything for the gallery. She promised me I wouldn't be left stranded, even though I don't think I've got any rights.

I turn the vacuum cleaner off, step back to admire my handiwork and almost collide with Barbara. When did she get here? What gave her the right to wander into the living room? Maybe she feels entitled because it's not actually my house. Or she could have been hammering on the back door for ages, with me unable to hear over the noise of the vacuum.

'Interesting.' She stares at the snow-scene on my canvas. The snow outside has completely melted now, apart from the ruins of Jason and Ben's igloo and the odd drift on the hills.

'It's quite minimal –'

'I like the style. I can see it in the gallery.'

'Maybe…'

'I had to tell you,' she beams. 'My offer on the old garage has been accepted. It should be a quick sale – it's a cash offer.'

'That's great.' I'm obviously not showing as much enthusiasm as Barbara was expecting. She looks disappointed. Then she smiles mysteriously.

'I'm not surprised you're shaken up. I knew there was something you weren't telling me.'

My heart jumps with alarm. She's staring at me as if she knows everything about me already. I know the game's up.

'Marilyn Richards called me about the gallery. She's got her finger on the pulse of contemporary art. You're big news. Returned from the dead!'

'I've just been keeping my head down.'

'This is so exciting, Keziah – or should I call you Kaz now?'

I unplug the vacuum cleaner and wind the cable back up. I feel so tired, I want to go to bed and hide under the covers until everyone has forgotten about me. But that's not going to happen.

'I'm scared of being public property again.'

'That's how I feel sometimes. I think we were brought together by Fate.'

'Marilyn Richards called me, too. She's writing a book about my band. Jason wants me to talk to her.'

'I'm thrilled for you, Kaz.'

'I'm not ready. I'm not even ready for my parents coming – and that's tomorrow.'

Barbara looks around the living room.

'The house looks lovely.'

'I've got to talk to Ash and Pete – the other members of Mission Control.'

Barbara peers at me through her oversized glasses.

'I looked you up on the internet. You've still got a lot of explaining to do, haven't you?'

'I just wanted everyone to forget me.'

'But it's fascinating.'

'I was trying to be boring.'

'Look, you need a break from all this cleaning. Come for a walk.'

'Sorry. I've got too much to do.'

'Do you think they're going to notice every speck of dirt?' Barbara asks.

'I need to make a good impression. I want to show them I'm capable…'

Barbara laughs.

'Relax. Be yourself. I think it would be a good idea to talk to Marilyn Richards.'

'That's up to me, isn't it?'

'I'll call you on Monday.'

Barbara smiles as she leaves, leaving me alone in the middle of the room. I stare at Marilyn Richards' number, scribbled by Jason on my sketchbook. I could call her. She sounded desperate to talk to me. Perhaps it would be easy.

If only I could talk to Ash. I could tell him everything. He would understand. It used to be easier than talking to Daz, because Ash filled up any silences with his endless enthusiasm. Marilyn Richards must know where he is. I pick up the phone and get halfway through dialling her number but then I realise that Ash wouldn't be the same person now, would he? There's a loud beeping sound from the receiver: a female voice says mechanically "the number you have dialled has not been recognised". I slam down the receiver, annoyed with myself for being so scared.

The smell of furniture polish is overwhelming and the disturbed dust irritates my nose. I need fresh air. I've got to tidy the garden up a bit and harvest some vegetables for tomorrow's lunch. A couple of cauliflowers and big main-crop potatoes, I think. I push open the living room window. The wooden frame is stiff. I'll have to look at it soon.

I walk into the kitchen. Everything's shining in the here

too. I put my jacket on and open the back door. With a twinge of regret, I realise it's a perfect day for a walk. The sky is clear blue and the breeze is mild, with a hint of spring; a day for filling your lungs with air that smells of moss and leaf mould. I get my gardening tools from the shed.

Chapter 17
Cauliflower Cheese

Jason

I practise the piece I've learned for Gran and Grandad in the living room, which is so clean, I barely recognise it. Mum has gone mad with cleaning this week. Everything's so tidy and neat, it feels like we're about to sit an exam in being a perfect version of ourselves.

Mum said Gran and Grandad were into folk music when they were young. I asked Mrs Lyons about it on Wednesday lunchtime. It turns out she's into that sort of thing too and she told me about a band called Fairport Convention. She lent me an album called *Liege and Lief*. I wasn't sure if I'd like it but she told me the album was recorded after the drummer was killed in a motorway accident. I thought it was sort of appropriate. Their songs are all about murder and stuff. It's actually really cool. I learned a song called 'Tam Lin' which is about a fairy, but he's not a girly fairy with wings – he's a knight under an enchantment. Ben thinks it's pretty good as well, but he's a bit jealous that I managed to learn the song so quickly. I'm not so confident about singing it though. My voice has gone a bit growly recently, so I've left the singing out for now. I'm playing the lines that are sung, and the violin melody on the guitar. It's kind of my own version and it sounds good on my Stratocaster.

I hope Gran and Grandad like it. I feel like I did before I went busking for the first time. I'm too nervous to do anything except play my guitar. My hands shook so much this morning, I spilled tea on the living room rug. Mum was just as bad. She fussed over the stain on the rug and scrubbed at it with a cloth. It's not like I haven't done my bit. My bedroom's really tidy and I cleaned the bathroom. I polished my guitar. It feels like Sunday night never happened, like I'm meeting Gran and Grandad for the first time today.

I've played around with the melody of 'Tam Lin' a bit. You could change the words around too and it would start to become a new song. That's how Ben got started and he's written about five songs now. I don't know why he's so jealous of me, because his voice is great. Mine's all over the place at the moment. It's a good job I can let the guitar do the talking. I'll play it for Mrs Lyons too. Maybe Ben could sing it. It could be another song for our band. I haven't told Mrs Lyons about Mission Control yet. I told Ben not to. She probably hasn't even heard of Mission Control but I want her to know I'm taking music seriously, not just doing it because of my parents.

'They're here!' Mum shouts through the living room window. She went into the garden with her secateurs half an hour ago, so she could keep herself busy with pruning while she was waiting for Gran and Grandad's car.

I put my guitar down on the sofa and rush outside. I stand next to Mum while Grandad parks the car. He seems to take a long time doing it, even though there aren't any other cars parked on this stretch of road. Gran waves at us. I put my hand on Mum's shoulder. She's trembling, terrified, like the live mice the cat brings into the house in her mouth that we sometimes manage to rescue.

'It'll be fine,' I say.

'I hope so.'

I run down the steps as Gran and Grandad are getting out of the car. Gran gives me a hug. She takes a long, serious look at me.

'You take after both of them, don't you?' she says. 'The best of both.'

I'm not sure what to say. Grandad smiles and pats me on the back.

'Recovered from your adventures, young man?'

'Yeah. Thanks.'

Gran struggles with a large shopping bag in the boot of the car. There are packages in wrapping paper inside it. My heart gives a little lurch of excitement. Gran sees me staring at it.

'Do you want a hand?'

'No peeking though,' she smiles.

I lug the bag up the steps. It's not too heavy, just bulky.

'What a lovely garden!' Gran stops for breath at the top of the steps.

'We didn't know what to expect,' Grandad says. 'This is lovely. What a view!'

'I can't take all the credit.' Mum bends down to examine the cabbages. 'Everything belonged to Elsa – the lady I looked after. And it's not at its best.'

'It's beautiful – all the sculptures.' Gran's eyes are wide with amazement.

'Let me get this straight,' Grandad says. 'You looked after this old artist woman and lived in her cottage, and then when she died, you just kept on living here? You don't pay any rent or anything?'

Mum looks uncomfortable.

'She asked me to look after it.'

'You don't own the house?'

Mum looks really flustered. Grandad takes the hint and looks admiringly at the vegetable patch.

'Are those Brussels Sprouts?' he says. 'You used to hate them when you were little.'

'I was lucky with Jason. He'll eat anything.'

'I don't really like marrow,' I say.

Mum laughs. 'Now he tells me!'

'I had to eat marrow with everything last autumn,' I grumble.

'It was a bumper harvest.'

They wander around the garden, looking like they're really enjoying it. But they're in coats and I'm just in a t-shirt. It's sunny but really cold outside today. Looking at the half-melted igloo just makes me feel colder. Gran catches me shivering.

'Look at you. You'll catch your death of cold standing out here!'

'I was practising something for you on the guitar when you arrived.'

'We'd better come in then.'

Mum shepherds Gran and Grandad through the back door. It takes them ages to get anywhere because they want to stop and look at everything. I want to get them into the living room so I can play the guitar for them, but they seem fascinated by the AGA. It radiates warmth, and the delicious smell of cauliflower cheese and jacket potatoes cooking.

'What a nice old fashioned kitchen,' Gran says. 'It reminds me of being a little girl. So nothing's been modernised?'

'When Jason was little, she turned the attic into his bedroom and got the AGA converted to heat up water, but apart from that…'

'It's like a time capsule. It's wonderful.'

'Are you sure everything's safe?' Grandad asks, staring at the light fitting with its old brown electrical cord.

'We're still alive! You never stop fussing, do you, Dad?' Mum laughs, but I can tell she's itching with frustration. 'Honestly, Jason. He used to drive me mad.'

Mum fills the kettle at the sink. I use it as an excuse to get Gran and Grandad into the living room. This visit is stressing Mum out. I put the bag of presents down, pick up my guitar and sling the strap around my shoulder.

'What a lovely guitar,' Gran says.

'I got it for Christmas. Mum sold a painting.'

They gasp as they look around the living room. I suppose it is full of paintings and old stuff and I made a nice fire in the fireplace, but I want them to hear me play.

I start playing 'Tam Lin'. I can't wait to open the presents but I've been learning the song especially for Gran and Grandad and I can't put it off any longer. They both sit down on the sofa and listen to me intently.

'That was wonderful,' Gran says when I've finished. 'It sounds like one of those old tunes we used to listen to at the Umbrella folk club.'

'Mum said you might like it.'

'You've only been playing since last September?'

'I practise a lot though.'

'Darren was like that – gifted,' Gran says.

Mum comes into the living room with a tray of mugs.

'He's good, isn't he?' she says.

'How about those presents?' Grandad says. 'Fourteen presents – to start making up for all those Christmases we missed.'

Kaz

From the kitchen, I can hear Jason talking excitedly to Mum and Dad. He's telling them all about his band with Ben. He seemed a bit shy with them earlier but now he's beaming away, like a little boy again. Jason hasn't been so chatty for ages.

He's thrilled with his presents. Mum and Dad didn't meet Jason for very long last weekend. We've only had a couple of phone conversations since Sunday but they've got most things spot-on: some really cool books, including a Star Wars graphic novel he kept reading in Cromford Books, mountain biking gloves, a tin of plectrums, blank CDs, Lynx shower gel, a Toblerone, and a black woolly hat with a skull on it. He's even pleased with the notebook and new pairs of socks. Jason's happy with any clothes you buy him, as long as they're black. He takes after me and Daz like that. Most of the clothes going round in Elsa's old twin tub washing machine are black, so Jason's school shirts look a bit grey.

I take the cauliflower cheese out of the oven. The jacket potatoes are already sitting there on the plates. It all looks pretty good. I grip the heavy stoneware casserole dish as tightly as I can through my oven gloves. I push open the living room door.

Mum and Dad stare at me expectantly. I wasn't much of a cook when I was a kid. When I was in Mission Control, I made things like spag bol with lentils, when I wasn't living off toast, chips and takeaways.

Jason set the table with the best Crown Derby plates

from the back of the cupboard. We've never used them before. They have gold edges. We brought proper napkins in a deep red colour. I bought a bottle of red wine. Jason insisted on having some. He constantly surprises me – a kid one moment, an adult the next. Dad's got red grape juice because he's driving. The whole thing looks really pretty, including the cat sitting on the windowsill, washing her paws nonchalantly, pretending to ignore the smell of cheese sauce.

My heart flutters and my hands start shaking. As I reach the table, the dish slips and crash-lands on the table. Dad's glass topples over, spilling grape juice on his lap and onto the carpet. Somehow Jason's plate gets smashed cleanly into two halves.

'Shit! I'm so sorry!' I shriek.

'Way to go, Mum!' Jason's mouth gapes, as if he can't believe how clumsy I am.

Dad dabs at his lap with his napkin.

Mum is out of her seat before I can do anything. She grabs a cloth and a tea towel from the kitchen and manages to have everything mopped up in seconds. I stand there, flapping, still wearing the oven gloves.

'Sit down, Karen. Everything's fine. Jim's trousers won't stain. This looks delicious.'

Jason takes the halves of his plate back into the kitchen.

'I didn't want anything to go wrong,' I say. Before I know it, I'm crying. I wipe my eyes with the oven gloves.

'When you turned up on the doorstep last Sunday, we didn't know who you were anymore. Anything could have happened to you. But Jason's so nice – and you've done so well for yourself,' Mum says.

'I haven't. None of this is mine.'

'Jason showed us your paintings while you were in the kitchen.' Dad says.

Jason comes back with a chipped blue and white plate. He rolls his eyes towards the ceiling.

'Chill out, it's just a broken plate.' He helps himself to a large portion of cauliflower cheese and rescues his jacket potato from where it's rolled halfway down the table, sawing through it with his knife. 'We can probably glue it back together.'

'It was certainly a novel way of serving a meal,' Dad says, a wry smile on his face. 'It looks delicious, anyway.'

'All the vegetables are from the garden,' I say. 'Cauliflowers aren't easy to grow but I seem to have the knack.'

I take a deep breath and serve Mum and Dad with the cauliflower cheese. I don't feel hungry but I put some on my plate anyway. I manage to gulp down a few mouthfuls. I pour myself a glass of wine. Everyone else seems to be enjoying it, like a normal family having lunch together.

'You'll be choosing your GCSEs soon, won't you?' Grandad asks.

'I'm definitely doing music – and art. I don't know what else. We've still got a couple of months to decide. I hate exams,' Jason says, through a mouthful of potato and cauliflower.

Gran laughs.

'You sound just like Karen did. It's great that you've got a passion for things you love.'

'I don't know if I want to go to uni or anything. I want to be a musician.' Jason stares at me accusingly.

'Jason told us about the lady writing a book about your band,' Dad says. 'She tried to contact us a few years ago, but we didn't want to talk to her.'

'I'm not talking to Marilyn Richards until I get in touch with Pete and Ash,' I say. 'I don't think anyone will care anyway. It's too long ago.'

'She's going to get the band back together,' Jason says.

'How could I?'

Mum and Dad exchange glances.

'We've got something for you, Karen,' Dad says. 'I went to Singh News on Monday afternoon. I told them about you.'

I put my knife and fork down and stare at him.

'Jason's guitar teacher said Ash had gone a bit weird.'

'He lives in Devon, apparently. He's in touch with his parents.' Dad looks at me searchingly and I stare guiltily at my plate. 'They haven't seen him for a while but he calls them regularly; sends them cards and emails.'

'Is he okay though?'

Dad sighs. 'It's funny but before this week, we'd hardly spoken to the Singhs since you went missing. We didn't even know Ash was in hospital.'

'Hospital?' I gulp. My hand shakes as I grip the wineglass and lift it to my lips.

'They didn't really want to talk about it. Can't blame them. Anyway, they gave me this. They said it was for you.'

Dad gives me a small blue envelope. It says "to Kaz" in the middle, surrounded by symbols: smiley faces, lightning bolts and skulls and crossbones. It looks a little faded, as if Mr and Mrs Singh have been keeping it for me for a long time. I tear the envelope open as carefully as I can.

I want to run away and read the letter in the garden. Instead, I try to ignore Jason and my parents staring at me expectantly over the remains of their dinner, and I focus on Ash's note.

Kaz

If you're reading this, that means you're alive. If you weren't alive, I'd feel it somehow, so obviously you're alive. I told Mum and Dad to keep this letter and not let anyone else open it. I wish I'd been able to stop you from slipping away. When I realised you'd gone, I freaked out. Why didn't you leave a note? Did you sell the van? I want my share — only kidding!! I did something far worse.

You might have heard about the fire in the studio. After you disappeared I locked myself into the studio. I held it together until Daz's funeral. After that, I didn't even let Pete in. I let Bob in though — remember Bob? He brought me everything I needed. I managed to hold out for three months, not leaving the studio at all. The worst thing was that I started to sell Daz's stuff to Bob — records, Daz's jacket and even his guitars. I knew the records belonged to both of you which made it feel worse because I knew you were still alive. I justified it because I couldn't stand to be surrounded by Daz's stuff now he was gone. Also because I didn't want to leave the studio, not even to go to the cashpoint. I couldn't stop thinking about that argument. I didn't mean to come between you and Daz. I blamed myself for his death. I made him lose trust in you.

Pete, Mum and Dad and uncle Vik kept trying to get in. I spoke to them through the door. They were about to call the funny farm when I finally snapped out of it. The studio had turned into a mess. I'd spent the whole summer in there. I'd not even been on the roof for weeks. I was paranoid. The whole place had become evil to me. I needed sunshine and people and music.

I put that old copy of '1984' Daz used to carry around with him through your Mum and Dad's letterbox. I thought I needed to return it to you somehow.

The fire was supposed to be symbolic. I didn't realise that it might spread to the rest of the building. I didn't know that until later. I packed a bag, got the flames going and called the fire brigade from the phone box on the corner. I finally remembered I could use my cash card, travelled to Birmingham and got a flight to Goa. I partied so hard that by the time uncle Vik found me, I'd gone a bit loopy. I thought I'd be difficult to find. Obviously I find it quite difficult to blend in.

I didn't particularly mind ending up in hospital. They give you quite interesting drugs.

So what am I doing now? I'm in Devon. Not heaven. It rains more here. That's okay. I like the countryside. I'm making music again. Noise art, I suppose you'd call it. Some of my new tracks would sound great with your basslines on them. Are you still playing? Come to see me here. I've got everything I need. Except you. It would be nice to see Pete too. I really left him in the lurch.

I hope writing this letter will make you come back.

Yours Forever,

Ash

There's an address at the bottom: Pennywell Farm. No phone number. I hope he's still there. No mention of whether he's married or has any kids. It could be a lot worse. I was prepared for incoherent rambling, but he sounds almost like his old self.

224

'What does he say?' Jason asks.

'I'm going to write to him, tonight. He's been waiting for me to contact him. I don't know when he wrote the letter. It could have been years ago.' My eyes start streaming again and I dab at them with my napkin, but I know I'll feel better after this.

Chapter 18
Pete

Jason

'She just wrote to him. By hand. It could take days – weeks – for him to get back to her. That's even if he's still living there.' I put my apron on. Sam's face is red, clashing with his hair. The pub's really busy and Sam is trying to fry his way through loads of orders. He looks like he's struggling.

'It's brilliant that she's done it though. When did she post the letter?'

'I did, on my way here.'

'So what did Ash's letter say? Did she let you read it?' Sam sounds excited. He whirls round the kitchen cutting burger buns in half.

'He sold loads of Daz's stuff to a drug dealer when he locked himself in the studio. He acted like a dick and went a bit mental. At least he admits it.'

I wash my hands and get on with chopping up the salad.

'His guitars could still be out there – they might not have been burned in the fire.' Sam sounds excited. I imagine Dad's guitars sitting in Cash Converters in Coventry, being bought by strangers. But I'm glad Ash sold them rather than destroying them.

'I don't know why Mum doesn't call Ash's parents to get his number. We'd be sorted then.' I start slicing a cucumber. Sam stops me and shows me how to hold the knife properly so I can do really thin, precise slices.

'Let her take her time.'

'We need to find Pete now, don't we?'

Sam laughs.

'That's easy. He's on Facebook.'

My hand slips with the knife, millimetres away from slicing my thumb. My head's whirling. Does Sam actually know Pete? Why didn't he tell me last Sunday?

'Hey, careful!' Sam says. 'Concentrate. Music will help.' There's a stereo in the kitchen; a boom-box I didn't notice last Sunday. Sam presses "play". It sounds great. Heavy and quite slow. I sort of recognise it.

'Black Sabbath. 'Paranoid'.' Sam smiles. 'Heard it before?'

'Not all the way through.'

'Tony Iommi is an awesome guitarist but when he was just a few years older than you, he had an accident at work. He lost the tips of two of his fingers in a machine.'

'Ouch!' I start slicing the tomatoes. I'd better be ultra-careful. 'How could he carry on playing without his fingertips?'

'He was fed up at first – thought he'd have to give up, but then he made thimbles for his fingers out of washing up bottles, used different strings and changed the tuning on his guitar. The result is what you're listening to right now. He invented heavy metal.'

'Invented it?'

'Black Sabbath put all the ingredients together – heavy blues riffs, gloomy lyrics, crazy drumming. I'll teach you to play some of their stuff in the lesson.'

'Thanks!'

Sam takes two burgers and portions of chips out of the deep-fat fryer and puts them on plates with a bun. I arrange salad around them.

'Can you take those out to the pub?' Sam asks. 'Table two.'

'Which one's table two?'

'It's near the window. The numbers are on the corner of each table.' Sam smiles apologetically. He reads the next order and puts more stuff into the fryer. 'I'm sorry – Judith must be stuck behind the bar.'

'It's okay.'

I feel a bit self-conscious, stepping into the pub with my apron on. I'm not sure I'm supposed to be working in a pub when I'm not even fourteen, even though I'm just doing it for my guitar lesson. I find table two – a middle-aged couple in biker leathers. They smile and say thank you, although the man mumbles something about having to wait ages. Now I'm out of the kitchen I can think, without Sam telling me about Black Sabbath, when I really want to talk about Mission Control.

Sam looks really busy in the kitchen. So much for having a chilled-out time listening to music. He's got three more plates ready to go out into the pub. He's frantically chopping more salad, slicing burger buns, getting stuff out of the fryer, arms whirling.

'Table five,' he pants. 'Sorry.'

'I don't mind.' I pick up two of the plates. 'So does Pete know?' I blurt out. 'Did you tell him that Mum's alive? Does he know about me?'

Sam stares straight at me. There's a look of desperation in his eyes as he glances around the chaotic kitchen.

'Sorry, Jason. You've got to take that food out.'

'But…'

Judith looms through the serving hatch from the bar.

'There's going to be a bloody riot out here if you two don't get a move on!'

I scuttle out into the pub. I don't want to annoy Judith any more than I've already done by breathing and existing. It looks like I'll have to wait before I can ask Sam anything.

My arms ache by the time I'm sitting in Sam's studio with my guitar on my knee. I glance around the room. He's taken down Mum's anti-fur poster, but replaced it with another Mission Control poster, the band lined up against a graffiti-covered brick wall. Daz is staring over to his left, his expression grim. Mum is wearing a fluffy coat with the collar up and big shades so you can't see much of her face. Ash is looking up, shielding his eyes, as if he's searching for something in the sky. Only Pete is staring at the camera, a big grin on his face. The *NME* logo is in the bottom right-hand corner.

Sam looks up from his guitar.

'I thought you'd find that poster less distracting.'

'I feel sorry for Pete. He kind of got left behind, didn't he?'

'He's a drum teacher – he still lives in Coventry. He

started a Facebook group for music teachers. I don't really know him. I just asked him for some advice on setting up. I wanted to respect his privacy. But he's responded to a few of my questions.'

'So he doesn't know Mum's alive?'

'Not unless Marilyn Richards has told him. She interviewed Pete years back – hopeless – one interview was hardly going to make a book.'

'Mum needs to talk to Pete.'

'Are you on Facebook?'

'Don't use it much. Not much point when you don't have your own computer.' I set up my Facebook account at Ben's house two months ago.

'Why don't you send him a message now?'

I put my guitar down and go over to the computer. I log into Facebook. Sam finds Pete's page for me. It's definitely him. In his photo, he's still got red hair and he's sitting behind a drum kit.

I send a friend request with a message: *Hi! I'm not sure if you'll believe this but I'm Kaz's son. Kaz is fine and she lives near Cromford in Derbyshire.*

I think for a moment and then I type our phone number. That's probably the quickest way. *If you want to talk to Kaz, this is our number. She doesn't do computers. This isn't a hoax. Please get in touch.*' I press "send". I hope he'll read it. It probably doesn't help that my Facebook name is "Baby Alien", and my profile picture is a drawing of Jabba the Hutt I did myself and scanned in. We set up Facebook profiles to enter a competition on a Star Wars fan page. It seems a bit silly now.

'Do you think it'll be a shock for him?'

'Jason, you'd better have your guitar lesson while you've got the chance. You worked much harder than you should have done in the pub.'

'Yeah, sorry.'

'Maybe it's a mistake for you to work in the pub first. Not fair on you.'

'I'm fine.'

'Maybe we should pay you properly. Judith had you running round like a blue-arsed fly.'

Sam plays the opening riff from 'Paranoid' on his guitar. Something sounds different about the way he's playing. Sam looks up and smiles, when he's finished.

'You tuned your guitar differently,' I say.

'Downtuned by a semitone. Toni Iommi did it because it made it easier to play with his missing fingertips – but it sounds darker and heavier.'

'So the E string is tuned to D-sharp?'

'You've got it.'

Sam plays his bottom string and I turn the tuning peg until it sounds the same, then I change the tunings on all of the other strings to match. I think about the first day I got my acoustic guitar. I nearly gave up because I couldn't tune it. Now it feels like I've been doing it for my whole life. Sam shows me how to play the riff again, slowing it down so I can see what he's doing. I let myself get totally absorbed in playing. This is worth all that time running around in the pub.

Kaz

The living room is looking a bit crazy again. Barbara wanted me to do an inventory of Elsa's work so she can decide what to display in the gallery. It seems a bit premature – the old garage is still full of pigeon poo, but she's meeting the architect on site this week and she wants me to come too. Barbara wants the gallery to be open by the summer. She seems very optimistic to me.

I've emptied out the cupboard under the stairs. The winter sun shows thousands of particles of dust, undisturbed in the darkness since Jason was a baby, dust made from Elsa's skin, spiders and disintegrating cloth and paper. I'm surrounded by Elsa.

I open a fragile cardboard box. It was sealed with sticky tape, now brittle and yellow. Inside are items wrapped in newspaper, stacked carefully. I unwrap the top parcel. The tall vase inside is in the shape of a trout with its mouth gaping open, standing on its tail. It would look startling on a table, with a spray of gladioli spewing out of its jaws.

Out of curiosity, I straighten out the sheet of newspaper. It's from the Independent, July 1995, when Jason was five months old and just starting to crawl. A small article catches my eye: SHADOWS ALLOWED TO GATHER OVER FATE OF PREACHER JAMES. It's a pointless article really, explaining that there was still no news following Richey Manic's disappearance. My heart beats faster. I don't remember seeing this at the time. Elsa must have wrapped it. What if I had read it?

When the postman came up the steps this morning, I thought I was going to collapse, my heart beat so fast. Ash has probably not even got my letter yet. It's only Tuesday, and it was just some junk mail. I imagine a postman cycling down a narrow Devon lane with my letter in his bag. I can't imagine Ash living on a farm somehow. He liked the countryside but only if there was a rave happening in it.

The next package is a bowl shaped like a cabbage. Memories of these objects return to me. The bowl once stood on top of the radiogram, next to the stripy lighthouse table lamp. Jason started pulling himself up on the door of the radiogram, wobbling the ceramics dangerously close to the edge. Elsa didn't seem particularly bothered about her creations, but she didn't want Jason banging his head, so we packed everything away, to make it childproof.

I pick my way across the room to fetch the pad I'm using to make my list and almost trip over a small, square canvas. Gasping, I grab tightly onto the radiogram, making the lighthouse table lamp wobble, just like it used to do when Jason was a baby. I regain my balance and steady the lamp.

I examine the canvas. It's one of my first oil paintings. A portrait of Elsa. It's crude, nothing like my style now, but I've managed to capture Elsa's face: her china-blue eyes, high cheekbones and the crinkled crow's feet spreading out from the corners of her eyes. Elsa looks wise and mysterious, a mischievous look in her eyes. I stare at her, and she stares back knowingly.

I put the painting on one side, and concentrate on unwrapping Elsa's treasures. I can't help thinking that she left everything here for a reason, like a breadcrumb trail. There's nothing definite, only the certainty that everything's changing.

●

I swapped the van's number plates with an abandoned Fiesta in a country lane when I was on the run. No one's caught me yet. I got the garage in Cromford to give the van a coat of dull green paint.

My hair is brown and cropped. I'm dressed in paint-splattered jumble sale clothes, six months pregnant, starting to waddle, feeling the heaviness of the baby inside me. I park the van in the Somerfield car park in Matlock.

Elsa sits in the passenger seat, watching the copper and russet beech leaves twirling down onto the windscreen while I fetch her walking frame from the back of the van. She gives me a wry smile.

The back of the van is stripped out and scrubbed, but I get a vision of us all, huddled in sleeping bags, swigging from a shared bottle of cheap cider to keep out the cold, bedded down in a layby between gigs, hopelessly skint, but full of adventurous confidence.

I pick up the walking frame and slam the doors as hard as I can, screwing my eyes up so tight to stop the tears that when I open them again, stars explode in my vision.

I open the passenger door and help Elsa down the steps. She clings to the door for support. I get a vision of Daz, drunk at the Spiral Sun festival. I try to concentrate on the golden autumn light; on Elsa. I lock the van – not that anyone would steal it.

'I used to think about Pierre all the time,' Elsa says, her blue eyes piercing my thoughts. 'Until I was almost drunk on the past. But no amount of thinking ever brought him back.'

We walk, slowly. The sunshine doesn't warm the air any more. I button my long grey cardigan over my bump. I've had a whole summer of mourning and hiding. I've decided I don't want to go back to whatever's left of my old life. Elsa's an enthusiastic conspirator. After a few weeks of staying with her, when I realised I was pregnant, we came up with our story: I'm studying art with my Great Aunt, Elsa Day. After a vaguely alluded to troubled past, I'm here to have my baby, bring him up in the peace of the Derbyshire hills. He's going to be a boy. They checked at his last scan. How would Daz have acted, if he'd known?

I need a new name. I nearly didn't go to the hospital, but Elsa said I had to – she likes to do things properly. No one's found me out. The NHS has to be confidential anyway. It's not as if I'm a criminal, apart from the thing with the number plates, and that didn't hurt anyone.

Elsa came up with my name. I wanted to keep my alliterative initials. Keziah, a strong, Old Testament Name, with a hint of the exotic. Knight, valiant: the opposite of Day; Elsa's little joke. It feels right. It sounds like an artist's name. Elsa says my paintings are good. In my faded floral skirt, I'm not Kaz K, or Karen Kenning anymore. This isn't the missing rock star you were looking for.

The solicitors' office is tiny, above a stationery shop near the bridge, with gold-leaf lettering on the first floor windows: Draper and Ferris, and a polished brass plaque on a dark green door. I leave Elsa's walking frame at the bottom of the dusty stairs. She's going to need my help to support her up every one of those creaky, uncarpeted steps. But I couldn't have got this far without her help. When I come back down these stairs, I'll be a different person.

●

Jason

Mrs Lyons hands out the worksheets to our form. She looks stressed, waiting for the class to stop talking. I don't know

233

why she doesn't get us to hand out the worksheets for her but if I offered to help, people would say I was sucking up to her.

The worksheets say "Writing a Song – Lesson One". I look at Ben and he rolls his eyes. I can't help grinning. If we'd had this lesson last month, it might have saved me a lot of hassle, with all those words I crossed out and rubbish chord progressions I tried before I came up with something good.

Mrs Lyons stands at the front of the classroom again. She puts her hands on her hips and tries glaring at a few people, especially Kevin Sanderton, who never shuts up. She reaches under her desk. There's a flash of polished metal and the entire class is stunned into silence by a blast from her trumpet. A B-Flat, I think.

Josh is drawing surfboards on his exercise book but the noise makes him jump so much, his pen leaps out of his hand and clatters onto the floor. He scrabbles to pick it up, while everyone else looks obediently at Mrs Lyons at last.

'Before we start, I've got an announcement. As you know, we could do with some new equipment in the music department. Wouldn't it be nice if everyone could try the guitar or have a go on a trombone? Most classes do try to look after the instruments but they're getting worn out. I'm organising a fundraising concert at school, on Thursday 12th February. It's in the evening, so your parents can come along. It doesn't matter if you're a beginner or if you're grade eight – or you do classical, heavy metal or hip hop. Let me know if you'd like to perform. I'm sure it'll be brilliant.'

The rest of the class visibly shrink into themselves at the thought of performing on stage, apart from Alicia Jones, who plays the flute in the Derbyshire Youth Orchestra. Her hand shoots up straight away, her plait bouncing. Mrs Lyons nods and notes down her name. Ben and I exchange glances.

'Are you up for it?' I whisper.

'Course I am.' Ben grins.

I glance across the table.

'Josh – do you fancy playing the drums for us?'

Josh turns pale – he's only messed about on the drums on a few lunchtimes when it was too wet for him to play football. Then he nods and smiles shakily. I stick my hand up with as much confidence as I can manage. Mrs Lyons smiles.

'We'll do it. Me, Ben and Josh – he's our drummer.' I say.

'Excellent. You can do two songs. So have you got a name for your band?'

I stare around the room, desperately trying to think of something. We've been trying to think up band names for months but nothing sounds right. I can't just tell her we haven't come up with anything.

'Erm, the Organ Detectives, miss,' I say, looking at the giant electric organ that doesn't work at all anymore, apart from making an ominous low hum when you switch it on. A giggle ripples around the room but Mrs Lyons writes it down.

'That's shit,' Ben hisses.

'Sorry, I panicked,' I say. 'We can change it.'

'I can't believe you didn't even ask me.' Ben crosses his arms and glares at me.

'I think it's quite good.' Josh smiles at me. It's not. Ben's right. It wasn't even on the list of possible band names we've made.

'Right.' Mrs Lyons shouts, just as the class is starting to slip into gossiping and sidelong staring at me, Ben and Josh. 'Let's get on with it. You've got five minutes to write the name of your favourite song on the worksheet and write down five things you like about it. I'll put some ideas on the whiteboard. Make sure you pick a song with lyrics – what are lyrics, Arron?' she says, catching Arron Reeves just as he's about to flick a bit of rubber at Alicia.

'Words, miss?'

'That's right. Starting…now.'

I write *Motorcycle Emptiness*' on my worksheet. Then I cross it out and write *Rootless in Babylon' by Mission Control*.

235

I write the reasons why I like it:

Amazing bass riff that makes you want to go crazy.

Brilliant singing with loads of emotion and attitude.

The guitar playing mirrors the melody line and then just goes mental.

The drumming's really funky so it makes people want to dance.

But it's about loneliness and not fitting in.

There are loads of other reasons why I like it too but Mrs Lyons only asked for five. I look across at Ben's worksheet.

He's chosen 'Subterranean Homesick Blues' by Bob Dylan, which is a bit of a shock. I mean, it's alright but it sounds too much like something his dad would like. I know I like old stuff but that's ancient. Bob Dylan doesn't even sing properly and his voice gets on my nerves. I thought Ben would choose 'Supersonic' by Oasis, which has been his favourite song ever since we were in playgroup together. Mind you, Liam Gallagher's voice gets on my nerves as well.

Kaz

The phone rings. It'll be Barbara, checking on my progress with the catalogue. I stretch. My back is aching from sitting hunched on the floor. It's absorbing work, seeing these things that haven't see daylight for so many years. Some of them have been in boxes for my whole lifetime, never mind Jason's, wrapped in newspapers from the early seventies. The room is disappearing under piles of crumpled yellow newspaper.

I can just about reach the phone without disturbing anything.

'Hello?'

'Who is this?' The voice is suspicious, male. Should I recognise it?

'You rang me. You should know who I am.'

'Bloody typical.'

'Who are you?'

The man laughs. I recognise his voice but I can't place it.

'I got a Facebook message to call you. Some ninety-year old guy who looks like Jabba the Hutt gave me your number. He says he's your son.'

'Jason?' My heart jumps. Jason's on Facebook and he's contacting random strangers? I know this voice.

'He calls himself Baby Alien...' The voice falters. 'You have a son?'

'I'm sorry – he was probably joking around.'

'You've still got no idea who I am, have you?'

I can't think. I daren't even hope.

The man laughs again. 'Oh for fuck's sake!' he says.

'Pete?' I whisper.

'Jesus, you took your time working that out.'

'So...how are you?' I sit on the rug, knees drawn up to my chest, not daring to move.

'I'm fine, I think...'

'Where do we start?'

'You live in Derbyshire?' he asks.

'How do you know?'

'Your son told me. In his message. '

'Where are you?' This could win prizes for the most stilted conversation ever.

'Still in Cov. I've got kids. They're only young. I'm married.'

'That's great.' I say.

'Are you married or anything?'

'No one since Daz.'

There's a pause, a sharp intake of breath.

'How old is Jason?

'He's thirteen.'

'Is he...? I mean, did you...?' I can hear Pete breathing. 'Is he Daz's son?'

'He looks just like Daz.' I shiver.

'So, you were...'

'Daz never knew. Neither did I.' My head's spinning. I wish I could sit on the sofa but it's across a minefield of precious china.

'Why didn't you tell us you were okay?'

'I'm sorry.'

'Bit late for that, Kaz.' I can hear the bitterness in his voice.

'I know.'

'I had to carry everything on my own. I didn't want to do music anymore. I was glad when everyone forgot about Mission Control. I got a job in a garden centre. I met my wife…'

'I stuffed my bass in a cupboard. Don't even own any records.'

'When my son was born, I felt like I had to start playing the drums again. Start teaching. Kids like me. Give them a chance.'

'I wrote to Ash on Sunday. He'd left a letter for me in Singh News.'

'He wrote me one too. Apologising for shutting himself in the studio and then running off. That was about ten years ago.'

'Ten years ago? Does he still live on that farm?'

'Fuck knows. Why should I care?'

'Sounds like he was depressed. I've been thinking about him.'

'Ash was just milking it for attention.'

I wish Pete didn't sound so angry.

'I'll let you know if Ash writes back.'

'Don't hold your breath. God, Kaz. I thought you were dead.'

'My son found out about me. His guitar teacher had that anti-fur poster on his wall.'

Pete laughs. I remember the reaction when I told the rest of the band that PETA had asked me to pose as the latest celebrity for their campaign. Daz was angry, even though there was nothing he could do to stop me.

I should have read the signs. Daz was starting to see me as his private property. Ash was supportive. He thought it would raise the profile of the band. Pete joked about why PETA hadn't asked him too.

'That's how Jason found out about Mission Control? Poor kid.'

'His guitar teacher is a massive Mission Control fan. Sam Baxter.'

'Shit – yeah. Red hair. He's posted on my Facebook group a few times. Wanted business advice. Something about his in-laws.'

'I'm back in touch with my parents again.'

'That's good. That's great, Kaz!'

'We had lunch together on Saturday.'

'It wasn't too late then, was it? It's so good to hear from you,' Pete says.

'I thought you were angry.'

'Just wake me up and tell me this is real. I still don't believe it. I'm actually talking to you?'

'Jason was desperate to find you and Ash. Marilyn Richards wants to interview us for some stupid book she's writing.'

'It's not so stupid. When I talked to her, there was nothing to say, really. But now…maybe we can get hold of Captain Fruitloop too.' Pete sounds suddenly excited.

'Who?'

'Ash. We'll find him. Can't be that difficult. After all, they managed to find him in Goa.'

'I said I wouldn't do the interview on my own. It has to be the three of us.'

'Let's fucking do it, then.'

I can hear noises in the background now, as if someone's opened a door. Tinkly music like a kids' TV theme tune; excited footsteps and small children yelling.

'I wish you wouldn't swear when you're on the phone. And shouldn't you have gone by now?' A woman's voice.

'Bollocks. Sorry, love, I'll explain later,' he tells her. It must be his wife. 'I can't believe the time. I've got to go. I've got a drumming workshop at a special school on the other side of Cov. I'll be late but fuck it. It's been fifteen years, Kaz. Call me tonight.' Pete gives me his number and I scribble it on my sketchbook.

'We need to meet up. As soon as possible. We've got shit-loads of catching up to do.' Pete says. 'This weekend?'

'Okay. Jason really wants to meet you.'

'We'll work something out. Fuck – sorry – I've really got to go. Sorry Kaz.'

The phone goes dead. I stare at the receiver in my hand, not quite able to believe what just happened. A churning feeling rises in my chest. I drop the phone and pick my way through Elsa's ceramics on wobbly legs to the bathroom, but then I realise I don't actually feel sick. I start laughing and crying at the same time, leaning against the bathroom door, wiping my eyes on the folds of Jason's towel.

Chapter 19
Rabbit Food

Jason

The stale smell of the charity shop envelops me as soon as I close the door behind me. Mavis smiles at me from behind the counter.

'I haven't seen you for a few weeks.'

'The snow stopped me. It's a bit lighter at night now.'

'Not much. You be careful, cycling all that way in the dark.'

I go straight over to the records and CDs. I don't want to get trapped in an endless conversation with Mavis. She'll only start talking about old people who fell over in the snow.

Ben's waiting outside with the bikes and our guitars. He's on his own and it's raining. I only took my acoustic guitar to school today but I still don't want it to get soaked, or stolen by Bradley Smeed. I want to get home. Ever since I sent that message to Pete, I've had a nervous tingle, like butterflies in my stomach.

There isn't much interesting music in the shop today. Maybe the supply of good stuff is running out. It doesn't really matter anymore. I can just ask Sam for anything I like and he'll copy it for me. I miss the randomness of getting stuff from the charity shop. The only thing I find today is a CD single of 'Nancy Boy' by Placebo. I take it to the counter but then something catches my eye on the £1 rail. A black shirt – a woman's blouse, in black stretchy lace.

Mavis nips into the stockroom for a second. I take the shirt off the rail and hold it against my chest. It looks like it might fit. This has to be done. I suddenly crack up laughing. I must look mental but I don't care. I imagine the school concert, with me wearing the black lacy shirt, showing the whole school that I'm Jason Knight, guitarist – not a little kid anymore. The choice of the CD is perfect. I put them both on the counter.

Mavis looks puzzled. I'm not surprised. Teenage boys in Wirksworth don't usually buy women's clothes.

'Is this a present for your mum, dear? I haven't seen her for a while.'

'She's been quite busy.' I hand over the money.

'You've grown such a lot.'

'Er…thanks.' I stuff the CD and the blouse into my bag. I don't want to show it to Ben yet. 'See you,' I say to Mavis, and I leave the shop. It's really chucking it down now, and Ben's already got his bike helmet on.

'Anything good?'

'Just a Placebo single.' I fumble with my cycle helmet, my fingers already numb from the freezing wind. I zip up my new black waterproof and put on my gloves.

'Pikey!' a familiar voice shouts. I look over the road and see a figure huddled against the wall by the bus stop. Bradley Smeed. He's on his own, looking a bit miserable without his mates. I get on my bike.

'Tosser!' I shout at Bradley as I pedal away. I'm not even sure he heard me, because the wind is almost knocking us sideways. We have to pedal furiously to stay on our bikes tonight but I can't help feeling a bit sorry for Bradley standing there in the rain. No, that's stupid. I hope he gets soaking wet because the bus breaks down before it gets to Wirksworth and then a tractor comes past and dumps a load of manure on him. I spend the rest of the bike ride thinking of terrible things that could happen to Bradley Smeed while he's waiting at the bus stop. I stop myself before I imagine things that are too terrible. I'd feel guilty if he was murdered or something.

I bump my bike up the garden steps. I'm almost out of breath; the wind was tearing the air away before I had chance to breathe it. Ben follows me. His dad is still picking him up from our house on his way home from work. It's usually a good chance to practise – and yeah, I know, do our homework.

'I've got my first lesson with Sam tonight,' Ben says.

'Watch out for his mother-in-law.'

242

'I can't believe we've got our first proper gig. We've got to change the band name though.'

'Don't ask Sam for advice. His band was called Trampoline Nightmares.'

Ben laughs.

'That's pretty bad. Maybe we should ask your mum.'

I put my bike in the shed. Ben leaves his in the front porch as usual. I open the back door. Mum rushes out, hugging me tightly, even though my waterproof has a river of water running down it.

'Pete called! You sent him that message and he called me!'

'That's brilliant.' I take my waterproof off and hang it on the back of the door. The AGA's hot and the kitchen smells like baking. Ben comes inside.

'What's brilliant?' he asks, staring into the living room at all the paintings piled up against every surface.

'Pete. The drummer in Mission Control. I messaged him on Facebook yesterday in my lesson with Sam.'

'I made an apple cake,' Mum says. 'I thought we should celebrate. You too, Ben.' Her eyes are too shiny. She's in one of those moods where she's a bit over the top. Who can blame her, today?

'So what did you talk about?'

'He's a music teacher now. He's still in Coventry. He wants to come and see us this weekend.'

I can't help grinning. I've managed to reunite half of Mission Control in one day. I can't wait to meet Pete.

'Why didn't you tell me? About the Facebook thing?'

'I thought you might freak out. We could try to find Ash on Facebook too. He was into computers.'

Mum takes the cake out of the AGA and upturns the tin. The cake steams on the cooling rack, making my stomach growl.

'He'll write back. I know he will.'

'You can't rely on snail-mail,' I tell her.

Mum goes back into the living room and starts moving Elsa's junk and her paintings so we can at least sit down.

'You're meeting Pete?' Ben asks. 'Excellent!'

'Can I use your laptop to search for Ash? I mean, it worked for Pete. I've nearly got the whole band back together.'

'You only hang out with me because I've got stuff you want to borrow,' he says. He stares at me accusingly. I don't know what I've done to piss him off. The worst thing is, it's true. I've always taken it for granted that I can use Ben's computer and eat food at his house. I've always been the poor little boy that Ben's family feels sorry for.

Knowing about Mission Control has changed all that. The only reason why I want to find Ash and Pete is so Mum can be happy, like she was when she was in the band, before Daz died. She needs to talk to Marilyn Richards too. Then more people will want to buy her paintings and we won't have to worry about money all the time. She might even play her bass again.

I cut a slice of the cake and I give it to Ben as a peace offering. He's still glaring at me but he takes it anyway and starts stuffing his face with it, letting crumbs drop on the kitchen floor. I put the kettle on the hotplate to boil.

'We'll change the band name if you like – any better ideas?'

Ben shrugs. He can't talk – his mouth is full of cake.

Kaz

I'm late for the site meeting at the garage. The rain cleared this morning. It's windy and black clouds are still visible on the horizon. After Jason left for school, I put my wellies on and inspected the garden; got carried away with pruning the forsythia, lost in thoughts about seeing Pete again. I wasn't even wearing my watch.

I hurtle down Cromford Hill in my gardening clothes, already twenty minutes late. A quarry lorry crawls up the hill as I ride blindly around the corner. Luckily, the brakes work perfectly on this bike. Jason made me have it serviced.

Something about riding a boys' mountain bike makes me cycle like an idiot. I make myself slow down, imagining myself as an old lady on a heavy iron bicycle.

Barbara's right, in a way. I'd rather be cleaning someone's kitchen than going to this meeting. When I reach the old garage, the yard is surrounded by temporary metal fencing – the sort of stuff you always get on building sites. I haven't been here since Barbara's bid was accepted. A buttercup yellow skip stands next to the main doors. I get off my bike and wheel it past the skip. The calendar with the permed topless model lies on top of a broken desk, her features deformed by the paper which has crinkled in the rain.

Barbara's four-wheel-drive and a shiny BMW are parked, side-by-side, in the yard. I chain my bike to the fence. I unbuckle my helmet and sling it around the handlebars.

The main gates of the garage are open and I can see people inside. A short figure in a hard hat and a high visibility jacket walks out stiffly towards me. I realise it's Barbara. I'm sure nothing is going to fall on her head in the garage, apart from pigeon shit. I look at her feet and realise she's wearing brand-new steel-cap safety boots.

'Site regulations, Keziah. You're already wearing boots but I've got a hard hat for you.'

'I was already wearing a hard hat too.' I point at my cycle helmet.

There's a yellow hat and jacket waiting for me on the back seat of the car. I put them on, feeling comically dwarfed. Barbara looks just as ridiculous. She stares at me and laughs, realising what she must look like.

'This isn't doing my hairstyle any good. And these boots are ridiculous.'

'It's pointless. We're the only people here.'

'We have to prove we're doing everything properly. Dominic's the site manager.'

'Who?'

'The architect.' Barbara sighs, as if I'm a child.

Inside the garage, a tall man makes notes on a paperback sized electronic device. He stares at the metal roof joists as if he's envisaging what could be there in the future. I snatch a glimpse of a diagram on the computer screen. The garage has been swept and cleaned. Rat poison has been put down in the corners of the space. Light floods in through the open doors.

The architect turns towards us, and pockets his computer. He stares at me uncertainly, and then his features stretch into a wide grin.

'Kaz!' He stretches out his hand for me to shake. 'I mean Keziah. It's an honour to meet you. 'I'm Dominic Smeed.'

I stand back, staring at the masculine, yet nicely manicured hand; a squarish face, with warm brown eyes. His clothes look expensive under his bright yellow jacket – a dark green cashmere sweater; a checked shirt made of thick, luxurious material.

'There's a kid at my son's school called Bradley Smeed.'

Dominic Smeed laughs, thrown off his stride.

'He's my step-son.'

I fold my arms and press my lips together.

'He's been making my son's life a misery for nearly ten years.'

Dominic Smeed stares at his outstretched hand, then lets it hang by his side. He smiles again, but this time I can see panic in his eyes.

'Barbara told me about you. I remember Mission Control – you were a great band. You've been here all along, living in Bolehill?'

I stare at him, the obvious wealth in his clothes and his car. Architects don't come cheap. He's obviously worked hard; made himself a success, like Barbara. I feel pathetic, standing here in my old jeans and my jacket falling apart at the seams.

I stand as tall as I can, my full five foot two inches; my shoulders back. This stupid hard hat perched on top of my head adds some extra height.

'You have no idea. I bet you don't even know your stepson and his idiot friends covered my son in egg and flour on Boxing Day, in the middle of Matlock Bath.'

'What?'

'I got the truth out of Jason in the end. He'd been keeping it to himself. He didn't want to worry me.' I take the hard hat off and throw it on the floor. 'Because Bradley has been bullying Jason since the start of primary school – just because I can't afford to buy him the right kind of trainers.'

'I'm sorry, Kaz – Keziah. If I'd known about it…'

'You can talk about this later, Keziah,' There's a desperate look on Barbara's face. 'We need to show you the gallery plans now.'

I take the hi-vis jacket off and I run out into the yard.

I fumble with my bike chain. Dominic Smeed catches up with me.

'I didn't know Bradley was bullying your son. I feel terrible. I would have stopped it,' he sighs.

I leave the bike lock and look at him, my back pressed into the metal fence.

'Are you just saying that because Jason is my son? Because I used to be someone?'

Dominic Smeed shakes his head.

'His behaviour's always been bad. He's not like that all the time, but…' He means it. He really is sorry.

I laugh. I can't help it. Dominic Smeed is honest about Bradley, at least. He was pretty quick to deny Bradley Smeed was actually his son. I wonder what the story is, what happened to his real father.

'You look just the same as ever,' Dominic Smeed says. 'Barbara's been showing me your paintings. You deserve a showcase.'

'I thought Elsa Day was the main attraction.' I'm not impressed by the obvious flattery.

'We were about to show you the plans – before you exploded. Then you'll understand,' Barbara says.

'Okay, then. Go on.' I walk back to the old garage, but I refuse to put the bright yellow outfit on again. I look at the roof of the cavernous space. The hole in the corrugated roof has already been patched, making the pigeons homeless.

Dominic produces his computer and presses a button to awaken it. He shows me an architect's impression of a white gallery space under a roof with huge skylights. Elsa's delicate ceramics are displayed on glass shelves, glowing like jewels. The larger pieces of sculpture stand on pedestals, and there's space for Elsa's paintings.

The main gallery space is downstairs with paintings on white walls. There's a glass-roofed café on the side of the building, instead of the lean-to office.

I look around the dingy garage. I can almost imagine it transformed into Barbara's dream, but it's going to take a long time.

'You're going to put a whole floor in? It looks great, but it's going to cost so much.'

'I knew you'd like it.' Barbara smiles. 'The upper floor is for Elsa's work. A permanent gallery. The main space is for contemporary artists – you'll have the first exhibition.'

'A whole new roof?' I'm speaking from the perspective of someone who's had to think twice before buying a tin of beans.

'That's my job,' Dominic Smeed says. 'Barbara wants to flood the building with light.'

'How are you going to clean the windows on the roof?'

Barbara laughs. 'Trust you to think of something down to earth. She really does have a practical way of thinking about things, Dominic.'

'Self-cleaning glass. If the pigeons are a problem, we'll use rope access cleaning,' Dominic Smeed explains. 'Rock climbers who like dangling off cliffs so much, they formed their own companies to dangle off roofs.'

'So what do you want me to do? Apart from loan you Barbara's artwork and keep painting pictures?' I ask.

'The sculpture garden, remember? I'm giving you a free rein to make the sculptures; plant what you want. I want it to have the same feel as your garden – Elsa's garden, but on a larger scale – and I need you to help me find the best contemporary artists. People who need more exposure.'

'You're going to pay me?'

'Don't be silly, of course I am,' Barbara says. 'You've got an edge. I'm tired of designing matching kitchenware. It's become a monster I can't control. I need you. You can help me attract the right people.'

'My mum's got your oven gloves. Thousands of people must have them.' I can't say I'm sorry for Barbara. She must be a millionaire. But she's become successful in a way she didn't want. She's brave, investing so much money in something different.

'I'll start working on the garden ideas.'

I've already got plans to transform that old Nissan Micra into something really special, filled with earth and plants. I wander outside, leaving them to their plans. I get my sketchbook out of the bike's saddle bag, and start making a plan of the yard. There needs to be space to park, but the garden should be full of colour and life. I wonder about the thickness of the cracked, oil-stained concrete. We'd need to hire a JCB to drill through it and break it up.

I want to hate Dominic Smeed. I want the father (or step-father) of Jason's bully to be a horrible man. Even though I was pretty harsh about Bradley, he was friendly and calm. Maybe I should give him a chance.

Jason

Mum waits at the top of the garden steps, watching the purple campervan climb up the hill, weaving between the parked cars. It pulls up outside the house. The man behind the steering wheel has a thatch of orange hair. As he gets out of the van, Mum flies down the steps, but I hang back, behind the shrubbery, suddenly shy.

Pete is even bigger and taller than I expected, wearing an Iron Maiden t-shirt under a black and white lumberjack shirt. A lady, Pete's wife, fusses over two small children. Pete hugs Mum and she almost disappears. The top of her head only comes up to his chest, and his arms wrap around her like anacondas.

Pete's rolled-up shirt sleeve reveals elaborate tattooed scales. I'll have to ask him to show me the whole tattoo. I wonder if it covers his whole arm. It looks like a Chinese dragon. His face is lit up with joy and relief.

They haven't seen each other for fifteen years. In that time, Mum could have become massively fat, or lost all her teeth. She's made a special effort today. Mum asked me to cut her hair. Usually, she just gets me to trim it at shoulder length so she can tie it back. I cut it into a bob with a straight fringe. She seems to like it, anyway. Her fringe hides the small scar on her forehead from the bike accident.

Even though she was busy all week, throwing herself into the designs for Barbara Fleming's sculpture garden, she cycled to Superdrug in Matlock to buy animal friendly black hair dye. She wanted to cover up her grey hairs – not that there were many. She stained the bath black too. She says it was worth it. She bought a short black dress from a charity shop on the same shopping trip, and she's even wearing eyeliner.

'Have you been drinking formaldehyde or something? You haven't changed at all.'

Mum laughs. She's trying to hide how nervous she is.

'This is my wife, Emma.' Pete's wife is big too and Mum has to crane her neck to look at her properly. Emma's skin is the colour of milky coffee, and she wears a brightly patterned scarf around her head. She looks kind, holding onto the hands of the chubby children so they don't run into the road. Not that there's any traffic right now.

It's weird how Mum looks almost like a child herself, small and delicate. In contrast, Pete and Emma's children are sturdy and robust. Mum gives Emma a hug and bends down to greet the children, smiling.

'This is Nicko," Emma says. 'He's four.' He's wearing a jumper with a hand-knitted picture of Animal from the Muppets. 'And this is Karen.'

'You named your daughter after me?' Mum gasps. The toddler in the pink dress and the woolly mauve cardigan stares back at her with gobstopper-round eyes, wild light-brown hair and a raft of freckles across her nose. She's about two years old.

'Well – you and Karen Carpenter,' Pete says. 'The only really famous female drummer. I'm hoping she'll change that. I won't mind if she turns out to be a bass player.'

'And this is…' Mum says. I step out from behind the cotoneaster bush. I feel stupid and awkward.

'Fuck me!' Pete says, his eyes wide. Emma frowns at him and kicks him hard on the shin, but he doesn't seem to notice any pain at all.

'I'm Jason.' I know what he's thinking, but now I know what Daz looked like and how much he meant to Pete. I walk to the bottom of the steps and Pete hugs me. I was right about Pete having anaconda arms – it feels like I'm being crushed by a giant snake.

'I hear you're getting pretty good at playing the guitar,' Pete says.

'I've only been playing since September but I'm in a band with my friend Ben. We've got our first gig next month at the school concert.'

'What does Ben play?'

'He's the main singer. He plays acoustic guitar. We've got our friend Josh on drums. He's just learning.'

'Sounds interesting. You've got to start somewhere. At least at a school concert you should have a guaranteed audience.'

'We've been busking already. In Matlock Bath, before Christmas. We made about seventy pounds each.'

'That's pretty good.'

'There are loads of tourists. My guitar teacher – Sam – he always gave us money. He wasn't my guitar teacher then, of course.'

Pete grins.

'You found me through him.'

'He's a massive Mission Control fan. You have to meet him.'

'You must get your confidence from Kaz,' Pete says. 'Daz never believed in himself.'

'I've listened to the albums lots of times now. I know them by heart, almost. And I'm working out Daz's guitar parts. Can I show you?'

Pete scoops up the little girl and swings her, giggling, onto his shoulders.

Mum and Emma walk up the steps slowly. The little boy stomps up slowly, one-by-one, in his bright blue wellies.

With one hand, Pete points his keyring blipper at the van and locks it. The back window is tinted and it says "Big Pete's Drum School", with his mobile number and a website in curly silver writing and cartoons of people drumming. The van's quite new. Pete must be doing okay as a teacher.

'Do you miss being in a band?' I ask.

'I don't miss all the hanging around. It makes people fall out with each other.' Pete smiles at me, as we follow the others up the steps. 'But if you want to be a musician, you can't beat the feeling of being on stage in front of an audience – of everything coming together at the same time.'

In the kitchen, Mum's already got the kettle on the AGA. She's offering Emma a ginger biscuit from a batch she made earlier. I wonder if Mum made them as a kind of joke about Pete's hair, but Emma doesn't say anything.

The little girl wanders towards the AGA and Emma snatches her away, just before she puts her hand on the hot metal. I take the kids into the living room. Immediately, I know it was a mistake. Little Karen makes a bee-line for the cat, dozing on the settee. Patti wakes up just in time, before she has her tail grabbed by a sticky hand. The cat leaps out of the way and bolts out of the door. Karen starts to wail.

'You've got to be gentle with pussy cats,' I say, trying to sound gentle, and hoping it doesn't come out as too much of a growl. Karen immediately wobbles towards the low table where Mum puts her painting stuff. She grasps a tube of paint and tries to take the lid off. I wrestle it away from her. Her face crumples again, but I stick my tongue out to distract her. She seems to like that.

Nicko is standing over the cardboard box where Mum has left Elsa's ceramics loosely wrapped, their bright colours peeking from the newspaper like toys. He pulls off the newspaper and grabs a bright orange model of a crab with its claws in the air.

'What does this do?' Nicko sticks one of his fingers into the little firing hole in the bottom and waves his hand around. I've got a sudden memory of being around Nicko's age, pushing something into one of those holes, with Elsa watching me, smiling.

'It doesn't do anything.' I grab him before he can run around with it. 'Careful. It might break.' Mum and Aunt Elsa packed these things away in case I smashed them. So why has she left everything lying around? I know she's been busy this week, but has she forgotten what young kids are like?

I gently prise the crab out of Nicko's hand and put it back in the box. Mum told me how much Elsa's surrealist ceramics might be worth and, as she's reminded me, they don't actually belong to us.

'I'll find something better for you to do,' I tell him.

There's a twanging crash from the other end of the room. My guitar! I left it leaning against the sofa, ready to show off to Pete. My fault for leaving it there. The guitar falls onto the rug. I pick it up. There seems to be no harm done. I quickly put it in the cupboard under the stairs.

By the time I get back to little Karen, she's got hold of one of Mum's pencils, and is scribbling in a sketch book. There are already some drawings on the page. I hope it's not anything important.

Mum's still talking to Emma and Pete in the kitchen. I haven't heard the kettle whistle yet.

'Pete's mum loves knitting. It really keeps her busy and the kids are never short of anything to wear,' Emma says.

'I never really got beyond scarves. And the wool was more expensive than jumpers in charity shops.'

I've brought them together for the first time in fifteen years and all they can talk about is knitting? I need to make sure Mum and Pete talk properly, alone.

What am I going to do now? I can't leave Nicko and

Karen in here trashing the living room. I can't shout for help. I'd sound pathetic. I grab both children by the hand.

'Let's go and play in the garden,' I say, as cheerfully as possible. I feel like my head's going to explode. No wonder Mum was stressed out when I was little. I've got an idea for entertaining them without wrecking anything. The firewood cart. I can pull them around the lawn. They'll love it. Just like I did.

Nicko and Karen giggle as we run through the kitchen. Mum and Emma look at us approvingly, and Pete laughs.

'This is the least child-friendly house ever!' I shout, as I open the back door.

'You're doing a grand job!' Pete says. 'Come and babysit for us anytime.'

Kaz

'A pretty decent meal for rabbit food.' Pete winks at me, as a massive plate of cheesy homity pie and pasta salad is put in front of him.

'Pete!' Emma digs him in the ribs. 'Don't listen to him. He's actually been vegetarian for years. And that's not rabbit food. It's carb-tastic.'

'Jason's been brought up vegetarian,' I say.

'I'm veggie at home,' Jason mumbles, through a mouthful of his own pie. 'Not the rest of the time.'

'You're free to make your own mind up.' I can't help feeling rejected. I never managed to convince Daz to turn vegetarian. I felt like a hypocrite, not even being able to convince the man I loved.

'This place is great.' Emma looks around at the recipe books lining the café walls. 'You could get lost for days among all these books.' She tucks napkins firmly into Nicko and Karen's t-shirts as their veggie sausage sandwiches are delivered.

The children are already muddy from their adventures in the garden. Emma had to pick wet leaves out of their hair.

Jason sponged his skinny jeans clean in the kitchen before we set off for the café in Cromford Books in Pete's camper van.

He didn't seem to mind getting mucky. It looked like he was enjoying looking after Pete's children. It gave him an excuse to be silly for a while. There are wheel marks and footprints all over the lawn, but it'll grow back in spring.

'I used to think it was magic – going through the secret door from the bookshop into the café,' Jason says.

Pete's kids happily chomp into their food, their faces and hands slathered in tomato ketchup.

My vegan calzone and salad arrives. I can't remember when I last ate a meal in here. We've been far too skint for years. The calzone is good.

'These two make so much mess,' Emma laughs. 'The washing machine's constantly on the go.'

'Jason was constantly covered in mud and paint.'

Jason blushes.

'You encouraged me.'

Sometimes I wish he could be a little boy again. He's nowhere near as tall as Pete yet, but his voice turns into a growl at the end of his sentences. He's all knees and elbows.

'Have you got any tips for our drummer?' Jason finishes off his pie. 'He can't stay in time.' He seems relaxed with Pete, happy to be himself.

'Don't be too hard on him. Some of the best songs speed up or slow down. He'll get it eventually. Just have fun.'

'He needs lessons, really. He's just making it up as he goes along,' Jason grumbles.

Pete laughs.

'That's what I did! Hanging round, pestering people who worked in music shops.' Pete smiles. 'Remember all that time we used to spend in Express Music, Kaz?'

I can't help smiling back. Today has been a whirlwind of activity so far. No time to talk to each other.

'We couldn't afford anything apart from a few plectrums. Daz used to spend hours there on Saturdays, trying out guitars and effects pedals. The guys in there didn't seem to mind.'

'They were thinking of offering him a job, remember?'

'Ash convinced Daz the studio could be successful and the band started taking off.'

'They were nice, those guys in the music shop. We must have been really annoying.'

Nicko finishes his sausage sandwich. Emma is poised, ready to clean his sticky fingers and face with wet-wipes produced from the depths of her bag. He tugs on Jason's sleeve.

'Take us to the magic book room,' he demands.

The children's book room is opposite the café, with pages from books stuck to the wall and silver-painted branches suspended from the ceiling. Jason spent hours in there when he was younger. Nowadays, he usually disappears to the music book department on the top floor.

'Me too!' Karen shouts, waving the crust of her sandwich around. 'Want *The Gruffalo*.'

'She's obsessed by *The Gruffalo*,' Emma laughs. 'We know it by heart – and the sequel.'

'Nicko likes Thomas the Tank Engine,' Pete says. 'I try to do Ringo Starr's voice when I read the books to him.'

'Daddy's funny,' Nicko says.

'He's not very good at doing the accent,' Emma explains. 'Nicko doesn't know any better.'

'Jason's favourite was *Mog the Forgetful Cat*,' Mum says.

Jason flicks his fringe out of his eyes.

'I loved all the stories,' he says. 'Still do. Mog rocked. I used to wish she was a real cat. Then our cat Patti turned up at the back door as a stray. I started writing stories about her and drawing pictures.' I can't believe Jason's freely admitting to his Patti stories in front of Pete. Usually, he'd be too embarrassed, even though when he was eight, Jason was so proud of his stories.

'Jason's got a brilliant imagination,' I say.

'He takes after you – and Daz, of course.'

Jason glances at me meaningfully.

'Tell you what,' Jason says to Nicko and Karen. 'I'll read a Mog story to you. You'll like it.' Karen grins, her mouth still full of chewed-up bread. 'Mog is a cat and she's a bit rubbish and can't remember anything.'

'Yeah!' Nicko shouts, grabbing hold of Jason's hand. The kids both pull on Jason's arms. Jason seems to be coping with them remarkably well.

'I'll keep an eye on them,' Emma says. 'They know they need to be careful with books, but they're a bit giddy today. I don't want to have to pay for half the shop.'

'You two can stay here and talk about Mission Control.' Jason gives me a stern look.

Pete's plate is scraped clean. He takes it back to the counter. He seems so at ease with himself.

'Do you want pudding?' he asks.

I shake my head. Pete orders chocolate cake and cream. He comes back to the table with a generous slice. The fork looks tiny in Pete's hand.

'How are you? Really?' he says. 'You look good.'

'I'm busy now – with the gallery – and there's always something to do in the garden. Being a mum used to take up a lot of time, but now it feels like Jason's looking after me.'

'It gave me a shock at first, seeing Jason. But Daz would never volunteer to read to a couple of toddlers.'

'He's got an ulterior motive.'

'Only forcing us to talk.' Pete sighs. 'Daz was out for himself most of the time.'

'You know what he'd been through!'

Pete stares at me, stopping me short, his eyes as blue as the china jug on the table. After all, Pete had been Daz's best friend since primary school. He knew Daz better than anyone.

'He was a selfish git. Even down to dying and leaving us to deal with everything.'

Pete watches me keenly for a reaction.

'You've done a good job with Jason,' he says.

'Have I?'

'He seems pretty well balanced, considering he didn't know anything about his family two weeks ago.'

'I was trying to protect him.'

'Jesus, Kaz! What from? You can see how proud he is of Mission Control. He needed to know about Daz – you needn't have told him the bad stuff at first.'

'I know. He was bound to find out. I couldn't stop him from getting into music and playing the guitar. It was only a matter of time before he found a picture of me.'

'It had to be that poster, didn't it?' Pete laughs. 'Poor Jason. What a shock.'

I remember Pete in the hospital, the hours we spent around Daz's hospital bed, listening to the beep of the monitor, Pete compulsively drumming his fingers on the plastic chair.

'I just wanted Jason to be normal.'

'And you thought bringing him up without any of your family or friends would help with that?'

'I had Elsa.'

'How do you think I felt when you disappeared – and your parents? What if when you left, it pushed Ash over the edge?'

'He hasn't written back yet.'

'Give it a few weeks.'

'What about the internet? That's how Jason found you.' I stare at him fiercely. 'I'm not talking to Marilyn Richards until we've found him.'

'I'll try, Kaz. I'll put out a few feelers. We'll find him. It's not like he's deliberately gone missing –' Pete raises his eyebrows. He stares at me, as if he can't believe I'm real. I take a deep breath.

'I've got to tell you something. I know Daz got paranoid about it, but I never slept with Ash.' Saying it make my heart hammer in my chest; brings me back to those destructive arguments in the Watermill Studio.

'I told Daz it was all in his head. He was so angry – with his dad – with himself. It was stupid, but Daz always blamed himself for his mum leaving. He was only nine years old. It was horrible for him.'

'I made it worse.' I'm unable to hold it in any longer. My eyes fill with tears.

Pete holds my hands. His fingers are like massive freckled sausages, but he's gentle. I feel safe with him. I don't care that we're in a café, with people trying not to stare at us. I allow myself to cry. Pete hands me a serviette and I blow my nose; rub my eyes. I'd forgotten I was wearing make-up and the eyeliner smudges off on the tissue. My eyes must be smudged with black rings like they were half a lifetime ago, waking up with a hangover in the back of a van.

'You were so dedicated to him, it was scary. Without you pushing Daz, he would have been too scared to get up on stage. Ash always fancied you, you know?'

'Did you ever see Ash again? After the fire?'

'I went to see him in hospital, after his uncle brought him back from Goa. It was like a switch had flicked. He wasn't making sense any more. I think he got better – partly, anyway.'

'He sounded okay in that letter.'

'We'll have to see, won't we? Let's give it until half term.'

'I'll write to him again. Let him know how important it is. For all of us.'

'Then we can tell Marilyn Richards what really happened,' Pete says.

Chapter 20
The School Dinner Explosion

Jason

There's a massive queue in the canteen. Josh and Ben are already waiting for me in the music room. They have packed lunches but I'm still on the stupid free school dinners list. It saves Mum money but we've got to rehearse for the concert and I'm just wasting my time here.

A Year Seven kid in front of me is trying to hide his biscuit in a bowl of custard. He's useless at it. I can still see the biscuit rising to the surface. Ben's an expert. It saves 40p every time.

The kid gets to the front of the queue. Mrs Mellors blinks, her eyelids caked in bright blue eye-shadow. She spots the biscuit and charges him for it. His shoulders slump a bit, but he pays for it, as if he was never pretending to hide it in the first place. I feel sorry for him, even though he's not on free school dinners.

Mrs Mellors smiles at me and crosses my name off the list. The ham and pickle sandwich looks squashed, under the layers of cling-film, and school sandwiches are always made with slightly stale bread. Not that I care, as long as I can eat my lunch fast and get on with playing. Mum would have a fit. She doesn't like me eating crap.

I put the sandwich, cherry Bakewell slice, bacon Frazzles and a bright blue raspberry flavour drink in my bag and try to dodge past all the kids trying not to spill stuff from their trays, looking for places to sit.

The kid with the biscuit heads for a gap between the tables where Bradley Smeed and his mates are sitting. My senses are ultra-sensitive about Bradley Smeed, developed over years of avoiding him and hiding. I see the look in Bradley's eyes.

Bradley sticks his foot into the gap, just as the kid is passing, concentrating on his tray. The fall happens in slow motion. There's a loud crash, the sound of smashing crockery, and a split second of silence until people start talking again. The kid sprawls on the floor. Bradley's table erupts into nasty laughter. I know I should stay out of it and go straight to the music room but no one else is doing anything to help.

I go over to the kid. He's trying to get up. Custard is splashed up the front of his coat and the biscuit is squashed onto it. He looks like he's about to cry. Custard and baked beans have splashed over the floor like a Jackson Pollock painting. I crouch down to help the kid. His dinner is totally ruined. There's no point in trying to pick anything up but I put the pieces of the broken plate back on the tray, getting a gross mixture of bean juice and custard on my hands. Now I'm going to be later than ever. The kid stares at me blankly.

'Are you trying to lick food off the floor now, Kenny?'

I look straight at Bradley Smeed. He gives me a smarmy, patronising smile. I stand up and bang the kid's tray down on his table with a crash.

'This jacket cost two hundred quid, Kenny!' Bradley inspects a tiny custard splash on his sleeve. 'I bet your whole house isn't worth that much.'

'Haven't you got anything better to do? Is that going to be your job when you leave school, tripping people up?' I say, hardly believing I'm daring to do this. But I'm not scared any more. 'Pathetic.'

I turn away from him slowly. It's not like he can do anything to me. Quite a few people are watching, and a dinner lady has finally come to clear up the mess. The little kid is open-mouthed. I open my bag and I hand him my Bakewell slice, even though it was the part of my lunch I was most looking forward to.

'Thanks!' he says.

'Just watch where you're putting your feet next time,' I tell him.

I wash my hands in the toilets and run to the music room. There's only half an hour of lunchtime left. Josh and Ben are eating. Josh's sandwiches are balanced on the snare drum. My mouth waters slightly at the sight of them. Thick, fresh bread and chunky slices of cheese. I've got no time to eat now.

'What happened to you?' Ben asks.

'Queuing for free flipping food hand-outs. I hope Mum makes a success out of this gallery, so –'

Ben gives me a cold stare.

'You'll soon be eating caviar sandwiches and going to private school.'

'What's that supposed to mean?' I get my guitar out of its case and plug it into the amp. What's got into Ben recently?

I turn up the amp and start playing the intro to Ben's song. We won't get anywhere if we stand around arguing. Josh comes in with the drums, slightly too late because he's had to take his sandwiches off the snare.

He's not quite got the hang of playing in time with my guitar playing, or is it me who hasn't got the hang of playing in time with Josh? I've practiced with loads of CDs. I'm still trying to work out all of the Mission Control songs. I'm nowhere near as good as my dad but I can keep time with Pete's drumming. Josh seems to speed up and slow down all the time. We'll get there eventually, I'm sure. I stop playing.

'Let's start again. Are you ready, Ben? Is the microphone set up?'

'Yeah. I did it while we were waiting for you,' Ben grumbles. It's his song. He should be more excited about it.

'Good work, Josh. Just come in straight after the second bar. Make it sound really strong.'

'Cool. I was just a bit surprised when you started playing.' Josh grabs another bite of his sandwich. My stomach rumbles.

'Stop bossing us around, Jason,' Ben says.

'It's okay,' Josh says. 'I don't mind you telling me what to do. I need you to tell me.'

'Yeah, well. Let's give it another go.' Ben smiles, but it's like he's forcing himself.

I play the intro again. Josh comes in, more or less on time and then Ben starts singing, strumming his acoustic guitar. It's going to sound good. We just need to practice and play more. Every lunchtime if we need to. Ben had better just grow up.

Kaz

There's a small portacabin at the old garage now, a site office, where the builders can make stewed tea and eat their sandwiches in the warmth of the electric fan heater. In Mission Control, we used cabins like this as our dressing room at festivals, if we were lucky.

The windows are steamed up and the chipboard walls are hung with safety notices. Barbara looks out of place here, dressed smartly, with her fluorescent site jacket folded neatly by her side. A huge crane lorry blocks the forecourt, delivering the steel girders for the mezzanine floor. There are men with hard-hats shouting and hammering. Barbara's grand dreams seem real now.

I take a sip of cold tea and open my sketchbook. I've never done anything like this before and I feel horribly nervous. Barbara peers at my sketches though her oversized glasses, squinting at the labels I've written to show what plants I want. Time seems to pass very slowly as she turns the pages. I've read enough gardening books to know how to lay out a plan, and the shapes for trees, bushes and flowerbeds are washed in watercolours. Ideas for the sculptures are sketched out, along with imagined views of the gardens. I enjoyed working on it, but reality overwhelms me. What if Barbara thinks it's rubbish? I bite at the skin around my thumbnail.

'You see?' Barbara says. She trains her penetrating blue eyes on me.

I feel like a wood mouse, cornered by Patti in the kitchen.

'This garden is going to be the making of you, Keziah.'

'I did my best.'

'You're too modest. People will come for miles to see

this gallery and the gardens. Let's go outside – you can talk me through everything in situ.'

I put on my yellow waterproof, glad of its powers to repel the biting winter wind. Thin sunlight glances through the patchy clouds, but it doesn't bring any warmth.

We walk up the slope from the garage, to the part of the yard that hasn't been used in years, apart from as a dumping ground. Underfoot, there are ankle-turning stones and chunks of brick.

The top yard is a tangle of brambles and rough grass, faded and dried, twined around the rusty carcasses of cars and old machinery. Over the past week, I've investigated it all, designed sculptures using the scrap metal. Barbara was busy with her plans for the building. I was relieved she let me get on with it, in my own way.

'How many cars will be able to park here anyway?' Barbara asks.

'At least forty.' I have to hand it to Barbara. She's always got one eye on the business side of things.

I guide Barbara through the undergrowth and debris to the pond, overhung by a large willow tree. The pond is half-full of old tyres and jagged rusty objects but it could be beautiful. Barbara blinks in surprise. I know more about this place than she does. I don't think she's ever seen the pond before.

I've been here every day. A heron often perches on a half-submerged car door, although I haven't seen any fish. I sat on an old lorry tyre and sketched him for a new painting.

Barbara looks at my plans for the pond, for the rill I've designed to make the water run down towards the gallery, using an Archimedes Screw to pump the water back up. That's going to take some figuring out. Perhaps it's a bit overambitious, but I got carried away.

'The pond needs dredging. All this rubbish needs removing,' Barbara says.

'When do you want me to start?'

'As soon as possible. The plants will need time to grow.'

Barbara compares my plans to the derelict reality.

'Think of the people who'll come here.' She smiles, proudly.

'Won't Cromford Books be angry with us for taking away their business?'

'We'll add to it, Keziah. People will park here, buy some art, enjoy our café, and then have a lovely potter around the village. The sort of people who love a good bookshop.'

'What about the people who are expecting the Barbara Fleming collection?' I ask.

'They need something new. Something with an edge.'

I think of my painting of the heron. It's a work in progress. Underneath the surface of the rusty water, the heron's sharp beak spears a tiny, human-shaped creature. Its companions struggle to save it from the heron's attack. I don't know what Barbara would make of it. Would anyone buy my paintings on a tea towel?

I start laughing. Barbara stares at me, concerned.

'What's the matter?'

'I can't imagine my paintings having the same appeal. How about a teapot shaped like a skull covered in moss?'

'You could be onto something there.' Barbara scribbles in a tiny notebook.

I show Barbara the path of the stream – how I want it to run in front of the gallery, with a smaller pond, with the Archimedes screw turning as a huge piece of sculpture. Barbara looks entranced. When I was designing it, I saw the trailing water weed, vivid colours. I could almost hear Elsa's voice, telling me where to plant things, just like she did when I was working in her garden. It will take years before it looks like it's always been here, but it'll be worth it.

'I want to use native plants where possible. It needs to look as if everything just grew here naturally.'

Dominic Smeed waves from the lower yard. His other hand is clamped to his head. He must be on the phone. Barbara waves back. She rushes over to meet him, looking like a bee in her yellow fluorescent jacket and smart black trousers. I trail after her. I still feel like a traitor whenever I talk to Dominic Smeed. Jason doesn't know about him yet.

'Keziah's plans are marvellous,' Barbara says, above the noise of the contractors moving the girders. He puts his phone in his pocket and Barbara thrusts the sketchbook into his hands. He turns the pages, nodding with approval.

'I'll get someone to help you. There's a contractor I've used for hard landscaping. I think you'll like him.'

'I'd rather do it myself, to make sure it looks right.' I say, surprised by my own assertiveness. I know I'm being stubborn, but if this is really a tribute to Elsa, I don't want it coming out all wrong, with any old bits of metal welded together and the wrong plants in the wrong places.

Dominic Smeed pushes his hard-hat off his forehead and scratches his head. His smile is warm, genuine.

'You'll need someone who drives a mini-digger. Someone who can break up all this old concrete.'

'I suppose so.' I shrug.

'You'll be calling the shots.'

'Can I have a welding torch?' I ask, like a wildly optimistic kid at Christmas.

'You're going to build the sculptures yourself?' His eyes widen.

'Elsa built the sculptures in her garden. And this garden's in her honour.'

Dominic Smeed grins widely.

I glare at him. I don't like his patronising attitude but he doesn't seem daunted. He turns to one of my sketches – a rhinoceros welded from old car parts. Children will be able to climb on it.

'You don't keep having to ask us for things,' Dominic Smeed says. 'You're in charge of this garden.'

'I'll give you a proper budget to work to,' Barbara says.

'I can't wait to see you in action, creating all of this stuff,' Dominic Smeed says. I allow myself to give him a small, tight smile. I've never used a welding torch in my life. This could be a disaster.

'We need to start spreading the word about what we're doing here. The significance of it; the work of Elsa day and Keziah Knight coming together here in public for the first time.'

I look at Barbara with dread – but there's nothing I can do. Jason's right. I've just got to learn to deal with publicity.

Jason

I'm doing my Geography homework, filling in a worksheet about wind farms and then drawing and labelling a turbine. I'd be interested in it if we actually went and visited a wind farm. I'm sitting on the sofa, trying to balance my homework on one of Mum's drawing boards. The cat is curled up tightly against my leg.

Mum is working hard on her garden design, her hair curtaining her face as she sits, hunched over her desk with the old lamp angled over her plans. Maybe she's working too hard, getting herself stressed over this.

I've got my eye on the fire, keeping it well stoked. Otherwise, Mum just lets it burn down to the embers. It's nice, concentrating like this. The wind is blowing down the chimney, making the fire glow. It's cosy. I put a record on the radiogram – the Cardiacs, a really weird, wobbly sounding band. Sam lent me the record; he trusted me with the vinyl. I think he wanted Mum to hear it, but she's off in another world now, thinking about the garden for the gallery.

There's a knock on the back door. Patti dashes upstairs, her fur sticking out in startled tufts.

'Are you expecting Barbara?' I ask.

'No.' Mum looks up. It can't be Barbara; she doesn't even bother knocking any more. She must think she's being friendly, but Mum always knocks before she comes into my room, doesn't she? I walk through to the kitchen and open the door.

It's Rachel, Ben's sister, shivering in a long velvet coat, her hair whipping into her face.

'What…?'

'I've got to talk to you. About Ben.'

'Come in, it's freezing.'

Rachel wipes her New Rocks on the mat. I don't know how she can drive in them. They add several centimetres to her height and the heels are made of steel. It's the only way she still manages to be taller than me.

'What's the deal with you and Ben?'

I sigh.

'I dunno.' Ben didn't come back with me after school tonight. He said he needed to get back and he just cycled off through the railway arch, like he couldn't even stand being with me.

'He says you're showing off all the time.'

'Showing off?'

'Who is it?' Mum shouts from the living room.

Rachel stares at me, as if she's noticed something new. She bounds to the door, her heels gleaming.

'It's only me,' Rachel smiles as she sticks her head around the door.

'Rachel. How lovely to see you.' Mum frowns slightly. 'Is Ben with you?'

'Have you got any books on Matisse?' Rachel asks. 'I need them for an art project.' She's staring at Mum as if she's never seen her before. She's seeing her as Kaz K for the first time.

Mum glances at her bookcase.

'I think so. Elsa met him, before the war. Said he was a miserable old git. We've got plenty of books and copies of paintings if you want them.'

Mum gets up and crouches in front of the bookcase. She pulls out a thick book about Post-Impressionism.

'There might be something in this. The wider context.' Mum sighs. 'Some of these books haven't been opened since Elsa died.'

'Really?' Rachel says.

'I'm sure you'll find what you're looking for,' Mum says. 'Do you want a cup of tea?'

'Yes, please,' Rachel says. 'It's so cold out there, and the car didn't really warm up. Two sugars, remember?'

Mum pulls a face.

'I don't know how you can stand it that sweet.'

She walks into the kitchen. I listen to Mum filling the kettle and stacking the pots from tea into the sink.

'I copied the Mission Control CDs for my mates too.' Rachel whispers. 'I love them. I can't believe I've known Kaz since I was like, six.'

'You didn't know she was famous then,' I say. Has Rachel just come round for a glimpse of my mum?

'She was always cool. I mean, she reads to you and makes things with you.'

'That's because we've always been poor. I had to go round to your house to watch TV.'

'My parents are so boring.' Rachel taps the spines on the books with her purple fingernails. 'I mean, they'd never listen to cool records like this.' She picks up the record sleeve and looks at it, longingly.

'Tell Ben nothing's changed. Not with me, anyway. He seems to think we're going to get rich and I won't want to hang out with him,' I say.

'What about this gallery thing?'

'That's nothing to do with Mission Control. She's working really hard.' I look over to Mum's desk, piled with gardening books, plans and sketches. She's even built miniature sculptures from little scraps of wood. 'She deserves it. It's not like Ben's ever had to worry about the electricity being cut off and eating nothing but sprouts for months.'

'Why did she put you through all that?' Rachel asks. 'When she could have…'

'She just wanted to be left alone. And I was fine. I still am fine.' I snap.

Rachel puts her hand on my arm. I don't know how I'm supposed to react. I just stare at it. Her nail varnish is chipped and there are marks on her fingers from a leaky biro.

'You would never show off, Jason,' Rachel says. 'Not about this, anyway.'

'Why can't Ben get it out of his head, then? I just want things to get back to normal.'

The door creaks. Rachel grabs a book at random from the shelf – a green, material-covered book with *The Death of Modernism* embossed on the spine in gold lettering. A piece of paper flutters out of it, onto the rug. There's a pencil sketch on it. Rachel picks it up as Mum comes back into the living room with the tea tray.

'Look what I found.' Rachel shows the sketch to me and Mum. The drawing shows a boy about four years old. Mum's done lots of drawings of me, but I've not seen this one. I'm wearing patched corduroy shorts, and my hair is a shiny black mop.

'You look sweet,' Rachel says. I narrow my eyes at her.

'I haven't seen this since I drew it,' Mum gasps. 'Elsa must have hidden it.' She puts the tray down on the rug. 'I never forget a drawing.' She smiles.

In the sketch, I'm reaching up for something on top of the radiogram. The table lamp shaped like a lighthouse.

'There's some writing on here too, but I can't make it out,' Rachel says. She shows me. The writing looks like mine did when I sprained my wrist falling off my bike.

'Elsa's handwriting,' Mum frowns. '*One day, Jason will reach that thing. Not yet, I hope, it's not quite time, my dear.* Her mind was wandering a bit before the end, and she liked riddles.'

I pick up my cup of tea from the tray. Mum hands a mug to Rachel.

'Have you found anything useful on Matisse?' she asks.

'Yes, thanks Ka...Keziah,' Rachel says.

'You can borrow some books if you like. I know you'll be careful with them.'

'Keziah...?' Rachel asks, in a nervous voice. 'Since I found out about Mission Control, I've wanted to ask you something.'

'What?' Mum says, biting her lip and looking away.

Rachel sips her tea and fiddles with the lace on her long black skirt.

'Can I see your bass?' she asks.

Mum laughs, relieved. I wonder what she thought Rachel was going to ask.

'It's under my bed.' She sounds almost proud that Rachel asked about it.

Rachel follows me upstairs. I switch the light on in Mum's room. Patti is curled up tightly on the patchwork quilt, her nose tucked into her tail. As we enter the room, the cat opens her eyes, glares at us, stretches her front paws, extending her claws, and then curls up again, stiffly, resenting our presence.

I pull out the flight case from under the bed and open it.

'It's beautiful! Can I try playing it?' Rachel asks. She straps the bass over her shoulder. 'It's really heavy.'

'Mum chose it. I'm surprised she didn't give herself back strain.'

'It looks cool though.' Rachel admires herself in the mirror, flicking her purple-streaked dyed black hair over her face. She fumbles with the strings but doesn't even know how to put her fingers on the frets.

'I could learn to play. You need a bass player in your band.'

'I don't think Ben would let you.' That would be a disaster.

'It's not his band though is it? More like your band, from the way he was moaning about it.'

'I wasn't bossing them about. The concert's in two weeks' time and Josh isn't playing in time yet. Anyway, if you really want to learn bass, you should form your own band.'

'Until I found out about Mission Control, I didn't even think about learning an instrument. It just seemed like something that guys do. Your mum was amazing. She still is. Do you think she would teach me?'

'You'd better ask her. I know she's been practising but she's not got much time at the moment.'

Rachel squeezes me around my waist. I know it's meant to be affectionate but it feels like she's bruising my ribs in some kind of wrestling move. She ruffles my hair. Soon she'll have to reach up to do that. Or buy taller New Rocks.

'You're like my little brother, Jason.'

'What about Ben?'

'He'd better give it a rest soon. You're supposed to do everything together. It wouldn't feel right, otherwise,' Rachel says.

'I want to do the concert with him, more than anything. I just want everything to be back to normal.'

'It's not going to be normal though, is it?' Rachel says. 'Kaz is definitely going to be famous again, one way or another. Everyone's just going to have to get used to it.'

Rachel puts Mum's bass back in the flight case and pushes it gently under the bed.

Chapter 21
The Pond

Kaz

The work on the sculpture garden-cum-carpark starts today. It actually feels like I've got a proper job at last.

In the privacy of my shipping container workshop, I change into my brand new red boiler suit, ripping open the clear plastic packet. I ordered it from a building supplies catalogue, in the smallest size they had, along with my steel toe-capped work boots and welding equipment. I bought new gardening tools too, wondering if I was going wildly overboard, but Dominic Smeed didn't bat an eyelid when he approved my order.

The boiler suit fits me well, but I have to roll up the bottom of the trouser legs quite a bit. The boots are stiff around my ankles, but I've padded them out with thick socks to stop me from getting blisters.

I push open the door of the container, letting in the crisp late winter sunlight. I couldn't stay in here with the doors shut for too long. But it's my own space, for now. There are two deckchairs and a folding table to make it more inviting, and I can make tea next door in the site cabin.

I tape my garden plans to the wall and wait, watching the builders working on the old garage. I hope this contractor knows what he's doing. We've got some catching up to do; the building work seems to be progressing so quickly.

An orange Transit van with a mini-digger trailer drives into the yard, five minutes early.

A young man gets out of the van. He's tall, broad-shouldered, in his mid-twenties at a guess. He has a dark, curly ponytail, and he's wearing a Metallica hoodie, faded to a pale grey.

'Are you Keziah Knight?'

I nod.

'I'm Jeff Middleton – the landscaper. Dominic Smeed called me.'

He holds out his hand to shake, and when my hand's in his, it feels shrunken, like the paw of a tiny animal.

'The mini-digger gave it away.'

Jeff smiles, looking directly into my eyes. His eyes are brown and wide. He reminds me of a young bull, placid at the moment, but full of explosive energy.

He breaks away from me and looks around, taking in the busy building site, and the overgrown desolation of the old yard.

'I've never worked with an artist before. Most people who hire me have more money than taste.'

He looks straight at me again.

'You've not done this sort of thing before, have you?' he asks.

'What gives you that idea?' He's right though. The welding kit is still in its box. I haven't even tried it out. I suddenly feel out of my depth.

'Brand new overalls and boots. Before I worked on my own, that's what they always said about management. Never got their hands dirty.'

'I'm going to be clearing the site with you. I'm turning the scrap metal we find into sculptures.' I show him the plans for the garden and show him some of the designs in my sketchbook.

'It's going to be an outdoor gallery?'

'And a car park. They want it to look nice, so they've got me to do the gardening and the sculptures.'

'It's more than that. I can tell,' Jeff says.

'Really?'

'The village needs something like this. This place was an eyesore. The bloke who owned this place let it get into a right mess.'

'We've got to turn it into a garden by May.'

Jeff whistles through his teeth.

'We'd better learn quick, then.'

'Come on. Take a look round for yourself.'

I lead Jeff up the slope.

'Let's start work in the top yard.'

274

'There's a lot of undergrowth to clear,' Jeff says, pulling up a dried-up ragwort stalk and kicking at the rubble underfoot.

'I suggested reclaimed cobbles for the car park.'

'That's going to cost them.' Jeff raises his eyebrows. 'It'll look good though.'

'Barbara's happy to pay for it. She reckons we might find some old ones under all this junk.'

I lead Jeff towards the pond. He stares at it and sighs, hands on hips.

'It's an old mill pond,' I explain. 'I know it takes a lot of imagination, but it's going to look great when it's been cleared and restored.'

'What a twat – mind my language –'

'I don't mind,' I say.

'Filling a pond full of old tyres. Shitting in his own back yard. Still, we can make things right now, can't we?'

Jeff's sudden anger startles me, but I'm glad of it. He seems to really care.

'You're into nature?'

He laughs.

'Grew up round here. Sort of in the blood, isn't it?'

'A heron comes here sometimes. I can imagine this pond teeming with wildlife.'

'Let's get started, then.' Jeff turns and starts ripping up armfuls of dead undergrowth.

'You don't want a cup of tea first?'

'This place could be beautiful. You're right.'

I walk back to the container unit and fetch my industrial-strength gardening gloves, secateurs and a bowsaw. By the time I return to the top yard, Jeff has already made a small pile of rusty scrap metal.

The pond needs a gentler approach. We've scared the heron away for now but, around Cromford, he has streams, a river, a canal and a huge duck pond to choose from. Why does he come back here? Some kind of ancestral memory?

Balancing on the bank of the pond, I prune back the willow tree, not too hard. I want the first visitors to see a cascade of leaves, not a brutalised stump. Then I pull out the dead remains of the Himalayan balsam. I'll need to watch that carefully to keep it under control.

I add any rubbish I find to Jeff's pile. Then I start to roll as many old tyres out of the water as I can reach from the edge. The pond is full of them. Moving things stirs up the silted water, turning it as brown and thick as gravy.

I pull out bits of metal, twisted and rusted into abstract shapes. Maybe I could weld them into some of the sculptures, once I actually teach myself to weld.

I reach out from the bank of the pond as far as I dare and tug at the old car door, but it's stuck fast in the silt. Perhaps it should stay there. It's the heron's perch. It would be a shame if things were tidied up too much.

The pond will need dredging properly. There's only about a foot of water in there over the top of a thick layer of sludge. I wonder how deep things would sink. It's probably full of hibernating creatures.

Sometimes you have to destroy to create. That was one of Elsa's sayings, her way of making sense of the world after so much destruction: Paris occupied, London bombed; her beloved Pierre crushed under tonnes of rubble as he fought to control the fires. The sculpture garden was a tribute to him, a private outpouring of grief and hope. This is my tribute to Elsa, creating new life by dredging the pond and clearing the land.

I stand up and stretch, noticing that the patch Jeff is clearing already looks bare.

A car pulls into the bottom yard. Barbara comes out of the site office and greets the man who gets out of the car. She's been planning something over the last few days, spending a lot of time on her phone. We've hardly talked. It's almost like she's avoiding me, we're both so busy.

I concentrate on cutting back brambles with stems as thick as my thumb, an impenetrable fairy thicket. Anything could be hidden inside here – but it's just more old tyres. I take hold of a stem, carelessly and spear my thumb through my glove on one of the curved thorns. I untangle myself, take the glove off and a bead of blood blooms on my skin. I suck my thumb until it stops bleeding, watching Barbara showing the man around. I haven't seen him before.

Barbara sees me and waves. She's leading the stranger up the slope, towards the pond. He's balding, wearing a green waterproof jacket with suit trousers. Barbara's talking to him. He's taking photographs of everything with a large, professional-looking camera.

A stab of fear goes through me, heightened by the metallic taste of blood in my mouth. Barbara told me she wanted to get some publicity for the gallery. She didn't say when. She didn't say it would be now.

'There you are, Keziah!' Barbara calls, picking her way over to me through tussocks of dry grass. 'I didn't expect you to be so...hands on.'

'I'm Nick Price,' the man says. '*Wirksworth World*. You've got a very exciting project going on here.'

My heart flutters. Why didn't Barbara give me any warning? Did she think I would just smile and pose for the camera?

'Keziah Knight is the inspiration for all of this. Did you know she was the last student of Elsa Day?'

The journalist looks blank for a second, then covers his expression with a smile, as if he's kidding himself that he's an expert on art. Barbara stares at me. She's keen to reel in the media interest. She wants me to help her, but instead, I bend down to cut a bramble stem.

'Your press release was very interesting,' the reporter says. 'I remember the whole Mission Control mystery. I never thought I'd meet the elusive Kaz K.'

'What?' I stand up and stare at both of them.

For a few lines in a tatty local newspaper, I feel betrayed. I wanted to find Ash first, before the news spread in the press, if anyone still cared what happened to me.

The reporter gives me a smug smile. I'm so angry, I could smash his teeth in.

'So we've got an exclusive. One of those unsolved cases...solved. Brilliant. Have you got Shergar around the back?'

I turn away and snip through another bramble stem. At least my family know about me now; and Pete.

'I can't talk to you.'

I've promised I'll talk to Marilyn Richards. She's been patient so far. She knows I'm waiting to hear from Ash. She knows what I went through.

There's something faintly creepy about this guy, with his mismatched coat and trousers. He's got that grasping tabloid reporter look. He reminds me the hacks lurking outside the hospital, while we kept vigil over Daz.

'We just need a photograph,' Barbara pleads. 'You could come down to the site office and take your overalls off.' I look down at my boiler suit and hi-vis jacket. I'm streaked with mud from the tyres I've been wrestling out of the pond. At least it makes me look like I'm doing something.

'You didn't say anything about the *Wirksworth World*. What press release? Who else have you sent it to?'

Barbara laughs.

'No harm done, surely?'

The reporter starts climbing up the bank of the pond. He's wearing smart lace-up shoes. I should warn him he might slip. He starts taking photographs. The flash bounces off the greasy surface of the water. I hold my gloved hand in front of my face.

'My daughter liked Mission Control. Your boyfriend died, didn't he? Some kind of accident…'

'Keziah's not just an artist. Her garden's in Bolehill village,' Barbara says, low and soothing. 'It's magnificent. Stuffed with Elsa Day's sculptures and champion vegetables. She's creating something even bigger and better here. It might look like an old scrap yard at the moment, but…'

'It's just a going to be a glorified sodding carpark!' I snap.

I run down the bank of the pond. I want to escape. I see the panicked look on the reporter's face. He must think I'm lunging at him with the secateurs. I drop them. He swerves, slips on the mud and catches his foot on a loop of bramble, snagging his trousers. He flails for balance. With a dull splash, he lands, bum-first in the pond, blinking in surprise, slowly sinking into the mud, holding the camera above his head.

Barbara shrieks. I just stand and stare at him, frozen.

Jeff runs across the yard and climbs to the edge of the pond. The reporter throws him the camera. Jeff deftly catches it and puts it down gently. Then he takes the reporter's hands and hauls him out, with a loud sucking sound from the mud.

'I'm so sorry,' Barbara says. 'Let's get you to the site office.' The journalist looks a complete state, dripping wet and covered in brown sludge and green pond slime. At least he didn't get impaled on a shard of metal lurking beneath the surface. I've cleared everything within reach. He picks up his camera and clasps it tightly in his hands. Barbara stares at me balefully as she leads him away, shoes squelching.

Jeff wipes his hands on his trousers.

'Are you okay?' he asks. 'They were giving you a hard time.'

I feel terrible. Maybe I should have been nicer to the journalist, or at least warned him about slipping on the mud. Just as I was starting to enjoy this garden project, I've ruined things for myself. I'll either have to go back to cleaning people's houses or resign myself to living off my own vegetables and painting by candlelight again. I pick up the secateurs.

Jeff is quaking with silent laughter as he looks around the pond, at the work I've done this morning; the pile of tyres I've removed.

'You have to admit – it was funny. And it was his own stupid fault.'

'At least he wasn't hurt,' I say.

'You've worked hard,' Jeff says. 'Maybe we should do something with these tyres.'

'Put them in the skip?'

'Build something. A retaining wall between the two levels of the garden. Filled with trailing plants? I saw something like that on *Grand Designs.*'

I smile. It's a good idea.

'I think Barbara's going to give me the sack after this.'

Jeff puts his large, dirt-streaked hand on my shoulder. The weight of it feels strangely comforting.

'You didn't do anything wrong,' he says. 'That guy's an idiot.'

Jason

Today's rehearsal's actually going well. I got up early and made a packed lunch. Cheese sandwiches made from yesterday's emergency scone bread. A bit stale, but better than another close encounter with Bradley Smeed. We all got here at the start of lunchtime, which is good, because the school orchestra use the main music room after one pm. We're practising my song this time: 'Bring the Lightning'. It sounds good, with me on my Stratocaster and Ben with his acoustic guitar. Josh is still a bit wobbly but he's definitely improving. He says he's been practising by hitting his bedroom carpet with his drumsticks in time with his favourite Muse tracks.

'One day, I'll show them. Prove them wrong in every way. I'm going to show them – I'm going to have my day.' I sing the chorus. *'I bring the lightning.'*

I go into the guitar solo and I'm about to launch into the second verse when I see a face in the round window of the music room door. An anxious face, staring right at me. I stop playing.

'What?' Ben says. He seems to have calmed down since yesterday. We cycled to school together and, in science, he offered me one of the headphones on his MP3 player and we sneakily listened to The Clash while we were writing up our experiment. With our heads close together, it almost felt like old times. The face is still pressed against the window.

'We've got an audience,' I put my guitar down and open the door. It's the kid from the canteen, his grey eyes staring around him. His chest is heaving, out of breath.

'Kenny?' he asks.

'My name's not Kenny,' I'm surprised at how deep my voice just sounded, like a growl. The kid backs away from me.

'That lad who tripped me over in dinner yesterday. He called you Kenny.'

'He's a dick. My name's Jason.'

'He said he was going to get me, so I wanted to find you. I thought you might help.'

'You'd better come in. Don't know what I can do, though.'

The kid looks up and down the corridor, as if he's a secret agent afraid of being watched. Then he slips through the door. He stares shyly at Ben and Josh.

'Some girls said you would be in here,' he said. Girls? He must mean Alicia Jones, desperate to get in here to practise her flute, or someone else from the orchestra.

'What did Bradley Smeed say? How long's he been picking on you?'

'Just since yesterday. Thanks for the cake.'

'He's been picking on me since I was four. He's a total nob-end. But now he's too scared to pick on someone his own size.' I remember my fight with Bradley at the start of term. 'Actually, I'm taller than him now.'

'He said he'd smash my face in.'

'He wouldn't dare. Just try to avoid him.'

'Can I stay in here?' asks the kid.

Ben plays an exasperated chord on his guitar.

'Jason, we're running out of time already,' he says. 'We'll be crap if we don't practise enough.'

'Can I have a go on the drums?' the kid asks.

'No!' Josh and Ben chorus.

'Maybe another time,' I say. 'We're a bit busy now. Do us a favour. Sit here and don't mess around with anything. Then you can tell us what you think.' I strap my guitar back on.

'Cool!' The kid stares at my guitar as if it's the most

amazing thing he's ever seen.

If Bradley and his henchmen come in here to beat him up, they'll have to deal with the three of us first. At least I always had Ben as a friend. The kid sits on a brown plastic chair. He's wearing a grey anorak, clutching his school bag on his knees as if someone's going to snatch it off him at any moment.

'What's your name?' I ask.

'Lance. Lancelot Gawain Thomas,' He blurts out, as if he's making a confession.

'Poor you. What were your parents thinking?'

Lance stares at me.

'That lad said your mum was mad and you lived in a shed,' he says.

'Bradley Smeed is a complete tosser,' Ben says fiercely. 'He's just jealous. Do you know who Jason's mum is?'

I'm glad Ben is defending me, even if it's a bit embarrassing. I keep my head down and adjust the tuning on my guitar.

'She's a rock star. Used to be in a band called Mission Control. They were brilliant. Now she's an artist. She lives in a really cool cottage with paintings everywhere and an awesome record player.'

'Is she really famous?' Lance asks, his eyes wide.

'They played at Glastonbury and everything,' Ben says. 'Google them if you don't believe me.'

I bet my face is as red as my guitar. I'm proud of Mum and I don't want Lance to believe that I live in a shed, but it feels like Ben is showing off on my behalf.

'Can we just get on with it now?' Josh says. 'You two can practise the guitar whenever you want but the orchestra will be here in ten minutes and then I can't play the drums. It's not fair.'

Josh starts playing the drum part to 'Bring the Lightning'. I start playing along with him and Ben joins in.

A girl comes into the music room, carrying a violin case. I know her, a bit. She always gets picked to do the violin solos in the orchestra and sometimes she practises on her own, in one of the little music rooms. She's in the year above us. Her name's Tracey, which doesn't seem to go with what she looks like – tall, with straight light-brown hair. She sits on the edge of a table, busy with her phone, but I can tell she's listening to us. When I go into my guitar solo, she looks up at me and nods, with a bit of a smile.

We are sounding better now, more in time with each other. Maybe it's because Josh started first and had a chance to get into his stride, but we're meant to start at the same time really. Maybe I should ask Mum for some advice, as a musician. Who's meant to make sure everyone stays in time? Or does it just take practise?

Chapter 22
The Headline and the Letter

Kaz

I watch from the pond, as Barbara flaps about, offering the reporter plastic bin bags to stop him from getting slime on his car seats. Her hands are held out, as if she's pleading with him. He slams his car door and drives away, rubble crunching under the tyres.

'I'd better face up to this.' I sigh.

'I'm coming too,' Jeff says. 'You need someone to back you up.'

He walks with me to the site office. We've done a lot of work this morning. We've barely started, but it would be a shame if I couldn't continue, when I've worked so hard on it already. Jeff seems cheerful. I think he must be one of those rare people who can stay calm when things go wrong.

Barbara turns her head as we approach. She's leaning against the site cabin, smoking one of her posh cigarettes. I still can't get used to her in a hi-vis jacket and safety boots, so unlike her usual elegant self.

'What's he going to write about us now?' Barbara stares at me accusingly.

'You sent a press release about me and you didn't even let me read it first. Who else have you sent it to?'

Barbara just shrugs.

I walk into the site cabin. The door is open, and there's a trail of mud on the floor. A piece of paper lies on the table, crumpled and stained.

I straighten it out. It's the press release. The reporter must have left it behind. I straighten it out and start to read it – Barbara going on about her vision for the gallery and its projected economic benefit to the village.

'I saw what happened,' Jeff says to Barbara. 'It wasn't Keziah's fault at all. And if she hadn't cleared so much junk out of the pond this morning, that guy would have been seriously hurt.'

It feels good to have an ally.

I find a paragraph about me in the press release:

Keziah Knight trained with the influential yet reclusive surrealist Elsa Day. She became Elsa Day's carer and confidante in her final years, absorbing her skills and wisdom. In 1994, Keziah Knight walked away from an acclaimed music career with rock band Mission Control, as the band ended in tragedy with the death of her partner and collaborator, guitarist Daz Lightning. She found solace with her artistic mentor and now, in partnership with acclaimed wildlife artist Barbara Fleming, Keziah Knight will find the exposure she deserves at the Elsa Day gallery.

I stand in the doorway, the piece of paper in my hand.

'Why didn't you tell me you were doing this? I could have written something.'

'I know you too well, Keziah. You wouldn't have been very nice about yourself.' Barbara laughs.

'He just wanted to know about Mission Control. Not the art at all.'

'But it's out in the open now, surely?'

'I ran away because of the reporters. They wouldn't leave me alone, after Daz died...'

My leg throbs suddenly; feels as if it's going to collapse underneath me. My head swims. I put my hand on the doorframe, to steady myself.

'You okay?' Jeff asks.

Fuzzy dots are moving around in front of my eyes.

'Hey. What's up?' he says. 'Maybe you did too much work in one go.'

●

I stay by Daz's side in the hospital. I don't care what goes on around us – the bleeping machines, the nurses. Even Pete and Ash seem like shadows. The only thing I see clearly is the figure in the bed, swathed in white. I cling onto his pale hand.

I'm nothing without Daz; incomplete, broken. He's gone already, I know. We've shared the world since we were fifteen and now I've lost him.

I could have stopped him, let him talk, even though Daz wasn't seeing things straight. Too much of his dad's anger in him. His dad lashed out but Daz turned the anger in on himself, until he'd poisoned his own mind. If we had listened to each other, maybe we could have got over our problems.

Nothing ever happened between me and Ash. Just a silly kiss. I tried telling Daz so many times. Loving him wasn't – isn't – enough. By the time I found him, lying on crumbling Tarmac, under a sheet of rain, it was too late. I don't know why they're keeping his body alive like this. I can't leave him.

The line on the monitor screen goes flat. Everything seems to happen automatically. The machines are turned off, one by one. Daz's body is on the bed. I'm clutching his left hand. It still feels warm.

'Goodbye, mate.' Pete stands over the bed like an awkward priest.

Ash doesn't say anything. I turn towards him. His head is in his hands. He sits up, rubbing his eyes roughly with his knuckles. I look away.

'We have to move him now. We're sorry,' someone says.

They want to wheel Daz to the hospital morgue. They don't say that's where he's going, but I know. Refrigerator cold. A whole room of dead bodies that don't mean anything anymore.

I extend my fingers, so my hand is pressed against Daz's palm. My hand is small and stumpy, nothing like those long, elegant, guitar-playing fingers, calloused at the tips. Daz's hands had an intelligence of their own. Now they're dead and useless, like the rest of him. It doesn't matter how long I stay here, I'll never feel any movement in those hands again.

The porters part the curtains and wheel him away. The bed has a squeaky wheel. When I can't even hear the squeak any more, I know he really is gone. I stare at the empty space where the bed was, expecting to feel something, but there's just a void inside me.

Pete and Ash both hold my hands as I leave the hospital. Nobody warned us about the reporters; photographers lined up at the exit, blinding flashbulbs; a torrent of questions:

'What happened?'

'How did he die?'

'Was it an accident?'

'Are you splitting up?'

'Is there any truth in the rumours?'

'Keziah? Are you okay?' Barbara's voice wakes me.

I'm in the site cabin, propped up on the bench, leaning against the wall.

'Did I pass out?' I ask.

'A bit,' Jeff says. 'I caught you before you fell over.'

'You've over strained yourself. You're still getting over that bike accident,' Barbara says.

'I can do this job. I'll prove it to you.' I stand up, but my head spins so much I have to sit down again. Jeff plonks a mug of tea in front of me, patterned with oily fingerprints.

'I should have talked to you about the press release. I didn't realise it would affect you like this,' Barbara says.

'Is it possible to actually have a phobia of journalists? I felt trapped. I'm sorry.'

'I shouldn't have mentioned Mission Control like that. If someone wrote something about me that mentioned my ex-husband...'

'I'll be Googling Mission Control now though,' Jeff says. 'If that's okay with you.'

I take a sip of syrupy tea.

'Mission Control was a long time ago. I want to put it behind me, focus on the art.'

'If we can,' Barbara says. 'The *Wirksworth World* will spread this story as far as it can go.'

Jeff folds his arms, leaning back against the work surface.

'He shouldn't have even been allowed on site in those slippy shoes. With no hi-vis. The accident wouldn't have happened if you hadn't been so keen to show him around, Barbara.'

'Don't carry any more tyres around this afternoon, Keziah.' Barbara stands up and leaves the cabin, bristling about being told she's in the wrong.

Jason

I unlock my bike. It's quite sunny now, but freezing cold, so I pull on my fingerless gloves. Ben's Velcroing himself into his cycling jacket and gloves. We're going back to my house for tea, to work on our songs.

I strap on my cycling helmet and get on my bike. I look around, in case Bradley Smeed is lurking around, not that I'd be bothered if he was. I've proved I can stand up to him.

'I think I've got another idea for a song,' Ben says, as we weave around groups of chatting kids and slowly escape through the school gates.

'What's it about?'

'Bradley Smeed. He's obviously picked that Lance kid out as his next victim.'

'I won't let that happen.'

Lance was so pathetically grateful to us this lunchtime. When the orchestra came in, we moved into the little practise room and we let Lance come with us, even though there's not much room in there. He thought we were brilliant, which cheered Josh up no end. Lance said he doesn't have any friends in his own year.

'We could let him hang out with us a bit, until he realises Bradley wouldn't actually smash his face in.'

'Wouldn't he?'

'He's done some shitty things to me but he hasn't actually beaten me up.'

'He pushed you into Cromford canal when you were in

Year Four. And remember the snowball full of ice that nearly broke your hand?'

'I had you. I had friends. Lance is an easy target without anyone to stick up for him.'

'He did put us off a bit. Everything we did, he was just sort of staring up at us. Maybe we could get him to join computer club.'

'We've got the insider knowledge about the best geek hang-outs at school.'

'Hasn't he realised he can hide in the library? I don't think Bradley Smeed even knows where it is.'

When the road clears, I pick up speed and overtake Ben, the wind scything into my cheeks. It's good to get fresh air into my lungs.

When we get home, the house is freezing cold and dark. I let Ben get the fire going in the living room fireplace, while I stoke the embers in the AGA and load it with logs. I fill up the kettle. It'll be ages until the water boils.

Still wearing our coats, we get our guitars out in front of the fire. It feels like we're camping. I wish Mum was here, with the house all warm and bright and something cooking in the AGA. She's so busy and stressed.

This gallery thing should be great but she seems scared, like something really bad is going to happen. I feel like that too sometimes. Mum hasn't heard from Ash yet, either. Would she tell me if he had written back?

Patti curls up next to us, her nose tucked into her fluffy tail.

Ben tunes his guitar. He looks at me.

'You look kind of fed up,' he says.

'Well, you know,' I say. I want to tell Ben that how I feel is a bit like when we go up to Black Rocks and dare each other to stand right on the edge of the cliff, looking down at the trees at the bottom.

'Rachel gave me a massive bollocking when she got back last night. I've been a total twat, haven't I?'

'I hadn't noticed.' I hope Ben doesn't miss the sarcasm.

'What will it be like though? If your mum really does get famous again? Will you still live here? Will we still go to the same school?'

'I'm not going anywhere else.'

I fetch my acoustic guitar and sit cross-legged while I'm tuning it. The kettle starts whistling and I go into the kitchen to make tea. When I come back with the mugs, Ben is strumming a chord sequence. I don't recognise it but it sounds good.

'I thought of some words for my song. The one about Bradley Smeed.'

'Does it go *I really hate you – you're a bell-end – and you smell of sweaty trainers?*' I sing along to Ben's chords.

'That's why I'm a much better songwriter than you.' Ben laughs. I poke him with the headstock of my guitar.

'I don't understand how the songs just come out of you,' I moan. Ben has written about ten songs now, not counting the novelty ones we wrote at Christmas. An album's worth.

'Your song's amazing.'

'It's just one song though. It took me so long to think of lyrics that didn't sound totally embarrassing. It sounds better if you're singing anyway. But I've got loads of ideas for riffs and solos and things to play on the guitar.'

'It just seems to come naturally to you. Like Daz Lightning.'

'What are the lyrics you've come up with, anyway?'

Ben plays the chord sequence again.

'Playing games with people – that's all you ever do,' he sings. *'No real friends, you just use them till you're through. See the weakest ones and ruin their lives. But what are you going to do when they reach your size?'*

I laugh. It's brilliant. It sums him up perfectly. Ben stares at me, uncertain, but it's a million times better than his first attempt at song writing.

'We've got to do this at the school concert.'

'We're only supposed to do two songs.'

'So? Mrs Lyons wouldn't pull the plug if we did three songs. She thinks we're great, remember?'

'Bradley Smeed's probably going to be there. He'll be dragged along to watch his sister.' Ben looks a bit worried.

'That's the point. This is our chance to get our revenge. And what can he do?' Helping Lance has made me realise that Bradley Smeed is just a prat.

'He's too thick to notice the song's about him anyway. Yeah, let's do it. He needs to hear it.'

Kaz

It's pouring with rain as I reach the old garage. I chain my bike to the fence. The lights are on in the site office and the windows are running with condensation.

I open the door. Barbara is sitting at the table, reading a newspaper. She stares up at me.

'You haven't seen it yet?'

She holds up the *Wirksworth World*. My stomach takes a sickening lurch. I drop my dripping hi-vis waterproof and cycling helmet on the floor.

There's a picture of me on the front cover – one of the photos the reporter took two days ago, with my hand in front of my face as if I'm a fugitive. It's alongside a picture of me from my Mission Control days, my hair in multi-coloured dreadlocks, scowling into the camera lens. The music press always liked us to look mean and moody.

'Missing Rock Star Assaults Journalist', the headline shouts. It doesn't even make sense.

'We couldn't have planned it better,' Barbara says. She looks pleased with herself, as if she actually did plan it.

My hands are numb with cold and dripping wet. I wipe them on my overalls and hold them over the electric heater. Barbara hands me the newspaper, but the words won't stay still. I feel faint.

'Don't you want to read it?' Barbara asks.

'Read it out to me.' I screw my eyes shut, trying to stop feeling like my head is spinning out of control. I hand the paper back to her.

'Former rock star Kaz K from 90s indie band Mission Control, reported missing and feared dead 15 years ago, is alive and well, living in the picturesque village of Bolehill near Cromford. Now an artist and sculptor, she is involved with plans to turn a derelict motor garage on the Via Gelia in Cromford into an art gallery.

'Two days ago, a *Wirksworth World* reporter was invited to see the development take shape by the gallery's director, local luminary and wildlife artist Barbara Fleming. At the building site, Kaz K (birth name Karen Kenning), assaulted him and knocked him into a pond full of toxic waste and debris.

'Kaz K, now 36, changed her name by deed poll to Keziah Knight whilst under the wing of reclusive artist Elsa Day, an eccentric fixture of Wren Cottage in Bolehill village for many years, where the ex-rock star now lives with her teenage son. The assaulted journalist is recovering well from his ordeal, after attending hospital for a tetanus booster.'

Barbara stops reading. I open my eyes. I feel sick.

'They've got it all wrong. I didn't touch him.'

'People will want to come to the gallery now. They'll come in droves, just out of curiosity. That's enough to get things going.'

'How did they know where I live?'

'They must have asked around.' Barbara puts the newspaper down.

'People will think I'm a psycho.' A horrible thought strikes me. 'What if I get arrested for assault? What'll happen to Jason?'

Barbara laughs.

'Jeff and I witnessed it. An accident. That reporter didn't have a scratch on him. He's got a massive scoop out of this. Everyone's a winner.'

I run out into the rain, straight to my storage container. I open the heavy door and pull it shut behind me, until I'm trapped in the dark, with all the rusty car parts and scrap metal.

There's a loud bang on the door, making the whole

container reverberate.

'Let me in. I've made tea!' Jeff calls. I push the door open a crack. I feel better instantly, seeing his cheerful face.

'How many sugars have you put in it?'

'Upset about the paper?' He comes inside and puts the tea down on the camping table; turns the lights on.

'I don't like people knowing who I am. They're getting it all wrong.'

'It's bollocks. Don't worry. I won't let it happen again. Hey, I went on YouTube. Listened to both Mission Control albums. You were amazing.'

'Maybe.'

'People loved you. You played in front of thousands of people.'

'There are bits I'd rather forget.'

'You don't need to tell me. I read about most of it online.' Jeff looks away from me as he hangs up his waterproof. The internet seems like a strange place, where people are obsessed with chasing ghosts of other people's pasts.

Rain hammers on the container roof. I pick up an old car bumper from the top of the pile of scrap.

'We could start doing something with this lot today. Ever used a welding torch?' I ask.

'No.' Jeff laughs. 'How hard can it be?'

Jason

I hold my head up and try to chat to Ben as we walk down the corridor towards the music block. I'm trying to act normal but loads of kids are staring at me, nudging each other; pointing. Even people I don't know. The school rumour-mill must be in overdrive. Even some of the teachers give me funny looks.

I can feel my cheeks burning.

'I can't believe the concert's only a week away,' I say.

'Yeah.'

'What are you going to wear?'

Ben doesn't say anything. I think he's a bit freaked out. He saw the newspaper article when he got back from school last night. I told him what Mum told me – that it was an accident. I believe her. But when she showed me the newspaper, I thought most people would probably believe what it says.

I'm not upset though. It's a weird feeling. Really embarrassed, but pleased that people know about Mum. I'm proud of her.

I hold my head up, start looking people in the eye; smiling at them. What have I got to be ashamed about?

Bradley Smeed walks towards me up the corridor, his gang lined up behind him, like a cartoon baddie. He glares at me with so much hate I half-expect to wither up like a scorched plant. I just stare back at him.

'Think the sun shines out of your arse, don't you?' he says.

I carry on walking, as if he's a ghost and I'll just be able to walk right through him. He stands with his arms crossed, blocking my path.

'It proves your mum really is mental, Kenny,' Bradley says. 'Have they taken her away yet?'

A few months ago, I would have tried to run away and let his comments get to me. Deep down, I actually thought I was a worthless loser. I won't let him do that to me or anyone else.

I stare at Bradley Smeed; feel myself getting angry. For the stuff he said years ago, not just now. The things he said to me when I was a little kid that made me doubt everything.

'Do you believe everything you read in the papers?' I roll my eyes towards the ceiling. 'I knew you were thick, but –'

There's a delicious danger in my words. Bradley doesn't like being reminded how stupid he is. He lunges at me, his red beefy face right in mine.

Mrs Lyons walks down the corridor with a sheaf of photocopying in her arms.

'I've got the programmes for the concert.' She smiles at me and Ben. 'I could do with some help with folding them.'

Mrs Lyons doesn't even notice that Bradley was about to deck me. Bradley Smeed and his mates are clustered around the vending machine, as if they'd been there all break time.

'We'll help,' Ben says.

It pays to suck up to Mrs Lyons – we need more rehearsal time in the music room. She's a great trumpet player too. It's not just about school – that's what stupid kids like Bradley don't understand. You have to be nice to everyone who helps you on the way up. Mum told me that. Even though I'm not thrilled about spending time folding programmes instead of playing our songs. Maybe we can get Lance to help us.

I open the door of the music room for Mrs Lyons. Bradley Smeed's sister Mary is already here, sawing away on her cello. She smiles at me; then stares down at her strings, flicking her long plait over her shoulder.

'So, is it true?' Mrs Lyons asks, putting the programmes down on her cluttered desk. 'Is that really your mum on the front page of the newspaper?'

I imagine all the teachers passing yesterday's *Wirksworth World* around in the staff room, gossiping about meeting Mum at parents' evenings.

I nod.

'I had to look Mission Control up on the internet. I'd never heard of them.'

'Not many people have. They were brilliant but they didn't make it big or anything. I just want to be as good as my dad at playing the guitar.'

'I'm sure you will be. Is your mum coming to the concert?'

'She promised me.' I feel myself glow with pride.

I get my electric guitar from the locker. The lock is actually broken, but it's pretty safe. Everyone keeps their instruments here. Musicians trust each other. That's why Mrs Lyons doesn't mind people rehearsing in here while she's not there. She knows that if anyone tried to trash the room, we wouldn't let it happen.

'Can we do three songs at the concert?' Ben asks. 'We've got a great new one.'

'As long as they're not too long.'

'We like to keep things snappy,' Ben says.

Mrs Lyons bustles into her storeroom to get ready for the next lesson.

Ben smiles at me.

'I thought I'd ask her about it while she's all excited about your mum. We've got to take advantage of this situation.'

I plug in my guitar but it's hardly worth it. There's only five minutes left of break time, and we've got history next, which is all the way across the yard.

'Mum didn't push him, you know.'

'It didn't do Liam Gallagher any harm,' Ben says. 'It might make more people come to the concert.'

I remember reading in the Manics biography I got for my birthday last year that Nicky Wire once smashed up a video camera with his bass, when he was young and gobby.

'I'm not sure I want people coming to the concert because they think my mum pushed someone into a pond.'

'There's no such thing as bad publicity,' Ben grins, launching into the chord progression of our song about Bradley Smeed. Mary packs her cello away while we're practising. I wonder if she can hear the words.

Ben's got a lesson with Sam at the Fishpond tonight, so we part company at the railway bridge where I turn off for Bolehill village. The pink and orange sunset turns everything a weird colour, like something's on fire. It's freezing cold and an icy wind is blowing right into my face.

I bump my bike up the steps and I'm relieved the lights in the house are on. The kitchen window is steamed up: even better. I put the bike in the shed and open the back door.

The AGA is warm and there are pans lined up on top of the stove, boiling away; as many as we had for Christmas dinner. When Mum makes something elaborate, she's usually in a weird mood and needs to get it out of her system by throwing herself into cooking. Loud classical music plays on the radio.

'Am I notorious?' she asks.

I take off my coat and hang it on the hook on the back of the door. There's no point in lying.

'Everyone knows. You were on the front page. It was quite exciting, really.'

Mum goes back to violently mashing potato. That's good, because I don't like lumps, especially when she leaves the skins on, but she's holding the masher like she's imagining the pan of spuds is someone's face. Maybe she is capable of throwing someone into a pond after all.

'We should tell Pete. He'd love it,' I say.

'Would he?' She dumps the potato masher in the pan and sighs deeply, putting her hands over her eyes.

'Mum?' I touch her arm, gently. I thought she was coping quite well with all of this.

'I've written Ash two letters. There's no word – nothing. Doesn't he care?'

'You said you'd give it until half term. That's only two weeks away.' I swallow hard. The concert will be over by then.

I've been acting like the concert is the most important thing in my life so far. My birthday's at half term. We're going to stay with Gran and Grandad. Pete's promised I can jam with him in his studio.

'I just want to talk to him. It doesn't feel right.'

'Go into Singh News and ask his parents. We'll find him. Don't worry.' I put my arms around her. I've grown so much, it really feels like I'm the adult and Mum is the child. 'I'm glad people know about you.'

Kaz

A shaft of bright sunlight makes me look up from my new picture. I was absorbed in painting the feathers of the heron and the gleam of its beak. It was raining heavily this morning when Jason set off for school, but he was wearing his new waterproofs, full of excitement about the concert. It's only two days away now.

God, it's nearly lunchtime. I put my paintbrush down and check the letterbox. Nothing. Why hasn't Ash written to me?

I go into the kitchen and wash the breakfast pots. I look out of the kitchen window at the bird feeder. Greenfinches cluster round it, driven off by the resident robin, fighting for pole position. A wood pigeon flaps lazily to the ground, gobbling the scattered seed like a fat businessman finishing off the buffet. The feeder is almost empty.

I pull on my wellies. Stepping outside the back door, I can feel the warmth of the sun. I turn my face up and bask in it. The lawn is boggy but there are signs of spring in the borders: shoots from bulbs waking up in the soil, sensing the growing day length; buds on the willow tree starting to swell like the joints on Elsa's fingers.

As I come closer to the feeder, the birds scatter. The wood pigeon flaps to keep his balance on the frail twig he's landed on.

I unhook the feeder and take it into the shed. It feels cold in here now the morning sun has moved round, but the seed potatoes are sprouting nicely on the windowsill. I've been neglecting this garden recently.

The gallery garden is starting to take shape. Jeff's working on the tyre wall that's going to separate the two levels. We designed it together. This year, it will be planted with annual geraniums and pelargoniums, the brighter the better. It's going to be a real statement. Who said gardening had to be tasteful? I wish I was there now but Barbara insisted I had a rest; time for my own painting and to finish cataloguing Elsa's ceramics.

More newspapers have contacted Barbara but I'm not

talking to anyone apart from Marilyn Richards. I won't even do that unless I find Ash – unless all the members of Mission Control are ready to talk. By that time, all the fuss about the pond incident will have died down.

Jason made me call Marilyn Richards. She said she doesn't mind waiting. She told me she didn't think our story is finished yet. It sounds like she's holding out for a band reunion. She shouldn't get her hopes up.

I fill the bird feeder with more seed, careful not to spill any out of the bag. We had a problem with mice in here last spring, eating old cardboard boxes and out-of-date seeds. We had little else that was edible to attract them, but they seemed to think they had a very comfortable home. Until Patti discovered their hide-out.

The regulars, as I call the greenfinches, have settled on the bushes and tops of trees, watching as I carry the feeder outside again. They don't mind me, as long as the cat isn't hanging around. The sound of someone slamming a car door in the lane scatters them.

I look down into the lane. Not Barbara. A sleek hatchback in midnight blue. Too clean for a country-dweller. A tall, slim Asian man in a suit is crossing the road. He looks like Ash. My heart leaps. He's come to see me. Why would he be dressed like that?

It's not him. This man is young, with a mild, patient face and a brown leather satchel slung over one shoulder.

He looks up and sees me.

'Miss Knight?' he asks.

I don't answer. I turn around and hang up the bird feeder. My heart thuds like the bassline to 'Rootless in Babylon'.

The man starts walking up our steps.

Who is he? Another journalist? They're usually scruffier than that.

'Don't worry. I need to speak to you.' His voice is gentle, as if he's trying not to scare me.

Whoever he is, I don't want to talk to him. He looks like someone bearing bad news.

I run for the back door and bolt it behind me. I hear footsteps on the path. He knocks on the door.

'Miss Knight. This is important. It's about Elsa Day's estate.'

The house. This is the moment I've been dreading.

'Please, Miss Knight. I'm acting on behalf of the Treasury.'

He starts knocking again.

I run upstairs until I reach Jason's room. I crouch in the window gable, the pain from my knee suddenly shooting through my leg. I can still hear the knocking.

I hold my breath, until I think I might be able to stop myself from breathing forever. It's silent. The house seems to be holding its breath too. I curl into a ball and hide under Jason's bed, staring at the dust and old school worksheets that have ended up here.

There's a creak on the landing. I gasp.

Patti pushes the door open with her head and trots into the room. She gives me one of her owl-like glares, as if she's surprised to see me under the bed.

I hear the slam of a car door, and the sound of the blue hatchback driving off.

I don't stand up until the car disappears from view. I feel so wobbly, I have to grip the banister tightly as I walk downstairs. *This is real. This is happening*, I tell myself. *Deal with it.*

A white rectangle is lying on the old mat by the front door. A crisp white envelope with the official government logo of the lion and the unicorn. Addressed to me. I open it with trembling hands.

It's from the Bona Vacantia Division of the Treasury Solicitor's Department. A London address and telephone number. The letter is very short. After an official reference number, there is no "dear" or "yours sincerely". It just says:

Vital information has recently come to light about the Estate of Elsa Day. The Treasury Solicitor urgently requests to speak to Miss Keziah Knight regarding this Estate, which may be of interest to the Crown.

It must be important, if they've sent someone to deliver the letter in person. I tear the letter and the envelope into little pieces and scatter them in the fireplace. The paper curls and crisps in the embers of the fire that Jason laid this morning. If the worst is going to happen, it's going to happen whether I let it or not.

Chapter 23
The Concert

Jason

It's ironic that I'm getting dressed in the PE changing rooms because I hate most sports, apart from mountain biking, and I'm getting changed to play the guitar, not for charging round like a muddy idiot on a football field.

I'm still in my school uniform. My face feels greasy from the chips I shared with Ben and Josh once we'd set up the drums and done our sound-check. I didn't have many chips but I feel a bit sick now, really. This is the first time in my life I haven't wanted to eat anything.

'It's going to be alright,' I tell my reflection in the tiny changing room mirror. I feel myself shivering in my grey-tinged school shirt. I look scared, with the beginnings of a spot in the corner of my nose. Just a scruffy school-kid, whose mum can't even wash his shirts white. I lift my arms and sniff my pits. A whiff of cheap spray-on deodorant and chips. Could be worse. I look around, checking I'm alone.

Ben's putting new strings on his guitar and Josh is practising his drum patterns on a plastic chair in the music room. The school drum kit is set up on the stage now, with my guitar next to it, on a proper guitar stand. All I have to do is plug it in. We're the only rock band playing at the concert. There's another band at our school, a metal band called Skullbreath who are in Year Eleven. The singer, Adam Stammers, said they wouldn't be seen dead playing at the school concert. His loss. Their songs are mostly made up of swearwords.

I can hear a faint murmur from down the corridor. Parents are starting to come into the hall. Mrs Lyons said people could get changed in here but it's empty so far. Most people are staying in their uniforms.

I unbutton my school shirt, and bundle it into my bag. Underneath, I'm wearing a black t-shirt – one I grew out of a couple of years ago, so now it's almost skin-tight. I change from the suit trousers with safety pins at the bottom I've been wearing to school, into a pair of ultra-skinny jeans I persuaded Mum to buy for me. I don't feel so bad asking for new things now she has a job.

I take the black lacy shirt out of my bag. I stare at it, almost bottling out. My greasy-feeling face is putting me off. I squeeze the chemical-smelling soap from the dispenser into my hands and rub it all over my face. I turn on the tap, careful not to get the water so hot that my skin turns red, and splash my face until it feels tight and smooth. If I look closely, I can still see the red point of my spot but, if I listen to Mum's advice and don't squeeze it, no one will notice it.

I put the lacy shirt on. It's tight, but stretchy. I button it halfway up so you can still see my t-shirt. I found a silver skull and crossbones necklace in the 50p box in the charity shop, which I clasp around my neck. I got a cool skull ring in the charity shop too. It fits on the middle finger of my right hand so it doesn't get in the way of playing guitar.

Hair gel next: a handful of Shockwaves. I mess up my hair at the back, smoothing down my long fringe at the front so it almost sweeps into my eyes. Bradley Smeed calls me "Emo Kenny" now. I guess he's right, but this is my own look. I unzip my pencil case and take the stub of eye liner that fell out of Rachel's bag the other week. I draw it carefully under my eyes. I practised at home in the bathroom but wiped it off before Mum could notice. This time, I'm ready to face the whole world – well, virtually everyone I know.

I can only see my face and my shoulders in the tiny mirror, but I know I look different; like someone who can really play the guitar.

'It's going to be brilliant!' I shout into the mirror, surprised I really believe it. I start singing the words to my song, 'Bring the Lightning'.

The door creaks open and my heart jumps. It's only Ben.

'I thought I'd –' He looks at me properly. 'What the fuck?'

'I told you I was getting changed.'

'You didn't say you were going to put makeup on.'

'So?' I stare at Ben. He must have got changed in the music room. He's wearing his favourite denim shirt over the Oasis t-shirt he's had since he was ten. The logo's almost totally faded. His hair's a bit longer than it used to be and he's jammed a peaked corduroy cap he got from the charity shop on his head. An old man probably used to wear it to walk his dog. He's got his guitar case with him.

Josh follows Ben through the door, in a Muse t-shirt he got when his dad took him to see them, and his usual baggy jeans. His eyes widen in surprise.

'Jason! Cool!'

Ben glares at Josh. 'He looks like a girl.'

'You look like a…like Bob Dylan or someone,' I say. I don't exactly mean it as a compliment because I think Bob Dylan's singing sounds like a tone deaf tramp.

Ben grins, and I feel like I've mended something between us, for now.

'It's time we went down to the hall,' Ben says.

'Is Mum here yet? Your mum and dad were giving her a lift.'

'I saw my dad's van in the car park,' Josh says.

'Sam said he'd try to be here.' He warned me his mother-in-law might need him in the pub.

'Why don't you look for yourself?' Ben frowns at me.

I want to surprise Mum; put on a show for her. Prove I'm not a nerdy little kid any more. Do I look too much like a girl? I never felt more like myself. But we don't really look like a band. Band members should have a look that works together. Like the Ramones, with their tight jeans and white sneakers. Mission Control didn't all dress the same, but they looked good: a bit of metal, a bit of Goth, punk and rave. I look at Ben. We should feel like a team but something's not quite right.

'Let's go down to the hall and check from the wings,' Josh says.

I sling my school bag on my back and we walk down the corridor until we get to the stage door. Two Year Eight girls from the wind band are sitting on the chairs laid out for performers, sharing a bag of crisps. They stare at me as I walk through the door. Mrs Lyons is backstage, talking quietly but urgently to the Year Eleven lad who's in charge of the lighting. She's pointing at the lamps attached to the lighting rig and he keeps nodding. She's got pages of notes about the concert in a blue folder clutched to her chest.

'The Organ Detectives!' she whispers. My insides groan at the terrible name I chose for the band. We couldn't agree on anything else. 'Brave costume choice, Jason.' She smiles at me. 'The concert starts in ten minutes. You can sit with your parents, but be backstage as soon as the advanced recorder group start their piece.'

Maybe Adam Stammers was right. I mean, who played their first proper gig after a recorder group? It's crap. It's the best we can do, apart from busking. Like Mum keeps saying – everyone has to start somewhere.

'I don't want people seeing me until we're on stage.' Rachel lent me a bottle of purple nail varnish. I've definitely got time to put it on before it's our turn.

'Can we look through the curtains to see if they're here yet?' Ben asks.

'Don't twitch the curtains. And try not to trip over anything!' Mrs Lyons tells us.

We stand behind the curtains at the side of the stage. I put my eye up to a frayed hole in the heavy old red material. The school curtains are so faded – something else we could have a concert to fundraise for, I suppose.

The hall is almost full. In one of the front rows, Bradley Smeed looks incredibly bored in a big puffer jacket, his arms folded, trying to look like a rapper. A woman with long blonde hair and too much make-up sits next to him – his mum. I recognise her from the primary school gates. She looks like she's looking down her nose at everyone in the room. Next to her, a posh-looking bloke with glasses. He must be Bradley's dad.

There's Mary, prim and perfect with her plait, like a girl in one of those really old books about boarding schools we've got in our house. I don't get how a brother and sister can be so different. The Smeeds are a bit too close for comfort in the audience. I can't see Sam but he said he'd probably be late, if he could make it at all.

Mum walks in, with Ben's parents and Rachel. Rachel and Mum look more like sisters. Mum's wearing her fake leather jacket and black jeans. Someone whispers something and nudges the woman sitting next to him. Loads of parents are staring and murmuring. They all know who she is.

I expect Mum to run out of the hall. I hold my breath. She keeps walking, her head held high, talking to Rachel. She points out the empty seats, right in front of Bradley Smeed. Why? Mum knows Bradley hates my guts. They're not even the only seats left.

She's talking to Bradley Smeed's dad, as if she knows him. They start laughing. I can't make out what they're saying. Bradley thrusts his jaw out and stares at the curtain, as if he can sense my presence. I feel the same as him for a second. I clamp my mouth shut, to make sure my expression doesn't mirror his.

Ben pulls me away from the curtain.

'Are they there?' he hisses.

'Yeah.'

Ben looks through the hole in the curtain.

'Why's she talking to Bradley's dad?'

'I don't know.'

I take a deep breath. The light from behind the curtain glints off my guitar, enticing me to play it. I'll have to wait until after the sodding wind band and the advanced recorder group. I stroke the neck of my guitar, for luck.

Kaz

'Kaz – can I have your autograph?' Before I have a chance to sit down, a man is waiting for me in the aisle between the seats. He's in his thirties, with sandy hair cut into a fin on top of his head. He must be the dad of one of the kids at the school. He stares at me with fascination and fear. I can sense the nervousness in his voice.

Brenda and Kevin look at me expectantly. I stare back blankly. Rachel gently nudges my arm. I make eye contact with the man. His eyes dart away, wondering if he's made a mistake in standing up and coming to talk to me in front of all the other parents and teachers. I can feel their eyes on my back.

'I'm sorry to disturb you. I thought you might be here, that's all. So I...' From his deep jacket pocket, he pulls out a clear plastic envelope. Inside it is the sleeve from a 7" vinyl copy of 'Rootless in Babylon'.

'Oh my god.'

The man smiles at me, wide-eyed, hardly believing his nerve and his luck. I take the record from him, clutching it in both hands. I haven't seen a copy of this single for almost fifteen years. Every detail is familiar, as if it's been sitting on a shelf in the back of my memory. Daz's cut-up artwork of riot police with alien faces. The blue and yellow cartoon background and our early band logo, based on the NASA insignia.

On the back of the record sleeve is a polarised black and white photograph of the band rehearsing in our studio. Just a snap, taken by Ash. Daz is concentrating furiously, improvising a guitar solo, and I'm staring at him with a questioning look on my face.

I remember that moment. I was playing a variation of the bassline to 'Rootless in Babylon', but Daz started jamming. I was trying to anticipate his next move into a sudden key change or different pace.

I look up and smile at the man. I take the record sleeve out of its protective plastic.

'Have you got a pen?'

He fishes in his pockets and pulls out a fibre-tipped pen, slightly chewed at the end.

'What's your name?'

'Steve.'

I sign the plainest section of the sleeve: *To Steve, with love from Kaz K".* My old name seems to come out of the pen automatically. This is so weird. I shiver. I turn and almost expect Daz to be waiting here next to me, ready to sign his scrawl over his own artwork. Rachel is standing next to me. She takes the record sleeve from me, reverently.

'This is so cool. I want one.'

'I was a big fan,' Steve says. 'I went to loads of your gigs.'

Rachel hands the record artwork back to him. He hugs it to his chest.

'I'm a graphic designer,' he says. 'Daz inspired me. And I sell a few collectable bits on eBay. I always keep an eye out for Mission Control stuff.' He looks at the single in his hands and can't stop himself from smiling. 'But I've had this since I was fifteen.'

'The concert's about to start,' Brenda says. The curtains are being jerkily drawn back and the music teacher is stepping onto the stage. I can see Jason's guitar.

'My son's playing with his band.'

'I know. I've heard from my daughter that they're pretty good. Thanks so much. You've not changed, Kaz.'

I laugh. Daz died fifteen years ago, I've got a teenage son and I've been too scared to make a public appearance, until now. And he thinks I haven't changed.

'It's so cool that you're back and you live here,' Steve says, before scuttling back to his chair. I settle into the empty seat next to Rachel, trying to ignore the people in the audience who are still craning to catch a glimpse of me.

There's a mumble of discontent in the row behind us, a screechy chair scraping on the floor as if someone is about to leave.

'Shhh, Bradley,' his mum says, in an angry whisper. 'It's about to start.'

Rachel turns her head and gives Bradley Smeed a withering death-stare, making him shrink back into his seat.

Jason

I blow on my fingernails as I wait in the backstage corridor on a plastic chair. Ben's sitting in the chair opposite me. The nail varnish has gone a bit blobby and smeared on my fingertips as well as my nails. It's not even properly dry yet. My hands were shaking while I was doing it.

It was a stupid idea really. I should have got Rachel to do it for me yesterday. It was better than just waiting, gripping the edge of the chair while being tortured by the sound of the wind band. The student and staff choir sounded pretty good actually. Who would have thought that Mr Banks, our English teacher, had such a deep voice? My voice is still a bit all over the place but I'm going to sing 'Bring the Lightning' as well as I can. I just try to sing all-out like James Dean Bradfield. I know I'm hitting some rough notes when my voice goes all growly but I'm going to give it everything. I wonder what my voice will be like eventually.

Now it's the advanced recorder group. I'm trying to keep my breathing steady but, with every squeaky note of their medieval medley, I know our performance is coming closer. Part of me can't wait to get out there and do it. Part of me wants to run out of the school gates screaming.

Ben rolls his eyes at me.

'Why did you have to put that muck on? As if you didn't look like a freak already?'

'Don't forget the chords in the middle eight to 'Someone Your Own Size'. And what if I want to look like a freak? Isn't that the point?'

'It's my song. I'm not likely to forget it, am I?'

'Just saying.'

'Don't boss me around, Jason.' Ben's sitting with his acoustic guitar on his lap. Its new strings look shiny and fresh. I wish I hadn't left my guitar on the stage. What if it's gone out of tune? I take a deep breath and blow on my sticky finger nails. Don't be stupid. It was perfectly tuned an hour ago.

'We're a team, aren't we?' Josh stares at us. He's practicing drumming in mid-air. He has got a lot better over the past week or so. Now he's actually got to do it in front of people.

Josh points at each of us with a drum stick.

'When I've got a windsurfing competition, my dad just tells me to get out there and do my best. I'm sure we'll be fine.'

I nod. My mouth is really dry. Sometimes I wish I saw the world like Josh. Everything seems so complicated: wanting to show Mum my guitar playing and my song and make her proud of me; attempting to show Bradley Smeed I'm not someone to mess with. And I just want to be myself and look the way I want to. So what if I've got a flag sticking out of the top of my head telling everyone I'm different? I wonder what Daz would think of me, if he could see me. What would he say to me?

It doesn't feel like me and Ben and Josh are a team; even though I desperately want us to be.

'It's been sounding really good in rehearsals. Let's just go for it!' I say, with more confidence than I've really got.

Ben gently strums the chords for his song. I can tell he's nervous because his eyes are darting around the corridor.

'We did alright when we were busking, didn't we?' I stretch my mouth into a forced smile. 'Josh is right. Let's give it our best shot.'

The squeal of the recorder group stops abruptly and the audience breaks into applause. I stand up and grip Ben's shoulder. He looks up at me, biting his lip.

Mrs Lyons opens the stage door.

'Come on, you lot,' she whispers. 'Good luck.'

We walk through the door. The curtains are closed. I strap on my guitar and plug it into the amp, and put my mic stand into position. Josh sits behind the drum kit and Ben adjusts the height of his mic stand. I stare at the curtains, trying not to think about all those people on the other side.

'Ready?' Mrs Lyons asks, putting her thumbs up.

I nod. Ready as I'll ever be.

The curtains are pulled back. I stare into the audience. The stage lights are bright and hot. The back of the hall is in darkness. I can see Mum, and Rachel, and Ben's parents. Mum grins and gives me a "thumbs up". She doesn't seem surprised to see me in the lacy shirt and the eyeliner. Rachel laughs, in a good way.

Behind her, Bradley Smeed stares straight at me, eyes narrowed. I ignore him. I make eye contact with Mum instead.

'We're the Organ Detectives,' I announce. I launch into the intro to Ben's song and Josh comes in, with the drums in perfect timing. Ben strums his guitar and starts singing. It's as sweet as clockwork. I start to feel like all those rehearsals; all those arguments, have paid off. I concentrate on playing my guitar lines, while Ben sings:

Your hair reflects the golden sun, you're always having all the fun.

Waiting in the dinner queue – the only thing I'm waiting for is someone like you…'

Ben's voice sounds good, like he's really singing to Hayley Green, even though I can't see her there in the audience. People are leaning forwards; listening, liking it. I daren't look at the others, so I lose myself in my guitar parts. My fingers feel a lot more confident than the rest of me. They know what to do. I move my head so my fringe flops over my eyes while I'm playing.

It's almost time for the first chorus. I move up to the mic stand.

'One day I'll have a girl like you, I'll know exactly what to do, to love you, to keep you – but I'm just another boy waiting in the queue.'

My voice growls a bit, but it sounds okay. Ben glances across at me and smiles.

Josh speeds up a bit towards the end but Ben isn't distracted. He sings with passion, looking straight into the audience, and he seems to be enjoying himself. The song sounds great, and a few girls in the front row are clapping along.

I spot Lance, the Year Seven kid, in the second row, left hand side, his eyes glued on the stage. He catches my eye but I look away and stare at my guitar.

Then it's over. The applause sounds like a rainstorm on

the roof. There's a whistle – Rachel, with her fingers in her mouth; even a few whoops and screams from the girls at the front. Not girls I've talked to before – girls from Year Seven and Eight who I've seen hanging around. Some of them dress a bit emo, with Converse trainers and black and white stripy socks.

I turn around and grin at Josh, and he smiles back. He looks a bit more relaxed now.

Ben steps up to his mic stand and strums a decisive chord.

'This song is dedicated to someone who's made our lives a misery. Now it's time for us to have our say.' Ben stares directly at Bradley Smeed.

'When we were new and little, you used to look so tall. You looked at us and thought you could kick us against the wall,' he sings slowly, just accompanied by his acoustic guitar. His new guitar strings sound fresh and zingy.

A chair squeaks against the floor. Bradley Smeed stands up. I think he's going to storm out. His mum tugs his coat and he sits back down again, staring at the stage with pure hate.

I turn back to Josh at the moment when we crash in with the drums and lead guitar. It sounds good but Ben has made it absolutely clear to everyone in the whole room who the song is about. Bradley won't let us get away with this. Lance glances over at him anxiously. We told him about the song and swore him to secrecy.

'Playing games with people – that's all you ever do,' Ben sings. His voice is confident and strong. *'No real friends, you just use them 'til you're through. See the weakest ones and ruin their lives. But what are you going to do when they reach your size?'*

Apart from succeeding in winding Bradley Smeed up, I realise it's our strongest song. That last line of the chorus seems to soar above the audience's heads, like something they could catch in their hands. Ben might not have much confidence in his guitar playing but he's a really good songwriter. We've got lots of work to do on the band, but this is a good start. I smile and I don't care what Bradley, or anyone else, might do to us.

I can't stay in my comfort zone at Ben's side for long. As Ben sings the last line, I feel like I'm gradually turning to ice; the feeling starting in my stomach, then spreading to my toes and fingertips. I almost lose balance and my fingers slip a little bit. I play a bum note but quickly cover it up. I glance up. I don't think anyone noticed. Ben's voice fades away and the clapping starts.

It's time for 'Bring the Lightning'. I cough into my shoulder, double-check the tuning on my guitar, and step up to my mic stand. Everyone is looking at me.

'Bring the Lightning,' I stammer. Before I lose my nerve, I launch into the guitar riff. Behind me, the drums crash in and Ben plays the chords I taught him perfectly. I take a deep breath and start to sing.

'Sitting alone in my room at night. I want to play and don't want to fight. But every day, I lose, not win – feels like my life will never begin.' It sounds alright. I concentrate on singing and playing. I can't even see the audience now – they've gone all blurred. Perhaps this is how Daz saw the world, without his glasses, lost in his guitar playing.

'Will anything work out right? It's a fight to the end. It's a fight for my life,' I sing. It's like I am Daz. It sounds stupid but I can really feel him inside my head, even though I never knew him. *'Just trying the best I can. It's never enough for my old man.'*

My playing feels spikier, angrier, more inspired than normal.

'One day, I'll show them. Prove them wrong in every way. I'm going to show them – I'm going to have my day.'

I sing the chorus. *'I bring the lightning.'* Ben worked out a harmony and it sounds great. Mrs Lyons was really impressed when she overheard one of our rehearsals last week.

There's a clatter behind me. Instead of a solid drum beat, there's suddenly silence. I turn my head. Josh's drumstick is rolling across the stage and he's crawling to retrieve it, red faced. Josh glances at me, apologetically. Ben's strumming falters.

Sam told me that when something goes wrong, the best thing to do is to carry on.

I step on my effects pedal, turning up the distortion, and turn up the volume on my guitar. I play the solo, making it as loud and heavy as I can. I can sense Ben's panic but I can't let myself look at him. I'm playing the way I do when I'm in my bedroom, making things up as I go along, mixing in Daz's jagged style with bits of James Dean Bradfield's epic rock guitar. Even though I'm covering up for a disaster, I'm really enjoying myself. I bend over my guitar, my fringe flailing around, wide-legged, centre stage. I'm getting lost in my playing, but I also want to distract attention from Josh.

I vaguely hear whoops and cheers from the audience. I can't hear Ben, even though I've stayed in the same key. I feel bad that I've lost him, left him behind. But what else can I do?

The drums join in with my solo, with a rumble on the floor tom that sounds quite good. The audience are clapping and cheering. I look up and see Mum's face. She looks really upset and intensely happy at the same time.

Looking at the audience, I almost panic, and my scalp prickles with sweat, like that time a lorry almost knocked me over on Cromford Hill. I launch back into the main riff, and Ben starts playing again.

I start singing the third verse. Ben glares at me. I don't know why he's angry with me. I know I got a bit carried away, but I was only trying to save our gig.

Kaz

I'm glad I stuffed my pocket with toilet roll before I left the house. Jason looks so natural on the stage – a few nerves, but that's not surprising. It's his first time in front of a proper audience. I was already crying by the time he started singing the song he wrote about Daz but, when he covered up for Josh dropping his drumsticks, I felt so proud of him.

I felt for Ben, though, completely out of his depth,

terror written across his face as he mimed strumming his guitar and tried not to lose face. Just like me trying to keep up with Daz. I'll have to give him lots of praise in the interval. I feel proud of Ben too.

I feel strangely sad. Jason is changing. His voice is breaking, changing his singing voice into something much more powerful. He's tall and strong, and he's growing in confidence; making his own decisions. I lost Daz and now I've lost my little son, my life-saver. He looks so much like Daz, apart from the black lace blouse which he would never have worn in a million years. Jason manages to pull it off, even though he and Ben look like chalk and cheese on stage.

The song ends, with the last line of the chorus. The applause starts; the girls at the front are squealing. Next to me, Rachel whistles, her fingers in her mouth like a shepherd calling a sheep dog. I clap until the palms of my hands are sore, and I stand up, not caring any more about people in the audience staring at me.

Jason smiles shyly, and makes a tiny bow. Josh grins. He's already unscrewing the nuts on his cymbal stand, obviously glad it's all over. Despite Jason's worries and the mistake he made today, he's shaping up to be a pretty good drummer. Ben looks upset, his smile not reaching his eyes.

I dab at my eyes and blow my nose. I don't want to look like a complete mess. I'm just a sentimental middle-aged mother. What if more people ask for my autograph over the coffee and biscuits?

The curtains close and the lights come up. The music teacher comes on stage.

'They've been working very hard, and I'm sure you all enjoyed their exciting musical debut. A trio of promising young musicians – Jason, Ben and Josh!'

There's another round of enthusiastic applause.

'Fucking show-off tosser,' mutters a voice behind me. Bradley Smeed.

'They were brilliant. Even Ben,' Rachel says, loudly. 'I think they need a bass player though.'

There's a scuffle of chairs scraping against the floor as

the audience make their way towards the serving hatch. Sam waves at me from the back of the hall and he bounds towards me. He gives me a hug, almost knocking the breath out of me.

'I told you Jason had potential,' he grins.

Sam smiles politely at Ben's parents.

'Ben's developing a great talent. His singing, his song writing…'

'He's certainly surprised us,' Kevin jokes. 'No one else in the family has any musical talent. I think those guitar lessons are worth it.'

Sam nods.

'I just wish he was more confident in his own abilities. He says he feels like he's standing in Jason's shadow,' Sam says.

'Jason is better than him though,' Rachel says. 'I can't believe he's only been playing the guitar for six months.'

'They're different, that's all,' Sam says. 'They sound good together, don't they?'

Jason

I help Josh to dismantle the drum kit and stack it backstage.

'Thanks for covering up for me. I don't know what happened. The stick just slipped out of my fingers.'

'I don't think many people noticed, anyway.'

'They were all watching you showing off,' Ben mutters, carrying two cymbal stands and putting them in the pile behind the curtains.

'Ben, I wasn't –'

'Yeah, right.' Ben shoves his guitar into its case and throws it over his shoulder.

He picks up the amp he's been using and staggers offstage. He can't go very fast carrying the amplifier, so I zip my Stratocaster and my effects pedal into my gig-bag, pick up my own amp and start to follow him. The rush of excitement I was feeling has shrunk like a shrivelled balloon.

We should be celebrating together, not arguing.

Josh frowns.

'See you in the hall. I'm going to find my dad.'

'You're getting really good, Josh,' I say.

'I dunno. And you two arguing all the time does my head in.'

'Why's he being such a prick?' I realise my voice is too loud. People might be able to hear me from behind the curtains.

'He's jealous, isn't he? That's all.'

'But –'

I walk out of the door at the back of the stage, squeezing past members of the school orchestra who are carrying stacks of chairs.

'You guys rock!' Tracey Monks says. It's the first time she's actually spoken to me. The other orchestra members murmur their approval.

Tracey is really pretty, with big grey eyes, and lashes spidery with mascara. She smiles at me warmly as we shuffle past each other, our arms brushing; the nylon of my lace shirt against the polyester of her school blouse.

Our eyes lock for a millisecond. She's far nicer than Hayley Green, and she's a great musician. I've heard her playing on her own in the practise room, wild, swooping melodies. Perhaps we could use a violin player in our band.

But my right arm feels like it's falling off from the weight of the amplifier, and I've got to catch up with Ben. We need to talk, now.

Ben is already half way down the dimly lit corridor. I can't go any faster than a slow, unbalanced waddle, because the amplifier I borrowed from school is bigger than his. Another reason for him to be jealous. Stupid. Really stupid of him.

'Ben!' I shout.

He carries on walking, ignoring me.

When I catch up with him in the music room, it's crowded with orchestra members fetching their instruments. It's a relief to put the amp on the floor, and I put my

317

Stratocaster down carefully on a table so I can rub my arm. I probably shouldn't have carried the amp in one go but I didn't want to look like a wimp.

Ben bolts out of the room, without even looking at me. I follow him back towards the hall, dodging more orchestra members carrying their instruments. Will Hardcastle turns towards me, his French horn blocking my way.

'I wish I played the guitar. But my dad won't let me give this up. It belonged to my grandad. It's so cool your parents were in a band.'

'My mum's waiting for me – and I've got to catch up with Ben,' I say, trying not to sound rude as I push past him. I don't want anyone else to think I'm big-headed. Mum will be desperate to see me. She's the only person who'll really understand the crazy mix of emotions going through my head right now.

Ben's ahead of me. I run and almost catch up with him, just as he walks through the double doors into the hall. The girls who were cheering us in the front row suddenly surround us, as if we're a boy band. I add another emotion to my list: panic.

'Ben – you're such a great singer.'

'Can we come and watch your next rehearsal?'

'Brilliant guitar playing, Jason.'

I glance across the hall. I can see Mum, with a paper cup in her hand, talking to Sam. He did make it after all. Sam sees me and waves, and I wave back. I try to walk away but a girl with long mousy hair and freckles across her nose stands in front of me.

A scruffy paper booklet and a chewed biro are thrust into my hands.

'Jason, will you sign my homework planner?'

This is ridiculous. I mean, what am I supposed to write? *Jason Knight, 9RB. Great Geography homework*?

I hand the planner back to her. The girl's face goes from being happy and excited, to looking like a sad clown with her mouth painted on upside down. I feel terrible for a second.

I'm just a kid from another class. It would be like asking for someone's autograph just because they won a race on sports day.

'No. Sorry. I mean, what's the point of doing that?'

It came out more growly than I wanted it to. I smile at her, to show I'm not a complete bastard. Ben gives me the dirtiest look imaginable.

'You'll sign it though, won't you, Ben?' the girl pleads.

I make a run for it. Actually more of a fast walk, dodging around people standing in the aisle between the seats towards the tea urn at the back of the hall.

'Well done, son,' says a bald man I've never met before. I'm not anybody's son. Definitely not his. I bet Daz Lightning wouldn't feel so guilty about not signing a little kid's homework planner.

What am I supposed to have done to upset Ben? I can't see Josh anywhere. He seemed pissed off too, but I don't know what I've done to deserve it.

'Cracking little guitarist,' another man says. People's parents give me sidelong glances and whisper things, glancing towards Mum.

Chapter 24
The Fight

Kaz

Jason rushes towards us. He looks almost out of breath, as if he's being chased.

'Those girls. Total nightmare,' he says.

'Groupies already,' I tell him.

Sam laughs but Jason stares at me like a stunned animal, his eyeliner-ringed eyes wide with horror.

'You played really well,' I tell him. 'And it was good that you covered up for Josh. Perhaps a little over the top –'

'Don't listen to her, Jason,' Sam says. 'I'm really proud of you.'

Ben walks towards us. He freezes and stares at Jason.

'You were great, Ben. You've got star quality. We should record some of your songs for the Young Songwriter of the Year Awards,' Sam says.

He's right. Ben's got an impressive singing voice, good tunes and witty lyrics. He's better than most people twice his age. But he just gives Sam a small, disappointed smile. Jason looks almost as if he might cry. His head and shoulders have drooped. He should be really happy now.

This fall-out with Ben has been brewing ever since Jason discovered the truth about me. Ben's got an inferiority complex, according to Jason, but I feel partly responsible, even though I can't help being who I am. Perhaps I should have praised Ben's musical abilities more; given him more faith in himself?

Brenda, Kevin and Rachel fuss around Ben. It's obvious how pleased and proud they are, and Ben smiles, but his expression seems pasted on.

I hug Jason, with my empty paper cup still in my hand. I don't care about embarrassing him, or that he's too big for hugs.

'I really enjoyed the gig, Jason. The first of many.'

Jason leans into me, just like he did when he was little

and I came to pick him up from school. He'd leave Ben and come running across the playground. I always felt overwhelmed that I was responsible for this miraculous little life.

Jason pulls away, sharply.

'Well, what a talented young man,' Dominic Smeed says, rather loudly, as he approaches us from the direction of the tea table. 'He obviously takes after his parents.'

Bradley Smeed stares across at Jason; his eyes so cold they could be dead. There's a pile of biscuits in his hand and his lips are covered in crumbs.

'He works very hard. He loves playing the guitar. It's permanently welded to him.' I notice Jason hasn't got his guitar case with him now. 'Did you leave it in the music room?'

Jason looks rooted to the spot, he's so angry. He gives me an accusing stare.

'Dominic's the architect on Barbara's gallery project,' I explain.

'And we're very lucky to have your mother on the team.'

'You didn't tell me,' Jason mutters.

The school PA system crackles. Mrs Lyons walks on stage from behind the curtains, holding a microphone.

'Ladies and gentlemen,' she says, with a smile. 'The concert will resume in five minutes with a performance from the Senior Orchestra. They've been practising hard on Holst's *Planets Suite*, so it should be a real treat.'

Dominic Smeed turns to his step-son.

'Bradley. I told you to fetch Mary's cello. Have you done it? They're about to start.'

Bradley mutters something to himself. It does seem a bit harsh, making him fetch and carry for his sister. Bradley starts walking, shoulders slumped. As he passes Jason, his face brightens with a combination of glee and malice.

Jason

As Bradley walks past me, his eyes lock with mine. With his finger, he makes a tiny movement in front of his throat.

'You're dead,' he whispers.

He's going to the music room, to fetch his sister's cello. But I can see he wants to hurt me; to get his own back. People are starting to head back to their seats.

'I'm just going to the loo,' I say.

'Be quick. The orchestra will be on in a minute.'

I try to catch Ben's eye, but Rachel is talking to him, and I'm better doing this on my own anyway. I keep my eyes on Bradley's puffer jacket. He's walking quickly and he's already out of the doors into the foyer.

I walk faster. Those girls are sitting down again now but they turn their heads to watch me. Maybe they'll stop bothering me if I refuse to sign anything. Ben thought I was being stuck up when I didn't sign that girl's book. I used to be able to be myself with Ben, but now it feels like I have to watch everything I say and do.

Bradley is walking down the corridor. His footsteps echo. It's quiet; the classrooms are dark, empty. I hang back. Bradley turns right, towards the music room. I follow, treading carefully. The soles of my Docs hardly make a sound.

The music room light is on. I look through the window in the door. Bradley Smeed has unzipped my guitar case and he's picked up my guitar. The thought of him touching my guitar feels like an icy-cold hand pressing into my stomach. I make myself watch. He sits on the table and holds my guitar clumsily, the wrong way up. He strums it, frowns, and tries moving his hand around. He stares angrily at my Stratocaster, grabs it by its neck, then swings his arm.

I run into the room and try to grab the guitar from him. He's not letting go. I try to prise his fingers away but Bradley seizes my wrist. I can't escape from his sausage-fingered grip and he twists it in a Chinese burn. I try not to gasp in pain. I hang onto my guitar and try to pull it away from him.

'You think you're all clever now? Just because you can string some fucking words together. Pathetic.'

'We can say what we like about you.'

'Big mistake, Kenny.'

He suddenly shoves the body of my guitar into my chest, knocking my breath away. Bradley lifts the guitar above his head and throws it, as hard as he can, across the room. There's a sickening crack and a twang as it hits the wall opposite. I run over to it. The neck has snapped off, and there's a crack running along the body.

I burst into tears. I can't help it. I try to wipe my eyes with my sleeve but the nylon lace isn't very absorbent.

'Fucking poof!'

'What the fuck have I ever done to you?' I meant it to come out as a threatening shout, but it just sounds pathetic; a hysterical squeak.

I'm so angry: with myself, for leaving my guitar in here, for allowing myself to be Bradley Smeed's victim my whole life; with Ben, for abandoning me.

I look up at Bradley's doughy face and his small, stupid eyes. He looks like a pig. He's laughing.

I charge at Bradley. I try to grab hold of his shoulders but his puffer jacket is too slippery. I slam him backwards into the piano, making it rock on its feet. Bradley blinks with surprise. Then he pushes me back, making me lose my balance. I quickly scramble back onto my feet.

I stand and square up to Bradley, staring at him at point-blank range.

'You can hurt me, but you can't scare me,' I say.

Bradley tries to push me again.

My fingers lock into a fist. I pull my arm back and punch, with all the force in my body. My fist connects with his face, right into his nose. There's a crunching sound. A trickle of blood comes out of one nostril. I remember I'm wearing the skull ring.

Bradley's eyes open wide with shock. He touches his nose with his hand and stares at the line of blood, dripping onto the pale grey material of his jacket.

'You fucking…' he growls.

He aims a punch at me, too fast for me to dodge. It hits me square in my right eye, in an explosion of pain and a flash of light. I stagger backwards. I can't see anything, out of either eye. My ears are filled with a ringing sound. Everything in front of my eyes is grey and full of dots, like looking up into a snow-filled sky.

'Fucking mummy's boy. Just because your mum's got people chasing after her to sign autographs, it doesn't mean she's not mental. They must be mental too.'

Bradley pushes me again and I collide with a chair, knocking it over. I get tangled up in its metal legs. I'm on the floor again. I feel sick. My head's spinning. I don't even know where I am in the room.

Maybe because I can't see, I get an image of Mum crouching down in the playground, on my first day at school, her arms wrapped around me. My dark blue parka was like wearing a hug too. Bradley must have seen me. Even then, he knew what would hurt me. Because I had something he didn't.

The door opens. I raise my head at the sound. My vision's starting to clear. I can see shapes moving around, gradually forming themselves into people.

'What's going on?' Mrs Lyons shouts. Bradley's dad is here too.

You would have thought it was obvious.

She gasps as she sees my smashed guitar. I look at Bradley. There's blood running from his nose, leaving a trail of red on the floor.

'You were supposed to be bringing Mary's cello. The concert can't go on without her. They're all waiting. The whole school is waiting.' Mr Smeed's voice is low, threatening.

'You'd better take the cello to the hall yourself, Mr Smeed. The show must go on. And fetch Jason's mum,' Mrs Lyons says, flatly, like she's struggling to control her temper.

'I can't trust you on your own anymore,' Mr Smeed says, as he picks up the cello. 'You're grounded.'

Bradley stares at him. He blinks, once. Bradley's dad walks away, down the corridor.

I'm sitting awkwardly on the floor.

Mrs Lyons turns the chair the right way round and I get up and perch on the edge of it. I must be in trouble too. I don't care.

'Sit down,' she orders Bradley Smeed. She takes a handful of tissues from the box on her desk, and gives them to him. 'Perhaps your step-dad should take you to hospital, when we've sorted this out. Your nose could be broken.'

Mrs Lyons looks over at me. There's a trace of a smile on her face.

Step-dad? I hadn't realised. I look over at Bradley. He's holding the wad of tissues up to his nose. It's gradually turning red.

'Jason. What happened? Your eye looks nasty.'

'I followed him to the music room, and when I got there, he was about to smash my guitar.'

'I just wanted to play it. And then when he saw me, he went mental. And then…' Bradley's voice is muffled, like he's got a bad cold.

'He smashed it!' I say. But he was trying to play it, it's true.

'Don't panic, Jason. It can probably be repaired.'

Mr Smeed comes back, with Mum.

'Your guitar!' she yells. She kneels down, looking closely at the damage. I stagger towards her.

'Can it be mended?'

Mum hugs me fiercely.

'Did he do that to your eye?'

She glares at Bradley. Then she notices the blood coming out of Bradley's nose, the scarlet-stained tissue.

'Nice work, Jason,' she whispers.

Mr Smeed stands there with his arms folded.

'I'll pay for repairs – or a replacement. We'll stop Bradley's allowance. Is it expensive?'

Mum looks up at him.

'I know a guy in a music shop in Derby. I'll take it there.

It's a budget guitar – but a good one.'

'Bradley, it's nothing but homework and chores for you until the summer,' Mr Smeed says.

Bradley shrugs his shoulders, refusing to look at Mr Smeed.

'You can't stop me from going out. You're not even my dad.'

I wonder what happened to Bradley's real dad. Bradley doesn't look anything like Mr Smeed; clever-looking, and turning bone-white with anger.

'We've given you everything, Bradley. We've given you all the right chances in life. And you're still no better than…'

My right eyelid throbs. I put up my hand to touch it and it feels all puffed up.

Mum picks up my guitar as if it's an injured bird, and puts it gently inside my guitar case. My eye waters, and it stings like hell.

'It'll be okay, Jason. We'll go and see Andy at the music shop tomorrow. He's fantastic. He'll know what to do.'

I smile gratefully at Mum. Even though my guitar is in splinters and Ben hates me because he thinks I'm a show off, I'm proud to be Jason Knight.

We arrive back at our house. It's dark, and it'll be cold, but I can't wait to get inside, to make sure my acoustic guitar is still okay. Part of my brain's running on overtime, imagining that Bradley's wrecked that too.

Ben jumps out of the Land Rover so I can get out of the middle seat. We haven't spoken much since the end of the concert. Ben's been really quiet. Mum's still talking to Ben's parents, in the car.

'It's my fault, isn't it?' Ben says. 'That song about him. I pushed it too far.'

'It doesn't matter. You were great.'

'I could have come with you. He wouldn't have dared take on the two of us.'

'I shouldn't have left my guitar in the music room.'

'You wouldn't have, if I hadn't –'

'Mum said the music shop might be able to mend it.'

'Is it true? You broke his nose?'

I nod. It makes me dizzy. I can only see out of my left eye.

'There was lots of blood. Made a mess of his jacket.'

'Nice one.'

Mum gets out of the car. She's holding my guitar case carefully so the broken bits don't get shaken up. It's like the guitar case is a body bag. Ben's dad unloads my bike from the boot and wheels it up the steps for me. Without Ben's family looking after us, we'd have to cycle everywhere.

'Come on,' Mum says. 'Let's get you an icepack. There's a bag of frozen blackberries that'll do.'

Ben gets back into the Land Rover, but leaves the door open.

'Are you coming to school tomorrow? Will you be well enough?'

'Course I am.' I grin.

'To bask in the glory?' Ben raises his eyebrows. He's smiling.

'You were brilliant too,' I say. 'That's what I wanted to tell you.'

'And you don't look like a girl – much,' he says.

Rachel hits him over the head, from the shadow of the third row of seats at the back of the car.

'Shut up, Ben. You won't be the only one with a black eye at this rate.' She cranes her neck out of the seat and stares at me.

'You really were amazing on stage tonight. Don't listen to this idiot. Let me know if he's ever out of line again, and I'll sort him right out.'

I laugh, despite the growing throb in my head.

Ben grips my hand in his. It's sore from being twisted by Bradley Smeed.

'I'll never let you down again, Jason. I promise.'

I squeeze his hand back. Ben has been a total pain in the arse recently but I know when he says something like that, he really means it.

Chapter 25
Bruises

Kaz

'This is amazing!' Jason's left eye grows wide as we walk upstairs into Andy's guitar department. His right eye is almost swollen shut and bruised the colour of livid purple eye shadow. It looks terrible. He keeps flicking his fringe over his bad eye, trying to hide it, but also wearing it like a badge of honour.

Sam and I picked him up from school. Jason was full of excitement about the concert and his renewed friendship with Ben. He must have been showing off a little today, about the drama of his fight with Bradley Smeed. Jason told us gleefully that Bradley has been suspended from school.

I was worried Jason might get suspended too but, luckily, the school and Dominic Smeed have taken his side. I can't say I feel sorry for Bradley though.

'It's a great shop,' Sam says. 'What Andy doesn't know about guitars isn't worth knowing.'

Andy comes out from behind his counter. He smiles warmly.

'Great to see you, Kaz. Shame about the circumstances but I'm sure I can mend it.' He sees Jason. He takes his glasses off and polishes them on his old checked shirt.

'Your mum told me what happened. Quite a shiner you've got there.'

Sam laughs. 'The other lad came off worse.'

'Do you think you can fix my guitar?' Jason says.

'I need to see it first.'

I put Jason's guitar case on the counter. Andy opens it up and whistles softly as he inspects it.

Jason pretends to look at a display of guitar straps.

I stand with Sam, holding my breath. The guitar looks pretty hopeless to me. I remember burying the pieces of Daz's white flying V copy that his dad smashed at the bottom of my parents' garden. It's probably still there, under the apple tree.

'I don't care if it costs a million pounds,' Jason mutters. 'Bradley Smeed's paying for what he's done.' I put my hand on Jason's arm. I thought he was alright, but I can feel him shaking with anger.

'The guitar only cost a hundred and fifty quid,' Andy says. 'You could ask them to pay for a replacement – if this lad's family really are rolling in it.'

'That's my guitar. I want it back. I want him to know I survived. That I'm not afraid.'

Jason is so determined. He's changed – for the better. He's been so guarded, self-conscious about what he's wearing, worried; asking me if I'm okay all the time. I wish I'd known Bradley Smeed was making him feel so frustrated and ashamed of himself. Just like Daz used to feel.

Jason's come out of this with his dignity intact. Nothing Bradley, or any other bully, could do, can hurt him again.

Andy frowns, his forehead creased.

'It's going to take a lot of wood glue and resin. It'll take a week or to set properly. I'm not sure I can save the neck. But you'll get your guitar back.'

Jason grins.

'How much is it going to cost?' I ask.

'Just make up a price – it's coming out of Bradley Smeed's pocket money,' Jason says.

'I've got a spare Stratocaster neck if we need it. I'd say about eighty quid,' Andy says.

'That sounds great,' I say.

'I'll bring my acoustic guitar to Coventry tomorrow. I'll play for Gran and Grandad. I wish I had my Strat for jamming with Pete. But it won't stop us.'

Jason's been learning more folk songs to play to my parents. He's excited about going away.

'You couldn't have brought two guitars with you on the train anyway.'

'Can I look round the shop?' Jason asks me, his voice turning from a growl to an excited squeak.

'In case you see another guitar you want after all?'

'I've never seen so many guitars.'

'I'll help,' Sam says, obviously glad of a useful purpose, apart from being a chauffeur. Sam explains the history of each make and model and Jason is entranced, gently stroking the lacquer of each guitar like it's a rare, beautiful animal.

Andy returns his gaze to me, steady and serious.

'I knew who you were that first day,' he says, too low for Jason to hear.

'You did?'

'I knew you were the real thing the second you walked up the stairs. A proper musician. Been playing your bass recently?'

'A bit. Sometimes with Jason, but mostly on my own. Just remembering the basslines. I was never that good anyway.'

'I put all the clues together. I recognised that riff you played. And the note I found. All I needed to do was look at my old Glastonbury programme for that year and do a bit of internet research. I'd forgotten about everything that happened to you...'

'Thanks for keeping it to yourself.'

'The *Wirksworth World* thing went viral, you know.' Andy stares at me, his eyes huge behind his glasses.

'What does that mean?'

'Shared on Facebook and Twitter.' Andy smiles, amused, at my obvious ignorance.

'Last night at the concert – everyone seemed to know about me. I got asked for my autograph.'

Jason comes back to the counter, a pristine white guitar tenderly cradled in his arms.

'Can I try out this Les Paul? It's just like the one James Dean Bradfield plays. I mean, I love my Strat, but...'

'You can try out as many as you want,' Andy tells him. 'Just plug it into the practice amp in the corner.'

'Thanks.' Jason stops, staring at a poster tacked on the side of the counter for a festival in May, called Bearded Theory. Weird name. I scan the line-up. Lots of names I haven't heard of, but Hawkwind? Neville Staple from the

Specials? The singer from New Model Army? It's happening somewhere near Belper.

'Can we go, Mum? Our exams finish that week. I'll work really hard on them.' Jason smiles hopefully. He deserves it. He needs to see some proper live music. I could use it to bribe him to spend more time on his school work, as well as his guitar playing. I don't want him to narrow his choices just because he has his heart set on becoming a musician. I want him to be able to write well and to fill out his own tax return without getting hopelessly tangled.

The festival tickets are quite cheap. If I can't cope, we could be home again within an hour. We'll have to borrow a tent, and get someone to give us a lift. What about Ben? He'll want to come too, and what will his parents say? Jason looks at the poster longingly.

'I'll take you both,' Sam says. 'I'll ask Judith for some time…'

'We'll see.' I fold my arms. 'I'd love to but…'

'Actually…' Andy looks uncomfortable. 'I've been meaning to call you. I know the organisers and I told them I'd met you. They've got a gap in their main stage line-up for Saturday night, and they wondered…'

'They want Mission Control to play?' Jason gasps. 'On the main stage?'

'It's impossible.' Everyone stares at me. I feel lightheaded. I put my hand on the counter to steady myself.

'Why?' Jason asks.

I stare at him. This is stupid.

Jason throws the strap of the Les Paul over his shoulder, quickly checks the tuning, and plugs it into the practice amp. He turns up the amp until the guitar sounds loud and distorted, playing power chords, smiling to himself with satisfaction. He bends over the guitar until his fringe flops in front of both eyes; launches into Daz's guitar part from 'Rootless in Babylon'.

We listen, transfixed. I knew he'd been practising the songs, but I didn't realise he was this good. He follows it up with 'Twisted Skin', playing Daz's chiming, intricate solo

331

note for note, but adding a distorted, heavier flavour to it. Then he plays something I don't recognise at first, frantic chords morphing into a surf-style guitar line.

I break into a smile. It's 'No Hope', from the second album. We only played that song live once, at Spiral Sun. Daz's melodic guitar line blended brilliantly with my Siouxsie-Sioux style screaming in the chorus.

Jason looks up at me and stops playing. He looks older somehow; the bruised, swollen eye making him look more like a wounded hero than a vulnerable, beaten-up kid.

'I know I'm not perfect, but I'll work really hard on all the songs until I'm good enough. I promise I'll be ready…'

I rush forward and hug him. I can't believe he's only been playing the guitar for six months. He wants to take Daz's place in Mission Control. He might just be able to. He's got grit and the determination, and the self-confidence Daz never had.

'You're brilliant, but we need Ash.'

'We'll find him. Next week. We'll keep looking until we do.'

'What about Pete?'

'He'll love it. I know he will.'

'This is amazing,' Sam says. 'The start of a whole new chapter.'

Andy's magnified eyes sparkle behind his glasses.

'Shall I call them?' he asks. 'Tell them you're up for it?'

I feel myself shaking.

'Please, Mum? You can do it. I won't let you down.'

The idea is terrifying but somehow thrilling, just like it always was: the nerves and nausea before going onstage and the euphoria of performing. Jason got a taste of it last night: the buzz, the craving. He's hopelessly addicted already.

Jason

Gran and Grandad are waiting for us on the platform at the train station. I catch sight of them as the train is still rolling gently to a stand-still. We're standing by the doors, other passengers jostling my acoustic guitar hanging on my back in the new padded gig bag Mum bought me as an early birthday present. My school bag is stuffed with clothes and books. Mum made me bring homework.

The train from Birmingham was running a bit late, and Gran and Grandad are craning forward to check we're there, worried expressions on their faces. Maybe they look anxious most of the time. After all, they've had to put up with years of searching for Mum, not even knowing if she was alive.

We step off the train and the coldness hits my face. Even the diesel-smelling air seems fresh after the musty railway carriage.

Mum gives me a nervous look. It's the first time she's been away from home in my entire life, apart from my other trip to Coventry. This time it's different. We're a proper family, with grandparents. Just like everyone else.

Mum locked the house up carefully, hiding Elsa's artwork in the cupboard under the stairs. Rachel offered to cat sit and look after the house. Mum told Rachel she could stay overnight if she promised not to have any parties while we we're away. Rachel rolled her eyes, just like she does at home.

Gran rushes forwards and hugs me but I'm weighed down with bags sticking out at awkward angles, so she may as well be giving my guitar case a hug. I bend down as she stretches up to kiss my cheek, and I flick my hair out of my face.

'Jason! Look at you!' She stares at my black eye. It's turning an interesting colour – greenish around the edges. I got some funny looks on the train. Some people looked sorry for me and tried not to stare at me. I think they thought I'd been beaten up by my dad or something. Or people thought I was some kind of psycho and looked a bit scared of me. I just covered my eye with my fringe and read my *NME*.

Gran looks so much like Mum.

'It doesn't hurt much. It's already gone down a bit.' I've got a few other bruises too but they're not on my face, and I feel fine. I won't be fourteen until the middle of this week, but I feel like I'm sixteen or something. I wish I was. Then I could spend all my time making music.

Grandad gives me a handshake, staring at my chipped purple nail varnish. Then he hugs me, gripping my shoulders with his bony hands. He offers to take my bag, but he's so old and skinny, I don't want to tire him out.

'I hear you were standing up for yourself. And doing a pretty good job of it, too.'

I grin. We start walking through the train station. Gran puts her arm around Mum. She's even shorter than Mum, wearing soft lace-up shoes, even though Mum's worn-out Doc Martens don't give her much extra height. I've got a few inches to grow until I'm as tall as Grandad, but his shoulders stoop.

The ground is icy, with a thin dusting of snow. Our feet crunch on grit scattered on the pavement as we walk towards Grandad's car.

'It's not a long walk from the station, but you've got luggage.' Grandad unlocks the car doors with his blipper. 'The pavements are slippery.'

'We can't wait to hear you play the guitar again,' Gran says. 'Such a shame about your electric one.'

'It might be mended by the time I get home. Then I'm going to need to rehearse like mad.'

'Have you got another concert at school?'

Mum glares at me as she puts her holdall in the car boot. She obviously didn't tell Gran and Grandad when she was on the phone last night. Maybe she wants to wimp out of the whole thing. I won't let her. I put my school bag in the boot but I'm going to hang onto my guitar.

'I'm going to be playing guitar in Mission Control, at a festival in the summer,' I say. I can't help grinning. Gran and Grandad look shocked. Mum turns pale.

'Nothing's certain, Jason. We don't even know what Pete will say – and even if we find Ash, it might be the last thing he wants to do.'

'We'll do it, Mum. Even if we have to get Josh to play the drums with us.'

We get into the back seat of Gran and Grandad's car.

'Josh is shaping up nicely, but he's not quite ready for the main stage of a festival. What if he drops his drumsticks again?'

Mum laughs. She's talking to me casually, as a musician; the way she talks to Sam, as if she thinks I am ready. I hug her, before she can change her mind. I'm glowing from the inside, despite the ice outside.

'Karen, you can't be serious – surely not?' Gran says. 'You're getting the band back together, with Jason?'

'Why not?' Mum suddenly sounds defiant, like me when I don't want to tidy my room. 'It's his idea.'

'He's a child,' Gran says. 'Are you sure you know what you're doing?'

I stay quiet. I don't want to start our visit with an argument. I thought they'd be pleased.

Kaz

I push open the door of Singh News. It's early; Sunday morning. Jason is still asleep in my old room. And I need to do this alone.

It used to smell of dusty spices in here, mingled with fresh cooking from the maisonette upstairs. Shelves were arranged haphazardly, according to Mr Singh's unique logic, tins of cat food next to model aeroplanes and packets of Bombay mix.

When Daz worked here, he was in charge of the video corner. He was quite proud of it, very methodical, with an ordering system he'd made up himself.

Mr and Mrs Singh were kind to Daz, making him snacks to eat at work; giving him little bonuses, knowing how difficult life was for him at home. When we lived in the studio, Mrs Singh would bring us curries in Tupperware containers, plastic bags filled with samosas.

Daz's video corner is long gone. Wine bottles on shelves line the walls now. The shop is white-painted, fresh and neat.

A woman about the same age as me stands behind the counter, sorting out a stack of newspapers, while an old man in a nylon overall stands in the aisle, bent over a stack of cardboard boxes, a price gun in his hand. He slowly puts packets of biscuits on the shelf.

The glare from the harsh strip-lights is reflected in his shiny brown scalp, through thin skeins of white hair.

I step forward.

'Mr Singh?' When I knew Mr Singh, he still had thick dark hair, streaked with grey. It's a shock to see how much time has changed people.

The man unbends stiffly, his hand on his back. He pushes his wire-rimmed glasses up his prominent nose. His eyes are clouded with confusion, and he stares at me. Gradually, his eyes light up with recognition.

'It is you! Your parents said you were back.' He smiles, sadly.

'Kaz?' the woman behind the counter says. I recognise her. Ash's sporty sister.

'Kavita?'

We make eye contact and smile, awkwardly. Kavita looks harassed, her hair scraped into a ponytail. She's dressed in a pale green Nike sweatshirt. I never knew her that well, even at school. She was always at running practise, or in the gym. Everything about her was clean and tidy. The idea of getting drunk or stoned, going to live in a dirty old warehouse or being bundled into a smelly van for weeks on end, made absolutely no sense to her. We could never think of much to say to each other.

'You look well,' she says.

'You don't look any different,' I tell her. I'm lying. She's still slim, but there are dark shadows under her eyes, and hollows in her cheeks. She sighs, in mock exasperation.

'I've got three kids. That's the only running I do now.' She glances at her dad and gives me a meaningful look. 'The shop keeps me busy. Mum and Dad are getting on a bit, and someone's got to –'

'I wrote to Ash last month. I haven't heard from him yet. Is he okay?'

'For years he waited,' Mr Singh says. 'Then he went to a place where no one could reach him. To save him the disappointment.'

My heart stabs with panic.

'He's not...? What happened? I'm so sorry...' I glance wildly from father to daughter. Mr Singh goes back to pricing his biscuits. I feel Ash's letter in my pocket. The paper crinkles under my fingers.

Please, no. He loved me. And all I could do was throw it away, ruin his life.

'It's not that bad!' Kavita says, with a bitter, dry laugh. 'He's still in Devon – sometimes.'

'He ran away to sea,' Mr Singh says.

Kavita sighs. 'The *Sea Shepherd*. He signs up for bloody months on end to work on some boat. For free. Trying to save the whales or something,' She sounds completely bored by the whole thing.

I try to breathe normally. He's alive – unless he's been harpooned at sea, or fallen overboard. He's got his own life, doing something useful. He's probably happy.

'When does he get back?' I ask.

'The day after tomorrow, as it happens.' Kavita makes a face. 'He won't come back here though. He should be the one stuck here. He's never had a proper job.'

I can't help smiling. I can't wait to tell Jason that Ash is alive. I take the letter out of my pocket and show Kavita the address at the top of the letter.

'Is he still here? At this farm?'

Kavita snorts.

'Not much of a farm. Unless they're farming hippies.'

'Thanks – that's brilliant!'

Kavita must spend too much time reading the shop's copies of the Daily Mail, but I don't care. Ash probably doesn't even know I sent him a letter. Not yet. I can find him.

'Is he on the phone?'

Mr Singh smiles.

'You must come upstairs; have tea. I can tell you all about Ash. He sends us emails, you know. From the middle of the ocean.'

I follow him, meekly.

Jason

'Do you want to see our studio? Find out what happened to it?' Mum says.

I nod.

'It's only ten minutes from here.'

I glance at Gran and Grandad. We're in Debenhams, just finishing off a coffee. Gran bought me a slice of chocolate cake. We look strange, like two mismatched pairs: Grandma in her smart coat, with her Barbara Fleming shopping bag with pictures of ducks on it, next to Mum, wearing her falling-apart fake leather jacket.

'Do you mind if we go off on our own for a bit?' Mum asks. 'We'll meet you by the entrance in an hour.'

Gran smiles. I wonder if she's worn out, or fed up with us by now. We're staying until Thursday. It's my birthday on Wednesday.

Grandad has dragged us around every possible visitor attraction in Coventry. This morning, it was the cathedral. Both cathedrals. And the visitor centre for one that hasn't even existed since medieval times, where you can just see the medieval floor plan laid out on the ground.

In the ruined cathedral, I just wanted to be quiet and think about what it meant. All those people who died; all those buildings burned. It must have been terrifying. Grandad wouldn't stop talking, explaining everything, pointing out every little detail. Sometimes you don't want to know everything. You just want it to wash over you.

'That's fine.' Gran nods. 'I've got the measurements for the living room curtains with me.'

'I don't know what's wrong with the old ones,' Grandad says.

'We've had them over twenty years! The lining's perished. We've had the same curtains since Karen was Jason's age.'

Mum wraps her scarf around her neck, and pulls on the gloves that Gran bought her. We leave them, gently arguing. I bet it wasn't like this before Mum came back, before I found them. It must have been horrible to live their lives without knowing what had happened to their daughter.

Away from the city centre, Mum leads me down scruffy, derelict-looking streets. The cold wind blows old crisp packets and chip papers around. A few people pass us, and they're scary, hard-looking. A man carrying a four-pack of lager in a plastic bag has home-made tattoos on his knuckles. Mum walks briskly, her gloved hands deep in her jacket pockets, her eyes shining.

'This way!' she says.

We climb the steps of a metal bridge high over the dual carriageway. It makes me feel dizzy, looking at the cars whizzing below me and I have to concentrate so I don't slip on the thin covering of snow.

'Daz used to skateboard over here,' she says.

'He had a skateboard?'

'It was Ash's skateboard. They had this stupid game. Doing a trick jump just before the steps. Or they'd skate down the ramp. They used to dare each other.'

'I wouldn't fancy it in this weather. Sounds like fun, though.'

'Daz took too many risks.'

We climb down the steps on the other side, carefully. They've been gritted, but they're still slippy. Daz would probably say I was a total wuss.

'The canal's over there,' she says. She knows exactly where she's going, along a street with old warehouses built with dark brown bricks.

'You sound like Grandad,' I joke, but she keeps on walking, faster now.

We follow the concrete ring road, passing a tall white tower block. There are some leafless trees, and dried-up, frozen weeds in the pavement cracks. I feel like such a country boy, lost without green fields.

She turns left, over a little bridge. The steel-grey canal water reflects the sky. She walks down a small scruffy side street. Mum suddenly stops and looks around, confused.

'I was looking for the telephone box.' She stares at an empty patch of Tarmac. She looks up. 'It's gone.'

I don't know what she wants me to look at. In front of us is a breeze-block built single-storey unit with steel shutters over a loading bay. It's the least exciting building I've ever seen in my life. Purely functional.

Mum walks up to the building and stares at the sign, blue lettering on white plastic: *Nagra Wholesale Fruit & Vegetables.*

'This is it. They must have rebuilt the whole thing.'

'Ash burned it down. It did sound like a bit of a shithole,' I say. Mum's told me about mice chewing through cables and cereal boxes.

'Our bedroom was up in the loft. Ash and Daz converted it themselves.'

'It can't have been worth saving.'

Mum sits on the edge of the pavement, staring at the warehouse.

'I haven't been here since I ran away.'

We'll be late for meeting Gran and Grandad. Mum hasn't got a mobile. I don't even know where I am. I really wanted to come here. I knew it wouldn't be the same but I thought something might be there to connect me to Daz, to the songs and the music that was made here. I don't know what to do. I look at the warehouse building, at the view of the white tower block in front of the grey sky. Why do some things get destroyed: the studio; Daz, while some things go on existing, like Gran and Grandad's curtains?

I've been drinking tea out of the same mug Daz used but

I'll never know him.

I sit down next to Mum. We must look like a right pair of pikeys. It's a good job the street is quiet, or people might start chucking spare change at us. I put my arm around Mum and she leans her head on my shoulder.

'It's okay. I know it's something you had to do.'

'You were probably conceived here, you know.' She laughs, and pulls me to my feet. I'm not sure I wanted to know that, but maybe I needed to. To know I came from here too.

Chapter 26
The Road Trip

Kaz

I press Pete's doorbell. He lives in a semi-detached thirties place, like my parents' house, further out of town. I can see toys and brightly coloured wellies through the frosted glass of the porch door.

I clutch a carrier bag, with a bottle of red wine from Singh News. Dad dropped us off. It made me feel like a teenager again, getting a lift to a party where I would end up under a pile of coats in a back bedroom with Daz.

Jason's acoustic guitar is slung on his back. He's gelled his fringe over his bruised eye.

'Pete might not want to get the band back together,' I say. 'He's busy.'

'We won't know until we ask him.'

The light in the porch is suddenly blocked out by the massive shape of Pete, standing in the doorway. He opens the front door. He's holding little Karen on his hip. She reaches her hands out towards Jason.

'Horsey!' she shouts.

'She remembers me pulling her round the garden on the cart!' Jason beams. He bends down to say hello to Karen, pushing his hair out of his eyes through force of habit.

'Fucking hell, Jason!' Pete gasps, seeing his purple, puffed-up eye, turning a nasty shade of yellow around the edges. Pete reaches out and holds Jason's fringe aside. He examines the bruise closely, anger growing on his face. Jason blinks.

I remember the way Pete used to protect Daz.

'Kaz told me what happened. That little bastard needs to be taught a lesson.'

'I broke his nose,' Jason says.

'He smashed up your guitar.'

'We sang a song taking the piss out of him at the school concert.'

'It's a brilliant song,' I tell Pete.

'It was war. And I think we've won.' Jason smiles.

'It's great to see you, Kaz. How are your parents?'

We follow Pete into the house. It's warm, painted in bright, earthy colours, with African style paintings on the walls. The hall floor is laminated dark wood, tidy apart from an overflowing toy box. A smell of spicy food comes from the kitchen.

'I must know everything there is to know about Coventry now,' Jason says. 'I'm surprised Grandad hasn't set me an exam.'

'He's just catching up on lost time. Showing you around the cathedral is his way of saying he loves you,' I say.

'I don't mind,' Jason smiles. 'I've got some new ideas for songs. Mum took me to the studio today. There's nothing left.'

'We're still here – and it was a crappy old building anyway.' We follow Pete into the open-plan kitchen-dining room. The table is already set for dinner and Nicko is playing underneath it, pulling a toy train through the chair legs.

Emma rushes forward and hugs me. It's surprising but lovely to get so much affection from someone I've only met once before. She's wearing a brightly printed wrap-around dress that flatters her statuesque curves. Pete is in his usual old jeans and band t-shirt: Slayer, this time.

I give Emma the wine bottle.

'It's freezing.' She touches my cheek. 'Cold night. And he kept you talking on the doorstep.'

She puts the bottle on the kitchen work surface and pours wine from an already opened bottle into glasses.

'Do you drink wine, Jason?' She looks at me for guidance.

'I love wine!' Jason says. 'Great – Shiraz.'

'Just a small glass, then,' I say. 'He's not even fourteen until Wednesday and already he can tell the difference between different kinds of wine.'

Pete laughs. 'It was cans of Woodpecker cider in the park

for me and Daz.'

'He gets all this from eating tea at his best mate's house. His dad thinks that if kids learn about wine, they won't binge on crap stuff.'

I remember Daz, how he struggled every day with his dad's drink problem. When he left home, he seemed okay, at first. Daz seemed free; happy. He helped Ash to build the studio and our living space in the loft. He spent the rest of his time playing the guitar. We'd write at least one song per week together.

As we got more successful, Daz started to drink, to stave off the boredom of long journeys in the van, waiting for gigs to start. When the venues got bigger, he drank more, to numb the fear of performing. There were large lonely spaces inside himself, where I couldn't reach.

Jason hasn't gone through life with so many hurts that he needs to drink like Daz. What if it's genetic? What if Jason's got a taste for it?

'I need to put my guitar somewhere kid-proof,' Jason says.

'I'll put it in my studio,' Pete says. 'We can jam after dinner.'

'Can I see the studio?'

'Wait a bit,' Pete tells him, firmly. 'Dinner first.'

Jason slips the guitar case off his back and gives it to Pete. He opens a door off the kitchen and puts the guitar inside a room, without turning the light on. It's as if he doesn't want us to see what's in his studio.

'We got a Thai recipe book for Christmas,' Emma says.

'I made vegetable tempura.' Pete explains. 'It might go soggy if we leave it much longer.'

'It smells wonderful.'

As we sit down, we have to carefully negotiate Nicko, who's weaving his train in and out of the chair legs.

Jason takes a sip from his wine glass.

'Can we have a jam later, though?' he asks.

'You bet!' Pete grins. 'Help yourselves.'

There's a large serving plate in the middle of the dining

table, piled with delicate pieces of battered golden vegetables.

'You did this?' I ask, somehow not being able to imagine Pete's meaty fingers finely chopping slices of aubergine and dipping coriander leaves into batter.

Pete nods.

'Remember those tinned curries me and Daz used to like?'

'Yeah. Gross. And you turned your nose up at the food Ash got from his mum.'

'I liked the samosas.'

I bite into a piece of battered cauliflower. It's spicy and crisp, with the cauliflower inside tender and aromatic.

'They were lovely. These aren't bad either.'

'You said you'd give it until half term to find Ash,' Jason says, with his mouth full.

'There was a good reason he didn't get in touch. But he's back now,' I say.

Pete looks puzzled.

'He's been on a boat,' Jason says. 'Like Greenpeace. No wonder he didn't get Mum's letter.'

'He comes back tomorrow. To Devon,' I add.

'Great. I hope he gets back to you.'

'I've got his mobile number. I've left a message for him.'

'So what's he been doing on this ship, then?' Pete opens a bottle of lager and pours it into a green glass tumbler.

'His dad said he was some sort of electrician. Gets involved in anti-whaling protests too, from what I can gather.'

'He lived on protest sites a lot after the band. Bob told me. He used to go down there and visit Ash – sold him a bit of weed and some trips.'

'Pete.' Emma says warningly. 'Don't talk about drugs in front of the kids.'

'They're too young to understand.'

'Jason's not too young. I don't want them thinking it's normal,' she says. 'Sorry, Kaz. I don't want Pete to be a bad influence on them. I'm trying to bring them up well and…'

'Don't worry. Mum's really boring now.' He flicks his fringe out of his eyes and smiles hopefully at Pete. 'I want to hear some stories about the old days, though.'

'I want to hear about your gig,' Pete says.

I eat tempura, savouring each mouthful, as Jason tells Pete all about the school concert, showing him his skull ring, and his fingernails, still coated in chipped purple polish. Jason gives him a detailed account of his fight with Bradley Smeed and how he broke Bradley's nose.

'Too fucking right, Jason. Just watch those guitar fingers.'

'I was upset about my guitar. Angry that I'd let him bully me all those years.'

'He won't bother you again,' Pete tells him.

'I'll be ready for him.'

Pete roars with laughter. Some people become a shadow of their former selves as they get older, mourning former glories. Pete is a larger than life version of himself.

Little Karen copies him, throwing her head back; banging a spoon on her high chair, until Emma gently prises it out of her hand.

'Already drumming,' Pete says, proudly. 'You'll have to see her on the kit. Nicko's more interested in trains at the moment.'

'Your drumming sounds awesome on the records,' Jason says. 'I can't wait to see you play.'

'Later, mate.' Pete gives me a conspiratorial wink, although I've got no idea what it's about. Jason notices Pete's glance and stares at me.

'Does Pete know yet? You did mean it, didn't you?'

The festival. Jason was bursting to ask Pete straight away. I think we've waited long enough now.

'You tell him, then,' I say.

'So there's something else we want to tell you.' Jason smiles and smooths his fringe over his bruised, swollen eye.

Emma pauses, halfway between sitting down and standing up, on her way to the kitchen.

'When I went to get my guitar fixed, we found out about a festival in Derbyshire and they want Mission Control to play!'

Pete stares at us with his mouth wide open.

'They want a non-existent band to play a festival? Who's going to headline, fucking Nirvana?'

'They read about me in the local paper. I told you about the gallery thing –'

'That guy you knocked into the pond?'

'They're serious about it. Sam – Jason's guitar teacher – he spoke to the organisers,' I say. 'If I can get the band back together, we'll be on at eight o'clock, Saturday night.'

I should have known. Pete looks angry, as if he might storm off.

'How can you get the band back together, Kaz? It's impossible.'

'I'm going to do it. I'm going to take Daz's part.' Jason smiles proudly and bravely, like a soldier volunteering for war.

The room falls silent, apart from Nicko making steam train noises under the table. I glance at Pete but he's staring at the bubbles in his lager.

'No one could ever take Daz's place,' Pete mumbles.

Jason's shoulders slump. He stares at the table. When he looks up again, he's turned pale. He rubs his good eye savagely with his fist, as if he's bruising it to match the other one.

Pete looks at Jason. It's as if he's seeing Daz instead. A smile slowly spreads across his face.

'No one apart from you, mate. You were born to it.'

Jason glows from within.

'So you'll do it?'

'When the fuck is this festival anyway?'

'May,' I say. 'Mid May.'

'I haven't played the old tunes for years. I didn't want to. We'll have to find Ash – drag him away from saving the whales.'

'You're serious?' I say. 'You really want to do this?'

'It's about time, Kaz. Unfinished business. We're not too old yet.' Pete turns to Jason. 'It's going to be a lot of hard work. But I know you can do it.'

Jason nods gravely.

'Are you going to call Ash?' he asks. 'We need him.'

'We'll do better than that,' Pete says. 'Let's jump in the campervan and go down to Devon and find him. How about Wednesday?'

'My birthday. Cool.' Jason grins.

'You promised to take the kids swimming on Wednesday,' Emma sighs. She lifts her wineglass to her lips, takes a sip and laughs. 'Oh, sod it! Go and find Ash.'

Emma gets up and starts collecting the plates. I help her.

'What if you get there and he doesn't want anything to do with the band anymore?' she asks. Jason helps her to stack the dishwasher.

Pete puts on some oven gloves (not Barbara Fleming ones but plain black quilted ones) and carries an array of oven-warmed serving dishes to the table, being very careful not to trip over Nicko and his train.

'Ash will want to be in the band again. I know he will,' Jason says.

'At least we'll have tried,' I say.

Jason

Pete switches on the lights in his studio. He stands in the doorway with a weird look on his face. Maybe he's drunk, but he wasn't drinking that much.

They let me have two glasses of wine with dinner, in the end. They were big ones, too, but this is an important moment in my life. Even if it's just for one gig, I'm going to be the guitarist in Mission Control.

My hands are aching to hold my guitar in my hands. My acoustic's going to have to do for now. My Strat's probably still in pieces in Andy's workshop.

'Come in. Look around,' Pete says. 'It used to be the garage, but I soundproofed it.'

I step into the room. There's a big drum-kit in the corner

and the walls have got carpet on them. On a stand in front of the drums, is a black electric guitar, its paintwork scuffed and gouged, covered in stickers. I think about Mum's photo album; the photos of Daz in the early days of the band.

Mum gasps. I turn around and look at her, her eyes wide; staring at the guitar.

'What do you think?' Pete grins at her.

'Daz's guitar!' Mum says.

I pick it up gently, examine it. There are hand-drawn skull stickers covering the name on the headstock, and the varnish on the fretboard has been worn away from intense playing. From my dad's fingers.

I look up. Mum is crying, wiping her eyes on a napkin. Too much wine.

The guitar is already plugged into an amp. I switch it on; give the guitar an experimental strum. A tingle goes through me. This is the closest I've ever felt to my dad. I try out the riff from 'Rootless in Babylon'.

Pete smiles at me.

'I've had it for years. Put new strings on and everything for you.'

For me?

'I thought everything in the studio was sold, or burned.' Mum blinks. 'Ash's letter…'

'He sold it to Bob. Bob's not stupid. He knew he'd only get a tenner for it down at Cash Converters. So he brought it to me.'

'This is the guitar you told me about?' I ask. 'The one Ash gave to Daz?'

Daz smashed some expensive guitars, but he kept this one. I've memorised the photos from Mum's album and this angular, beaten-up guitar is there in almost all of them, right up to the Earth Calling days, just with more layers of stickers as time went on. He drew these stickers himself. I trace the outline of one of the skulls on the headstock.

'I hope you don't mind a cheap fourth-hand guitar for your birthday present,' Pete says.

'I promise I'll practise all the time. I'll make Daz proud

of me.' I can't believe he's giving it to me.

'We're already proud of you,' Mum says. She hugs me, then the guitar, as if it's a long-lost child. 'I had no idea, Pete.'

'It's been waiting for its moment. Somehow, I knew it would come.'

I can't think of anything to say, so I play the intro to 'Twisted Skin', and Pete jumps behind the drums. I turn to face him and I feel my face split into the world's biggest grin as Pete plays the little drum fill I've heard so many times on the CD.

The bassline is missing. Mum should have brought her Thunderbird but I suppose it would have been awkward on the train. Instead she grabs my acoustic guitar and joins in, perching on the edge of Pete's desk.

It doesn't matter that we can't hear her above the racket of the guitar and the drums. It's the look on her face that counts; her eyes shining, staring at me as if she can't believe what she's seeing.

Kaz

An unfamiliar alarm clock rings, waking me from an uncertain dream where I'm driving down dark lanes, following a map that doesn't make sense. I sit up and turn on the desk lamp.

Dad's study is claustrophobic, the shelves stretching up to the ceiling, overflowing with history books and journals, the desk jutting out and barely leaving enough space for the narrow folding bed.

It's 6.00am and completely dark outside. The house is silent apart from the groaning and plinking of the central heating pipes, reminding me of winter mornings as a child. I never wanted to get out of bed then, either. Pete is picking us up in an hour. We have to make the most of our time to find Ash. I wriggle free from the blankets and sleeping bag and roll carefully off the end of the camp bed and out of the door, grabbing the bundle of clothes I laid out on the desk.

I tiptoe downstairs. I left a message for Ash; gave him Mum and Dad's number. In the hallway, the answerphone machine is dark. No flashing light. No message. Mr Singh said Ash was definitely in Devon. I take a deep breath. Whatever happens today, at least we'll have tried. For Jason's sake as much as mine.

I climb the stairs again and open the door of my old bedroom.

'Jason,' I call softly. 'Time to get up. Happy birthday.'

There's no response. He sleeps deeply, even on a day like today with so much happening.

Before I get into the shower, I re-tune the bathroom radio from the Today programme to a station playing loud rock music. That might penetrate Jason's dreams.

Jason

Someone's singing 'Livin' on a Prayer'. Mum's voice. She sounds good, but it's embarrassing. Her singing is louder than the noise of the shower and the radio. She's probably woken Gran and Granddad up too. I don't know if she sings in the bathroom at home because it's downstairs, not right next door to my bedroom. We don't have a shower. Singing in the bath would be weird.

I switch on the light. The first thing I see is Daz's guitar, leaning against the bookshelf. Even though I've not got an amplifier, I played it all day yesterday.

I get out of bed and pick up the guitar. I work out the chords to the song on the radio. Then I stop. I want to start my fourteenth birthday by playing a better song. So I block out Mum's singing and play 'Rootless in Babylon' instead.

The door opens. Mum walks in, wrapped in a towel.

'Your turn for the shower. Hurry up, Jason.'

'You only just got out of it.'

'Pete'll be here in half an hour – and you've got presents to open.'

'Really?'

'It is your birthday.'

I don't need telling twice. I put my guitar down and run into the bathroom.

I walk into the kitchen, following the smell of bacon cooking.

Gran is standing at the cooker, in her dressing gown and apron. She gives me a big smile as she sees me and puts the perfectly fried rashers onto the buttered bread with a squirt of brown sauce, and cuts the sandwich in half. I give her a little hug as she hands it to me. She pours me a cup of tea, from a teapot.

'Happy birthday, love.'

Mum smiles, but looks slightly disapproving. She's sitting at the kitchen table with a bowl of cereal and a black coffee. She doesn't like Gran giving me meat. I do feel a bit guilty sometimes, for Mum's sake, mostly.

'I wish you weren't haring off like this,' Gran says.

'We'll be back tomorrow – we'll see you before we go home.' Mum scrapes her spoon on the bowl, and then goes to the sink to wash it up.

I sit down and Gran puts the tea down on the coaster with a picture of Coventry Cathedral's spire on it. There's no getting away from history in this house.

'We've got a little surprise for you, before you go,' she says. 'You thought we were just buying curtains on Monday, didn't you?'

I take a big bite out of my bacon sandwich. Grandad comes through the door, still in his pyjamas, carrying a bulky parcel wrapped in red sparkly paper. He puts it down on the kitchen table, beaming with pride.

'Go on, open it,' he says, smiling at my difficulty of trying decide between my present and my bacon sarnie.

I tear the paper as delicately as I can. Mum always likes to re-use it. Some of our wrapping paper is probably as old as me.

'A laptop!' I smile up at Gran and Grandad.

They smile back, even more pleased than I am, like

they've never given a present to anyone that really made a difference to them before. I'll be able to go on the internet, if Mum pays for broadband, make a Facebook page for our band, which is definitely NOT called the Organ Detectives, and do my homework without jostling for a place in the library at lunchtime, when we could be having valuable rehearsals. They've given me a laptop case as well, black with a skull on it. They definitely know the sort of thing I like.

'Thanks so much!'

Gran starts dabbing the corners of her eyes with a hanky. Something Mum used to do all the time. Mum's smiling too, in the slightly over the top way that means she'll probably start crying too.

I turn to Grandad, while I open the cardboard box and carefully take out the laptop. It's black, sleek and compact. They've even bought me Microsoft Office to go with it. Grandad spends a lot of time on his computer, making his local history presentations.

'It's got Windows Seven,' he says. 'The latest version. The young man in the shop was very keen on this computer. It's a fine model.'

'I want to record my music on it,' I say. 'It's difficult playing something and then trying to remember it. I tried doing it on my tape deck, but that's a bit retro, isn't it?'

'Cutting edge technology in our day,' Mum laughs. 'Handier than carrying that thing about. I'd record a bassline and Daz'd listen to it on his Walkman.'

'I'd just be able to email things to Ben. If we had the internet at home.'

'It's time I embraced the twenty first century,' Mum says. 'Maybe you can give me a go on your laptop.'

'Every time anyone mentions the internet, you look scared to death.'

'You need to teach me.'

She can use it when I'm at school. I'm not cycling with a guitar and a laptop.

I pick up my bacon sandwich again. It's getting cold.

Grandad's talking about the laptops's RAM memory and Gran's rabbiting about the nice young man who sold it to them. I just eat and nod.

The doorbell rings. Grandad shuffles off to answer it, in his slippers.

'Come in,' he says. 'How are you?'

'Fine, thanks, Mr Kenning. It's good to see you again.'

I wonder when Pete last saw my parents. Was it in the hospital, with Daz on the life-support machine, or was it at his funeral, without Mum?

Pete steps into the kitchen. It's beginning to look very crowded.

'Ash still hasn't rung.' Mum's pale, anxious face deflates my mood.

'We won't come back until we find him. I promise.' Pete folds his arms. Mum drains her coffee mug and rinses it into the sink.

'Let's go then.'

'Happy birthday, Jason,' Pete says.

I chew the last mouthful of my sandwich, and reluctantly slide my new laptop back into its box.

It's almost light outside now.

'The weather report said there were icy patches on the roads,' Grandad says. 'I hope you're not like that other young man Karen knows. Didn't even have an ice scraper.'

Pete laughs, the sound echoing off the kitchen cabinets.

'Don't worry. Emma makes sure I'm equipped for a blizzard. Even though I'm usually only off to a school on the other side of Cov.'

Kaz

The roads around here have changed since I ferried the band everywhere in the van. Ash could drive. It was his van, really, but he preferred getting stoned with Daz and Pete, especially on the way back from a gig. I became an expert in negotiating Coventry's ring road system, with all its weird turn-offs.

Pete confidently negotiates an entirely new junction onto the M40, an Orbital track playing on the van's stereo. It's a dull, grey dawn now. The motorway verges are black with traffic dirt.

After years of hardly going anywhere, my navigational skills have re-surfaced. When you get teenage dreams of stardom, no one tells you about all the days you have to spend driving, waiting around, sleeping in laybys and using toilets as a dressing room. Some rock biographies mentioned the gritty details but we lapped it up hungrily. It all seemed wildly glamourous compared with dull, suburban hell. We thought we had it sorted, kitting our van out with beds and a stove.

Pete sails effortlessly onto the motorway. If only he'd been able to drive when we were in the band.

'Remember Castlemorten?' Pete asks, too casually, the way you'd talk about a trip to Alton Towers.

'As if I'd forget.'

It was just before we recorded *Calling Earth*. We'd been flogging the toilet venue circuit for a couple of years and we'd put out a couple of EPs ourselves. We'd got a dedicated following, mostly around the Midlands. Playing anywhere else was a bit hit-and-miss.

It was Ash's idea to go to the free festival. He'd heard rumours about it being massive and he'd called the people running the stage to get us a slot to play: 4.30 on Friday afternoon. We had a few gigs lined up in London later that week anyway, so we thought we'd do it on the way.

'The *Select* magazine article said something about Castlemorten,' Jason says. 'Some of the photos in your scrapbook are from there but you haven't told me anything about it.'

Pete shakes his head in disbelief.

'God, Kaz. You really have been keeping this kid in ignorance.'

'An amazing festival. May, '92. We turned up to do one gig and ended up staying there for a week.'

'Ash had to keep calling them to find out where it was. When we got closer, you could hear it for miles.'

I reach down into my holdall and get out the photo album. It might help persuade Ash to join the band again, on the strength of the good times in the past.

It's worth a shot. I open it at the pages of us at Castlemorten. It's lucky I took so many photographs. What just seemed like a laugh at the time became a key part of the band's mythology; helped us to get hyped in the *NME*; gave us an edge.

There's a picture of the band performing on the Wango Riley's travelling stage. I took it myself. I jumped into the crowd, hanging onto my camera for dear life.

I managed to catch Daz mid-guitar solo, Pete grinning at me from behind his kit. There's a crowd of sunburned, shirtless lads in front of me, gurning and making "peace" signs.

'Is that Ash?' Jason asks, 'Wearing the crash helmet?'

Pete chuckles.

Behind the keyboard, Ash is wearing a lime green crash helmet with pink swirls spray-painted on it. He'd found it in a ditch and claimed that, if he wore it with the visor open, it made everything sound amazing.

'I made him take it off when I got back onstage. It was funny at first but looking at him from the audience made me realise he looked like a twat.'

'She doesn't mince her words, your mother.'

'I threw it into the crowd. Good job too. Marilyn Richards was in the audience. She'd come down on her own to experience a bit of genuine alternative culture. She discovered us – even though we'd been going for years already.'

The photos used in the review were taken on Marilyn Richards' own camera, the rest of the *NME* slow to embrace the rave scene. I'm wearing a black vest, cut down from an old Cult t-shirt, and tie-dyed cycling shorts, screaming into the microphone.

I've got my old bass, the one covered in stickers – I

collected them. One from every gig I'd ever played. People started bringing them for me: Greenpeace, Twyford Down, other bands' stickers, fans' home-made Mission Control stickers, and fruit stickers, advertising Granny Smiths and exotic mangos.

It was probably burned in the fire but I hope that Ash sold it to Bob and, that maybe, a teenage girl somewhere is learning Joy Division songs on it in her bedroom, puzzled by the ancient layers of peeling stickers.

'So you just sort of camped there?'

Jason stares at the photos and points at one where we're all sitting around an open fire, with our van in the background. Daz is laughing, cross-legged, and Pete is deep in conversation with an old guy wearing a hat who looks like Worzel Gummidge. We're part of a big circle of people, the friends and neighbours of our temporary world: hippies, punks, ravers, bikers. Our kind of people. Ash is squatting over a griddle pan, making food for everyone.

'I like camping. I went with Ben. And when we were in the Scouts…' Jason blushes. He only left the Scouts six months ago. Before he discovered rock 'n' roll, he'd come home carrying something he'd carved out of wood, a new knot he'd mastered, or delightedly covered in pond slime.

'Why were you there for so long?' Jason asks.

'We arrived to do the gig and by the time we got back to the van, it was stuck, parked in by a lorry,' Pete says.

'The cars and buses went on for miles,' I add. 'It would have been impossible to get out.'

'So we joined them,' Pete says.

Pete turns off onto the M42. We're getting closer already. He smiles at the memory as he concentrates on the road ahead. The traffic is slowing down, crawling to a standstill. He puts the radio on.

'This bloke taught me to do African drumming. It was fucking awesome.'

'What would Mission Control have sounded like if you'd carried on?'

'Who knows? Some kind of world music folk metal

mash-up?' Pete wonders, with a wry smile.

'What would Daz have made of that?' Jason says.

The van comes to a complete standstill, hemmed in by lorries. The traffic update on the radio says there's been an accident, with long tailbacks.

'Bollocks. We could be stuck in this for hours.' Pete slams his hands on the steering wheel.

'I'll look for another route,' I say, grabbing the map. Pete's using one of those Sat Nav things, but sometimes the old skills are the best.

'Let's start a rave!' Jason says. Pete grins. They give each other a high five.

'Turn the music up loud. You can be the DJ. There's loads of great stuff on my iPod.'

Jason turns the music back on. Being stuck in a traffic jam is a terrible way to spend a birthday, but he seems to be enjoying himself.

Jason

We crawl forward again. Orbital are still blasting out of the speakers, nice and loud. Pete's been telling me about the raves he went to.

'I think I'm starting to understand dance music,' I say.

Pete grins.

'You won't really understand it until you're actually dancing. In a field, with hundreds of other people. That moment when the bass kicks in and the vocals soar above everything.'

'And you all turn and look at each other, the music fills you up and it's the only thing that matters,' Mum says, in the faraway voice she used to use when she was talking about the band.

'It took a while to convince Daz,' Pete says. 'Especially with all those people saying guitar music was dead.'

'What a stupid thing to say.'

'Ash took us to a rave near Birmingham airport and Daz

was hooked. He saw what Ash wanted to do with the band, combining dance music with heavy guitars.' Mum stares out of the window, at the remains of an old farm next to the motorway.

'And real drums,' Pete adds.

'That sort of thing's more normal these days,' I say.

The traffic jam thins out and suddenly we're moving again. Pete accelerates. I see relieved looks on the faces of other drivers as the densely packed vehicles break apart. Before long, we break onto the M5, following signs to the South West. It's just past ten o'clock.

'Now we're really on our way,' Pete says. 'I'm bursting for a piss but I think I can make it to the next services.'

'Can I phone Ash?' Mum asks. Pete picks his phone up from the dashboard and I pass it to her. She stares at it. It's blank, like a black mirror.

'You have to sort of wake it up,' I say. I take the phone off her and press buttons until the screen lights up.

'Now what do I do?' she wails.

I realise how stressed and scared she is.

'Just dial the number.' I can't help sounding impatient.

'I don't even like using the home phone,' Mum says. 'Now everyone's on at me to get a mobile.'

'The band had a mobile phone in the nineties,' Pete says.

'That was massive. It had proper buttons. This thing just has glass.' She stares at Pete's phone, bewildered, until it goes black again.

Mum fumbles in her bag and pulls out a folded bit of paper. It's printed with a spreadsheet that says *Stocktake October 2008*', but she shows me the mobile number written by hand on the other side. I dial it, and press the green button on the touch screen. The phone starts to ring.

'Hello?' A man picks up. He sounds sleepy.

Pete turns the stereo down.

'Is that Ash?' I say.

'Depends who's asking!' The man laughs.

'Is it him?' Mum shrieks.

'Did you get the message? From my mum?'

Mum grabs the phone. 'Ash? It is you, isn't it?'

I hear a muffled shout but I can't make out any words.

'We're coming to find you. Pete, me and…'

There's an inaudible reply.

'Yeah. My son. You'd better be in Devon.'

I wish I could hear what he was saying.

'We're on our way. We've just got out of a traffic jam.' Mum listens to Ash, scribbling directions on the scrap of paper. 'We'll be a few hours. Can't wait.'

Mum puts the phone back down on the dashboard. Her eyes shine.

'I can't believe I actually spoke to him,' she says.

'I don't know about you, but I fancy a second breakfast. I'll treat you,' Pete says, as we emerge from the gents in the service station. We wait for Mum in WH Smiths.

Pete flicks through Rhythm Magazine and finds an article on John Bonham from Led Zeppelin.

'He's my biggest influence.'

'I've read *Hammer of the Gods*,' I say.

Pete looks impressed.

Mum appears.

So women aren't interested in music?' She looks up at the heading above the shelves. 'Putting music magazines under "men's interest".'

I look up at the sign. Just above the music magazines are lads' mags with women in bikinis. I quickly look away. If they make me feel embarrassed, they're definitely going to put off any girls who want to buy an *NME*.

'I'm starving,' Pete says. 'I've promised Jason a birthday fry-up.'

'Can't we just get a sandwich?' Mum stares at us intensely. 'Ash is waiting for us.' She's been really on edge since she spoke to Ash, desperate to get there.

It's not even lunchtime yet. There's plenty of time, especially if we're staying in the campervan tonight. I really want to meet Ash but I'm enjoying spending time with Pete, learning about music, being treated like an adult. I'm starting to feel like I could actually be a member of Mission Control.

'I'm paying,' Pete says, firmly. Mum gives him a mardy look but follows us to the restaurant.

We each pick up a tray, just like in the school canteen, and push it along the counter. A man with fat red cheeks stands behind the cooked food, with a spatula in his hand. Pete's in front of me.

'Veggie breakfast, please,' he says. 'As much as you can give me.' He winks at the man, who piles up his plate with hash browns and mushrooms.

The bacon and sausages on the hotplate look shrivelled and greasy.

The man turns to me with a smile.

'I'll have the same. No beans.' I've gone off beans since the thing with Bradley Smeed in the canteen.

Mum smiles at me and squeezes my arm. Maybe I could be a full time vegetarian. I might give it a go.

Chapter 27
Ash

Kaz

Pete turns off the B-road, onto a muddy lane. The van rocks on the potholes, its tyres crunching into icy puddles. There are high embankments on both sides, with snow-dusted moss and the brown remains of last year's bracken. The hedge is so overgrown that the bare branches meet in the middle.

Pete's sat nav is stuck onto the dashboard, but its screen doesn't show the lane. We seem to be driving through the middle of a green field.

'This is it,' I say. 'He told me to turn left at the big oak tree.'

'Okay.' Pete grimaces as the sides of the van scrape against twigs. We're driving down an even narrower lane now. Its muddy ruts have frozen like concrete and I have to grab onto the door handle to stop me from colliding with Jason.

'Fucking hell. I thought you were a hermit, but this really is the middle of nowhere.'

'He's here though. Definitely.'

The lane stops abruptly at a dilapidated gate, held together with orange nylon twine. There's no sign but it's just the way Ash described it on the phone.

I jump out to open the gate, wondering if Ash is waiting on the other side of it to meet us.

The farmyard is parked up haphazardly with a collection of rusty vans and trucks. Some of them are half-dismantled, covered in tarpaulins.

Snow is scraped into greying piles, the remainder muddied with tyre tracks.

I try to untangle the loop of string holding the gate closed. There's an instant volley of barking: a pack of assorted dogs, including a lurcher and a tiny Jack Russell, rushes to the gate, jumping up, growling and yapping. I flinch, backing off.

A man comes to the gate; cropped grey hair, wearing a camouflage jacket, smoking a thin roll-up with stained fingers. He stares at me with pale grey eyes.

'We're here to see Ash,' I say.

The man doesn't respond. This is the right place. It must be.

'Ashok Singh. He lives here. He's been with Sea Shepherd. Got back yesterday.'

'Clear off!' The man shouts. I feel my face flush with anger, before I realise he's shouting at the dogs. They scatter, diving behind the nearest truck. The man opens the gate to let me in and the thin line of his mouth bows into a grudging smile.

'You must mean Doc.'

'I'm Kaz. We're old friends.'

The man takes a long leering look at me, his eyes bulging.

'I know who you are. I used to have posters of you.' He jerks his head towards Pete's van. 'The drummer too. You took your time, didn't you?'

He holds the gate open, and Pete drives through. The man continues to stare at me, and I pretend he's not imagining that anti-fur poster. I shiver, and zip my jacket all the way up. He looks away when Pete jumps out of the van and stands next to me, his boots crunching on the snow.

'I'm Dave, if you need me,' he says. Some of the dogs follow him as he lopes back towards one of the rickety barns. 'You'll find Doc in the bottom field.' He nods towards a gate leading out of the farmyard.

Jason plunges his hands into the pockets of his fleece. He looks around uncertainly. Smoke comes from the chimney of ramshackle farmhouse and from the tin stove pipes of some of the caravans and trucks.

Once you get past the initial chaos of the farmyard, there's a settled look to the place, with rabbit hutches, and chickens scratching around in the snow.

'I was expecting something a bit more like an actual farm,' Jason says. 'Do people live here?'

'Looks like it,' Pete says. 'Over the winter, anyway.'

'I think it's this way.' I walk towards the gate. It feels like we're being watched from behind the curtains and blinds of the caravans.

The field slopes gently downhill, with a hedgerow full of old trees. Three rough-coated ponies munch on a bale of hay in the middle of the field. They ignore us as we pass the old railway carriage that acts as their stable.

At the end of the field is a large ash tree, full of jackdaws, croaking and cawing. There's someone down there, wearing white, camouflaged by the snow. He's concentrating, holding something up towards the tree.

The figure turns towards us and breaks into a run. He waves wildly. It's him.

I run too, crunching through the ice-topped snow. My foot gets caught on something under the surface. I can't stop myself from falling and I sprawl on the snow, unable to get up. Adrenaline courses through me and pain shoots from my knee.

A strong, slim hand reaches down to me, and I grasp it. I look into a face that's thinner, more care-worn than I remember. He has a full beard. I stare into his eyes.

'Great entrance, Kaz!' he says.

'I'm not sure I can walk.'

'I'll help you up.' I hang onto him and gradually rise into a standing position. My knee hurts but it'll bear my weight.

Ash brushes the snow off my jacket and jeans. We can't stop staring at each other.

He's wearing white painter-and-decorator's overalls, with a woollen cricket jumper and a white bobble hat. His hair is halfway down his back, in rope-like dreadlocks, tinged with grey. He bends down and picks up a device with a microphone attached, lying in the snow.

'I was recording the jackdaws,' he says. 'For a new sound collage.'

'I'm not sure about the beard.' I laugh and hug him. He smells the same as he used to: a musky, reassuring sweetness.

'You look exactly the same, Kaz.' Ash pulls away from me slightly. His eyes are full of pain and confusion.

'I've started dying my hair. It's going grey.'

'We've missed so much. Wasted so much time.'

I think of Ash's letter; the long talk I had with his dad a few days ago.

'You alright?' Pete asks, plunging towards us through the snow. He stops and takes a good look at Ash. 'What's with the face foliage?'

Ash smiles and they give each other a back-slapping bear-hug.

Then Ash turns and sees Jason. He's standing quietly, apart from us all. He's flicked his fringe over his bruised eye.

'It's true then,' Ash says. 'You're Kaz's son?'

Jason nods. Ash shakes his hand. It seems oddly formal.

'You're looking at a shit-hot guitarist there,' Pete says.

'I'm Jason. It's great to meet you,' Jason says. 'We're getting Mission Control back together. That's why we've come to see you.'

'What?' Ash looks shocked.

'We've got the chance to play at a festival in May, if we want.'

Ash stares at us.

'Tea. We'll need tea,' he says. He starts walking and we follow him. I move my feet cautiously, so I don't trip over on anything under the snow.

Ash rounds the corner of the wooden railway carriage stable. Behind it are three more carriages, making a kind of courtyard. There's a vegetable garden in the middle, cabbages poking through the snow like bald heads; rosemary and sage growing in pots. The middle carriage has a tin chimney coming out of its roof, with smoke spiralling into the grey sky. One of the other carriages has a small wind turbine, spinning steadily.

Ash opens the door. Even though this is his home, he still looks lost. I should have warned Jason to tread carefully. We shouldn't have upset Ash like this. But Jason's so enthusiastic.

I squeeze Jason's hand.

'It'll be alright,' I whisper. 'At least we're here.'

A rich aroma of wood smoke, coffee and weed envelops us as we follow Ash inside. It's warm in here, with light coming from leaded windows at the back of the carriage. Pine planks line the walls on the inside. Objects hang on the walls and sit on every surface: tiny Buddha statues, Japanese pen and ink drawings; strange tangles of rusty metal and plastic, things Ash must have rescued from distant oceans.

Ash fills an old fashioned iron kettle from a tap with a bucket under it and sits the kettle on the hotplate of a wood-burning stove.

'Sit down. You must have been driving for a long time.'

'Only about six hours – we got stuck in traffic,' Pete says.

It's really not far away at all. That's the bad thing. I know Ash spends half his time chasing whaling ships on the ocean but I could have done this years ago; made contact before he gave up hope.

We sit down on an old sofa covered with blankets. My knee throbs. I should have been more careful.

It's a squeeze, with Pete sitting at one end and Jason at the other, sinking into the cushions. At one side of the carriage is a trestle table covered with wires and cables, a laptop, more sound recording equipment and a keyboard. Down the far end of the cabin is a narrow wooden bed, covered with a patchwork quilt, surrounded by shelves of old paperback books.

'I've learned all the Mission Control songs. I'll keep practising them,' Jason says. He's sunk so low into the cushions that his knees are above his head.

I put my hand on his leg, to warn him not to go on. Ash obviously isn't ready to talk yet.

'I've got real coffee. And normal tea. And some mint tea I made myself from the garden. It's quite good,' Ash says.

'I'll have coffee.' Jason watches Ash closely.

'Me too, mate,' Pete says. 'Make it so I can stand a spoon in it.'

'I'll try the mint tea,' I say.

We watch Ash, in silence. He gets four chipped mugs from a cupboard and spoons coffee into a home-made filtering device made from a tin can. He takes a glass jar filled with dried leaves down from a high shelf and shakes some of the contents into a tiny sieve.

'I'm working on sound sculptures. Collages. Using found sounds.' Ash doesn't turn around as he talks. 'I'm putting it out online.'

'What do you call yourself?' Pete asks.

'Circuits of Forgotten Doom,' Ash mumbles.

Jason and Pete stare at each other in surprise.

'My band's called the Organ Detectives.' Jason says. 'It's a rubbish name. Your name sounds cool – one person but with a name like a band.'

'Thanks,' Ash says.

'I really like your railway carriage. I like all the things on the walls.'

Ash wraps his hand in a tea towel and takes the steaming kettle off the hotplate. He concentrates on making the drinks. In the old days, he hardly ever stopped talking, ideas constantly brimming over. I look around this place. Everything is home-made or recycled and repurposed. He might be quieter now but he hasn't run short of creativity.

Ash hands round the mugs. Mine says *"World's Greatest Dad"*, and the contents are a dark, rich green.

'You call yourself Doc nowadays?' I take the mug from Ash and look into his eyes, catching his look of desperation.

'They started calling me that at the Fairmile protest. I rigged up a communications system so the tunnellers could talk to people on the surface. It's what I do.'

'Like out of *Back to the Future*?' Jason asks.

'Yeah. Making stuff. Inventing stuff.'

Pete tastes his coffee and smiles. 'You remembered. Two sugars.'

Jason's coffee looks very strong and dark. I know what he's like with caffeine. He goes hyper. I'm not even sure if he likes it, or if he just likes the idea of it. He blows on it and balances the mug on his knee.

Ash perches on a swivel chair with stuffing coming out of it. He opens a desk drawer and pulls out a battered Cadbury's Chocolate Fingers tin. He licks Rizla papers and sticks them together.

I glance at Jason, Emma's warning about drugs ringing in my head, but Jason is staring around the room.

'Dave kept the letters you wrote to me. I read them yesterday, after I got your phone message,' Ash says.

I gaze at the multi-coloured rag rug on the floor.

'I waited,' Ash says. 'No news came. I began to think you'd killed yourself. That's what they were saying on the news. But there was nothing. No body. No van. After a while, I thought you must still be alive somewhere. And it was my fault you didn't want to come back.'

'How could you think that?'

'I'm ready to understand,' he says. 'Why did you leave it so long?'

I glance up at him, as he lights his joint.

'I want to know about my dad,' Jason says, not taking his eyes off Ash. 'What was Daz like?'

Ash shakes his head. 'Daz could be great. But he was a miserable bastard too. He didn't think he could trust me anymore.'

'Why?' Jason asks.

'He was jealous. He thought me and Kaz were...'

Jason stares at me, his eyes wide with alarm.

'It was nothing, Jason,' I tell him.

'What happened?'

I must have sounded too quick to deny it.

'That night, in the swimming pool, at the studio...' Ash says.

'I was watching TV. I didn't see anything.' Pete folds his arms, setting his mouth in a hard, thin line.

'Daz did,' I say. 'He thought he did.'

'I had to stop him from smashing up the house afterwards.'

'Something else you haven't told me?' Jason asks. He stares at me intently. I feel like I'm on trial. The truth is hard but I've got no choice. I've made such a mess of the tangle of half-truths Jason has been brought up on.

I can feel Jason shaking next to me. I wonder if he's capable of lashing out, the way Daz would. Maybe trying to cocoon him in love wasn't enough to protect him.

I turn to him. I can't read the look in Jason's eyes anymore.

'We thought we knew what we were doing back then. Drugs – and Daz drank way too much too.'

'It was in Wales, in the posh studio, when we were recording *Losing Control*,' Pete says.

'We were bored, doing each other's heads in.' Ash looks at me with raised eyebrows. He passes the joint to Pete, who accepts with a wry grin.

'Me and Ash took acid one night,' I say. I can't hide the details of life in Mission Control from Jason any longer.

'I took acid all the time,' Ash says. 'You weren't used to it.'

'I only did it because we were in a safe place.'

'What's it like?' Jason asks. 'Did you think you were going crazy?'

Ash laughs.

'It makes everything come alive. Your senses…'

I shoot him a warning glance. He's still glamorising it. Even after everything it did to him.

'It was your idea to jump into the swimming pool,' Ash says.

'I didn't know I'd forget how to swim. I thought it would be fun.'

I can still remember deciding to jump in, stripping off, feeling the cool air of the pool room on my skin.

The trip made everything hilariously funny. I thought that if I jumped into the water, it would feel like I was flying.

●

The living room's high ceiling echoes with the tinny keyboard stabs of the *Sonic the Hedgehog* theme tune, punctuated by tinkles, and whoops from Pete as he collects magic rings. I can't read my book with this noise and Pete is completely absorbed in the game, bent forward on the sofa with the game controller grasped tightly in both hands.

It's too early to go to bed. I slam the book down on the coffee table and pad down the hallway, my bare feet sinking into the deep pile of the carpet.

I can hear Daz playing from behind the closed door of the dining room, starting the same guitar solo over and over again, ending in a cry of frustration and the thump of furniture being kicked. I know better than to disturb him when he's in a mood like this, shut away with a bottle of whisky, striving for the perfection he can hear in his head.

I linger and listen outside the door. He's been working too hard over the past few weeks. I wish we could go back to how it was when we recorded *Calling Earth*. We were at home in our own studio and Daz was enjoying himself, not pushing himself to the limit.

'You okay?'

I turn around. I hadn't noticed Ash, walking down the corridor towards me on the soft carpet.

'Bored.'

'Come on.' He beckons me down towards the kitchen. I wish he hadn't, at first. There's a huge pile of washing up in the sink. I can't believe it's only taken one day for it to accumulate. I take the smeared plates and pile them into the dishwasher.

Ash puts his hand on my arm to stop me.

'Don't. Mrs Evans comes to sort all that out.'

'It's weird, having a cleaner. She gives us dirty looks, especially me.'

'So? We're here to record an album, not tidy up.'

Ash sits at the kitchen table, where we ate earlier. He starts to skin up.

'Fancy a trip?' he asks. 'Best cure for boredom.'

'I prefer swimming.'

'The novelty's still not worn off yet?'

'I love it. I can get away from you lot.' Maybe that's what I should do – backstroke, staring up at the stars through the glass ceiling, surrounded by terracotta tiles.

I walk over to the enormous fridge and take out a bottle of lager. I smile at Ash. It feels like we're co-conspirators.

'You know, I just might have a trip with you. You'll look after me, won't you? If anything goes wrong?'

●

Ash laughs, remembering.

'I jumped in to save you.'

'The pool was only chest-high after all.'

'We thought that was so funny. We hugged each other, dancing around and splashing. And then you kissed me.'

'I thought I'd never get the chance.' Ash blasts me with the full force of his sorrowful eyes. 'You didn't have a clue how much I loved you.'

The way he's looking at me, as if he's not quite sure I'm real; I know it's true. He did love me.

'Did Daz know that? When he saw us together in the pool, is that why…?'

Jason tenses up next to me. He struggles to escape from the sofa cushions.

'I need the loo,' he mumbles. He doesn't meet my eyes.

Ash gives Jason a slight, sad smile, as if he's apologising.

'The carriage on the left. Here.' He tosses Jason a loop of string with a couple of keys on it. It seems strange to keep it locked, when we're so far away from anywhere.

Jason scuttles out of the room, his head down.

'I did love you, Kaz,' Ash says.

I stare at him. The only time Ash actually told me he loved me was the night Daz died, when all I wanted was to turn back time so that Daz was safe and we'd be off on tour together.

'Daz had got so jealous of us hanging out together.'

'He said he didn't know why you stuck with him, when

you could have had anyone,' Pete says.

'I thought I was safe with you, Ash. I thought the kiss didn't mean anything – it was just the acid taking over. I told Daz that over and over for weeks because, as far as I was concerned, it was true.'

'Daz should have trusted you. I didn't want to hurt him,' Ash says.

'We all knew Daz had problems.' Pete nods. 'We were too young to cope with success. Sometimes I had to pretend it wasn't happening. I tried to stop him from getting on that fucking motorbike.'

'I blamed myself for a long time,' Ash says. 'Maybe it didn't matter what we did. None of us could have saved him.'

'This argument is fifteen years too late,' I say. It doesn't feel real, us being together in the same room after all these years. Are regrets about the past all we've got to talk about?

Pete gives me a sharp glance.

'It's different now. We can't be like this,' he says. 'How do you think Jason feels, Ash? He had such high hopes, and it's his birthday, for fuck's sake!'

'I can't pretend to be happy about everything, just for the sake of your kid!'

'He's Daz's son.'

'Fuck Daz.' Ash swivels his chair away from us, and turns his laptop on.

Jason was expecting an emotional reunion but we're bitter and resentful, unable to move on. Even Pete. At least he'll get the satisfaction of going back to Emma and his kids, knowing his life is solid and he can leave the wreckage of Mission Control in the past.

'We should go,' I say.

Jason

This is the weirdest birthday I've ever had. Last year, me, Ben and Josh ate pizza in Chesterfield, and then we went bowling. Ben's mum picked us up afterwards.

This year, I've locked myself into an old railway carriage because some nutter who I've never even seen before says he's in love with Mum and that they were on drugs in a swimming pool before I was born.

I wanted this adventure more than anything. I thought it was going to be easy – that I'd just get everyone together again and we'd play at the festival, and I'd just slip into place, playing Daz's guitar lines. I'm just a kid to them. In their eyes, I'll never be anything more than that.

The coffee has made my heart feel fluttery. I've got a jittery, empty feeling in my chest. I lean against the door and wait until I've calmed down.

I wish I could hear what Mum and the others are saying but the walls in here are covered with shiny silver insulation and there's a buzz, like the noise a fridge makes. That wind turbine on the roof must power something.

It's really warm in here, and it smells weird too, a bit like the railway carriage Ash lives in. I wonder if Ash smokes that stuff all the time. It's a heavy, sleepy smell, like a bonfire in the middle of a jungle. One of the girls in my form had some cannabis perfume once and we all had a sniff. It gave me a headache but this isn't the same at all.

There's a toilet, with a proper seat, on a sort of wooden platform. I lift the lid and peer down, but I can't see anything disgusting, only sawdust. It smells like the stables behind our house. I only came in here as an excuse to get away from everyone arguing and embarrassing me.

There's no sink. Just an old washing up bowl on a rough table, next to a plastic jug full of water. There's a bar of cracked soap and an old towel, so I wash my hands anyway. There's also a shower cubicle made of planks. I open the door and there's a wooden draining thing to stand on. Instead of a proper shower there's a bucket hanging up, with a watering can attachment on it. I wonder how Ash heats the water up.

Does he like inventing things, or is it because he's got no money? He reminds me of Mum, a bit, the way she never throws anything away when it gets worn out; the way she never buys anything new, but drags home things she's found in skips. No wonder Bradley Smeed found me easy to pick on. We need a shower at home. It's a pain having to run a bath all the time and if you're in a hurry you can't put enough water in to lie back and get warm.

The only other thing in the room is a tall airing cupboard. I open the door, expecting towels or clothes drying out, but instead there are shelves of green plant stuff, laid out on newspaper. I pick up a sprig of it.

I stand back. The cupboard stands against a false wall, which makes the carriage a lot smaller than it should be. There's a door-shaped join in the silver insulation next to the cupboard, and a keyhole but no handle. The other key on the bit of string fits into it. I turn it and open the door.

The humming is really loud in here, and the smell's the first thing that hits me. There are rows of plants, growing under bright, hot lights. I shut the door again. The smell is so strong, my sore eye is watering and stinging like mad. I know what it is. We had a drugs talk at school when the police came and showed us samples of cannabis in a little Perspex box.

I feel a bit guilty for poking around. Should I tell Mum, or will she find out for herself? He hasn't hidden it very well. Ash even gave me the keys.

I go back into the cupboard and put some bits of the dried plant in the back pocket of my jeans. I'm not sure why. I don't like the smell of it.

If I'm here any longer, they'll wonder what I'm up to. I open the carriage door and lock it behind me. The sky is dark grey, heavy-looking. A snowflake falls onto the sleeve of my fleece.

'It's starting to snow,' I say, opening the door to the main carriage. They turn around and stare at me, pasting fake smiles on their faces.

'Happy birthday, Jason,' Ash says. 'Sorry, I didn't realise.'

'You should show Ash what you can do on the guitar.' Pete gives me an encouraging smile but it feels like they're asking me to do a party trick to stop them from arguing.

'My guitar's in the van. I only brought my acoustic with me.'

'It doesn't matter,' Mum says.

'I would have liked to see my old Marlin again,' Ash says. They must have told Ash about my guitar, and the fight. 'I couldn't remember what had happened to it. I thought it must have gone up in flames, along with the tapes for the albums. All my samples, and my keyboards. That's why I can't join Mission Control again.'

Ash stares sadly at the floor. I feel like I've been punched in the chest. I think about the fire Ash started in Mission Control's studio in Coventry. He must have hated the band so much he wanted to destroy everything. Maybe he thought there was nothing left worth saving.

I slump down onto the sofa.

'Oh.' I feel stupid. Mum and Pete must have known this all along. Mum puts her arm around my shoulders. I want to shrug her off but I don't.

Pete stands up and walks out of the railway carriage.

Chapter 28
Snowed In

Jason

Pete comes back. He's carrying my guitar case. The shoulders of his jacket are covered thickly with snow.

'It's really coming down,' he says. 'We might have to stay the night after all.'

'I thought that was the plan anyway.' I stare up at him. There's food in the camper van and sleeping bags and the van has an electric heater. I was really looking forward to it.

Pete passes me my guitar. I unzip the case and start to tune up. It feels cold but no worse than it does first thing in the morning in my own bedroom. It's good to have something to do. I always feel better if I've got a guitar in my hands.

'Only if it's okay with Ash,' Pete says.

Ash smiles.

'If the weather's bad, this farm gets cut off,' he says. 'Dave says that a couple of weeks ago, it was about two feet deep. You might be stuck here for weeks.'

Mum gets up from the sofa. She's limping. She stares out of the window.

'We've got to feed the cat.'

'Rachel's looking after the house.'

'What if the snow's like this at home?' Mum presses her hands against the leaded windows, as if she's desperate to leave. The snow is settling on the window sills, like a Christmas card in February.

'It'll be good,' Ash says. He stands next to her at the window and puts his hand on her shoulder. He's quite tall, compared with Mum; slim but strong-looking. I can tell why Daz would have been jealous. 'We all need to talk – get to know each other again.'

Pete sits down, making the sofa creak ominously.

'What are you going to play for us?' he asks me.

'I'm learning this with Sam – my guitar teacher. It's called

'Anji'.'

I have to keep playing the bassline with my thumb, while I'm finger-picking the melody. I concentrate so hard I have to stick my tongue out but I manage to get through it with only a couple of mistakes.

Ash claps when I've finished.

'Not easy, that.'

'He's only been playing five months,' Mum says.

They all stare at me, and I can't think of anything to say. I start playing something else. I just slip into 'Bring the Lightning'. I haven't played it since the gig last Thursday.

As I'm playing the intro, I think about Bradley Smeed breaking my Stratocaster. It feels like ages ago now. I realise I'm singing the verse. I didn't mean to start singing the lyrics but they just sort of come naturally to me now.

'It's about Daz, isn't it?' Ash says, when I've finished playing the song.

I nod.

'I'll do one of yours.' I start playing 'Forgotten Alien'. They all stare at me in surprise. It's from *Losing Control*. I know they only played that song once, at the last gig.

Mum starts singing along. Hesitantly at first, not quite getting the lyrics right, but slowly getting more confident. She sits on the arm of the sofa. Ash looks at her and sings softly too. Pete grabs the bucket from under the tap and starts hitting it with his huge hands, like an African drum.

'It sounds great, Jason. Your voice, Kaz. It's better than ever,' Ash says. 'I haven't heard that song since…'

'I've heard it through Jason's bedroom door.' Mum looks at me. 'He must play *Losing Control* almost every day. He's learned both albums, all the way through.'

'And the B-sides. My guitar teacher copied them for me.'

'Mission Control fans are still out there. A man I'd never met before wanted me to sign 'Rootless in Babylon' at the school concert. He treated me like a celebrity.'

'It's not that strange,' I say. 'Mission Control were brilliant.'

'It was a bit embarrassing.'

'Do you think you could perform again? In front of people?' Ash asks.

'Maybe.'

'Have you been practising?'

'I've been running through the old songs. I play along with Jason sometimes. The Thunderbird weighs a ton.'

Ash picks up a couple of small logs from the wicker basket and puts them into the wood burner. It's so warm in here now, I take my fleece off.

'The songs stand up by themselves. You could do an unplugged gig,' he says.

'You've got a keyboard and a laptop,' I say. 'You could programme everything again, couldn't you?'

Ash looks at me, as if the thought hadn't occurred to him before.

'You've always been able to sing those songs without me. When we used to sit and jam on the studio roof, part of me always thought you didn't need me. You started off without me. You could be a three-piece.'

'We were just kids then, practising in my dad's garage. We wouldn't have got anywhere without you. Without you and Daz building the studio,' Pete says.

'So what's Circuits of Forgotten Doom like? What are sound sculptures?' I ask.

Ash sits down at his desk and fiddles with his laptop. He attaches a pair of small speakers.

'I was working on this while I was away. Whale song. I use a hydrophone to monitor the location of the whale pods. Keep one step ahead. Part of my job on the boat.'

'Is it like that New Agey stuff Emma listens to in the bath?' Pete asks.

Ash gives him a stony stare.

He opens a video file, and hits "Play".

It's like nothing I've ever heard before. Like the techno Pete was playing in the van on the way here, but all the beats and different sounds are noises made by whales: slaps and pops and eerie cries.

I watch the laptop screen over Ash's shoulder.

The video is cut perfectly to match the music. It shows a big ship, painted in blue and grey camouflage stripes with a sort of skull and crossbones logo on it. It rides up and down on huge waves, water crashing over the front of the boat. There are people on board, watching a group of whales rising out of the ocean through binoculars.

The music gets faster, more urgent. Another boat appears. A harpoon shoots out of the ship and the water turns red. The body of a whale is winched on board. Then there's a small inflatable dinghy with three people on it, putting themselves between the whales and the harpoon ship. The music reaches a crescendo before ending with footage of a whale diving into the water, its tail flipping up towards the sky.

'That's brilliant,' I say.

'Amazing. Like the Aphex Twin or something,' Pete says, with a whistle.

'How do you do all that, with all the different sounds?' I ask.

Ash smiles at me.

'Have you ever used music technology? Cubase, that sort of thing?'

'I just got a laptop today, from Gran and Grandad. My friend Ben's got a free music programme on his computer. We recorded some songs we were busking before Christmas. We don't really know what we're doing yet, to be honest.'

'I chop up the samples and drop them where I want them on the sequencer.' Ash opens a programme on his laptop. It looks similar to the one I've tried to use with Ben, with waves, blocks and wiggly lines on a grid. The shapes make different noises when he points the mouse at them.

'Is that what you used to do in the band?'

'This stuff had only just started in the early nineties. I did use Cubase a bit on *Losing Control*. Mostly, it was live. Analogue synths. Classic stuff. All gone.'

'You could re-create it. On this.'

'It's not the same. I could get this to sound like your

guitar if I wanted. What's the point? I'd just be a bloke stood behind a laptop. Go out there and let the songs stand for themselves. Kaz has an amazing voice. Let them hear it without me making weird noises at the side of the stage.'

'You're scared of performing?'

He shakes his head, making his dreadlocks move about like snakes. He looks a bit like a pirate crossed with a painter-and-decorator.

'I've got my life here – and on the ship.'

'Do you actually go out on those inflatable boats?'

Ash nods.

'Not all the time. I could be fixing the electrics on board, cooking, cleaning. Anything. It all helps to stop the whalers.' He sounds so passionate about it, so certain it's the right thing to do. I've never been so sure about anything, apart from playing the guitar.

'I've decided I'm going to go vegetarian.'

'You had a bacon sandwich this morning,' Mum says. I turn away from the computer screen and face her. She looks pleased and annoyed at the same time.

'I want to give it a go. Properly.'

'Good on you, mate,' Ash says.

'I'd better visit that shed.' Mum hauls herself up, hanging onto the arm of the sofa. She stretches her leg out.

'I'll get the food out of the van,' Pete says.

I pat the pockets of my jeans for the bathroom key. It's still in my back pocket. I fish out the keyring.

'What's that?' She stares at my hand.

I'd forgotten about the dried weed I put in my pocket. Some of it is now sitting in the palm of my hand with the key ring.

'You found our little harvest.' Ash smiles proudly and picks up the piece of dried plant. 'Help yourself, within reason. It's got to earn us some money.'

She snatches the keys from me.

I rummage around in my pocket and scoop out the rest of the weed. I give it to Ash.

'It's nothing to do with me. I just found it.' I say.

'Where?'

'In the shed – the bathroom. Loads of it.'

She glares at Ash.

He shrugs, like it's not important at all.

'Dave needs some money to restore the farm. It's going to be amazing once it's finished. Off-grid living. Renewable technology. It's all coming together. I get to live here free because I'm helping Dave to build it.'

'You never learn, do you?'

Mum walks out of the room so fast, she almost forgets to limp. Pete bolts after her. Me and Ash stare at each other. Pete shouts after Mum; she yells something back at him but I can't make it out.

'She's gone straight, hasn't she?'

'It's not like she works in an office.'

Ash reaches for his rolling papers again. I stare at him, trying to work him out. He's acting more mature than Mum in some ways. At least he's staying calm.

'I've never actually smoked it. I wasn't going to. I just wondered. Mum said you've been into it for a long time.'

'It gives me flow – lots of ideas.'

'It was my stupid idea to get the band back together.'

Ash licks the cigarette paper.

'We've all been hurt. Pete the worst, really. He lost his best mate, then he lost Kaz. And I was a twat.'

'I know I'm not as good as Daz. Not in a million years, but...'

'You can do it. You can play Daz's parts. Even on an acoustic guitar. Where did you get it from?'

'Charity shop.'

Ash picks up my guitar. 'No label inside. Weird. Someone must have made it.' He turns it around in his hands. 'It's not fancy, but it plays well.'

He strums an E chord.

'It's gone a bit wrong, hasn't it? This reunion,' I say.

Ash lights the spliff. It smells like hedge trimmings. I move away and stand by the stove, getting closer to the wood smoke smell that reminds me of home.

'It's happened. Kaz is alive. You exist. That's the important thing. It doesn't matter what I do now – whether I join the band or go back on the ship. It's not hanging over me anymore.'

'She's really angry with you.'

'If only she knew how angry I was with her.'

'What about now?'

'Still too angry to join the band. Sorry.'

Kaz

I open the cupboard and see the weed drying out on the shelves. Enough to fill a couple of bin bags. I unlock the hidden door and stare at the room where it's all growing.

Pete whistles through his teeth.

'Wonder how much that lot's worth?' he says.

'He's irresponsible.'

'Ash hasn't changed that much. Not really.'

'He hasn't grown up.' I lock the door; close the cupboard. Pete gives me a strange look.

'And you have? Chill the fuck out, Kaz. I'll meet you at the van.'

'We're leaving?'

'We've got food and stuff to fetch. I thought you needed the loo.' He leaves me alone in the shed. As he shuts the door, a flurry of white flakes blows inside.

When I stumble into the yard, I can't see anything through a whirling blizzard. I sink into the snow, past my ankles. The snowflakes melt on my cheeks, hot with panic and anger.

'Pete! Pete!' I see a bright purple van shape in the swirl of white. Footsteps crunch towards me. Pete's face looms out of the gloom, snowflakes caught in his eyebrows. He grabs my hand.

'Come on. Otherwise you'll freeze.'

Pete slides the van door back and steps inside, stamping the snow off his boots. He has to bend almost double to get through the door. Once I'm inside too, there's barely room for both of us until I sit on the sofa. Pete turns on the lights and the electric heater, and the air starts to warm up.

'Seeing as we're stuck...' He opens a cupboard and puts two cans of cider on the table. Pete opens his and takes a long gulp. He stares at the side of the can.

'Made in Devon,' he laughs. 'All the way from Coventry.'

'We can't stay in the van. I can't leave Ash alone with Jason,' I say.

'You used to trust him.'

'Jason's still a child. Ash is running a cannabis farm, in case you hadn't noticed.'

'Did you think you were a child when you were fourteen?'

'I had a perm. I didn't know shit.'

I open the can of cider and take a cautious sip. It's heartburn-inducingly sweet, but maybe I need to get a bit drunk to calm me down; help me to remember what being in Mission Control felt like.

'Jason's got his head screwed on,' Pete says. 'He's got more sense than you.'

'He'll be disappointed Ash doesn't want to join the band again.'

'It wouldn't be the same as a three-piece. We could give it a go...'

'I hurt a lot of people, didn't I?'

Pete looks baffled and lost, his deep blue eyes reflecting the falling snow outside the van. It's starting to get dark now.

Through the snow storm, I can see lights glowing faintly from the farmhouse; from the caravan windows. The people who live on the farm must be wondering what we're doing here.

'Ash hasn't done too badly. Rent free. Fresh air,' I say.

'All the weed he can smoke.'

'What if he gets caught?'

Pete stares out into the snow.

'It's none of our business, really.'

'He doesn't want us here.'

'It's too much of a shock for him. Everyone thought you were dead, remember?'

'Do you wish I hadn't come back? I've made such a mess of everything.' I can't help thinking about the letter I burned the other day: more running away.

'Maybe if you relaxed a bit with him, Ash would trust you. We told Jason not to get his hopes up for a reunion. Can't we just talk to each other, like civilised people? Or drink each other under the table…'

'But Jason…?'

'He's the guitarist in Mission Control now. Even if we end up as a three-piece unplugged tribute band to ourselves, we should start treating him like an equal.'

'You're right. I'll try to have fun.'

If Jason wants to be a musician, he'll find out about drink and drugs soon enough.

Jason

'It must have been amazing, building your own studio,' I say. I want to talk to Ash about being friends with Daz, not about when they were all falling out.

I watch the snowflakes through the window. Mum and Pete can't still be looking at all the plants, surely? Maybe they're arguing.

Ash spins around on his office chair, closes his eyes and breathes smoke in deeply, as if it's helping him to remember. He wheels the chair closer to the sofa.

'Daz had nowhere to live – he'd run away from his dad.'

'His dad sounds like a proper bastard.'

Ash nods.

'Mum and Dad must have sold him so much lager, it could have filled a swimming pool. But after Daz got beaten up that time, they banned him from the shop. He kicked off, called Dad all sorts of shit.'

'I know he's my grandad, but I hope he's dead. I never

want to meet him.'

'Daz was alright, though. We didn't really know each other until then, when I found out he'd formed a band with Kaz and Pete. I've not been very fair on him, have I?'

'What was he really like?'

'Quiet, but with great ideas. He could get absorbed in things for hours. He worked hard on the studio. He was good at art and making stuff.'

'It was your own place, and Daz was only sixteen. It must have been exciting.'

'Needed a lot of work though. Top floor of uncle Vik's warehouse. At first, we had to sleep amongst the pigeon shit. But I was desperate to leave home and Daz had nothing. Uncle Vik let us have it for free, as long as I worked for him as a driver. That's how we got the van.'

'You did it all yourselves?'

'We learned a lot. Plumbing, laying electrical cables, soundproofing. Daz loved it all.'

'What did Mum think?'

'She made us put in a shower before she moved in.'

'I've seen the one in your shed. The bucket one.'

'Works just fine. The one in the studio was made from a hosepipe. It wasn't fancy or anything, the studio – it was proper DIY. The only thing we spent any money on was the mixing desk and all the gear. We saved up for that, and got everything else out of skips.'

'Mum's good at that.'

'Don't I know it? One night we found a cooker on the pavement. She made us carry it half a mile and up the fire escape. Only two of the hobs worked, but it was something…'

The door of the railway carriage opens with a bang. Pete and Mum come inside, covered in snow, which swirls around them. The wind makes the stove roar. They've both got carrier bags of food from the van. I suddenly start to feel hungry. It feels like days since the service station.

Mum gives Ash a slightly forced smile.

'I know it's not fair on you, us appearing out of the blue,

but we're stuck here now. I thought we'd make some dinner. We brought food – tins and stuff.'

Ash looks at the plastic bags they've brought in and glances across to a rack near the door, filled with earth-covered swedes and potatoes and carrots.

'Fancy helping me make chapattis, Jason?'

I nod.

'He's good in the kitchen,' Mum says, stamping the snow off her boots. 'Even though you haven't really got a kitchen.'

'I manage,' Ash murmurs.

Mum rummages in a carrier bag and I expect her to bring out a tin of tomatoes or something, but it's a can of cider. She cracks it open, before sitting down on the sofa.

Ash stands up and rummages in his vegetable rack.

'Are you making one of your curries? Lovely. We'll help you to chop the veg and stuff,' Mum says.

I stare over at Pete, totally confused, but he smiles back at me.

'Don't worry, Jason. Your mum's decided to have a good time, rather than keep that poker shoved up her arse.'

Mum slaps his leg, laughing. I wonder if she's already had something to drink. This could be an interesting evening.

Kaz

I mop up the last of the curry with a scrap of chapatti and stuff it into my mouth. I stare at Ash, his mouth full of bread. Pete's right about him. This cannabis farm thing is really dodgy but he's basically okay, although he seems a bit lonely here.

Jason made him put on some more of his sound collages. The track playing in the background now is made of sounds Ash must have collected from around the farm: jackdaws cawing, the odd volley of barking, drowsy bees reminding me of summer, and wind blowing through leaves. I imagine the ash tree at the bottom of the field, dark green and majestic. It's not just a swirl of sound: there are beats, breaks; an insistent riff that sounds like it has been sampled from an old tractor engine.

'This is brilliant! Something like this could be part of Mission Control,' Jason says.

'It's fucking great.' Pete helps himself to more curry.

Ash stops chewing and stares at us.

'Dave wants me to rewire the farmhouse.'

'He seems like a bit of a tosser.'

Jason giggles, hidden behind his fringe, sounding like his more childish self. He's already finished eating and has picked up his guitar and is working out a melody, playing along with the sound collage, sitting on a beanbag on the floor.

'That sounds good,' I say.

Jason looks at me with his head on one side, hair falling over his black eye.

'Are you alright, Mum? You're not used to drinking.'

I try to stop myself from laughing. I stand up, and walk over to the tap, pretty steadily, and I put my plate in the washing up bowl. I fill the bowl with water, wincing as the icy jet touches my hand, squirt in a glob of washing up liquid and rinse the plate. Squatting down to wash up reminds me of our studio.

'I've only had two cans. Pass me your plate.'

'Coffee, Jason?' Ash picks up the plates and puts them gently into the washing up bowl.

I shoot a warning look at Jason. Too much coffee and he gets wired.

'Your coffee's great, Ash.'

'I get it on my travels.'

'Cool.'

After he's made the coffee, Ash makes another joint. His fingers seem to do it automatically, whenever he sits down. It's probably because he's living next door to a shed full of the stuff. Without anything else to do, his default mode was always getting stoned.

I look around. Jason is absorbed in playing the guitar and

Pete is still eating, lost in the world of the music. I wait, until Ash has taken a decent amount of drags on the spliff.

Not taking my eyes off him, I shuffle to the edge of the sofa.

'Can I have a puff on that?' I ask, quietly.

Ash smiles, and hands the joint over.

'I knew you weren't gone forever,' he says. There's an amused twinkle in his eyes.

Jason stops playing the guitar. He sweeps his fringe off his face and stares at my hand.

'Mum!' His lips are beginning to curl into a disbelieving smile.

'What?'

I take a drag, slow and deep, to show them I haven't completely forgotten what it was like to be Kaz K. The harsh smoke scratches the back of my throat, and I double up, eyes watering. I pass the spliff quickly onto Pete. Everyone laughs.

'Mum, you idiot.'

'Take it steady,' Ash says.

I stumble over to the door, open it and take gasping breaths of cold air, closing my eyes to stop the spinning in my head.

There's an arm around my shoulder; a hand stroking my hair.

'Maybe you'd better have some coffee.'

I turn around and almost find myself wrapped in Ash's arms.

Jason

I wake up to the sound of rain bouncing off the tin roof. I'm much warmer than I would be at home. I open my eyes. It's dark in here but there's a bit of greyness at the windows. I've got no idea what time it is.

I'm on the sofa in Ash's railway carriage, wrapped in a sleeping bag and a patchwork blanket. I sit up.

388

Mum is curled on her side on the bed, while Ash and Pete are lying on the floor, their heads sharing the beanbag. They're covered by the same enormous blanket. Looking at them, I can't help smiling. Pete is snoring a bit.

My head feels like it's stuffed with cotton wool. I think I must have been stoned last night from Ash's fumes. I ate most of a massive bag of crisps from Pete's van.

I kept playing my guitar for them last night. Loads of old songs I learned for busking, and I threw in a few Mission Control songs, but didn't make a big thing about it. Once Mum sobered up, she drew pictures of us all. It was funny, Mum getting stoned, but it was like she was trying too hard to prove herself to Ash. If she tries to tell me off about anything, I'll have the best come-back ever.

I wrestle my way out of the sleeping bag. I slept in my clothes last night. Now I feel weird, all crumpled. We all decided to sleep in Ash's railway carriage because it was warmer. Pete carried the sleeping bags out of the van but forgot my bag, so I haven't got my toothbrush and jogging bottoms, and I couldn't be bothered to struggle through the snow again to get it.

Me and Mum are supposed to be going home today, back to Bolehill. I'm not desperate to leave, but it would be nice to sleep in my own bed, with Patti curled up on my duvet cover. I want show Ben my new guitar.

Ash said we could be stuck here for days. I might miss the start of school next Monday. I wouldn't mind too much. Everyone will still be going on about Bradley Smeed's broken nose, taking sides.

I pick my way around Ash and Pete without waking them and slip my feet into my Docs, where I left them near the door. I don't know what Ash did with the keys to the bathroom shed, so I just open the door and shuffle through the snow to pee behind the railway carriage.

The rain is really chucking down now, and the air feels warmer. The snow is shrinking. Pete might be able to drive back to Coventry after all. I stand for a while, the rain washing stale smoke out of my eyes.

It's light now, mostly. I look over at the bare tree where we found Ash yesterday. The birds are waking, flying in a circle around the top of the tree, croaking and shaking the snow from the branches.

We've done it. Reunited the band. Except that Ash won't be joining us. There's nothing stopping him, really. It doesn't matter about the master tapes and his vintage keyboards. What he's doing now is totally brilliant. But he doesn't really want us.

There's a splash behind me. I jump. It's Ash, throwing the dirty water out of the washing up bowl, onto the vegetable garden.

'Come in – you're getting soaked.'

He's changed out of his white jumper. He's wearing a red one now, unravelling at the neck. I realise I'm staring at him.

'I've been wearing white for too long. Now Kaz is back, I'm celebrating.'

'With a jumper?'

'I'm not in mourning anymore.'

Rain drips off the roof of the railway carriage, down the back of my neck, making me squeal in a really embarrassing way, so I run back inside.

'It's been a bit weird, but I'm really glad we came to see you.'

Ash smiles.

'So am I.'

Kaz

Pete comes back from investigating the lane. His waterproof is dripping wet.

'We'll get through,' he says, opening the van door and hauling himself into the driver's seat. 'The ice has melted to slush. Good job. Emma needs me to look after the kids tonight.'

I nod, trying not to move my head too much. I've got a throbbing headache. Who was I trying to convince? I'm not a nineteen-year-old sleeping in a van anymore.

'You actually look green,' Jason says, without any sympathy.

'Two cans, Kaz,' Pete says with a grin. 'Total lightweight. And then you had that whitey from one drag of Ash's spliff.'

Jason laughs, clicking his seatbelt together. I've made a mess of things; bringing Jason up without any temptations, and then ruining it by setting a terrible example for him. I hope he didn't smoke any of it himself. But he seems fine, apart from dark shadows under his eyes. Emma was right, though. After one day with Ash, drugs must now seem as normal to him as having a cup of tea.

'You won't be laughing if I throw up.'

Pete starts the engine.

'At least we tried, Jason,' Pete says. 'We found him. Can't say fairer than that.'

'He doesn't want to join us. Would it work as a three-piece?'

'At the Spiral Sun festival, Daz said he wanted to chuck Ash out of the band. Take us back to basics again,' I say.

Jason stares at me; his eyes like puddles in the melted snow.

'We'll have to try it.' There's so much disappointment in Jason's voice it makes my heart ache. 'We can't give up now.'

The van creeps forward, splashing through the slush. Dave watches us silently from an outbuilding. A few of the dogs bark, but they don't move far from the doorway.

Ash stayed in the railway carriage as we gathered all our stuff up and got ready to leave. He made us toast and coffee but he didn't even bother waving goodbye to us. He was eating a bowl of muesli. He seemed glad we were leaving. He can get back to tending his cannabis plants or maybe just smoking them and looping birdsong and dolphin noises on his computer.

Pete drives through the gate, jumps out and closes it behind him. He drives the van, trundling slowly and carefully, crunching through disintegrating ice.

'Stop! Stop!' a voice shouts behind us.

Pete brakes. We jerk forward uncomfortably as the van slithers a couple of feet on the slush, and the front tyres bump into puddles.

'For fuck's sake!' Pete shouts.

In the passenger door mirror, I see Ash, running headlong towards us in his wellies, almost slipping over.

I open the passenger door, tangling it in the hedge.

Ash squeezes down the side of the van, holding the door open, hanging onto it to keep him upright.

'I know it's not the same now. But I could do something new, like you said.' He gasps for breath.

'Really?' I ask.

'I've been thinking. I need to be part of it. If you think you could give me another chance.'

I jump out of the van, icy water splashing up my legs and seeping into my boots. The coldness hits me, but I feel great, as if my hangover never happened.

I put my arms around Ash. He's soaking wet.

'I knew we'd change your mind.' Jason grins.

'Welcome back, mate,' Pete says.

Ash stands up straight and takes a deep breath. His mouth stretches into a wide smile, eyes closed.

'I've got a lot of work to do, then. New samples and synth parts for all the songs.'

'I'll get Sam to burn you a copy of everything on CD,' Jason says.

Ash laughs.

'You're so outdated, Jason. I'll download it. Our back catalogue's online already. Illegally, mind.'

'What about Dave – the farmhouse?'

'I'll work something out,' Ash says, with a shrug, like he's not really bothered about the farm any more. 'I'll see you next month, for rehearsals.'

I look up at Ash's face, filled with joy and relief.

Chapter 29
Black Ice

Jason

Sam's tyres spin on the ice as he drives up the steep road to our house, but he doesn't seem to notice.

'I can't believe it. The Mission Control reunion is actually going to happen.' His voice squeaks with excitement.

'Only one gig. And we've got a lot of work to do,' Mum says.

'You worked fast, getting everyone on board, tracking Ash down.'

'It should have happened a long time ago.'

'We need to ring Marilyn Richards,' I say. 'She can write her book now.'

'She'll be really pleased,' Sam says. 'I'll call the festival organisers in the morning – let them know it's all on.'

I feel bad for Sam. Mum called him from Gran and Grandad's house to see if he wouldn't mind picking us up from Cromford station. She's using him like a taxi driver, but he'd do anything for her. He worships her and Mission Control.

He parks the car outside our house. We've been gone since Saturday. The house has been emptier for longer than it's ever been in our lives. At least Rachel has been here, to feed the cat.

It's not as snowy here as it was in Devon but it's much colder. It says minus two degrees on the temperature gauge on Sam's car. The house will be freezing. I get out of the back seat but need to hang onto the car roof to stop myself from sliding down the road on black ice.

Sam opens the boot and hands me my acoustic guitar case. I sling it on my back and carefully climb up the icy steps to the house, concentrating on not slipping.

I lean my guitar against the back door and grab a bag of rock salt from the shed. I pour it on the path, down the steps and onto the pavement. I don't want Mum falling over again.

'Sam, what are you doing?' Mum stands with her hands on her hips, while Sam stares into the boot of his car, his face illuminated by the light inside it. He looks like he's found the Holy Grail.

'Daz's guitar!' he gasps. 'I couldn't help looking.' He's unzipped the case and he's staring at my black electric guitar.

'It was my birthday present. From Pete.'

'Amazing. He kept it all those years...'

Mum picks up her holdall, laughing.

'Come inside and stare at it. I'm too cold – that train journey seemed to take forever.'

'We woke up in Devon. We had tea with Gran and Grandad. It's been a long day.'

'Thanks for the lift, Sam,' Mum says. 'I really appreciate it.'

Sam hands the guitar case to me.

'Bring it to your lesson on Sunday. Can I have a go? You'll need to know every Mission Control song inside out and upside down.'

'I think he already does.' Mum gives Sam a hug.

I pick up my bag.

'I need to learn how to play everything again. I'm seriously rusty. I might need some lessons too,' she says.

'You'll be fine. I'd better get back to the pub. Jason – see you on Sunday.'

'Drive carefully,' Mum says. 'Especially down Cromford Hill.'

We watch Sam's car trundling slowly down the lane.

'I can't believe you dragged him out on a night like this.'

'So we should have walked back from the station?'

'We could have got a taxi. You can afford it now.'

The salt has dissolved the ice on the steps. I feel pleased with myself.

'Sam's happy to help.'

'It's not fair. You can't expect him to run around after you all the time.'

Mum lifts up the flowerpot, finds the key and unlocks

the back door. She turns on the light. I follow her into the kitchen and dump my bag.

A desperate-sounding mew comes from the living room. Patti leaps through the kitchen doorway and rubs her head against my legs. She glares at us accusingly.

'I'm sorry we left you.' I bend down to stroke her, and she pushes her head against my hand, purring furiously. She's only eaten half of her bowl of biscuits though, so Rachel must have been here today at some point.

'I'll get the AGA lit,' Mum says. She piles up kindling and adds logs from the basket.

A stack of letters is leaning up against the coffee jar on the work surface. Mostly junk mail. Rachel must have put the post there. The envelope in front of everything else is brown, with a picture of a crown on it. It looks kind of important. It's addressed to Miss Keziah Knight. Mum reaches out for it, and without opening it, she twists it up into a firelighter.

'What's that?' I ask.

'Nothing.'

'How do you know?'

She won't look me in the eye. I snatch the letter out of her hand.

I try to smooth the envelope out and I open it. The letterhead says: *Bona Vacantia Division, part of the Treasury Solicitor's Department.* That sounds serious.

I read on.

Dear Miss Knight,

Despite several attempts to contact you, we have been unable to resolve the issues regarding the estate of the late Miss Elsa Day.

Miss Day does not appear to have left a will, and furthermore, you have hitherto been unable to produce proof that you are Miss Day's next of kin. We will therefore take steps to sell the estate via auction, with the proceeds going to the Crown.

We urge you to contact your solicitor urgently as soon as possible.

'You were going to burn this?' I ask, holding the letter so close to Mum's face she has to read it. She's trapped, between me and the work surface.

She was just going to carry on pretending this wasn't happening. *Sell the estate via auction.* That's the house and the garden and everything.

I don't move while Mum reads the letter. Patti head-butts my leg. I grab the Go-Cat from the shelf and top up her bowl.

I hear a funny choking sound. I turn around.

Mum is crying, her hands over her eyes, as if she's trying to stop the tears from spilling out from behind her fingers.

'They're going to sell the house, aren't they?'

Mum nods. She makes a horrible sobbing noise. Patti stares up at her, as if Mum can suddenly speak her language.

I get the AGA lit, with real fire-lighters rather than life-changing letters.

Mum needs a cup of tea. She needs to be put to bed with a hot water bottle and the cat curled up next to her. When I was little, she used to get upset all the time. I didn't know what was wrong with her then. I worried she might actually be mental.

She is mental. Totally mental. That's the only reason why she would ignore something like this for years and not sort it out.

I fill the kettle and put it on the hotplate. Then I take my guitars into the living room. I unzip the electric guitar case. I stare at the sticker-covered guitar, trying to steady my breathing and calm down. It's amazing we've found Pete and Ash. I'm ready to take Daz's place in the band.

I know people are much more important than buildings but this place means so much to Mum. She's being so fucking stupid about it.

I walk back into the kitchen. She's still crying.

'They're right. The house doesn't belong to us. Maybe we should just get over it,' I say.

'Elsa told me it was our house!' she shouts, then sobs uncontrollably. I prise the letter out of her fingers and wedge it between the tins on the shelf.

I keep getting flashes of memory. Aunt Elsa beckoning me over to her armchair with a mischievous smile, making her wrinkled face look decades younger. If it was something to do with the will, why didn't she tell Mum?

If Elsa really wanted us to live here, she would have done something about it. She wouldn't want to put us through this, surely?

I look at the AGA, the pots and pans, the furniture, the familiar things I've known forever. None of it belongs to us. Once this house is sold, what's going to happen? I pick up Patti, needing to feel her soft fur against my face, but she yowls in protest, wriggles from my arms and runs out of the cat flap.

Mum is trembling. She looks so small and lonely. I should be helping her, but I feel so angry I almost want to slap her.

What if I turn out like Daz's dad? I shiver, horrified.

I run outside, slamming the back door as hard as I can. It's not even ours, so I don't care if it comes off its hinges. I run down the steps and march up the road as fast as I can without slipping over, until the houses run out and everything's dark. All I can see is the moon shining on the icy lane.

Opening my mouth wide, I shout as loud as I can. Not words, just sounds. My shout sounds deep and powerful. I wonder if anyone can hear me in the village or on the other side of the valley. What would they think?

I start laughing. Maybe I'm as crazy as Mum, but I start to feel better. I take deep breaths of the icy air.

I don't blame Mum for being so useless about sorting out the house. After Daz died, she changed from being a musician who performed in front of thousands of people, to someone so scared she couldn't even face her best friends. But she's made such a mess of things.

If I don't carry on trying to sort things out, they're only going to get worse.

Kaz

I walk through the gap in the fence surrounding the old garage. It's still too icy to risk cycling. Everything seems busy and normal, with hammering going on inside the building. The crumpled piece of paper in my jacket pocket will change everything.

'Kaz! Great to see you!' Jeff shouts as he wheels a barrow of crushed concrete down the slope. I give him a half-hearted wave.

The windows of the site office are steamed up. I open the door.

Barbara is sitting at the table with a laptop in front of her. She smiles, peering over the top of her glasses.

'Keziah! Welcome back to the madhouse! Things are really coming on. Did you have a good holiday?' She stares more closely at me. I focus on the health and safety notice behind her head.

'You look like you've been crying.' Barbara says.

'When I came back, I found this.' I give her the letter. It's a wrinkled, crumpled mess now, but at least I didn't throw it in the fire.

Barbara smooths out the letter on the desk in front of her. She reads it calmly.

'It's been weeks since the first letter. I didn't do anything about it.' I perch on the vinyl seat on the other side of the table.

I wait for Barbara to say something; anything.

'I'm glad this has happened,' she says.

A chasm of anxiety opens in my chest. I breathe in short gasps.

'I'm about to lose my home.'

Barbara takes off her glasses and rubs her eyes. Then she looks at me, lips pursed, as if she's about to make an important announcement.

'I'll buy Wren Cottage. And all the art. We need to secure it.'

She's so matter of fact, as if she's talking about doing a big shop at the supermarket.

'Then what?'

'Nothing. You'll still live there.'

'Elsa told me it belonged to me.'

I can still see Elsa clearly, her skin pale as paper against the white sheets on the hospital bed. My hand covering hers; so bony and frail.

○

'You're my family. There's no one else,' she says.

I nod. I know she hasn't got long left. I don't want to sort out her funeral, but I'll have to. She's already told me what she wants: a quiet cremation. No one invited. A bird cherry with dark fruits planted in the garden.

'Help me to sit up,' Elsa croaks.

I plump up the pillows; try to move her into a sitting position. Her blue eyes are still as sharp as sapphires.

'I've made sure you can keep the house. Everything is yours.'

'But –'

'I know how much you love it.'

'I'm not related to you,' I whisper. Everyone in the hospital thinks I'm her great niece.

'I've made all the arrangements. Don't worry about a thing. Just look after the garden.'

The window opposite the bed is open, just a small crack, but enough for the aroma of freshly-cut grass to overpower the disinfectant smell of the ward. The sky is fresh blue, and I've brought a vase of hazel catkins to stand next to Elsa's bed. One of the nurses keeps moaning about allergies but we're ignoring her.

'The dogwood needs cutting back,' Elsa says.

'The onions and potatoes need planting.'

Lots of jobs need doing. Elsa seems calm, knowing I'll be there to carry on looking after everything.

○

I looked after everything, as if Elsa would come back one day and claim it. I dreamed she wasn't really dead, or that Daz turned up, revving a motorbike.

I waited. Nothing happened to confirm that the house was mine.

Sometimes I thought it could have been Elsa's mind wandering. But her mind was so sharp. Only her body let her down.

Would I care about everything so much if it belonged to Barbara?

'It sounds like you've already thought this through,' I say.

Barbara sighs.

'When you told me Elsa Day didn't leave a will, I knew how threatened everything was – how much you relied on chance.'

'You planned all of this?'

'I didn't tell the Treasury Solicitors, if that's what you mean. Please believe me.'

'The house – the garden. It's my life.' As I say it, I know that maybe it's not even true anymore. It was the only thing protecting me and Jason from the real world. Our refuge. But now we've got my parents; Pete and Ash.

'I'm just trying to preserve it for you.'

'I don't like to feel trapped.'

'You can do whatever you like!' Barbara laughs. Patronising cow. I want to punch her. Instead, I force my fists into my jacket pocket.

'I've got to bid for the estate. If we can't use Elsa's art, this whole project is in jeopardy.'

I try to imagine myself as a tenant in my own house. Barbara is offering me a lifeline. I should be grateful, but my brain strains against my skull.

'I have to think.'

'It's the only way. I'm sorry, Kaz.'

I snatch the letter off the desk, and escape the stifling, steam-filled air of the site cabin. I leave the door hanging open by a few inches. I stand, bent forwards, trying to get the stingingly cold air into my lungs.

Jeff comes out of the container unit, whistling a tune I vaguely recognise.

'I found some interesting bits of old metal for your sculptures,' he says. 'Want to look? The ground's frozen, so…'

He stares at me more closely.

'Are you alright?'

'I haven't slept.'

I give Jeff the letter.

'Estate of the late Miss Elsa Day?' he asks, baffled.

'I live in her house. Now Barbara's going to buy it, with us still living there.'

'I'm renting too. Don't think I'll ever be able to afford a place around here.'

'Wren Cottage should belong to me. But it doesn't. I cared for Elsa when she was old and ill, and she said she was leaving the house to us. Nothing was left to prove it. So we may as well just be squatters.'

'It says to contact your solicitor.'

'I haven't got one.'

'Hey, you could find somewhere else to squat in. Take over another old building, do it up, move in. No one would ever know you weren't supposed to be living there. Might try it myself.'

'That's what I've been doing already. Hoping no one would notice – that something would turn up. Why did I open my big mouth to Barbara?'

'I think she's alright, myself. She brings me cups of tea while I'm working.'

'She says she hasn't been planning this. What if she's lying?' I'm almost shouting. My words are ugly, torn out of my mouth for Barbara to overhear.

'She's just trying to help.'

'Convenient for her, isn't it? Even without the will, she wanted everything in my house the moment she saw it.'

An icy wind blows across the yard. Even though I'm wearing a thick jumper and my jacket, the chill spreads right into my bones. I stare at my hands, the skin red and flaky from the never-ending coldness. I put my gloves on.

I pick my way up the slope, to the top of the yard. I want to look at my pond. The brown water is covered with a film of white ice. With the undergrowth cut back, exposing bare earth, and with all the junk removed, it looks stark and empty: ready for the new beginning of the spring. It was already thawing in Devon. I wonder where the heron is.

Things change, I remind myself. I try to take deep breaths. Maybe I should just resign myself to this. But how can I?

I poke at the ice at the edge of the pond with the toe of my boot, making little cracks that grow and spread.

I could get some advice, but where? I close my eyes, remembering gold leaf lettering, heavy mahogany furniture and dusty stairs.

There's a squeak behind me. Jeff's pushing the empty wheelbarrow towards a pile of rubble.

'Kaz – I listened to your band. Both albums in full, on YouTube,' Jeff says.

'I thought no one cared anymore. Turned out I was wrong.'

'Someone must be listening – they've both got thousands of hits. I can't believe I'd never heard of Mission Control.'

'You would have only been a little kid at the time.'

'I would have loved to see Mission Control live.' Jeff smiles regretfully.

I think I can trust him with the news. After all, everyone's going to know it soon.

'We're getting back together, with my son on guitar.'

'That's amazing! Can I be your roadie?'

I laugh. He's so young, so enthusiastic and keen to help me.

'We've only got one festival booked, in Derbyshire, but why not? Come and help us. We might even be able to pay you – a bit.'

Jeff laughs.

'I don't care about that,' he says.

'Can you do me a favour?'

Jeff gives me a sheepish grin.

'Shut up, you mean?'

'I need a lift to Matlock. I know I'm being...'

'I need to go to the builders' merchants anyway. What do you think of using wire gabions for picnic benches?'

'The solicitors – the ones I remember Elsa going to. Their office was in Matlock, near the bridge. There's a chance –'

'No worries. Whatever.' Jeff smiles.

Jason

I open the back door. Ben's standing there.

'Your eye looks better. Happy birthday, mate.'

'That was Wednesday,' I say.

'What's up?'

He comes into the kitchen, wiping his boots on the mat. He's carrying a large Tupperware box, with his guitar on his back, and there's no sign of his bike.

'Did your mum drop you off?'

'I wanted to cycle but she worried about the ice.' He puts the box down on the work surface. 'And she made this.'

I open the lid. A birthday cake, with white and blue icing, piped into the shape of a number fourteen. The sort of cake Mum would never make in a million years. All her cakes involve fruit or oats. Ben's mum makes a sponge cake for me every year. My mouth waters at the thought of the buttercream icing but I only manage to crack a small smile.

'You didn't find Ash, did you?' Ben puts his guitar case down. Good timing. The kettle has almost boiled on the AGA hotplate.

'He lives on a sort of...cannabis farm. Mum got stoned.'

Ben laughs.

'Awesome.'

'We're getting the band back together. We're going to play a festival – not far from here. They want Mission

Control to play, and we're going to do it.'

Ben wraps his arms around my shoulders, crushing my windpipe. It's more like a wrestling move than a hug.

'That's brilliant! The best thing ever. Can I come?'

I prise Ben away from me.

'Course you can. But if your mum won't even let you cycle up a hill…'

'I'll come. Even if I have to walk there and jump the fence.'

I make the tea.

'So what's wrong?'

I take both mugs into the living room. Ben follows me.

'What the fuck?'

Ben stares at everything. I dragged all the boxes of Elsa's ceramics out of the cupboard under the stairs. Mum says she's looked everywhere, but I've got that memory. I know I have.

'I'm looking for Elsa's will. Otherwise, the house is going to be auctioned off. They think she died without making one but I remember we hid something in one of these.'

'It could have been anything.' Ben rolls his eyes up to the ceiling.

'Will you help me to look for it?'

'Yeah, but –'

I sit down, cross-legged, amongst the boxes.

'Just shake it.' I unwrap a model of a hedgehog, check if it rattles; stare inside it and hold it up to the light. 'If there's paper inside, you'll hear it rustle.'

Nothing in there, anyway. I wrap it up again, put it back in the box. I take out the next newspaper-wrapped parcel. Patti wakes up from being curled up next to the fire. She tries to get into the cardboard box. I shoo her away.

'You're nuts. Don't you have to go to a lawyer or something to make a will? Mum and Dad are going to make a donation to the hospice…'

'I've already done two boxes.'

Ben sighs.

'I'll do one box and then we're eating cake.'

Ben's eyes meet mine. He's almost laughing, treating the whole thing as a joke, but then he sees how determined I am. I don't care how stupid this must seem, even to Mum. That's why I waited until she went to work. But I've got to try.

Kaz

It's gone. Draper and Ferris – the office where Elsa took me to change my name; the building next to the bridge, above the newsagents. It says "Summer Sands Tanning Salon", not in gold paint, but in curly pink letters on a vinyl banner in the bay window.

Jeff's bulky body deflects the winter wind as we stare at the building on the other side of the road.

If only I'd come here straight after Elsa died and asked about the house. There are a lot of things I should have done. The best I can do is to try to untangle the mess I've created.

'You must have been into Matlock hundreds of times since then. I thought artists were good at noticing things.'

'I'm usually in a rush – and trying not to get run over on my bike.'

'Let's go in there. They might know something.'

We cross the road, push open the door and walk up the stairs. They're not dusty now – they're painted a bright white gloss, with adverts and special offers in clip frames at intervals along the walls. They creak under Jeff's weight.

When we reach the reception, a girl in a pink tunic glances up from her computer in surprise. I see our reflections in the mirror behind her. We're both out of place: a heavy metal lad in gardening clothes, and a haggard woman, chalk-pale, with scragged-back hair.

'Do you want an appointment, madam?' the girl asks, tossing her silky hair like a mane.

'This place used to be a solicitors. We need to know about it.'

'Did it? I'll ask the manager.'

She disappears through a door and comes back shaking her head, showing off her hair.

'We've been open two years. Before that, it was a knitting shop. She says you could try the newsagents. He's been here like, forever?' the receptionist says.

'Okay, thanks.' Jeff steers me gently downstairs.

The oldish man behind the counter in the newspaper shop gives me a sour look.

''Scuse me, mate,' Jeff says. 'We need to know about the shop upstairs.'

'What about it?'

'It used to be a solicitors. What happened to it?' I say.

The man scratches his chin and leans on a pile of newspapers.

'Old Mr Draper died – about ten years ago now. Then the other guy –'

'Ferris. They were called Draper and Ferris.'

'I think he took off to Spain or somewhere. Retired out there.'

'So what happened to all their paperwork – their clients?' I ask.

'How should I know?'

'Oh well,' Jeff says. 'Worth a try.'

Jeff buys some tobacco. I stare at a small display of Barbara Fleming greetings cards and notelets. There's no escape from her.

The man suddenly stares at me.

'Hey – you're that woman. The one who pushed that reporter into the lake.'

I grab Jeff's arm. He gets the hint and we walk out of the shop, back towards the builders' merchants where he parked his Transit.

Jeff must have slowed his pace for me, even though I'm walking as fast as I can to keep up. The pavements are strewn with rock salt and grit.

'You could try another solicitor. They might help you to trace the will.'

'If there even is one…'

Jeff stops walking and points up a side street, towards an office in an old building, the door and a sign painted a glossy dark blue.

'There's a solicitors up here. They helped my sister to buy her house. She said they were alright.'

'What if it costs a fortune?' Still, it looks more inviting than Draper and Ferris used to.

'Just make an appointment – while we're here.'

I walk slowly up the icy slope, and open the door. Jeff waits outside.

Chapter 31
The Lighthouse

Jason

I can see the bright yellow Auction sign from the bottom of the lane. It's been there for a week now.

Everyone who passes the house must be talking about us, wondering what Wren Cottage is like inside. On Sunday, a group of hikers was just standing and staring, talking about the architectural features of the house in loud voices. It's only going to get worse.

I get off my bike at the bottom of the steps and wheel it up to the top. Ben's right behind me. The garden is coming into life again. Snowdrops are in flower and there are a few crocuses pushing up through the damp earth. Normally, that would make Mum happy.

The first thing I do is throw my bike down on the grass and take a flying kick at the Auction sign. It wobbles a bit. Pathetic, but I wasn't really trying.

'That's not going to do much damage,' Ben says.

'There's not much I can do, is there?'

What I really want to do is to karate kick the sign right over and smash it into little pieces, but it won't make any difference if I do. It'll only make the estate agents hate us more than they do already. We're just in the way. We don't have any rights, as far as they are concerned. The estate agents don't know Barbara Fleming wants to buy the house so we can stay here.

What if Barbara Fleming changes her mind and doesn't want us? Mum had better be nice to her. Otherwise, in two weeks' time, we could be evicted.

'We tried our best, didn't we? I helped you for hours with those bloody china things.'

'Mum's had no luck either. They can't trace what that solicitor did with his paperwork. He probably had a big bonfire in the yard and got rid of everything before he pissed off to Spain.'

Ben leans his bike in the front porch and I wheel mine around to the shed. I can hear music: 'Monkey Mind' from *Calling Earth*, with a deep bass rumble. Ben follows me through the back door.

'She's practising?' he asks.

'The gig's the only thing she's looking forward to.'

'The show must go on?' Ben raises one eyebrow.

I fill the kettle and put it on the AGA, before going through to the living room.

Mum stops playing, and presses the pause button on my stereo. I brought it down from my room so we could both play along with the Mission Control albums.

Ash and Pete are coming this weekend. We'll spend the whole time having proper rehearsals. We may as well use this house while we've got it, making as much noise as we want. I'd be really excited if it wasn't for the auction. Even if we get to stay here, it won't be the same, with Barbara owning everything.

'That sounds great, Kaz,' Ben says.

Mum sits down on the sofa with the bass resting on her lap.

'Thanks, Ben.'

She rubs her eyes. She looks really tired. There are plasters on her fingertips because she's been playing hard but hasn't managed to build up callouses yet. But she's still got the technique.

'How was school?' she asks.

'Bradley Smeed's back. My skull ring's in my jacket pocket, so when he passed me on the corridor, I just slipped it on so he could see it. So he knows I mean business.'

I don't tell her that even though Bradley's nose is still bruised, he was laughing at me, trying to act big in front of his mates. His step-dad must have let it slip, about the house. For a second, I felt ashamed like I used to, but my anger was stronger and I forced myself to hold my head up.

'Jason gave him the finger. It was really cool,' Ben says.

I smile at the memory. I had Ben by my side, and Bradley stopped laughing when I stood up straight with my eyes narrowed and a sneer borrowed from an old picture of Daz. I carried on walking, the skull ring glinting under the strip lights. Until I hid it in my pocket again.

'Be careful. If you cause any trouble, they might suspend you next time.'

'So?'

'You're supposed to be the good guy,' Mum says.

'The victim, you mean? I can't let him win.'

'You're a million times better than him. Acting the hard man doesn't suit you.'

'You're still working for his step-dad,' I say.

Mum plays a few notes on her bass, turning the tuning pegs a fraction. She was a tiny bit flat.

'I'm working for Barbara. She's our only lifeline. Unless the solicitors can turn anything up but they're still waiting to hear from the claims management unit.'

I pull a face. She's left it far too late to put her faith in paperwork and things happening the normal, legal way.

'I know the will's here somewhere.'

Mum sighs dramatically and stands up. I step backwards – for a second, I'm scared she's going to hit me over the head with her bass.

'We looked everywhere, Jase,' Ben says.

The kettle is whistling. I dash into the kitchen, before the whole room fills with steam. I know every centimetre of every surface in this house: every creak it makes – every draught; every stain and scuff on the walls. So why won't the house give up its secrets to me, before it's too late?

Kaz

'It finally feels like we're getting there,' Barbara says.

I stand up stiffly from crouching down to plant herbs in the rubble-filled wire baskets around the café area. I've got to hand it to Jeff. He has some great ideas. It'll look and smell great with lavender and rosemary spilling out; the drowsy buzzing of bees in August.

Now the ground has finally thawed, we've got a lot of catching up to do.

'The plants are really making it come alive.' She sniffs, as if she can already smell flowers. She must have a good imagination because we're using young plug plants, only just hardened off in their pots.

'Can I buy some irises and other plants for the pond? Forget-me-nots…'

'You don't need to ask me.'

'I'm glad we're getting stuck into the planting. It helps to take my mind off things.'

'You've got absolutely nothing to worry about. The auction will go like clockwork.'

I nod like a child, forcing myself to believe everything. It seems as far-fetched as a fairy tale. Barbara knows I've found my own solicitors to help me look for Elsa's will. It might have been lost by Draper and Ferris. Barbara just smiled when I told her.

Instead, I'm focussing on real things, like working on this garden and playing my bass, trying to recapture any talent I once had, cursing myself every time I fumble or my fingertips get so sore I can't touch anything.

'What if you get outbid?'

'You're always looking on the gloomy side, Keziah. Change is always good, in the end. I'll make sure you and Jason are alright.'

I nod. I sit on the edge of the rubble wall and look around. Barbara's determination has transformed this place. It's only two months since Barbara bought the old garage and already it's got a new roof with huge windows. A plasterer is inside, skimming over dingy brick and breezeblock walls and they'll soon be painted bright white.

In the garden, bare trees have been planted between the different levels, and my scrap metal sculptures stick out like sentinels, inspired by the figures in Elsa's garden. They must have looked as stark as this once, before they were softened by well-chosen plants growing up around them, wrapping tendrils around their bare metal. I'm suddenly filled with a strange exhilaration. Elsa didn't want everything to stay the same.

'I'm sure it'll be fine,' I say, smiling brightly to stave off the anxiety gnawing inside me.

It seems to take a superhuman effort to cycle up Cromford Hill. I'm aching all over from planting the gallery garden and the weight of the Thunderbird bass hanging around my shoulders every night when I get home. Even on this dull, drizzly afternoon, feeling worn out and used up, the first thing I'll do when I get in is press play on whichever Mission Control album Jason left in the stereo last night, plug in my bass and play until I've almost transported myself back to the past.

Steadily, I reach home. Every inch of the lane, every stone and tree is so familiar. It'll be strange when I'm just a tenant in Wren cottage, or when I have to learn to live somewhere else. I can't stop things from changing.

I drag my bike up the steps. The living room light is on, and I can hear voices. I look back at the cars parked on the road. I should have noticed. A new Mini Cooper with the estate agent's name emblazoned on it and a small, smart-looking van with *"Peak Experience Holiday Cottages"* written on its side. I had to give the estate agent a spare house key and allow people to view it. Until now, no one has bothered and I didn't think anyone actually would.

I hide in the front porch. I crouch low behind my bike and lean my head against the door to listen.

'This has got tremendous potential,' someone says. 'It could be very stylish – a weekend get-away.'

'You could keep a little of its rustic charm, but of course, it needs a complete overhaul – electrics and all. Can you believe the only heating is from open fires and that museum-piece of an AGA?'

'We'll have to keep that, if only for show. It's so authentic. We could put in a modern electric oven in case visitors find it intimidating.'

'What do you think of the artwork?'

The other man mutters something.

'The pieces by Elsa Day are worth a fortune. I've heard Barbara Fleming is planning on buying the whole lot – Wren cottage and its art.'

'I only want the cottage.'

'That's what I thought. Barbara Fleming isn't thinking about the prospective income from this place. Too much of a romantic, helping that nutty woman who's lived here scot-free for years.'

I shiver. Is that what people think of me?

'We've got a deal with Barbara Fleming's agent. Limited edition prints for our other properties. Ironic, isn't it?'

'That's business. This way, everyone wins.'

I bite the inside of my lip so hard my teeth break the skin. A tiny trickle of blood runs inside my mouth. Everyone wins except me. Except Jason. I reach into my bag. I pull out the mobile phone Barbara forced me to buy for work. It's the cheapest one I could find, small and grey, but sending text messages is quite liberating. Everyone has a mobile. I can get in touch without that heart-stopping moment of waiting for them to pick up the phone.

I punch in a message to Barbara.

There's going to be another bid on the house. Holiday cottages.

I turn it onto silent and wait for her reply but the two men walk out of the back door, lock it and walk down the path. I shrink further behind the bike. While I've been at work, loads of people could have viewed the house. They could be ready to make bids higher than Barbara's. We wouldn't know a thing about it until it's too late.

Jason

In the kitchen, the biggest pan is bubbling with leek and potato soup and the AGA smells of baking bread – the most enormous loaf of emergency scone bread I've ever made.

Mum checks her phone for the millionth time.

'Relax. They're on their way, aren't they?'

'They might be here any minute.'

'Come and have a jam – warm up a bit, while we're waiting.'

Mum doesn't move away from the kitchen worktop. Maybe she's changed her mind about wanting Ash and Pete to come here. But this is our first chance of a proper rehearsal together.

Mum's tidied away her painting corner and the sofa has been pushed to one side, making the living room look surprisingly big.

Both my electric guitars are leaning against the sofa cushions. I pick up my red Stratocaster and plug it into my amp. Pete's bringing a proper rehearsal PA with him. My guitar now has an actual Stratocaster neck, rather than a budget Squier one. Ben says it's hardly the same guitar at all. I can see faint lines on the body where Andy has glued it back together and repaired the lacquer. It plays really well, even better than before.

I run through a few scales to warm up my fingers, turn up the distortion on my effects pedal and then launch into a new song I've been learning: 'Fire Woman' by The Cult. Mum loved The Cult when she was young.

She comes out of the kitchen, lured by the riff.

'You've nailed that, Jason.'

She picks up her Thunderbird, but there's a knock on the back door before she has a chance to play a note.

'This is fucking lush, Kaz.' The soup slops out of the side of Pete's bowl with the force of the big lump of bread he's dipped into the soup. 'Perfect after a long drive at rush-hour.'

Ash stares around at the paintings and all the other old stuff in the room.

'This house is amazing. At least you get to carry on living here, right?'

Mum stares into her soup. She's hardly touched it.

'It's an auction. Anyone could bid. That holiday cottage

company were pretty keen.'

I nod. This time, Mum told me the bad news, rather than just pretending nothing was happening.

'Ben says I can share his bedroom if we end up with nowhere to live,' I explain. 'There's a spare bedroom for Mum.'

Mum looks at me as if it's a stupid idea. Ben means it, though. Brenda and Kevin would help us. They wouldn't want us to be out on the streets, even if they wouldn't be particularly thrilled about us living with them.

'And then what?'

'We'll rent somewhere. In Wirksworth maybe.'

'He's so bloody sensible sometimes. Don't know where he gets it from.' Mum says.

There's nothing we can do about it now. All we can do is wait and see what happens. I hack off a slice of bread and a doorstop piece of cheddar.

'We're looking for Elsa's will,' I say.

'What if her mind was wandering? I keep thinking – what if she was playing an elaborate practical joke on us?' Mum sighs.

I'm embarrassed I made Ben sort through all of Elsa's ceramics. It must have been a false memory, wishful thinking.

'She wouldn't have done that to us,' I say. 'We were her family.'

'You could always lock on if they're trying to evict you,' Ash says. 'Use your bike locks to attach yourself to the washing machine.'

I stare at him. He's actually serious.

'Or the AGA,' I say. 'It's the heaviest thing in the house.'

'Not a bad idea,' Mum says. 'If it comes to that.'

'Have you ever chained yourself to anything?' I ask.

Ash laughs.

'I was attached to a JCB with a D lock around my neck for six hours at Fairmile. I'd swallowed the key. The police had to send for industrial bolt clippers.'

'Gran and Grandad bought me a D lock,' I say. 'I'm sure

415

they won't mind me using it to save the house.'

Mum pushes her half-eaten bowl of soup over to Pete. He swallows it down in seconds, while we're clearing everything away.

This should be the most exciting thing I've ever done in my life – a full Mission Control rehearsal – but losing the house has made everything feel grey and hopeless.

I go outside, to help Pete and Ash to carry their equipment inside. Pete's van is parked on the kerb but there's a battered old van behind it, covered in flaking khaki paint.

'We travelled in convoy from Coventry, just like the old days.' Ash grins. 'Do you like her?'

He pats the van gently and proudly, the way you'd pat a horse.

'Yeah. Great,' I say, even though it's just a knackered van.

'There wasn't much point going back to Devon all the time, not when we're rehearsing.'

Mum stands at the top of the steps, her arms crossed. She stares at Ash's van in amazement.

'Have you bought that thing?'

'Four hundred quid. From a mate on the farm. It's a good runner.'

'You've moved into it?'

'I need to be closer to Mum and Dad. But I can make myself useful up here too.'

'I won't let you teach Jason how to chain himself to things…'

'That's up to me, isn't it?' I say.

Ash unlocks the back doors of the van and picks up a long case that must be his keyboard. Next to it is a square cardboard box.

'Careful – it's heavy,' Ash says. I'm determined to pick it up.

The box is so heavy I can barely lift it but I try not to show the effort on my face. I stagger up the steps with it and dump it on the living room floor, trying to act as if it weighed as much as the washing powder the box originally contained.

Pete brings in his bass drum and the cat scarpers from her comfy spot in front of the fire and dashes upstairs. She's going to be seriously angry with us this weekend.

Pete's drum kit takes up loads of space in the corner by the window and by the time the amplifiers are in place, there's hardly anywhere left to stand, let alone to throw shapes. Extension cables and leads snake all over the floor. Mum is backed against the wall, trapped by her microphone stand.

I stare at my guitars, unable to choose which one to play. I know my dad would want to be part of this somehow, so I pick up the black Marlin. If it was good enough for Daz, it'll always be good enough for me.

'Next time, we'll book a proper rehearsal room,' Pete laughs. 'What the fuck were we thinking?'

'We can make as much noise as we like here. It doesn't matter if we piss anyone off. When the house is sold, I'm sure executive couples on weekend getaways will make much better neighbours than we ever were.'

I'm not so sure about that. We're not bad neighbours really. We grow vegetables and swap them for eggs and milk and stuff, and I'm willing to do odd jobs for a bit of cash, which must come in handy. If anyone goes on holiday, we're always happy to switch their lights on and off so they don't get burgled. We don't even have a car, which makes more space on the lane, even though there are currently two large campervans on the pavement outside the house.

Ash sets up his keyboard and his laptop on the dining table, and then lifts the heavy object reverentially out of the cardboard box.

'What is it?' I ask.

'An analogue Random Noise Generator,' he says proudly, showing me a metal box with a discoloured white finish, with dials and switches.

I must look completely blank. It's like something from an old sci-fi movie.

'You've been listening to the albums, right?' Ash stares at

me intently.

I nod. 'Every day. At least.'

'So what are those cosmic noises – the far out stuff you can't translate into notes?'

'You need one of those?'

'I just bought it from eBay. Not the same as the one I used to have, but I've tested it. Works a treat.'

'Are we all ready?' Mum asks.

'Just about,' Pete grunts, coming up for air after assembling his hi-hat pedal.

'How are we going to do this?' Ash plays a run of notes to test out his keyboard.

'Jason decides,' Pete says. 'What do you want to play first?'

I launch into the intro of 'Rootless in Babylon', expecting everyone else to join in. But Mum is still fiddling with the tuning pegs on her bass, and Ash is thumping the top of the Random Noise Generator.

They look at me apologetically as I stop playing.

'Sorry,' Mum says. 'You took me by surprise.'

'Sure you're ready now?' I ask. Everyone nods.

I play the intro again, and this time everything goes well. I've practised it so many times, I know the riffs and the song structure by heart. Because my fingers know what they're doing, I can listen to everything.

Mum's voice sounds great amplified, full of raw emotion. Pete's drumming adds loads of power and I can hear Ash's swelling notes on the keyboard. The gaps in the sound are filled by a menacing low hum – that must be the noise generator. The guitar parts sound like Daz is playing them, even though it's me. This is brilliant.

A loud bang comes from the cupboard under the stairs with a flash of light.

Everything goes silent. I strum at my guitar but nothing comes out. Complete darkness, apart from a faint red glow from the fireplace.

'What the fuck?' Pete says.

I sniff. Something acrid in the air.

'Can you smell something burning?' I ask.

'Have you got a torch?' Ash says.

'The kitchen – you're closest. In the cupboard under the sink.'

I can hear Ash moving around, trying to find the door into the kitchen, swearing as he stumbles on something – probably an extension cable.

'It must be the fusebox,' Mum yells. 'It's in the cupboard under the stairs. There's loads of Elsa's stuff in there.'

Before the lights went out, I was standing near to the cupboard. I can reach the door, even if I can't see anything. I know my way around the house by feel. I mean, how many times have I gone downstairs in the middle of the night, needing the loo or a glass of water? I walk slowly forward with my hands outstretched.

Something crashes to the floor and lands on my foot.

'Shit!'

I wiggle my toes. I think I'm okay, but I can feel broken pieces of china crunching under my trainers. I forgot my guitar was still strapped on. The headstock must have knocked something off the radiogram. The only thing on there was the lighthouse-shaped table lamp. Bollocks.

The smell of smoke is stronger here.

'Jason, are you okay?' Mum shouts.

'I think I broke the table lamp.'

'There should be candles and matches in the side drawer of the radiogram.'

I fumble about until I've found the drawer. I rummage around, remembering the candles we used for Christmas dinner. My hand closes around one of them. I feel for a rectangular box. There it is. I shake it and it makes a noise. I find the wick of the candle and hold it upright. I can feel my hands tremble as I strike the match.

The candle makes a very small glow but it means I can find the candle-holder. I can put it down on the radiogram. I find the next candle and light it.

I kneel down and collect up the pieces of the table lamp, before they get crushed in the confusion. Something rustles under my fingertips as I put the bits down on the top of the radiogram.

'Please tell me we can we fix the lamp?' Mum cries.

'I dunno. Superglue?'

'Let me take a look at the circuit board,' Ash says. He's found the torch. Its wide beam seems dazzling. I shield my eyes. Our torch is a massive, old-fashioned thing that takes a huge, square battery. It would be good as a weapon in case we were burgled. Its size makes it easier to find in the dark. Even the torch is part of the estate of Elsa Day. Hardly anything actually belongs to us.

In the dim light, I find a safe corner where I can lean my guitar. Then I open the cupboard door and trapped smoke billows out, smelling of burned plastic.

'We need to pull all this junk out so I can get in there,' Ash says.

'It's not junk. It's Elsa's stuff. God knows how much it's worth,' Mum shrieks. I move the cardboard boxes, as gently as I can; the paintings, the suitcases, to give Ash room to investigate. The smoke makes me cough but I can't see any flames, so maybe everything's okay.

'Fuck! It's melted the casing!' Ash yells, sounding muffled.

'Be careful!' Mum shouts.

'I'm an electrician.' There's a clunk, as if a switch is being thrown. Then Ash emerges, wriggling backwards out of the cupboard, wiping his eyes on his sleeve.

Mum puts down her bass and opens the window.

'Everything's safe now,' Ash says. 'I can replace it, but not until tomorrow.'

'So much for a bloody rehearsal. Ancient wiring.' Mum says. 'Oh, what's the point of it all, anyway?'

'Hey, it's okay,' Pete says. 'You sounded fucking brilliant. If we can play like that at the festival…'

'That wasn't even one song. We've got to play for forty five minutes.'

She's right. Everything seems to go wrong for us, all the time. Now everything's calmed down a bit, I take another look at the table lamp. I've wrecked it. It's in at least ten pieces. Even if I use superglue, people will be able to see the cracks. It's worthless, and Mum will get into trouble.

'You were lucky. This wiring's so old, it could have caught fire at any time. These old fuse boxes can be very dangerous,' Ash says.

'Everything needs replacing,' Mum says. 'Even us.'

I try to arrange the fragments of the table lamp, to see if it might go back together anyway. The lighthouse tower broke off at the base, and halfway up. Something's sticking out of it. A bit of rolled-up paper. I force myself to stay calm as I pull it out of the tower and flatten it out so I can read it. It's actually two pieces of paper. They feel brittle, from being rolled up for so long.

I begin to remember, clearly. When Elsa asked me to roll the paper up really tightly, it was the lighthouse lamp she was holding.

One piece of paper is typed and the other is written in wavering handwriting. I sneak a peek at the typed sheet:

Last Will and Testament of Elsa Day, of Wren Cottage, Bolehill, Derbyshire, DE56 2RU.

'Bloody hell.'

My heart thumps so loud I mistake it for Pete's bass drum.

'What?'

Mum rushes over to the radiogram as fast as she can without going flying over a stray cable.

'What is it?'

Her face is pale in the flickering candlelight.

'Read the letter first,' I say.

I hold the letter flat on the top of the radiogram. It's difficult to read the handwriting. Gradually, I make it out.

Dear Keziah,

I expect you'll have received a copy of the will from Draper and Ferris by now, but this is a back-up copy. The table lamp won't last long with Jason running around bashing into things. Both of you have brought such life into my last years.

421

You came into my life by accident, when you needed the safe haven it was my pleasure to give, in return for the things I was starting to find difficult. In time, your talents came to the fore, too. I hope that, when I'm gone, you'll be able to develop as an artist to heights I could only imagine and reclaim the life of music you left behind in your grief.

I'm glad we pretended you were my great-niece. It feels like you and Jason are truly my family, which is why I am leaving the bulk of my estate to you.

It's tempting to turn one's back on one's former life after loss and trauma. After Pierre died, I came here. This little cottage was empty and unloved, so I bought it and made it into a simple home with everything I needed, where I could hide away from the world and continue to make my art. You are young. At some point, you will need to face the world. I intend you to do this with the greatest of confidence in yourself, knowing that, whatever happens, you'll have the security of this house.

Of course, you can do whatever you want with it but I hope you'll continue to look after the house and the garden when I'm gone and that in the very distant future, you'll pass Wren Cottage on to Jason.

I'm sure I'll get the chance to say everything I need to say anyway. But in case I don't…

All my love,
Elsa

Mum sobs, her eyes spilling tears which she quickly wipes away with the back of her hand. She swaps the sheets of paper around and reads the will.

'It's true,' she gasps. 'She left everything to us. The house, anyway. She's left the ceramics and paintings to Derby Museum and Art Gallery.'

'That'll piss Barbara off,' I say.

'I'm sure she'll find a way round it. But we're safe. We can stay here. This proves it.'

'You'd better put it somewhere safe until tomorrow.'

Mum folds up the letter and the will, and stuffs them into her bra.

'Sure it's safe there?' Pete laughs.

She takes the pieces of paper out, unfolds them, and

stares at them again.

'Look at it, Pete – make sure I'm not hallucinating. It does say *"I give to my closest friend and carer, Keziah Knight (formerly known as Karen Kenning), my house, garden and the sum of two thousand pounds towards the upkeep of the property."* That's me, isn't it? There's no chance of a mistake?'

She passes the will over. Pete nods, and she takes it back again.

'It's all signed and everything?' Ash asks.

'By Elsa, the solicitor, and someone else – don't recognise the name, but I reckon it's the builder from when she had the attic converted into Jason's bedroom.'

'So what are you waiting for?' Pete says. 'Crack open the Champagne!'

Mum laughs.

'I bought some cider. For old time's sake.'

'That'll do.'

Pete opens the window to let out the smell of smoke. I need fresh air. No one notices me slipping outside into the garden.

The streetlights make it brighter than in the house. I can hear Mum, Pete and Ash inside, talking and laughing, as if a spell has been broken.

Now I can do what I've been aching to do for weeks. I fetch the axe from the shed and chop the Auction board down. As soon as it falls onto the lawn, I jump on top of the sign until it splinters.

Chapter 32
Rewiring

Jason

Walking through the house by torchlight reminds me of the time when our electricity got cut off. We can survive without electricity, as long as we've got plenty of candles and firewood. At Ben's house, they'd be screwed. They wouldn't even be able to get the heating on.

Downstairs, they've moved the amplifiers to one side so at least we can sit down on the sofa. Ash is already making a joint. I bet Mum will have some again. The smell of it makes me feel a bit sick but it's better than the acrid smell from the fuse box.

I reach the top of the stairs and open the door to my bedroom, ducking as I walk through the low doorway. My acoustic guitar is propped against my bed and I grab it. I've only played half a song with the band. Tonight, I was going to show them I was good enough to replace Daz. I'm pleased and massively relieved about the house but I'm sort of frustrated too. I've put so much work into learning every song Mission Control did – every B-side, as well as the songs on the albums. All the guitar parts and all the lyrics. Not even Mum knows I've worked that hard but I have to be perfect. I can't let Daz down.

I take my guitar downstairs. The living room looks different; full of looming, bulky shapes in the dark, lit by a few candles and the glow from the fireplace. I sit on the sofa and fine-tune my guitar.

To prove what I can do, I play the intro to a B-side from *Calling Earth* called 'Starling Skies'. It's a bit more of an acoustic song, one I can imagine the band singing around a camp fire at a music festival. It's almost a love song.

Mum and the guys look confused. I sing the first verse.

'I haven't heard this in years,' Ash says. 'I'd forgotten all about it.'

I put everything into singing and playing the song, almost

forgetting the others are there. It's not difficult to play; not show-offy, but there are some unusual chord changes and some fiddly bits to remember.

'Fancy you learning that song.' Mum smiles sadly, as if she's been lost in memories.

'Sam gave me all the B-sides – and some old live tapes.'

'You've made the song your own. You'll have to play it live.'

Pete nods. 'We'll have to get the electrics fixed, or find somewhere else to rehearse. We can't waste this weekend.'

Kaz

'I think that's it.' Ash's muffled voice comes out of the cupboard. He's been in there for hours, squashed into the corner right under the stairs. It's a good job he's spent so much time crawling around in narrow spaces on ships and digging tunnels on protest sites. I'd panic in such a stuffy corner.

It seems a stupid place to put a fuse box. Ash says it hadn't been replaced since the 1950s. Dad was right. The house was a death-trap. I think of Jason coming home on his own, playing his guitar turned up loud in his bedroom. The fuse box could have blown then.

'Shall I try the lights?' I ask.

'Go for it.'

I flip the living room light switch and the bulb comes on, bathing the gloomy living room in warm light.

'It works!'

I hear Ash collecting up his tools. He slowly emerges from the cupboard, with a torch attached to his forehead with elastic, still shining, like a third eye.

He takes a deep breath and turns the torch off, peeling off the elastic, leaving a horizontal mark on his skin.

'We can try rehearsing again when Pete and Jason come back from Matlock Bath.'

'We'd better be careful. The rest of the wiring needs

replacing too.'

'It's taken ages,' I say. 'What do I owe you?'

He stares at me, and I stare back. A lifetime of loss and loneliness passes between us. How much do I owe him? Stupid question.

Ash looks so hurt and lost. I put my arms around him; kiss him on the cheek. His beard feels strange on my lips. I wish he was clean-shaven. I can't get used to him like this.

'The whole house needs updating, insulating...'

'That's what the holiday cottage guy said.' I laugh.

The will is upstairs now, safe in my bedside cabinet. I'm still a bit nervy though. I have to wait until Monday for the solicitors to open. I keep going upstairs to take a look at it. I still can't believe it – maybe I'll go up and find nothing, or a blank sheet of paper.

'I could stay. Mum and Dad need me in Cov, but not all the time. We could work on the house together – do what needs doing.'

Ash follows me into the kitchen. I fill the kettle and put it on the AGA. He spoons coffee into his tin-can filter. He can't seem to live without it.

'I've always looked after the cottage. Always mended things.'

'You've done a great job. But it's your house now. You can change it.'

He's right. Wren Cottage doesn't need to be a museum to Elsa any more. I suppose that's why she left her art to the Derby gallery. I told Barbara, and she sounded relieved. She said she would sort something out that would work to everyone's advantage. We'll have to arrange to meet the curators from the gallery – get everything valued.

The house and the garden are mine. I keep having to remind myself.

'I could have a proper studio for painting. We could turn the shed into a rehearsal room. We could have central heating!' With the money Barbara's paying me to work on her gallery garden, I can finally afford things like this.

Ash grins, and gets two mugs out of the cupboard.

Jason

The pub is much quieter than it is on Sundays. It looks strange without day-trippers and middle-aged people in biker leathers waiting for meals.

The smell of Sam's chips is drifting from the kitchen. My stomach rumbles. It feels weird being here as a customer. Judith does a double-take as we walk up to the bar.

'We weren't expecting you this week, love,' she says. She's thawed towards me. I think she feels sorry for me; always trying to feed me, but she likes the way I turn up at the kitchen on time and I'm polite to the customers.

'I'm treating him,' Pete says. 'Veggie burger and chips twice, please.'

'Who are you, then?' She eyes him curiously. 'Hang on, I've seen you before. On one of those posters in Sam's room. You're another one from that band.' She doesn't look very pleased about it.

'I'm Pete. Nice to meet you,' he says, with a smile, holding out his hand confidently for her to shake. She does.

'Pint of Brown Cow, please. And a diet Coke for Jason.' Pete sneaks a wink at me. I warned him she could be awkward.

'You don't need to be on a diet.' She stares at me, and gives a sidelong glance at Pete. 'Thin as a rake, you are.'

'I think he's got hollow legs,' Pete says.

'Can we talk to Sam?' I ask.

Judith scribbles down our order and nods, before shouting through the door to the kitchen.

Sam looks stunned as he comes through the door.

'Pete? Oh my God. It's amazing to actually meet you.'

'How's the teaching going?' Pete asks.

'I've got one or two star pupils.' Sam and Pete share smiles. Pete puts his arm around me and ruffles my hair. I'm pleased but I give him a pretend pissed-off look.

'You've done a great job with him,' Pete says. 'Nurturing

natural talent.'

I feel my cheeks burning.

'We've had to stop rehearsing,' I say. 'The electrics have blown. Ash is replacing the fuse box.'

'He probably didn't help it by plugging in a noise generator that looked like it came out of a submarine.' Pete takes his first sip of beer.

'That's all you need,' Sam says. 'With the house and everything.'

'We came to tell you about that. I knocked the table lamp over and the will was inside it. Turns out the house really does belong to Mum.'

'Really? That's brilliant!'

'You should have seen us rehearsing. There was hardly any room for us once we'd set up.'

Sam looks uneasily at Judith.

'You could use our function room. It's being renovated at the moment, so we've not got anything on. That's alright, isn't it, Judith?'

'Haven't you got meals to cook? There are other orders besides these burgers, you know.'

Sam gives me an exasperated glance.

Judith rings our drinks and the burgers through the till. Then she slams a key on the bar.

'I'll show them now. I won't be a minute. They can use it for the rest of weekend, can't they? Come on, it's Mission Control.' Sam sounds ridiculously excited.

Judith sighs.

'I want to have weddings in that room. Nice things. Not sweaty bands and people wrecking the place.'

'We're not that sweaty. Quite well behaved really…' Pete lifts up his armpit and pretends to take a sniff.

'Apart from blowing fuse boxes.' Judith folds her arms.

Sam comes out from behind the bar and picks up the key. We follow him up some stairs. He unlocks a door.

The room is halfway through being decorated; stepladders, dustsheets and pots of paint in one corner. It's much smaller than our school hall, with a low stage at one end and a curved ceiling. The old paint is peeling in places but, in my mind, I can see it full of people watching a band.

Pete smiles.

'This is fucking perfect. A great little venue, once you get it going.'

'I need to convince my mother-in-law first.'

'Mission Control could do a gig here,' I say.

Pete laughs.

'We've got a festival to play first.'

'It's far too small for you guys,' Sam says. 'But that would be amazing.'

'I can't wait to practise in here. It was stupid, trying to do it at home,' I say.

'The festival organisers called me this morning. They've asked me to help set up the stages – the mixing desks, PAs, that sort of thing. Live sound engineering too. You and Ben could help me, if you want.'

'That sounds like great experience, Jason,' Pete says. 'Don't work him too hard, though.'

'I'd love to. If I'm allowed,' I say.

Sam pulls the dust sheet off a small but professional-looking mixing desk. 'I'll get my PA system set up in here after lunch. Judith's going to kill me, but it'll be worth it.'

Chapter 33
Frogs and Mermaids

Kaz

The skylights in the roof of the gallery are open, letting in the fresh spring air. I take a deep breath of it. It feels like magic – the promise of life, every time I look into the garden and see something new that's pushed through the earth; each tree bursting into leaf.

There's art to install, and finishing touches to be made, but the Elsa Day gallery is coming together. We're opening it for previews and to gently spread the word in May, before the big launch in June.

It feels strange – all of Elsa's artwork being here, going on display. Our house feels empty, in a good way: ready for something new to happen.

I cleaned all of Elsa's ceramics painstakingly, with warm soapy water and soft cloths and brushes. The people at the Derby Museum agreed, quite logically, that the Elsa Day Gallery was the best place for Elsa Day's art. Apart from keeping a couple of larger pieces for display, Barbara was allowed to keep the rest on permanent loan. She seems happy with the arrangement. I'm glad too. It feels like Elsa has got what she wanted.

I'm arranging the small ceramics in glass cabinets, where people will be able to see them for the first time. Elsa spent decades making them in the garden shed. She sold some locally but the objects that weren't displayed on shelves in the house were fired in the shed, wrapped in newspaper and just put away in boxes.

When Jason was small, we put the rest of them away too. I should have questioned why Elsa wanted to keep the lighthouse lamp in the living room. It's a wonder it wasn't broken years ago like she wanted it to be.

Putting the ceramics on these shelves feels like saying goodbye to Elsa. The frail-looking but tough old lady who helped me when I had reached my lowest point; who understood what I was going through and my need to hide from the world. We both dealt with our grief at losing the loves of our lives in the same way.

Now Elsa's art is being flooded with light from every angle; vivid colours glowing with the sunlight from the skylights above. These little pieces are surrealist high kitsch, like Mrs Norton's Scottie dog collection. I'll have to invite her to the gallery and see what she thinks.

I unwrap a small figure of a mermaid sitting on a rock. Like most of the others, it's small enough to sit on the palm of my hand.

She almost matches the lighthouse table lamp. A lot of Elsa's objects are surreal versions of sea-side souvenirs. Elsa loved living here – near Matlock Bath, with its land-locked holiday atmosphere. I haven't looked closely at this figure before. It's been catalogued, documented and cleaned by me. There were so many, I didn't notice it.

The mermaid has wild black hair with streaks of seaweed in it. Her mouth is open, singing a siren song, wearing a corset made out of jagged black stones. She doesn't look malevolent; she's a mermaid who refuses to conform to the blonde hair, shell-bikini stereotype.

She looks like me. By the time I met Elsa, the kiln had been rusting away for years; the pottery studio turned into a potting shed. I turn the figure upside down and examine its base. She always signed and dated her work. 1972 – the year I was born. I'll have to show Jason. It's almost as if Elsa knew she was going to meet me. I place the mermaid on the glass shelf, where she can sing to her heart's content.

'Keziah – can you help me?' Barbara calls.

I turn around.

She's wheeling our old Hoover along the floor. Surely she's not going to use it? It barely works. The wooden floor is spotless.

'Can you help me lift this onto this plinth?'

'Seriously?'

'It's conceptual.'

'Elsa painted that frog face on the Hoover to cheer Jason

up when he had chicken pox. It's just a…'

'You said yourself it's the last thing she ever painted.'

'It's a good talking point, I suppose.'

'A feminist riposte to Duchamp's *Urinal*.' Barbara is deadly serious about this.

Who knows what Elsa had in mind when she painted the smiling face on the vacuum cleaner? Jason was three. He'd caught chicken pox at nursery. It's the worst illness he's ever had.

Jason was miserable, bundled up on the sofa, bored of being read to and having to wear gloves so he couldn't scratch the itchy red spots on his face. We kept smoothing white calamine lotion all over him. He said he looked like a ghost when he looked into the mirror. I thought he looked more like a tiny goth. I blame myself for his recent experiments with eyeliner and nail varnish.

Elsa found her oil paints and painted the Hoover to look like a frog. It made Jason laugh and he suddenly felt well enough to sit on top of the vacuum cleaner and let me tow him around the house. We made up stories about the frog and Jason spent hours drawing his own pictures in wax crayon, which Elsa declared to be works of genius. I kept them safe, like all his pictures. Maybe Barbara would like them in the gallery too?

Together, we lift the Hoover, complete with its nozzle, onto the plinth. It grins widely at the white walls.

'I think Elsa would love it. It'll make them laugh. That's what she wanted.'

Barbara pulls a crumpled piece of paper from the pocket of her neatly tailored jeans. Her latest to-do list. She writes a new one every day and sticks to it religiously. She peers at it through her glasses, and nods as she reads each item she's already crossed off.

'I don't want you to stop what you're doing up here but I need to know exactly where you want your pictures to hang downstairs.'

Barbara doesn't give me time to answer. Her feet clang on the metal rungs of the staircase, hurrying down to the main gallery space. I follow her.

Barbara loves the adrenaline of rushing around, organising things, ordering people about or, if there's no one available, doing things herself. She's taking too much on. Yesterday, I found her trying to move a catering oven in the café into the place she'd marked on her plan. She was absolutely determined and moaned when Jeff turned up to help her out. But why struggle on your own? That was the mistake I made for too long.

The space down here is unrecognisable. A polished concrete floor, dazzling white walls, flooded with light through the roof-to-floor windows. There's a rather unflattering view of Jeff's builder's bum as he plants the tyre wall with primary-coloured annuals.

My paintings lean against the walls, ready to be hung alongside the work of other contemporary local artists. There will be price tags under my pictures that would have made my jaw drop a few months ago. Barbara has told me, over and over again: my work is worth it. My latest paintings look good here, exploring the peaceful decay we disturbed: the Nissan Micra entwined with bindweed and brambles; the heron perched on the rusty car door; and the one I'm most pleased with: the topless calendar model transformed into the high priestess of the derelict garage, transmuted by nature and time into a ruined temple, worshipped by the ghosts of long-dead mechanics. I only finished it last week.

'I can't believe it's only four months since we stood here, ankle deep in pigeon shit,' I say.

'We make a good team.' Barbara smiles at me. She lifts up the calendar girl picture, and holds it at arm's length.

'I was scared of you at first,' I say. 'I thought you were going to screw me over.'

'I thought I was quite gentle with you, really.'

'Did you really want to buy Wren Cottage?'

'You'd preserved everything so carefully. Elsa's whole life was there and you were part of it. I thought I could stop everything from being destroyed.'

'Did you believe me, when I said the house was mine?'

'This one should go at the centre of the room – to catch the eye.' Barbara turns to me. 'I knew you were telling the truth but I never thought any documents would turn up. I didn't want you or Jason to suffer. I'm sorry if I seemed like a bully.'

I shuffle some of the paintings around, leaning them against the wall in the places where I think they should hang.

'The garden will really draw people in,' she says. 'People already stop and look at the sculptures. They can't wait for the gallery to open.'

'I thought you wanted to own me,' I say. 'But no one can do that now and I don't think you wanted to anyway.'

Barbara laughs.

'I can be bossy. You needed someone to believe in you.' She takes her glasses off and polishes them; she looks softer, a little anxious. 'You will carry on working with me once the gallery's opened, won't you?'

'The garden will need keeping in trim.' I look around this space. It's huge. 'There's so much we could do with this place. There's nothing for young artists round here. What about classes? Gallery space? Elsa helped me. It's what she would have wanted.'

Barbara smiles.

'There's no stopping you now, is there?' she says.

Jason

We've gathered an audience. I wish I could get rid of them, but I've got a reputation – I'm the good guy, like Mum says. It's annoying, though, when I'm just trying to work on a new song with Ben and Josh. We don't need Lance Thomas and a crowd of girls hanging round us like we're famous. I try to act like we're on our own.

'My dad's bought tickets to this festival called Bearded Theory,' Lance Thomas says. The emo girls seem to have adopted him and he's upgraded his school bag to a Vans rucksack. He's cool in their eye because he knows me. It's so embarrassing. He's started combing his fringe over his eyes.

'He's going to see this old band called Hawkwind – and Mission Control are playing too.'

'Yeah, we are,' I say, hoping Lance isn't coming. Sometimes, it's like having a shadow.

'You must be so excited.'

'Ohmigod!' squeals a girl – I think she's called Alice. She seems to have forgiven me for not signing her homework planner at the school concert.

I turn up my amp and launch into a new riff I've been working on. I yell the chords out to Ben and he picks them up quickly. Josh tries to play along; he's slightly out of time, but it sounds okay.

The door of the music room opens and the heads of all the younger kids turn. It's Mrs Lyons, balancing a pile of books, cling-film-wrapped sandwiches and a mug of tea. Lance rushes to open the door for her, but she's not falling for it.

She puts everything down on her desk with a sigh.

'You know the rules. You can't just hang out in the music room. You have to be actually playing a musical instrument.'

'But we're…' pleads Georgia, a girl with a triangular ginger bob.

Mrs Lyons crosses her arms and gives her a particularly impressive teacher stare. The kids reluctantly file out of the door, grumbling. I give them a wave.

'You encourage them,' Ben says.

'You gave them your autograph.'

'We can't win,' Josh says, practising a paradiddle. He still can't keep in time, but he's getting better.

I check my guitar's in tune. I've got Daz's Marlin with me today. I'm not letting it out of my sight for a second.

'I've been looking on the Bearded Theory website,' Ben says. 'We should email them to sign up for an open mic session at Tina's Café stage on the Friday.'

'It's my cousin's wedding that weekend,' Josh grumbles, bashing a cymbal.

'We'll do an acoustic set then, like we're busking,' Ben says.

'We can't be the Organ Detectives anymore. That's just...' I pull a face.

'What about The Organ?' Ben suggests.

'Sounds crap.'

'You come up with something better,' Ben says. I can't think of anything. I've got brain-freeze.

'The right name'll come to us.'

Mrs Lyons peers at us over the top of her glasses.

'Does your form tutor know you're going to be off school on a Friday?'

We always talk in front of Mrs Lyons. She's usually on our side. But I didn't realise she was listening. Our form tutor Mr Whitehouse is really strict and boring. He didn't even come to the school concert and he was the only teacher who told me off for getting into the fight with Bradley.

'The exams are over by then – and we'll only miss one day.'

'I know you're not playing on the main stage until Saturday, Jason.'

'We're helping to set up some of the stages. Our guitar teacher sorted it out for us.'

There's a sparkle in Mrs Lyon's eyes; a hint of a smile.

'Work experience, too. I am impressed. I could persuade Mr Whitehouse to put it down as an authorised educational activity.'

'Really?'

'If you're performing, it's good practise for GCSE music. It'll do you both good to meet more working musicians.'

'Thanks,' Ben says, his eyes shining.

'You'll even see a few faces you know. One of my Year Ten girls is going – I've been giving her permission to go to festivals for years.' I wonder who it is. No one apart from Lance has mentioned the festival at school.

'It'll be great to have Ben with me.'

'I don't want to hear that you've had your stomachs

pumped after drinking three litres of cider.' Mrs Lyons stares at us sternly.

'I'm playing on the main stage.' I suddenly feel nervous, thinking about all the people who'll be watching us. 'I've got to be sensible. And I don't even like cider.' I tried some on the night we found the will. It was sickly and too sharp at the same time.

'We could put your names down for this open mic thing right now if you wanted,' Mrs Lyons says.

She clicks onto the internet on her computer, finding the festival's website.

'It's a funny name for a festival,' she says. 'Do you have to wear fake beards?'

'I think so. It sounds silly, but it'll be fun,' Ben says.

'It's a great chance to show people what a great songwriter you are,' Mrs Lyons tells him.

Ben swells with pride. I realise why Mrs Lyons is making such a big fuss of this Friday open mic thing. She doesn't want Ben to feel jealous and fall out with me again. Ben is over all that now, but I'm glad he's pleased.

Kaz

The garden is looking just right, blossom drifting with the breeze. Everything is in place. The air is warm and fragrant and the sun is shining but I've got a massive knot of anxiety in my stomach.

Marilyn Richards is due here in half an hour, and I'm paralysed by fear.

I sit down on the bench. I try to tell myself she's just a normal woman; that she's not going to expect anything of me, other than a willingness to talk. I'm sure the others will say what she needs to hear if I falter.

I picture her in that portacabin at the Spiral Sun festival. I've re-read the interview. She knew something was wrong. She arrived just after we'd had a big row. Daz was losing the plot. He was going on at Ash again; not trusting me. There was so much anger inside Daz, and I had lost my faith in being able to change him. Part of me agreed with him. I had betrayed him in that swimming pool.

My eyes well up with tears. I shut them tight, squeezing the tears out. I hear the radio from the kitchen; pots clattering as Jason does the washing up. He's made pizza. Daz would never have done that. He's chatting to Pete in the kitchen, his voice a few tones deeper than it was a year ago, but bright and cheerful. Above the noises from the house, there's a chorus of bird song as the countryside wakes up for summer.

I take out a tissue, mop up my eyes and blow my nose. I'm going to get through a lot of tissues today. Marilyn Richards deserves the full story. I've spent all these years feeling guilty about Daz, feeling responsible for his death. The anger he felt was far older than anything I did. Deep down, Daz hated himself. His dad's fault. Daz's dad might still be alive. Marilyn Richards could have researched that for her book. Not that I really want to know.

Ash emerges onto the lawn with a loud clatter, carrying a wooden deckchair under each arm. He smiles at me hopefully. His clothes, and his beard, are full of cobwebs.

'We could sit outside for the interview – it's a shame to be cooped up on a day like this.'

'They're disgusting. They won't even hold anyone's weight.'

The deckchairs are filthy. The material is frayed and faded. They must have been buried beneath decades of clutter.

'I'll give them a clean.'

'Get some normal chairs and the folding table – she'll be here soon – and look at you.' I hear something sharp in my voice, and I don't like it.

Ash is clearing out all the junk that's accumulated over the years, taking it to the tip. He's working so hard on the house, without asking for anything in return apart from space to park his van on the pavement.

We're making plans to rebuild the shed. The wood is

rotten. I gave the rusty potter's wheel and kiln to Barbara for the gallery. I hadn't realised how much floor space there was. We could have a rehearsal space for the band, and enough room for me to paint; big windows so I can use it as a greenhouse, and proper bike racks.

Ash sits next to me and reaches into his pocket. I expect him to pull out a spliff, but he's holding a creased photograph. He smooths it out and shows it to me.

The photo shows the three of them: Ash, Daz and Pete. The Coventry skyline is in the background: tower blocks and spires, against a pink summer sunset.

Then I remember. The first night Ash and Daz moved into the studio – just the disused top floor of a warehouse back then. I took the photograph. We'd just pushed open the hatch and climbed out onto the roof, sneezing. We were covered in dust. Daz looks dishevelled but happy. There's still a trace of a bruise around his mouth in the picture. He'd only just left home.

We were sixteen; Ash was nineteen. All high on the excitement of being in a band, hoping we could escape the jobs and the suffocating lives our parents led. Ash had convinced us that if we worked hard on our dreams, we'd succeed. Even though he was skint, he had ambitious dreams and a lot of talk.

Daz had escaped from his dad and the possibilities were endless for the first time in his life. Even without any money, all he needed was a guitar, a mattress to sleep on in a safe place, and his friends.

'I kept these through everything,' Ash says. He's got a photo of me too, taken a few moments after the first one; newly-dyed black hair tied in a high pony tail and a baggy Cure t-shirt, contrasting with my tanned summer skin. I'm laughing, half-scared of being on the roof, hanging onto Daz's arm. Daz's face is out of shot.

'We thought we could do anything, didn't we?'

'I feel sorry for anyone who doesn't believe that when they're a teenager.' Ash smiles. 'Jason's got it in spades.'

'He used to be really shy, but now…' I realise how much

Jason has changed since he started learning the guitar.

'Daz stopped believing that. He thought he was going to end up like his dad. We tried…'

'What if he'd never seen us in that swimming pool? What if we'd never done anything so stupid?'

Ash tucks the photographs back into the breast pocket of his overall; snaps the press-studs securely shut.

'We can't change the past,' he says.

I stand up and stretch, feeling dizzy.

'I must look a mess. I need to put my makeup on again.'

'I'd better get those chairs.'

In the living room, Jason is playing Daz's guitar. I don't recognise what he's playing. It must be another new song. Pete is sitting on the sofa, listening to him. He seems pretty relaxed. Jason looks up at me as I run upstairs but he doesn't stop playing.

The house is full of the smell of baking pizza, but my stomach is tied in knots.

I sit on the edge of my bed and stare into the dressing table mirror. The cat is curled up on the bed. Despite it being such a lovely day, she's decided to hide from the world. I wish I could curl up next to her. I grab a tissue and wipe off the smudged eyeliner, before reapplying it, more thinly this time, in the rim of my lower eyelids. Panda eyes looked great when I was twenty, perhaps not now.

What will Marilyn Richards think of this outfit? Will she be able to tell that the leggings are from Primark and the black lacy dress is from a charity shop? I was hoping to wear this at the festival next week but what if I look like someone who's wandered onto the stage by mistake? Someone's mum.

Looking into the mirror isn't doing me much good. I pick up the Mission Control scrapbook from the dressing table and take it downstairs. Pete and Jason are carrying the folding table out into the garden. I look at the time. Marilyn Richards' train should have arrived in Cromford.

The dining chairs are in the garden now and everything looks ready. I put the scrapbook down on the table. I put my hand on it and close my eyes. It's going to be a difficult day.

'Mum,' Jason says. 'You're doing my head in. Just sit down or something.'

'Sorry.'

'It'll be fine.'

I try to smile at him but I can tell he's completely unconvinced. I get my gardening basket from the shed and start weeding the vegetable patch. With the wet spring we've had so far, the dandelions are going wild amongst the new shoots and young leaves. I pick off slugs hiding under the leaves and put them in a yoghurt pot. I'll empty it into the field on the other side of the road later. I can never bring myself to kill slugs, no matter how repulsive and destructive they are. I sometimes use beer traps, but at least they die happy.

I hear a car coming up the lane. It stops. The door opens with a familiar creak.

'This place is amazing. Look at the view.'

'I don't know why anyone bothers living in London, when they could have all this.'

'I bet you can't get a decent cup of coffee.'

'More artisan cafés round here than you can shake a stick at.'

They walk up the steps: Sam looks thrilled beyond words about playing a part in this but he's trying to play it cool.

Marilyn Richards steps onto the lawn. She's wearing skinny jeans, faded blue, and knee-high boots. A distressed Rolling Stones t-shirt under a leather jacket. The sort of rock 'n' roll style that looks effortless but takes years to perfect. The jeans and jacket will be designer; the t-shirt from a hip boutique; the shaggy blonde highlights created by a stylist.

I stand up so quickly I almost black out. My hands are covered in soil and slug juice.

'I'm sorry,' I say, showing her my hands. 'I must...'

Marilyn Richards takes off her sunglasses. She rushes towards me and hugs me.

'It's so good to see you…' She stands back and looks around – at Pete, at Ash and at Jason, smiling as if we're something precious and wonderful. 'I can hardly believe it.'

'Do you want a drink?' Jason asks. 'I made lunch.'

'I think I need wine.' She stares at him. He's put black nail varnish on and the pale skin of his arms contrasts against the black of his skinny t-shirt. 'You're Jason, aren't you?'

Jason nods.

'It's lovely to meet you. You're fourteen, right?'

'Yeah.'

'My son Marco is almost your age. He's just starting to learn the guitar.'

Marilyn Richards shakes his hand. Jason blushes, under his fringe.

'We're ready for you, at last. Sorry we took our time,' Ash says.

'I almost didn't recognise you with that beard.' She rushes forward to give Ash a hug. I'm glad he's brushed off most of the cobwebs from the shed.

'Pete. You look just the same.'

'Thanks – I think,' Pete says.

'Loving the ink,' she says, admiring his tattoo and kissing the air next to both his cheeks.

Marilyn Richards glances around the garden, taking a deep breath.

'This is such a beautiful place.' She looks at the vegetable patch; at the slugs. One of them is trying to escape from the yoghurt pot.

'I'm trying coffee grounds and eggshells to get rid of the slugs in my garden. It's only a bit of a courtyard, but it gets the sun.'

'Gardening saved me – after everything. My mind could go blank when I was weeding. It helped me to forget.'

Marilyn looks at me. She holds my hand, not seeming to care about the dirt.

'I won't make you talk about anything you don't want to. Don't worry about anything. I just think we need to do this.

Together.'

I nod.

'You don't look any older at all,' she says. 'This country air must be good for you.'

'Liar,' I say. But I'm smiling.

Chapter 34
Mud and Glitter

Jason

The rain batters against the windscreen of Pete's van but Ben can hardly keep still in his seat. He looks like a little kid who needs the toilet. Pete picked us up, straight from school.

Nicko is next to Ben, bored after the long journey from Coventry. He holds his plastic dinosaur up to the window, to watch the wet countryside passing by. Little Karen is fast asleep with her thumb in her mouth, her head on my knee, dribbling a little bit onto my jeans. I don't mind though.

'Are we there yet?' Nicko moans.

'It won't be long, I promise,' Emma says.

We follow the signs with hand-painted beards on them, stuck in amongst the cow parsley and long grass at the side of the road.

My excitement is mixed with nerves. It's been so wet today. If it keeps raining, the whole thing might be rubbish. What if people don't bother to come? What if something goes wrong at our gig? Sam says our rehearsals at the Fishpond have been sounding brilliant but I've got a lot to live up to.

Pete pulls over, through an open gate, the van's tyres crunching on gravel. Karen wakes up and looks around, confused.

A man wearing a hi-vis waterproof jacket checks the computer print-out from the organisers and nods. He checks it and gives it back to us but all the ink has run. There is water dripping off the brim of his hat.

'Park anywhere over there.' He waves over towards the hedge. There are a few caravans and soggy looking tents there already. 'This is backstage camping. What's the weather forecast? Any chance of it stopping tonight?'

'It doesn't look great, to be honest,' Pete says. I think of last weekend, when it was sunny for the whole time. Why couldn't it be like that?

Pete takes his phone out and makes a call.

'We're here,' he says. 'Great. I'll come and find you.'

Pete starts driving slowly towards the tents. I can see Sam's car, parked next to a big square blue tent in the middle of the field. He unzips the door and waves at us, until we're parked in front of the tent.

'That was easy.' Pete jumps out of the van and gives Sam one of those back-slapping hugs that men do.

'I've been here since this morning.'

I unclip my seatbelt and open the sliding side door. It's a bit of a squeeze because the back of the campervan is full of Pete's drums at the moment.

'You lads are in here with me,' Sam says, indicating the blue tent with a flourish. 'Don't worry – it's got a separate bedroom.'

'I'll put the awning up – looks like we'll need the extra shelter,' Pete says.

'Where are Kaz and Ash?'

'Coming tomorrow. We need to leave space for Ash's van.'

'I can't blame her for holding off a bit. My wife's only coming for Saturday night. She's a fair-weather camper. Likes her home comforts.'

'Where can I put my drums?'

Everyone starts to move at once. The kids unclip their seatbelts but Emma doesn't let them leave the van until they're fully kitted up with wellies, waterproof dungarees, bright jackets and sou'westers. They soon find a puddle to splash in, their faces lit up with joy.

I put on my black cagoule and jump out of the van, feeling the soles of my Doc Martens sinking into the wet grass. I wish I could be as happy as Nicko and little Karen.

'Come on, let's explore,' Ben says. 'I want to check out Tina's Café stage.'

Seeing the grin on his face, I suddenly can't help feeling excited too. I can see a row of colourful flags in the distance; a big white structure that must be the main stage.

Our first festival. I don't know what to expect. Even though it's only a few miles from home and it's pouring with rain, this is going to be an adventure.

'Evening,' Pete says to a fat man with dreadlocks and a bald patch who's trudging past with a full water container.

'Bloody Derbyshire,' he grumbles. 'It's not even summer. I don't know what I was thinking, coming here.'

When the man has gone into his caravan, Ben takes the mick out of his angry, stompy walk.

'Bloody festivals, more trouble than they're worth,' Ben says. I start to laugh.

It's dark now, and we can hear the sound of drums, cutting through the rain on Pete's awning roof.

'Are they doing a sound check?' Ben asks.

Sam takes a swig from his can. 'That's what you're helping out with tomorrow morning.'

'It's African drumming,' Emma says. 'Sort of. Doesn't sound like they're very good.'

'Good job I brought a djembe with me. You never know when one comes in handy. Coming with me?'

Pete slings a tall padded case onto his back. I hadn't realised what it was, and Sam was using it as a table for his beer can.

We've already explored the site once. Earlier, we helped to carry Pete's drums to a portacabin in the backstage area. We'll be working there tomorrow morning. We stood on the main stage and I mimed playing the guitar, trying to imagine the noise and the lights and a crowd of people going wild. Tonight, apart from the drums, everything's quiet, with a few people rushing around, doing jobs; talking about the jobs they'll be doing once the festival gets going.

The sound of drums is coming from a long white marquee – the bar. It keeps stop-starting and the drum beats can't seem to stay in time. The marquee is brightly lit and there are quite a few people inside, sheltering from the rain, even though the bar isn't open until tomorrow. The drums drown out everyone's conversations. Some people look a bit annoyed, especially when they notice Pete carrying another drum case.

Pete sits down on a plastic chair next to the drummers: an intense-looking young guy with a dark ponytail, and a beefier, blond bloke. Pete smiles and they give him high fives as he unzips his case. At first, he lets them take the lead, while he makes the drum beat more solid. Pete starts shaping the rhythm, until the other two are following him. The drums are following a definite pattern now. I look around at the other people. They're starting to look in the direction of the drummers, nodding their heads, smiling. I never realised how good Pete's drumming is before now. We did African drumming in music lessons earlier this year but we didn't get to do much.

Someone rushes into the marquee. It's Emma. At first, I think something's wrong. She takes off her cagoule and throws it at me to hold. She starts dancing; quick whirling movements, hips shimmying, her arms thrown up towards the roof of the tent and towards the crowd, who are now watching, open-mouthed. Pete smiles proudly. He makes sure the other drummers are following his rhythm: call and response. The drums build to a crescendo and stop suddenly, and Emma takes a bow.

There must only be about a hundred people in the marquee, but their applause sounds louder than the torrential rain we heard earlier, drumming on the campervan roof.

'I haven't done that for a while,' Emma says, laughing and out of breath.

A man in a rain-slicked fluorescent jacket walks into the tent.

'The festival doesn't start until tomorrow – you'll have to keep the noise down.' People give him sulky looks for stopping the drummers. Before Pete turned up, they would have cheered if the drummers had stopped.

'We've got to keep on the right side of the law. You know that, guys?' The man turns to leave, then stops and looks at Pete more closely.

'You're in Mission Control, aren't you? You haven't changed a bit. Remember me from Castlemorton?'

Pete grins, but it's obvious he doesn't have a clue – not at first, anyway. I can tell by the look on his face that he's trying to imagine what the man must have looked like seventeen years ago.

'Didn't you have a burger stall or something?' Pete asks.

The man grins. 'The Exploding Gerbil Café. Mission Control played on our own little stage.'

'Yeah – I remember now.'

'We could do with some of that weather this weekend,' the man says. They launch into reminiscing about that mythical festival.

People start to drift away, back to their tents, probably. It's getting late.

I give Emma her waterproof back.

'That was brilliant!' Ben says.

'He met me when I was dancing. He was just getting into playing the djembe, after a couple of years when he hadn't played anything. I didn't know anything about Mission Control.'

'He told you, though, right?'

Emma nods.

As we walk out of the bar tent, someone smiles at me, her face half-hidden by the hood of her purple waterproof; long wet hair straggling out of it. I smile back but I can't place her right now. It's the sort of place where everyone smiles at each other anyway.

This job is hardly glamorous, but the main stage wouldn't work without it. Ben is digging a trench in the wet turf, and I'm pressing the cables into the hole – the cables connecting the main stage to the mixing desk. Sam told us to make the trench quite deep, in case the ground gets really muddy and churned up with people dancing.

Sam's kept us busy since really early this morning, running around with cables, using lots of gaffer tape to stick things down; teaching us about how a live mixing desk works and why it's essential for making things sound good. I love playing the guitar but I'm totally happy doing this as well – laying the foundations to make things work. I take a turn with the spade. The ground is so wet, the mud splashes up when I put the spade in. Rain runs off the bottom of my cagoule, soaking my jeans.

Sam was right. I should have worn the waterproof trousers he tried to lend me. I only brought two pairs of jeans for the whole festival.

We've almost finished, though. We'll soon be doing live sound-checks on the main stage.

Ben looks up at me, his face streaked with mud. He laughs.

'Look at the state of you. No one would believe you're actually playing on that stage tomorrow.'

'I'm keeping it real.' I stop myself from getting the giggles like a little kid. Even though it's really cold and wet, it's starting to feel like a dream, where you're having a good time even though everything's weird and nothing makes sense.

'Can you imagine the guitarist from the Manics –?'

'James Dean Bradfield.'

'Would he be digging the cable trench?'

'I bet he would. It's a very important job. Can't see Noel Gallagher doing it, though.'

'He was a roadie, so he's probably done lots of things like this.'

The cable reaches the mixing desk at last; a gazebo in the middle of the field with all the sound equipment inside so Sam can make the bands sound great from the same viewpoint as the audience. The lights are operated from here too.

We go back along the trench we've dug, treading the turf so it squashes back down, hiding the cables. I'm glad Mum made me bring my wellies.

'I quite fancy learning how to do this properly. Sound engineering and stuff. You can do it at college.'

'What if Mission Control get really famous again?' Ben

asks.

'Anything could happen.'

Pete walks towards us, holding two small rain-slicked figures by the hand. The kids jump up and down, splashing muddy water everywhere.

'Having fun?' he asks.

Sam starts laying a thick rubber mat on the ground to protect the cables even more. He looks at us and laughs.

'You've done a grand job but I think it's time for you to dry off a bit, have a rest. You've got your gig this afternoon.'

'It's alright, I don't mind,' I say, but Ben is kicking me in the shin.

'I'm starving,' he whispers. 'And I can't feel my hands anymore.'

He's right. We need to practise; warm up and try to clean some of this mud off.

Kaz

'The van's packed,' Ash calls from the kitchen. 'Are you ready?'

I put the pencil down and stare at the canvas. I started a new painting last night. It's not going to be for sale. I've pinned up copies of Ash's photographs on my noticeboard: the ones taken in Coventry on the roof of our old studio. I'm still sketching the outlines on the canvas. I've added myself to the photo, changing Daz's position so his arm is around my shoulder. This is the way I want to think about the old days of Mission Control – happy and excited, full of possibilities.

I want to work on it all weekend, alone with the cat. Instead, I've got to start a new chapter of the band. I'm not sure I want to but I've come this far and I don't want to let anyone down.

'Come on. Pete texted me. They've saved a space for the van but the backstage parking is a bit crazy.'

Rainwater splatters the windows. Last night, it came down so heavily it felt like we were in an ark. We've worked so hard on the house – nailing roof tiles back in place, repairing the guttering. It looks like we were just in time.

I rang Pete, expecting to find them all flooded out and miserable, but they seemed fine. I spoke to Jason. He talked non-stop about the things he's already done and seen.

Patti is curled on a blanket on the sofa, ignoring the rain outside. She knows I'm going away. She acts like she doesn't care, her nose buried in her bushy tail like a small fox.

I ruffle Patti's fur, and she gives me a baleful look, resentful of being disturbed.

Rachel is going to feed her until Monday. She's coming to the festival on Saturday night, but says there's no way she's ever going camping again – Guide camp has put her off for life.

Ash leans in the doorway, his arms folded.

'You're dragging your heels.'

'It's going to be terrible – a total mud bath.'

'We had some great times together, remember? The weather didn't matter.'

'We were off our faces, then, and I'm going to be sober.'

Ash pats his jacket pocket and gives me a wicked grin.

'You don't have to be.'

'I don't want to fuck it up.'

Ash walks across the living room. He takes my hand, gently trying to pull me out of the house.

'Come on. Time to start again.'

I pull my hand away from his. Ash looks hurt. His eyes huge, his face half-hidden by that horrible beard.

'You're scared, aren't you?' he asks.

I nod.

'I'm bricking it – you're not the only one.'

'I think you should get rid of that beard.' I desperately want to see his clean-shaven face, but who am I to boss him about? I can't believe I actually said it out loud but, in Mission Control, I was always the bossy one who made things happen.

'What?'

'Shave it off. You could do it now.'

Ash laughs but he looks a bit taken aback.

'I've tidied it up a bit. My dad likes it – says it's traditional.'

I stare at him.

'Since when have you bothered about tradition? People don't recognise you. I think you're hiding behind it –'

'Says you.'

I stare at the picture of him pinned to the board. His smooth skin is golden in the light of the setting sun.

'Says me.' Ash picks up a sofa cushion and throws it at me.

I throw it back. The cat ignores us, but I see her tense up, fighting the urge to run into the rain.

'The festival's called Bearded Theory. You can't expect me to turn up without a beard.'

He's got a point.

'I can't see the real you. I've forgotten what you look like.'

Ash sighs, giving in.

'Well, what with? Jason's not shaving yet, is he?'

'You can use nail scissors and one of my razors. A new one – don't worry.'

'We'll be late.'

'We're not playing until tomorrow. You just want to take acid and watch Hawkwind.'

'I want to have some fun, Kaz. And you should, too.'

I follow him into the bathroom. Ash opens the bathroom cabinet and finds the nail scissors.

'Do you have to watch me?' he says.

I find a brand new razor and balance it on the side of the sink.

Ash starts snipping.

'Once I've done this, can we go?'

'I promise.'

I wander into the kitchen and find myself wiping down already clean kitchen work surfaces. Everything's already clean and, even though it's old and worn, it's home. Maybe I could paint the walls a fresh colour and replace the worn-out lino with something new.

'Finished?'

I open the bathroom door just as Ash is finishing off with the razor.

I gasp. I know it's a cliché but he looks at least a decade younger. I look at him and I can see the college student bouncing along the pavement, absorbed in the music on his Walkman. I can see his strong, high-cheekboned face, rather than a mass of greying hair. His lips no longer have that weird naked look; they fit into his face properly.

I take his hands.

'That's better.' We smile at each other.

'I'll have to find a fake beard to wear at the festival now.'

'It was worth it.'

I stand on tip-toes to kiss him. Crazily I want to kiss him on the lips, but Ash turns his head in confusion and I end up kissing him somewhere between the chin and the cheek. We both laugh, embarrassed.

Jason

The rain has stopped as we make our way across the arena with our guitars on our backs. An indie band is playing on the main stage. They're local and quite young. I think Rachel knows them. We saw them backstage earlier. They looked pretty nervous but you wouldn't know it from watching them perform. There's a respectable cluster of people watching them in the pale sunshine.

'Maybe that could be us in a few years,' I say.

'It already is you, dumbass.' Ben doesn't look pissed off though. He's looking around, smiling at everything.

The bar marquee looks pretty busy and, further around, there are kids playing with diabolos and trying to juggle with muddy bean bags. Not too long ago, that would have been us.

I smile at the secret knowledge that we laid the cable for the main stage. We actually made this happen. I'm sure Sam or someone would have sorted it out if we hadn't done it, but it still makes me feel proud.

There are two women tottering on stilts, dressed as fairies. A man with a can of beer in his hand is staring at them as if he can't believe his eyes. He looks drunk already. I suppose he's been stuck in his tent for hours, waiting for the rain to stop with nothing else to do.

The Café tent is on the far side of the arena. The tent is low and cosy, with bits of coloured material draped around to decorate it. There are quite a few people in here, their hands wrapped around steaming china mugs, or cans of cider.

An old guy wearing a woolly hat is already on stage, playing a harmonica. Some people are clapping and stomping along with him. He's pretty good.

A lady with pillar-box red hair looks up at us, noticing our guitar cases.

'You must be Jason and Ben.'

I nod, feeling suddenly tongue-tied. The lady is dressed in a red dress with a corset, and a tiny black top hat with a veil perched on top of her head.

She stares at us, taking in how young we look. I wish we'd made more effort with our clothes, but it's freezing. I'm wearing my fingerless gloves and my fleece, and my jeans are muddy from helping to set everything up earlier. The t-shirt I've got on underneath is okay but I'd be shivering without the fleece. Ben's wearing his corduroy cap with his cycling jacket and waterproof trousers. It's not a good look, but I don't want to tell him. We've been getting on so well again recently, just like the old days.

I feel like we have to impress this lady. She might be running the smallest venue on the site but we still have to put on a great show. I give her a smile and push my shoulders back to try to make myself look confident.

'We've got Dean Harwood next. He's a performance poet – and then you're on,' she says.

'Awesome.' Ben doesn't seem nervous.

The lady looks at us more closely, peering over the top of her tiny red sunglasses, which she's wearing even though we're inside a tent and it's clouded over again.

'Have you been playing long?'

'Only since September,' I mumble. I've made a promise to myself not to mention Mission Control at all at this gig. This is just about me and Ben.

She smiles. 'You've got twenty minutes to play. Do you both sing? I'll have to set up your mics.'

'Yeah – and Jason does all the complicated bits on guitar, but his is just an acoustic.'

'I'll get everything set up – don't worry.'

'Thanks,' I say.

'Do you want anything? A cup of tea?'

'I'm okay.' I'm scared I'll need to visit the Portaloo as soon as I get up on stage.

'Yeah, please,' Ben says.

'How about a bit of cake too? I'm Tina by the way. Just ask me if you need anything.'

We sit down with our guitar cases at our feet, on plastic chairs sinking into the wet ground, and wait our turn. Tina brings us slices of lemon drizzle cake and a cup of tea for Ben. I nibble at my slice of cake. It's delicious, but I can't eat it. Ben seems relaxed, which is really weird. He grabs the cake off me and swallows the slice in about two bites.

'What's up with you?' he asks. 'Just pretend we're busking.'

'I'll be okay,' I say, to convince myself more than Ben, trying to keep my breathing steady.

The man with the woolly hat leaves the stage, to a smattering of applause. I take off my gloves and clap really hard. Mum told me it's important to show other artists your support, not just to piss off back to your nice warm caravan or to hide backstage. I thought she'd be here by now. Maybe she is. I told her not to come to the café. This is something we need to do by ourselves, without people recognising her instead – and people at this festival are definitely going to know who she is.

Dean Harwood is a man about the same age as Pete, wearing an old tweed coat with a pork pie hat. Everyone apart from me seems to be wearing a hat. My head feels a bit bare without one, but my hair was the one thing I made an effort with before I left Pete's campervan. I used Shockwaves to spike it up at the back and to smooth out my fringe so it falls in a point over one eye. I put on a bit of eye liner. We must look really weird together as a band, me and Ben.

The poet has lots of pieces of paper that he takes out of a torn Tesco carrier bag and reads out, throwing them over his shoulder when he's finished. He seems quite angry about politics and there's a lot of swearing. Some people near the front cover up their little children's ears. Tina stares at Dean Harwood and gives him a lot of angry gestures. He goes red and apologises, which makes the audience laugh. He starts reading out his poems, bleeping himself where the swearwords should be. He looks a bit frustrated when a crazy-looking lady with lots of different coloured braids in her hair in the crowd starts to heckle him.

Ben laughs and digs me in the ribs. I wish I could relax and enjoy it but my hands are shaking so much I have to clamp them down on my knees. Over the top of the poems, the music booms from the main stage. What if no one can hear us? I wipe my wellies on the grass so I don't get the stage muddy.

Then it's our turn. The stage is bare and Tina quickly rearranges microphones and amplifiers. I rush up to help her, positioning the mic stands so they're the right height for both of us. It calms me down a bit. Pete, Emma and the kids come into the café and wave at us. Emma crosses her fingers and mouths 'good luck' to us. They sit down with mugs of tea and slices of chocolate cake.

Just as we're about to start, the light in the tent gets really gloomy, and rain starts hammering down on the canvas. People rush through the tent flap; the tables fill up.

'Shit,' Ben whispers to me. 'We'd better be good.'

We step onto the stage.

'I'm Jason, and this is Ben,' I say, into the microphone. 'We haven't decided on our band name yet, but maybe you can help us out.'

I know that's a bit of a mistake, especially because the crazy-looking lady is still sitting in the middle of the tent, but at least I said it confidently.

Ben launches straight into the chords for 'Someone Your Own Size'. It sounds great; his guitar sounding bright and loud over the PA system. As Ben starts singing, I can tell people are really listening; laughing in all the right bits and nodding during my guitar solo.

We wondered about throwing in some covers, but we've got twenty minutes worth of our own stuff now. Ben sings 'The Only Thing I'm Waiting For', about Hayley Green in the dinner queue, and a new song we've been working on together, 'Stuck Like Glue' about how we're best mates for life.

The audience seems to love it. Some people are even dancing, around the edges of the tent. Maybe they're just drunk. I forget how cold and nervous I was. I'm glowing all over. I wish I could take my fleece off now but I'm too busy playing.

Then we play 'Bring the Lightning', and it goes okay this time. I don't think my voice is as good as Ben's, but I put everything into it. When we finish, there are cheers and Pete stands up, with Nicko on his shoulders, his head almost touching the roof of the tent. Nicko's face is smeared with chocolate icing.

'Well done!' Pete shouts. 'Let's have another one!'

I glance over at Tina, standing at the side of the stage. She smiles and nods. We've got time for one more, but I'm not sure what to do.

'Play 'Reindeer Blues'. I've been working on something,' Ben whispers.

A Christmas song?

There's no time to hesitate. I play the chords for the song. Ben sings, in his gravelly, Seasick Steve voice:

'I've set up camp in the rain and damp.
My wife says I look like a tramp.
This festival scene's not much fun.
Without blue skies and lots of sun.'

I try not to crack up as I play the next bit. I'm sure he's based it on the grumpy man who's camping next to us.

'I've got the Bearded Blues,' Ben sings. *'Mud on my boots and up my nose.'*

He grins at me. People are laughing and they're starting to sing along with the chorus. Ben sings the next verse, and a couple of girls squeeze their way to the front. One of them is wearing a purple waterproof, with long light-brown hair hiding her face. Both of them are carrying something.

The girl with the purple jacket opens a violin case. She looks up at me just as she's tucking the violin under her chin. It's Tracey Monks – from school! She joins in with playing the chorus. With the fiddle, the song sounds like a hoe-down, and people are really dancing, whirling each other around. I don't recognise the other girl, but she's banging on a plastic bucket, roughly in time. We carry on for ages, with Ben repeating the chorus and making up new verses on the spot, until Tina finally signals for us to stop. There's a massive round of applause after we've stopped, with people cheering. I just stand there, with a stupid grin plastered all over my face.

'Well, you charmed the weather, anyway,' Pete says, clapping Ben on the shoulder. 'You were fucking fantastic.' He's right. The sun has come out again and people are streaming outside, towards the main stage. 'See you back at the campervan.'

The café tent's almost empty again now. I feel sorry for the act coming on next, unless it rains again. The weather was definitely on our side. I put my guitar away in its case.

'You were great.' Tina says looks genuinely impressed. 'That was a real festival moment. I can't believe you've been playing less than a year. All your own songs too.'

'Thanks for letting us play,' I say.

'It was a pleasure. I'll have to get you back next year.

Who are you here with?' she asks, pointing at my backstage wristband, visible now I've taken my gloves off and pushed the sleeves of my fleece back so they didn't get in the way while I was playing.

'Oh, we were helping to set up backstage earlier. Work experience.'

She frowns.

'There's something familiar about you. Can't put my finger on it.'

I just shrug.

Tina turns to the next act, three musicians in their early twenties; two boys with patterned jumpers and bum-fluff beards, and a tall pale girl with red hair.

Then she calls back to us, smiling.

'Have another drink and some cake. You've both earned it.'

When I get back from the counter, trying to balance two cardboard cups of coffee and slices of chocolate cake, Ben's already chatting away to the girl who was playing the plastic bucket. He's standing with his guitar lead coiled around his hand like it's a pet snake. He looks captivated by her, even though she's wearing a rainbow-striped woolly hat pulled round down her ears and a red waterproof.

I put the drinks down on the table where we left our guitars.

'Sorry for butting in,' Tracey says to me. 'I just got carried away.'

'We've had some Barcardi!' the other girl says. She turns to me. She's got bright blue eyes, curls of blonde hair under her hat, and the sort of face that dimples when she smiles. 'Do you want some?'

'Put some in the coffee,' I say, more to Tracey than to her. We haven't had much chance to talk since the school concert. Just said hello to each other a few times in the music room and I've heard her play in the rehearsal rooms.

'The violin sounded great. You didn't tell me you were coming here.' I remember Mrs Lyons saying a girl from Year Ten was coming. It must have been Tracey.

'My dad's playing on the campfire stage tonight – Dan Monks. I'm doing a couple of songs with him. I was trying to find somewhere dry to go with my fiddle. I didn't know you and Ben had a gig.'

The girl with the stripy hat sloshes Barcadi from a small plastic bottle into both coffee cups.

'I'm Cassi,' she says. 'With an I. Short for Cassiopeia. It's a constellation.'

'I'm Jason.' I can sympathise with her. People sometimes think I'm named after Jason Donovan, but Elsa was really into Greek mythology. My name means healer, apparently.

'Cassi's mum and dad set up the dance stage,' Tracey explains. 'We met years ago, at Glastonbury –'

'On the climbing frame in the Green Kidz field.'

Ben laughs.

'Me and Jase met at playgroup.'

'It's last summer since we saw each other,' Tracey says.

'We're celebrating our reunion.'

'Don't let me have too much. Dad'll kill me if I'm drunk.'

'What sort of stuff does he play?' I ask Tracey.

'He's a folk singer. Not sure if you'd like it.'

'I thought you guys were great. That last song was brilliant. Ben's got such an amazing voice, don't you think?' Cassi says, batting her eyelids at him. She looks a bit ridiculous, flirting, while wearing that woolly hat. It's like the weather has destroyed our fashion sense but we just don't care.

I take a gulp of the Bacardi-laced coffee. It's quite nice and makes my chest feel warm inside. I offer the cup to Tracey. She smiles. Her mascara is perfectly in place. It must be waterproof. I notice her cheekbones have a stripe of iridescent glitter on them. I realise I don't know anything about her at all. I don't know what clothes she wears when she's not in her school uniform and I don't know what music she likes, even though I'm sure she's got great taste.

'Do you get nervous about performing?' I ask. 'I couldn't do anything earlier, when I was waiting.'

'I try not to think about it too much. Shut my eyes and pretend I'm at home,' she says.

'I feel okay once I'm playing. Then it's all just happening. It's before a performance when I feel like my insides are tying themselves in knots.'

'What about tomorrow?' Tracey stares at me, her eyes wide.

'Today went alright, didn't it? You're right. I'll just concentrate on playing. I won't let anyone in the audience put me off. It was probably better for my dad – he couldn't see anything without his glasses.'

The next band starts playing. They look very serious on stage but the harmonies they're singing sound great. Perhaps they're as nervous as I was.

I eat my chocolate cake while I watch the band perform. I'm suddenly starving, even though Emma made me a veggie sausage sandwich for lunch. I want to eat the whole cake but I stop myself in time and offer half of the slice to Tracey.

'Thanks.' She takes the plate from me and breaks pieces of cake off delicately in her fingers as she eats. She smiles at me, closing her eyes. Her eyelashes almost touch her cheek. The mascara must make them longer.

'We're going to go over to the dance tent in a bit. Want to come?' Cassi asks.

'Just got to stash my fiddle somewhere safe first,' Tracey tells her. I like the way she calls it a fiddle and not a violin.

'We've got to put our guitars away too. Are you camping backstage?' Ben asks.

Tracey nods. 'I've seen your campervan.'

'Our truck's right behind the dance tent,' Cassi says. 'I'll show you, if you like.'

'Can I have some of your glitter?' I ask, hardly daring. She looks really cool but I don't look very festivally, dressed all in black, even with a few splashes of mud.

Tracey laughs and gets a tiny pot of glitter out of her waterproof pocket. I close my eyes while she dusts glitter on my cheeks, to match hers. The feeling of her fingertip on my face makes me shiver, in a really nice way. When she finishes, she stares at me, checking she's got it right; her face close to mine. Maybe this was the feeling Ben was trying to write about when he wrote his song about Hayley Green.

'You look pretty,' Tracey giggles.

'The ladyboy of Belper,' Ben says, scowling.

'Let's get Ben!' Cassi squeals, shaking her own pot of glitter. Ben stands up and tries to run away, but Cassi grabs him and together we manage to wrestle Ben to the ground and cover his face in glitter, making it look like a rainbow has exploded all over his face. I get mud all over my fleece. I must look a right state.

The people in the café watching the band on now give us disapproving looks. I smile apologetically at Tina. She gives me a wink, as if she doesn't really mind us messing around.

Kaz

Being at a festival again is like going back to an exotic country after years away. Some things are exactly the same: people with dreadlocks and waterproof jackets clutching cans of cider or plastic pint glasses; the smell of weed mixed with frying burgers and Portaloos; the lights and the noise of music from several different stages merging together, always with the thump of the dance tent in the background.

There's one change: everywhere I look, people are on mobile phones – shouting into them, texting, or staring at screens.

A lot of the people here look old enough to have been Mission Control's original festival audience; older than me, with lined faces and weather-worn skin; real festival veterans. Quite a lot of punters are trailing small sleepy children in their wake, with giant headphones clamped over their ears to block out the noise, wearing mini hi-vis tabards with their names and parents' mobile numbers written on them.

I'm glad Ash forced me to come down tonight. In the twilight, I feel anonymous, with an oversized woolly hat of Jason's pulled down over my ears and his old waterproof jacket. A fine drizzle is falling but the crowd around the main stage don't seem to care. They're drinking and dancing. The band who are playing are going down well.

In twenty-four hours, Mission Control will be up there.

'Who are these again?' I ask Ash.

He consults a small piece of card with all the running times printed on it.

'Three Daft Monkeys,' he says, nodding with approval.

They must be big, in this world anyway, with most of the audience singing along to every word of their songs. They really know how to work the crowd, especially their female violin player, in her corset and embroidered skirt, chatting to about a thousand people between songs like she's in her own front room. I watch them, starting to get sucked into Three Daft Monkeys' songs, rather than focussing on the fear of being up on that stage myself.

'Hawkwind are on next,' Ash says. He reaches into his jacket pocket and pulls out a small plastic zip-bag, licking his finger, dipping into it and putting his finger in his mouth. His action reminds me of Jason when he was little, eating a bag of fizzy sherbet, except that Ash grimaces slightly at the taste.

'Want some MDMA?' Ash asks, grinning.

As far as Ash is concerned, nothing has changed. He's at a festival. There's a whole day to party before Mission Control play. But what if Ash offered MDMA to Jason? He's offered him a spliff before, although Jason has always politely refused. Ash treats him like the reincarnation of Daz. It doesn't seem to sink into his head that Jason is a child, with over two years of school left. When we were rehearsing, Jason loved being treated like an adult and he worked so hard, determined to do justice to Daz's guitar parts.

Being in a band will change him but, so far, it's made him more responsible than ever. With or without Mission

Control, I can't stop Jason from growing up and discovering the world.

I scan the faces in the crowd. I can't see Jason. When we arrived, Pete said he was with Ben and a couple of girls. A double date, he joked.

I can't protect Jason anymore. I fight the feeling of worry in my chest. There's nothing I can do about it.

Ash is right. I need to relax; acclimatise. I look at him, and I nod. He stares back at me with a wicked grin and holds out the bag of MDMA. One small dab can't hurt, can it?

Jason

It's raining again. Tracey is onstage with her dad. It's getting dark. The audience at the campfire stage is quite small but enthusiastic, even though it was too wet to actually light the campfire.

I can't take my eyes off Tracey. It's funny, how you get used to the shape of people wearing waterproofs. It's a shock to see Tracey without them, wearing a short silvery dress with leggings, her hair loose, reflecting the colours of the stage lights.

She's absorbed in playing her violin; long, haunting notes entwined with her dad's voice. I expected him to be an old guy with a wispy beard but Tracey's dad has short scruffy hair and an earring, and his songs tell stories about things I recognise – the struggle of not having much money; about Derbyshire and Wirksworth; and what it feels like to fall in love. I wasn't expecting it, but I can't take my eyes off her. I mean, where else would I look?

I don't want to look at Ben, anyway. He's snogging Cassi. They've barely come up for air in half an hour and it's starting to do my head in.

Ben isn't in love. I can tell. He just fancies her because she's fun and bubbly, and her parents own a massive campervan they live in all the time. It even has a lounge, with a TV and a 1950s drinks cabinet shaped like a boat. Cassi keeps stealing Barcardi from it without her mum noticing.

I move closer to the front, to get a better view of Tracey.

The dance tent is brilliant now. I wasn't so sure earlier, when it was still light outside, with a scattering of people older than Mum, dancing like idiots, re-living their raving days from twenty years ago. Now it's full to bursting. They seem to know all the tunes. Dreadzone are on now. The music is heavy, like some of Mum's dub basslines. It really makes me want to dance. I know I'm a bit drunk, but I'm not off my face like some of the people in here.

Hawkwind were okay but it started to rain too much to be standing around in the rain listening to slow, spacy rock music. I saw Ash standing there with Mum. He was holding an umbrella over her head and he had a daft grin on his face. Mum didn't see me. She was staring at the purple lights coming from the stage. There was something different about Ash. At first, I didn't know what it was. He's shaved his beard off. He looks more like he did in the 90s. Definitely an improvement. I bet Mum had something to do with it.

I didn't want to disturb Mum. It's nice, the feeling of being independent but knowing that at any time I can come back to our little circle of vans and tents and feel at home.

In here, bright lights are flashing and it's humid, like a greenhouse in summer, from all those people dancing around in wet cagoules. I tie my waterproof and my fleece around my waist.

I turn to Tracey. She's smiling.

'You were really good tonight. It's weird that...' I say.

The music is thumping too hard for her to hear me. She puts her arms around my neck and pulls me closer towards her, until our faces are almost touching. Then we're kissing. Tracey's lips are soft and warm, tasting of Barcardi and coke. I've never actually kissed anyone like this before. I know you're meant to use your tongue but I'm not sure how, so I keep it firmly in my mouth. How long is this supposed to go on for?

Tracey pulls away from me, laughing.

'What?' I say.

She takes my hand and pulls me towards the doorway of the tent, into the rain, until we can hear each other again.

'I really like you. I'm having a brilliant time,' she says. 'But you've not been out with anyone yet, have you?'

I shake my head. She laughs again.

'You're really sweet. Let's just enjoy ourselves – take it as it comes.'

'Yeah.' I don't know what I expected. That rule about girls not going out with lads younger than them just can't be broken, can it? I was probably such a rubbish kisser I put her off me for life; made her realise I'm just a kid, even though I'm a few centimetres taller than her.

Tracey strokes my cheek.

'Come on, it's freezing out here.' She takes my arm and pulls me back into the dance tent again.

Chapter 35
Transformations

Kaz

There's an arm wrapped around my chest. A man's arm. I can feel its strength, and the warmth of a body curled behind my back.

I open my eyes. The first thing I see is the bright square of a patchwork blanket. I slip out from under the arm, sliding down the bed, until I'm free. Ash sighs and changes position, still asleep. I'm wearing a t-shirt and the leggings I was wearing under my work overalls. They're still lying in a damp heap at the foot of the bed. Last night went by in a blur. What possessed me to do the MDMA? After Hawkwind, we ended up in the dance tent and stayed there until the music stopped. For a few hours, I felt like I used to when we were just starting out. No one recognised me. I was free to enjoy myself, get absorbed into the music. I felt so safe with Ash.

I remember what happened now. When we got back to the van, I didn't feel like struggling into a sleeping bag on the narrow bunk by the door. I wanted the warmth of having Ash near me in the double bed. It's a relief – to find out that we just huddled together. Nothing happened. I can't remember if I wanted to get closer to him. That's always been the thing with Ash; my feelings hovering somewhere just past friendship, with so many factors stopping anything else from happening.

The smiley-faced clock on the wall says it's just after eight. Bright sunlight is shining into the van through the gaps in the rainbow-striped curtains left by the guy who used to own the van. I lean over the sink, draw the curtains aside and open the window. The sky is patchwork to match the blankets: ragged shapes of dark grey and white, mixed with strips of blue. A definite improvement on yesterday, so far.

A sudden gust of wind makes the van rock slightly.

Outside, Pete's awning shakes and shivers. Through the open window, I can hear the chatter of his children, and Pete trying to get them to eat their cereal.

I fill the kettle and turn on the gas stove. As I spoon coffee into Ash's tin can filter, he jerks upright and stares at me. His dreads are tied around his head in a huge knot, the ends trailing over his shoulders like snake heads.

'Tonight's the night,' he says. His smile is brave but unconvincing. I know he's nervous. 'How are you feeling?'

'Like shit.'

He laughs.

'No getting out of it now.'

'I didn't see Jason at all last night. I need to check if he's okay.' What a terrible mother. Giving him his independence is one thing, but completely neglecting him to have my own fun?

'He'll be fine. Let him have a lie-in.'

I stare at Ash. 'Don't tell Jason about last night.'

'Scared of what he'll say?'

'Ash – Jason isn't Daz. He might be in the band, but he's a kid. He's younger than we were when we started out.'

'He's not stupid. He knows the score.'

Ash sits on the edge of the bed and I hand him a mug of steaming hot black coffee, then tip the used coffee grinds into the bin and start again, because Ash's contraption only makes one cup of coffee at a time. Ash looks almost boyish now, without the beard. I know it's partly my fault, but there's part of him that never grew up.

'We've got an example to set. I've tried to bring him up the right way –'

'By depriving him of the truth about his own dad? By letting everyone that cared about you think you were dead?'

'You know what Daz was like. Things I didn't want Jason to know.'

'So you blocked everything out?' he says.

I can't look Ash in the eye any more. I look at my mutton-dressed-as-lamb stage outfit, hanging on the curtain rail. Everything feels wrong.

Jason

'So what happened to you last night?' Ben asks, his mouth stretched in a lazy grin as he lolls on his Li-Lo. There's something different about him. Something show-offy.

'What's that on your neck? Gross.' It looks like a dark purple bruise. Like something from a vampire film.

'Cassi really knows how to kiss.'

'She seems to have totally missed your mouth. I know it was dark, but –'

My brain feels like it's growing too large for my skull, and I'm really thirsty. I need a piss. I've been awake for ages but it's safe in my warm cocoon. Once I get up, I'll have to think about the gig tonight. I heard Sam get up ages ago. He probably had something to sort out on one of the stages.

Ben's annoying me now. He'll just carry on asking awkward questions that'll spoil the memory of last night's kiss if I don't get out of bed.

It feels almost painful to shuffle out of the cosy nylon of the sleeping bag and feel the cold air on my skin, even though I'm used to living in a house without central heating. I pull on my muddy jeans and put my fleece on straight away; stand up and get my balance as I step over my Li-Lo and Ben's legs and unzip the inner tent.

I know some of what I'm feeling must be to do with the Barcardi I drank last night. I didn't have much but I've never had a hangover before. A hand inside me seems to be grabbing my guts and twisting them. I'm going to be playing on the main stage tonight. I try to imagine it, like Sam says: visualise everything going well, and the crowd cheering, but instead it feels like I'm standing on the edge of Black Rocks and someone's trying to push me off.

I open the cool box, rummaging past the eggs and the milk, and find an opened carton of orange juice, nearly full and I neck the lot. For a second I think I'm going to spew but I take deep breaths. I unzip the tent and put my wellies on. I put them on the edge of the groundsheet in the porch last night. It's sunny outside, but windy.

When I come back from the Portaloo, the door of Ash's bus is open and Mum is sitting on its steps with her hands around a cup of coffee. She doesn't see me at first.

Mum's wearing an old jumper, pulled over her knees, and her face looks pale and tired. It sort of feels like I don't know her – like she's a stranger. She's staring into space and she looks so sad. Does she normally look like that, or is it because I haven't seen her properly for over a day? It feels like we've fallen out with each other. I only saw her when she was with Ash, watching that old band. I feel guilty about telling her not to come to our gig in Tina's Tea Tent. But tonight's about being part of something that's bigger than all of us.

She looks up.

'Want some coffee?' she asks.

I go over to the van. The dark green paint is starting to flake off, and I crumble a bit under my fingers.

'You okay?' I say. 'I think I'm a bit nervous already.'

'Relax. You've been working hard on those guitar parts.'

'I think I'm playing them in my dreams sometimes.'

'I heard about your gig yesterday. Pete said it was brilliant. Where's Ben?'

'Still in bed. His new girlfriend gave him a love bite.' I say it loud enough for Ben to hear from inside the tent, unless he's fallen asleep again.

Mum starts shaking and she spills some coffee. I grab her shoulders. I don't know what else to do. She looks up at me. She's laughing – she looks so different from just a few minutes ago. She's laughing too much to speak.

'Nasty things, love bites.' She wipes her eyes on the back of her hand. 'Ben didn't leave you to wander around on your own, did he?'

'I had a great time.' I don't really want to go into it. If we were at home, I might tell Mum more about it, but tents aren't exactly sound-proof.

I hear giggling from Pete's awning. It sounds like Emma's

trying to get the kids to brush their teeth while Pete's doing something silly to distract them. The awning unzips. Pete appears in the doorway, bent over, with little Karen on his shoulders, in Disney princess pyjamas and wellies.

'Run faster, Daddy!' she shouts. She can be really bossy sometimes. Pete sees us and looks a bit sheepish, as if it's wrecking his rock 'n' roll image.

'Morning,' Pete says. 'Grand day for it so far.'

Ash sticks his head out of the window of his van, waving at Pete. He's already got a spliff in his hand. He told me that when he's had a few spliffs, he feels like he can slow time down; his ideas flow and everything seems more intense. Part of me wonders if he's smoked so much weed he just needs it to feel normal. Maybe being stone-cold sober is a weird experience for him. I don't know if he'll be able to change, or if that's just the way he is.

Pete straightens up. Little Karen is bouncing up and down, kicking his chest in her wellies to make him run around the field. We're all together, Mission Control, about to play at a festival again, and it's like being in the middle of a big family. The thought makes my cheeks feel warm.

'Emma's cooking a fry-up. We'd better get a decent breakfast inside us,' he says.

'Sounds tempting,' Mum says, smiling. I realise I feel okay again. My headache and the horrible gut-wrenching feeling have gone. I'm going to concentrate on getting everything right today.

I can see Tracey, in her purple waterproof, picking her way between the tents behind Pete's van.

'Give me a minute,' I say. I follow Tracey, ignoring the smirk that Pete and Mum exchange.

Tracey hasn't seen me. She stops next to a small pop-up tent.

'Hi,' I say. I'm unsure exactly how we left things last night. I think she just wants to be friends, but that's okay. Better than nothing. She looks up, surprised.

'Is that your tent?' I ask, because I can't think of anything else to say.

471

'I got it for my birthday. I'm not sharing Dad's tent any more. I mean, look at it.'

She points at a faded orange ridge tent, patched and stained.

'Watch what you're saying,' says a gruff voice from inside. 'It's lasted me thirty years, man and boy.'

'You can tell,' Tracey shouts back.

'I thought you were camped round here somewhere.' I feel a bit self-conscious. I must look a mess. I'm wearing the same clothes as yesterday and I bet my face still has some glitter on it. I feel dirty, clammy from getting wet and drying out again all through the day. I must smell a bit. As soon as I've got some privacy, I'll have a washing up bowl wash. My hair must be sticking up all over the place. I try to smooth it down and make it cover my eyes at the front, but it just seems to curl up again.

Tracey laughs. She's managing to look okay, a bit wind-swept, but beautiful.

'I've got some Shockwaves in my tent. I can't go on stage looking like a tramp.'

'You're fine.'

'I just wondered. Do you want some breakfast? A proper cooked one?' What am I saying? I'm sure it'll be fine, but it'll be embarrassing. I'm sure everyone will be able to tell how much I fancy Tracey.

'With your band?' She seems a bit surprised.

'You'll like them – I hope. Ash is a bit mad, but he's nice. I hope you don't mind swearing.'

'Okay. Thanks.'

'It'll be vegetarian.'

'Sure they won't mind?'

I glance over towards our camp.

'They might start winking at each other though. I think Pete, our drummer, saw us all last night. Thought it was some kind of date. I'll set them straight.'

'They'll get over it.' She puts her arm around my shoulder and kisses me on the cheek. She's brushed her teeth and her mouth smells minty and fresh. I haven't, so I keep my mouth shut. I can't work out the way she's looking at me.

Kaz

The wind whips the flags so hard, they seem to be about to blow straight off their poles and fly into the air.

The performer on the main stage is singing a song called 'The Wind Is Getting Stronger'. That's the last thing we need.

Slate-grey clouds block out the blue sky, bringing raindrops like a hail of bullets. I dodge under the cover of a stall, not caring what it's selling. I just want to get out of the torrential rain shower.

'Ridiculous weather,' says a tall, blonde woman, arranging a row of jackets. They're patched together: pinstripe, denim and corduroy combined, artfully distressed, but well made, with sewn-on punk badges and corsages made from old lace. I look at her and smile.

'We make them,' she says. 'Everything's recycled.'

She's not really paying much attention to me. Her little awning is heaving with people sheltering from the rain and she rushes to tell a bloke off for smoking inside it. Eventually, the rain subsides and people slowly shuffle outside again.

'Why won't they buy anything?' the blonde woman complains. She handles the clothes, her own creations, so protectively.

There's another girl, near the entrance of the tent. She's busy with a small gaggle of customers, cooing over a black-painted cork board hung with jewellery sparkling in the sunlight and tinkling in the wind.

'The earrings are just two pounds each,' the girl says, smiling. She looks a few years younger than the nervy blonde designer; in her mid-twenties, with copper-coloured hair framing her face. 'We make them ourselves, out of tin cans and old toys and things.'

I have the rest of the stall to myself now. Towards the back there are dresses, made from beautiful material, embroidery, boning and corsetry. You could get married in one of them and so much work has gone into each one that it's reflected in the price-tag. They're so gorgeous, like works of art.

I can't stop looking at one dress, its embroidered black satin bodice descending into a bustle of ripped lace and strips torn from old band t-shirts. It's wild and beautifully made. I imagine myself wearing it on stage. Maybe I'm imagining myself the way I used to be.

I was going to put my share of the fee from playing the festival towards a solar water heater for the bathroom, and this dress would really eat into that – and when am I ever going to wear it again? We haven't got any more gigs lined up. Would any venues let us get away with an underage guitarist?

'Can I try this dress on?' I ask, before the cautious half of my brain knows what I'm doing.

'Of course. The changing room's just over here.' There's a curtained-off section at the back of the stall, with a full-length mirror hanging up and moving with the wind.

I look down at myself; my muddy gardening wellies, my red work overalls and waterproof, but the woman running the stall doesn't seem bothered. The weather makes glamourous dressing impossible, which is one of the reasons why trying this dress on is madness.

Flattened cardboard boxes have been laid on the ground to cover the mud. The blonde girl hangs the dress up in the cubicle for me while I struggle out of my boots. I pad towards the changing room and draw the curtains around me.

Goose pimples appear on my arms as I expose them to the air, peeling off the overalls, my jumper and thermal vest. I hold the dress up against myself. It's strapless. I take off my greying bra, repaired with bodged stitches. I can't remember when I last had a new bra. I feel like a sea-creature out of its shell, and I'm glad I can at least keep my leggings on.

I take the dress off its hanger and pull it on. The corset laces at the front, so I don't need any help to put it on. It fits perfectly: the feeling of the satin against my bare skin feels decadent. I take the bobble out of my hair and run my fingers through the tangles. I'm ready to look at myself.

'Are you okay in there? Just let me know if you need any help?' the blonde woman asks.

'I'm fine, thanks,' I say. I'm not fine, not really.

The woman staring back at me in the mirror has been a stranger for fifteen years. She can carry off an outrageous dress, the skin of her shoulders pale against the dark material and the unruly curls of her hair.

I can't keep this dress. It would be stupid. It's over £200, and worth it. Enough money to feed me and Jason for over a month. So why am I twitching back the curtains and stepping out of the changing cubicle with a big smile on my face?

The girls running the stall turn towards me, their mouths open.

'It is you, isn't it? I thought you looked a bit like her, but then…You look fantastic. It's as if I made the dress for you.' The blonde woman stares at me, before appraising the dress with a more professional gaze, adjusting some of the ruffles. I look at myself in the mirror again, noticing the silver laminated *Access All Areas* pass with my name on it tangled up amongst my scruffy clothes. I'd forgotten I was wearing it.

I hug myself, to keep warm in the icy wind, and I catch the red-haired girl staring at the scar tissue on my arm from the bike accident. I wonder how she thinks I got it.

She takes one of the jackets I was looking at earlier off the racks.

'Try this. You'll be freezing on stage later – at least at first.'

The blonde woman shakes her head.

'She can't wear that. No one will be able to see the dress.' She makes a beeline for a rail labelled "Genuine Vintage", and before I know it, I'm slipping on a black velvet bolero with a diamante clasp.

'Gorgeous. Just gorgeous.' She turns me round to face the mirror again.

The blonde woman takes my hair in her hands and holds it up, twisting it to the top of my head. I'm starting to feel like a Barbie doll. I remember this pleasurable but helpless feeling of being styled. I stare at the crumpled heap of clothes I took off like an old shedded skin.

'Who's doing your hair and makeup?' she asks.

I laugh.

'It's our first gig in fifteen years. We'd be carrying all our gear onstage ourselves if a mate hadn't volunteered to do it. I might let my son loose on my eyeliner, but...'

'I'll do it,' the blonde girl offers. 'I'll do a great job.'

'Lil is brilliant,' the other woman tells me. 'She's styled lots of artists.'

I bite my lip and stare at the mirror.

'I can't afford it. I shouldn't buy the dress either, really. I'm sorry to waste your time.'

'The dress is yours. And the jacket. I couldn't possibly take your money.' Lil touches my arm, and gives me an intense look, a mixture of pride, admiration and pity.

'We'd be thrilled to see you up there wearing our clothes,' the other girl says, rummaging for something in her money belt.

'Mission Control were the first band I ever saw. I was fifteen,' Lil says. 'Spiral Sun was my first festival.'

I nod. I don't want her to say anymore.

The copper-haired girl gives me a stylish business card. *Liliam: Recycled Couture and Vintage Heaven. Lilian Cooper-Cox and Miriam Smith.* Very upmarket.

'You could give us a little mention or a "like" on Facebook if you want, though,' she says. Lil looks annoyed for a second but then she smiles wryly.

'Miriam's got the business brains. Always an eye for an opportunity. I wouldn't have got anywhere without her.'

I look at myself in the mirror again, not wanting to

change back into my scruffy clothes. A few more hours trying to be anonymous before Kaz K returns from the dead.

'I brought my Doc Martens to wear on stage. They're a bit scruffy...'

'They'll be perfect. And no one'll be looking at your feet.'

'Can I leave the dress here? What time shall I come back, for the makeup and everything?'

'About half five,' Lil says.

I look out of the stall, at the mud and people trudging around in waterproofs. It's raining heavily again, although the sky has patches of blue.

'You'll look amazing,' Miriam says.

'Thank you,' I tell them. 'I can't believe it.' Until I put this dress on, stepping on stage in front of all those people didn't feel real. Now I almost feel I can actually do it. I don't want to tell the others about the dress yet. I can't wait to see the look on their faces when they see me in my stage outfit.

Jason

Waiting for nail varnish to dry is usually one of the most boring things ever. Not today. I sit with my hands spread out on the table in Pete's campervan.

'I'd love to do music at uni,' Tracey says. 'Music runs in my family but no one's really made a living at it. I'll be the first person in my family to go to uni. I want to prove I'm good enough, you know?'

'You have to get really top grades, don't you? And do all those proper music exams.'

'I'm already studying for Grade Eight.' She's not showing off. She's just not scared of being talented.

'Woah.' I say. 'So you'll walk your GCSE music exam?'

'You're the one who's almost headlining a festival. You've not even been playing for a year.'

'Don't remind me. It must be a fluke. Maybe I'm not actually any good.' I feel my thumb-nail. Still tacky, but almost dry.

I pick up the Marlin and check it's in tune. I don't know which guitar to use onstage. I'll run through the whole set on each guitar and see what sounds best. I've put a battery in my practice amp so I can do it properly. I try to ignore the sick, jittery feeling in my stomach. I just need to keep busy and be as well prepared as possible. Mum said she'd run through the songs with me. I don't know where she's got to.

'Can I stick around and listen?' Tracey asks.

'What about Cassi?'

Tracey sort of growls.

'She'll be with Ben, won't she? She's doing my head in. She doesn't take anything seriously.'

'It'll be boring. Just me playing along to our rehearsal tracks on Pete's iPod.'

'Can I make you a t-shirt to wear on stage? I've got some fabric pens in my tent. Random, I know. Me and Cassi used to do things like that together.'

Tracey is good at art. I've seen her drawings up on the wall of the art room. She understands where I'm coming from. My eyes widen.

'You could write the chorus of 'Rootless in Babylon?' on it.'

'I've got a plain white t-shirt. It'll stand out more.'

'Will it be tight on me?'

Tracey laughs, and nudges me.

'What are you like?'

Chapter 36
Survivors

Jason

It's forty minutes before we're due onstage. The singer from New Model Army is playing. I expected Mum to be watching him, and I scan for her red overalls in the crowd, but she's nowhere to be seen. She's not behind the barrier either with the photographers.

I show my backstage wristband and my *Access All Areas* pass to the security guard on the gate, and he lets me through with a smile.

Being backstage is not as exciting as you think it's going to be. There's a marquee with food but it's just sandwiches, crisps and fruit, and a few crates of beer. There are no famous people hanging around drinking champagne.

Jeff's here, though; the landscape gardening bloke who works with Mum. He's shifting amplifiers up a ramp leading into the back of the main stage. I feel lost. Tracey's not allowed back here and I couldn't find Ben. I've got my trainers in a carrier bag, so I can put them on when I go on stage, and my Marlin in its case, slung over my shoulder.

I can feel myself shaking. I thought I'd feel protected with the t-shirt Tracey made, my military-style charity shop jacket and a bit of makeup, but I feel more scared than ever.

'Jason!' Pete shouts. He's waving from the doorway of a portacabin. I walk over to it. He looks normal: jeans, an Iron Maiden t-shirt, a lumberjack shirt.

Mum comes through the gap in the fencing. She's not wearing the dress hanging up in Ash's van. She looks like she should be on an album cover, more like Kaz K than on any of the posters I've seen of her; the queen of goths, her hair piled onto her head like a back-combed nest, eyeliner sweeping towards her temples. My mouth hangs open. A group of people are hanging around on the other side of the fence, staring at her.

'Fucking hell, Kaz,' Pete says. 'You'll have all the blokes' eyes out on stalks.'

Mum smiles, the way she does when she's trying to pretend she's not scared.

'I'm freezing,' she says. She's wearing a short dress – the top of it's like a corset, which shows the cleavage part of her boobs. I feel myself blushing. Her dress and the little short jacket thing look amazing. The only thing spoiling it is that she's wearing her gardening wellies and carrying an orange plastic bag containing her red overalls and Doc Martens.

'Look what Tracey made,' I say. I hope no one notices my face is burning as I show them my t-shirt with its spiky lettering:

I'm nothing and no one and nowhere.
Take me away from this world that doesn't care.
Somewhere I belong, where I fit my skin:
Rootless in Babylon – let me begin!

Mum smiles, happy, but with that weird twist in her mouth. Shit, she's about to cry. I dig some bog roll out of my pocket and hand it to her.

She blinks.

'I can't ruin my makeup. And neither can you. Unless you want to look like Bob Smith.' She grins and we hug each other. Sometimes it doesn't feel like she's my mum anymore. We're bandmates, too, and that's just as important.

She looks really cool: vulnerable but tough. I'm aiming for a similar look. At times like this, we're equals. I hope she's not going to ruin it by fussing about whether I've had any tea.

Ash walks past, carrying his random noise generator. He stops dead when he sees us, but we're staring back at him. Half his face is covered in a tangle of bright green and pink wool.

'Pete's kids made it for me. It was a fun afternoon,' he says, through the woollen strands.

Mum raises an eyebrow.

'To make up for having to shave off your beard?'

'You look nice,' Ash says to Mum with a cheeky smile.

'Sure you're not going to fall out of that dress when we're playing?'

'I'm very well supported, actually.'

Mum swings her carrier bag at him, and he scuttles towards the back of the stage. We join Pete in the dressing room. We take our wellies off before we go through the door and leave them next to Pete's, on a bit of cardboard. I sit down on a plastic chair, fiddling with the zip on my gig bag, unsure whether to get my Marlin out or not, just to keep my hands warmed up. The New Model Army guy still has fifteen minutes of his set left, so there's loads of time left before I play my first chord up there.

The sky darkens outside and it pelts with rain. I watch the droplets splashing on the surface of the backstage mud. My stomach feel strange and hollow, even though I ate some cereal before I got washed and dressed for the gig.

'At least we'll be in the dry,' Pete says.

'That's what you always said,' Mum tells him. She stares out at the rain and I know she's thinking about Daz.

'I ran through the set earlier. I think I'm going to be okay,' I say.

'I can't believe I convinced myself to do this.' Mum bites her lip.

'No backing out now.' Pete puts his enormous hand over hers. I can't believe Mum's hands are big enough to play those heavy strings on her bass, but they are. Over the weeks of rehearsals, she's developed callouses on her fingertips and the strength to play a full set. We've worked hard.

The rain stops, as suddenly as it started. The main stage is pumping out dance music now. My stomach feels like it's doing somersaults.

Sam appears at the door of the portacabin, his waterproof dripping.

'You need to start setting up now. Everyone okay?'

We follow Sam up the ramp to the stage. I wipe my wellies on a mat and we stand in the wings. Even though there are still a few raindrops, there are quite a lot of people standing there waiting for us. Marilyn Richards is in the pit at the front of the stage, clutching a large camera.

Emma's standing near the mixing desk, holding onto each kid by the hand. I can see Ben, near the front, with Cassi holding onto his arm like she's won him in a fair. I want to wave, but that would spoil the moment when we come out on stage properly. Where's Tracey?

Pete gets to work, setting up his drum kit, with Jeff helping. Ash is already wiring up his equipment, deep in concentration, but still wearing his woolly beard.

'Where's your spare guitar?' Sam asks.

'I'm going to play Daz's Marlin,' I tell him.

'You'll need your Strat, too. If you break a string. I've got a spare bass for Kaz. Just in case.' He inclines his head towards a Fender Precision bass, already waiting by the side of the stage. I've seen it before, hanging on the wall of his studio.

'You've got time to fetch it, Jason,' Mum says. 'The Strat's a better instrument anyway, especially with that new neck.'

'Be quick,' Sam tells me. 'We've got to tune it, too.'

I dump everything next to the mixing desk and run down the ramp before making my way carefully through the mud – I've put on my clean jeans and I don't want to go on stage with them covered in splashes. It's only a short dash to the backstage campsite.

The light outside is weird but, after all the weather we've had this weekend, nothing surprises me anymore. The clouds on the far side of the stage look very dark. If it rains, I could throw on my cagoule before running back to the stage. I wish I'd remembered to bring my Stratocaster – I feel a bit cut down to size. It's just one of those things that remind me I don't know what I'm doing; I'm fourteen and probably too young to be in a band with my mum. I'm half glad to be doing something; to be moving, rather than just watching the seconds drag by until show time.

I left my Strat in its case in Sam's tent. I rush towards it. The black cloud sweeps overhead, blocking out the sky. It's almost dark. This is weird. I fumble with the tent zip.

The wind suddenly rips through the tents and knocks me sideways onto the mud. The tent starts to buck and strain against the guy ropes. I grab onto the tent pole. The storm batters my face. Whole tents are taking off. Pop-up tents, whirling into the sky. Gazebos, umbrellas, chairs; sheets of tarpaulin spinning through the air. Crashes and bangs everywhere, but the loudest thing is the rain hammering on canvas and the wind roaring. The crowd is screaming: proper frightened screaming.

I can hear screaming from just a few tents away, too. Someone terrified. I've got to help them. I try to struggle towards the scream, fighting the force of the wind, so strong, like an invisible wrestler. I push myself along, past tents squashed flat; vans rocking so hard they might fall over.

It's Tracey. Clinging on to her tent. It's flying above her head, like a fat kite. It seems impossible. The wind's so strong, it might take Tracey, too, but I feel like I'm in one of those dreams where I can't move, and I can't quite reach her.

The wind seems to die down a bit. I jump up and grab her tent, hang onto it, and manage to sit on it as the material flaps around me like a mad parachute, trying to escape. I stand up. The tent pops back up and rolls around. I keep my foot on it.

'My fiddle's in there.' Tracey's voice trembles. 'I was getting changed, and I –'

'You're hurt.'

A trickle of blood runs from her wrist, onto the pale nylon material of her tent. We stare at it for a second.

'I felt a tent peg dig into me, but...'

'Hold your arm up on your chest. I think it slows down the bleeding.'

She doesn't do anything but just stands there. I have to take her arm and put it gently in position, with her other hand on her elbow.

'Wait there.'

483

I grab her pop-up tent, and drag it through the muddy path between the guy ropes. I shove the whole thing into the porch of Sam's tent. I think about my Strat. It must be time for us to go on stage now but I can't leave Tracey like this.

I zip up Sam's tent again and look around as I make my way back to Tracey. The storm has calmed down, making it easier to see what's happened. Loads of tents have collapsed, and other pop-up tents that escaped are now rolling around at the side of vans like they're pissed and have forgotten where they're camping. Tracey's dad's old tent has survived, perfectly.

When I get back to Tracey, she's shivering. I put my jacket around her shoulders. I pull toilet roll out of my pocket, hold it against her wrist, and guide her between the tents towards the gap in the fence leading into the arena. The tissue gets soaked in blood quickly and I feel it trickling down my arm.

'You can't come through here,' a security guard says. I'm not really listening. I look straight past him. Where the stage was is now a mangled heap of white canvas and metal, already fenced off and surrounded by security. There's no one else to be seen but there's still music thumping from the dance tent.

'Mum – everyone…' I gasp.

Tracey stares at the destruction, totally stunned. The security guard sees the blood and lets us through.

'First Aid's over there. On the other side of what used to be the stage.'

Kaz

There won't be time for a proper soundcheck but I warm up my fingers by running through 'Rootless in Babylon'. Jeff has almost finished setting up our gear. He's just giving Pete a hand with the drum kit.

I wish I'd told Jason he needed a spare guitar on stage.

There's so much he needs to know, little things we just assume he knows. This festival is his first taste of rock 'n' roll reality and he's still in love with it, despite the dreadful weather and smelly toilets.

My fingers automatically find the notes. The song is hard-wired into my brain. It's only eight months since I played it on Jason's acoustic guitar, when he'd never played a note before. He works so hard and he's growing in confidence all the time. I'm doing this for him, because I let him down so badly…

'What the fuck?' Pete shouts. The sky above us has turned as dark as lead. The striped canopy of the cocktail bar breaks loose and flies low, skimming the heads of the crowd. Pop up tents and chairs sail through the air as if they weigh nothing. The sound engineers cling desperately onto their gazebo as it lifts into the air, and the crowd scatters.

'Get down!' Ash yells. He throws himself on top of me and we fall onto the stage. I land on top of my bass, breath knocked out of me.

The stage canopy starts to lift. Its supports groan, bend and snap. Ash covers the top of my head with his hands.

It seems to happen in slow motion. The metal rim of the stage comes crashing back down, folding back on itself like the hood of an old fashioned pram. Lights smash and crash to earth. Everything shakes.

Horizontal rain blasts into my face. I'm soaked. I lie there, not moving.

'Are you okay?' Ash says. I find myself lying in his arms and, for a second, I don't want him to let go.

'What happened?' I'm half-blinded by rain and mascara running into my eyes.

'I don't know.'

I sit up and stare at the pile of mangled metal and canvas. It just missed the drum riser. Pete looks gobsmacked, still sitting at his drum stool.

Where Jeff was standing, next to the drums, a figure is lying face-down, his body covered by the white canopy.

'Jeff!'

I pick my way over to the drum riser. Jeff doesn't move.

'Help!' I shout.

Two uniformed first aiders are already rushing towards the stage platform and they swiftly take over, examining the body.

We look at each other hopelessly, the rain soaking everything.

'Grab the gear. Get everything off and in the dry!' Pete shouts. He takes my bass.

Other people help us. The organisers, other musicians, crew, security staff, I don't know who, forming a human chain. Water runs down my face, my eyes stinging. I pass over drums, amps, mixing desks and effects pedals to the next person, in a numb blur.

Someone passes me a carrier bag with two black size nine trainers inside. My heart seems to stop.

'Where's Jason?' I wipe my eyes on my soaked sleeve. 'Has anyone seen my son?'

Not again. Not again. I don't realise I'm screaming until the next person in the chain grabs me.

A tall man with long dark hair and a lean wolfish face takes me away from the stage to sit down in one of the portacabins. He puts a padded hi-vis jacket around my shoulders. The bag with Jason's shoes inside is on my knee. He opens a bottle and pours something into a plastic glass. He gives it to me and I take a sip. I pull a face. Vodka?

'Drink it, to calm you down,' he says. 'We'll find him. I'm sure he's okay. He wasn't on the stage.'

When he leaves me on my own again, I realise he's Justin Sullivan, from New Model Army.

Jason

We walk to the first aid tent as quickly as we can. There's loads of damage out here.

'It was a twister,' a bloke with a can of lager is telling someone. He's right. It's as if a giant monster has stomped through in a huge circle, destroying as it went.

Tina's Tea Tent has gone. There are just chairs and tables and a piano left behind.

There's a queue at the first aid tent but people part when they see the blood and let us get to the front. My t-shirt is covered in it. They probably think it's mine.

'What's happened to the people on stage?' I ask. 'My band were setting up. My mum...'

A girl in a St John Ambulance uniform, only a few years older than us, makes us sit down, then pushes Tracey's sleeve back. There's a lot of blood but, after she's pressed a gauze pad against it for a while, she inspects it. I can make out a jagged cut several centimetres long.

'It's quite a deep wound,' the girl says. 'You'll need stitches. You might have nicked the vein.'

Tracey shuts her eyes and bites her lip. I hold her other hand.

The first aider starts to bandage Tracey's wrist tightly and I help to hold the ends of the bandage. I always thought I was squeamish but I'm actually okay. Just numb.

'Someone's been badly hurt, onstage,' the first aider says. 'We've called the air ambulance. Looks like you'll need to get on it too. What caused the injury?'

'A tent peg,' I say. 'Her tent almost blew away.' I've got to stay here and look after Tracey, at least until the helicopter lands. What if Mum's the one who was hurt? She'll be worrying like mad about me.

'This is nuts. Just nuts,' the first aider says. 'I mean, this is Derbyshire.'

'Where's my dad?' Tracey asks. She looks scared. Then she laughs. 'He's probably in the bar.'

'I'll fetch him,' says a man with a long ginger beard, waiting in the queue.

'He's called Dan Monks.'

I'm about to ask him to pass on a message to anyone backstage that I'm okay but Pete appears, his face bright red. He's soaking wet.

'Fucking hell,' he gasps, staring at me. 'What happened?'

'It's not my blood,' I explain. 'It's Tracey's.'

'Your mum's having a meltdown.'

'Is she hurt?'

'No, it's Jeff. Thank fuck you're okay. She thinks it's Mission Control's fault. Keeps going on about the band being cursed. Thinks you're fucking dead.'

'Go and find her,' Tracey says. 'I'll be okay. My dad'll be here soon.'

'Are you sure?'

'I'll see you later.'

'There is no later. The festival's wrecked.'

'That's what you think.'

She pulls me towards her with her good hand, by the neck of my t-shirt. Her t-shirt. She kisses me on the lips, in front of everyone in the first aid tent, like she really means it.

I pull away reluctantly. Tracey gives me my jacket back, glancing at the label.

'Top Shop.' She raises her eyebrows. 'You do know it's a girl's label, right?'

'I got it from a charity shop.'

'Jason. We need to go.' Pete looks freezing.

I put on my jacket and button it up, to tone down the zombie apocalypse look. I don't want Mum to think I'm actually dead and have risen from the grave.

Kaz

I can't breathe properly. People are loading so much rescued gear into the portacabin that I feel trapped. I can't stop shivering. Ash is here, holding my hand. He's still got the tangled wool beard – it's sticking out of his overall pocket but at least he's not wearing it. He seems very calm and still.

'It's a sign. We shouldn't have tried to play here.' I gasp for air.

'You can do a lot of things, Kaz, but you're not responsible for the weather.'

488

'I shouldn't have taken my eyes off Jason.'

'He wasn't on the stage. Going to fetch that guitar might have saved his life.'

'Where is he?'

'Pete's gone to find him. It's a mess out there. It's not just the main stage. It was actually a tornado, a twister.'

'See? It was out to get us. Mission Control were the eye of the storm.'

Ash sighs and takes his hand away from mine.

'Kaz – I've talked some bollocks in my time. I should know. This isn't helping.' He opens a small tobacco tin, pulls out a pre-rolled spliff, and lights it.

'I don't think you're allowed to smoke in here,' I say.

'Like anyone cares now.' All the same, he leans in the doorway, breathing smoke into the still evening air. The patch of sky I can see through the window is blue. We were never meant to play this festival. I take another gulp of vodka. The taste makes me retch but at least it makes me feel everything a bit less keenly.

'She's in here.' Pete booms. I rush to the doorway.

'Mum!'

Jason's hair's all over the place and his eyeliner has smudged thickly around his eyes. He's splashed with mud. I hug him tightly.

There's something red smeared on his face, too.

'You're hurt?'

'It's Tracey. She cut herself trying to rescue her tent. She's okay but she's going off in the air ambulance – with Jeff. They're going to A&E. We should go and watch.' He sounds more excited than traumatised.

'It's my fault Jeff got hit by that lighting rig.'

'How can it be?' Jason throws his hands up.

'He wouldn't be here if it wasn't for me.'

Jason exchanges a worried look with Pete and Ash. They obviously all think I'm nuts. They don't believe me.

'Is it your fault Tracey got cut by her own tent peg?' Jason says. 'I know it's really weird but it was just a storm.'

'The UK has more tornados for its area than any other

489

country,' Ash says. 'Just most of the time, they're in an empty field.'

'This one wasn't empty.' Pete opens a can of beer from the slab put in here for us. What's the matter with them? They're being so calm.

'I've wasted all of our time. Our equipment could be ruined.'

Jason grabs me by the shoulders. It always surprises me how tall and strong he's grown. It feels like I'm the child.

The eerie quietness is filled with the sound of a helicopter circling the site and approaching the ground.

'It wasn't your fault, Mum. I'm just glad you're okay. That's the air ambulance. You need to see Jeff. You can't blame yourself.'

'Fine. I'll come.'

Jason

Tracey waves with her good hand as she climbs into the helicopter. Someone's going to give her dad a lift to the hospital. The helicopter has landed in an empty field, where the grass hasn't been trodden on and turned into mud.

'I'm sorry, I'm so sorry,' Mum sobs.

Jeff's on a stretcher, his head inside one of those plastic things stopping him from moving his neck in case he's damaged his spine. Pete is right. Mum has flipped, but I can't blame her. It must seem like history's repeating itself.

Marilyn Richards films the scene of devastation with a hand-held video recorder. She hasn't spoken to any of us yet. This will make an exciting chapter for her book, even if it's the last one.

Pete drags Mum to a safe distance, as the paramedics wheel Jeff's trolley onto the helicopter. Her face looks distorted, twisted by grief and blaming herself for everything.

'I'm never playing again. We're not safe,' I hear her say, before she buries her face in Pete's jacket. His face looks blank, out of his depth. Me and Ash exchange a look, as if he's had enough of her behaving like this too.

There's not much I can do. I just hug myself, shivering as the helicopter blades start to turn, creating so much turbulence it feels like the tornado has returned.

'Jase!'

Ben runs towards me, Cassi stumbling along behind him as the helicopter starts to lift, flattening the wet grass and blowing the leaves on the trees.

Ben bundles into me. The air ambulance steadily rises into the air and then speeds off towards Derby, making it quiet enough to hear each other talk.

'After it happened, we went into the dance tent for shelter. No one even knew about the tornado in there. They thought we'd made it up, until they went out and looked for themselves.'

'Tracey's on the helicopter. She got hurt – her tent almost blew away.'

'Oh my God!' Cassi shrieks.

'I thought you were on stage. I didn't know what had happened to you,' Ben says.

'I had to go back to get my Strat. I didn't know I needed a spare guitar.' It seems like ages ago. I look at my watch. It's only half an hour since we were on the stage starting our soundcheck.

'Mum's in a real state,' I tell Ben, quietly. 'She's blaming herself for the tornado. Our roadie's head was cut open by the lighting rig. They don't know how bad it is.'

'Shit. It could have been you.'

Ben's right. I could have been standing behind the drum riser, soundchecking. I don't even know if my guitar is okay.

Tracey's dad walks towards me. His face is pale with shock and he doesn't look very steady on his feet.

'The medics have just told me about you,' he says. He clasps my shoulder. 'You did a grand job.'

'I'll make sure her tent's safe.'

'You're a good lad.'

He walks away, towards the carpark field.

'You saved her!' Cassi stands on tiptoe in her wellies and kisses me on the cheek.

We walk, not really knowing where we're going but staring at the fenced-off destruction where the stage used to be. After all the effort to get the band back together and all the work we put in, I feel like crying but somehow I can't, like I'm blocked up inside. Everything's too weird.

'I knew it!' A woman's voice calls. 'I knew you looked familiar.' It's Tina, standing in the middle of what used to be her tea tent, now just an empty stretch of muddy grass with chairs and tables already folded and stacked up. She's bundled up in a khaki coat that almost reaches the ground. 'You're the spit of Daz Lightning. I wish I'd got to see you play with the band.'

'Yeah, sorry, that's never going to happen now. Mum thinks we're under a curse or something. We're over, before we even started again.'

'But hundreds of people were waiting for you to come onstage.'

'I'll ask my dad,' Cassi says. 'He might be able to rig a new tent up.'

'My PA system's not as big as the main stage's, but it'll do the job.'

'Leave it to us,' Ben tells me. Suddenly, they're all smiling.

'Go and get warm,' Tina says. 'You look freezing.'

'Okay…' I slowly walk away, towards our camp, not convinced they can do anything. Even if they can make miracles happen, what if Mum, Pete and Ash refuse to play? I'm on my own now and everything seems hopeless. I hang onto the wire fence surrounding the stage and start crying, hoping no one notices me.

Kaz

I'm wearing my red overalls and thick jumper again. My beautiful corset dress is hanging up to dry in Ash's camper van. I wish we could go back home but we've been blocked in by about five tents and three cars now, parked haphazardly in the fire lane, and no one knows where they've come from.

Emma comes out of the camper van, carrying a box of red wine and two plastic glasses.

'The kids are shattered. Too much excitement for one day. The tornado actually knocked them over.'

She opens the wine box and pours a large measure for me, putting it in my hands.

'That'll warm you up.'

The awning is cosy, lit by a battery-powered strip-light. It's dark outside now and I can hear a faint hum of generators and the distant thump of the dance tent, which kept going; a heartbeat, through the tornado. At least it's keeping people warm and safe inside.

Pete and Ash are sitting at the table, several empty beer cans between them.

We should have been celebrating by now, or at least relieved it was all over.

My phone bleeps. A text from Mum – she's heard about the tornado on the news. I reply quickly, to tell her we're okay. Nothing from Jeff, but how could there be? He's probably in intensive care.

'Jeff got in the way of the curse,' I say.

'There is no curse.' Ash glares at me. 'Daz died because he was being a twat. End of story. It's been freak weather all weekend. We're all okay, aren't we?'

I stare back at him. Is it really that simple? I feel something give inside my head. Something like relief. Daz has been dead for a very long time. Ash can call him a twat if he likes. It won't hurt Daz – it didn't while he was alive.

'I felt that stage rig whistle right past my head. I'm really fucking lucky,' Pete says. 'Jeff too. He was only knocked out for a minute. A few stitches, a night in hospital, and he'll be right as rain.'

'What if it made me feel better to blame myself?' I ask, clinging to the shreds of everything I've believed up to now. He's right. There is no chain of events; just choices we

493

make and things beyond our control.

'Kaz – please…' Ash says. But I smile back at him, feeling free at last.

'Hey, at least you tried,' Emma says.

Someone tugs open the awning zip. It's Jason, wearing Pete's head torch, so it looks as if he's entering a cave. I put my arm over my eyes, dazzled.

'I pegged down Tracey's tent.' He turns the torch off, and puts a violin case down on the table. 'She hadn't used the guy ropes properly. She won't be coming back to the festival but at least it won't blow away. Can you put her fiddle in the campervan?'

Emma pours some wine into a mug and gives it to Jason.

'Don't worry, we'll keep it safe for her.' She smiles kindly at Jason.

Jason yawns, looking worn out. A year ago, I would have sent him off to bed, but now things are different. He sits next to me, on a canvas chair. I wish he was small enough to cuddle again.

'I don't think she really likes me, though. She's in the year above me.'

'She likes you, alright. You're her hero,' Pete says, turning to me. 'You should have seen her snogging him.' He roars with laughter.

'She seems very nice,' I say. It gave me a funny feeling this morning. Jason has really lost his heart to this girl. She's pretty, and she helped whisk eggs and make cups of tea without being asked first, with Jason buttering toast and giving her longing glances from under his fringe.

'Musical too,' Pete says.

'Why would she like me though?'

'I think that kiss said it all, Jason,' Pete says, a big grin on his face. 'Right there in the First Aid tent.'

Jason sips wine to hide his embarrassment. He give me the confiding look I remember from when he was little, when he was telling me a secret.

'I hope she does like me,' he whispers.

'She's not shy, is she?' Pete chuckles.

'The first impressive thing about Pete was that he was taller than me,' Emma laughs. 'He was so different from all those earnest types I knew at uni.'

'The other girls at school thought Daz was ugly,' I say. 'He was hardly the school heart-throb.'

'Until you saw his beautiful eyes behind his bottle-bottom glasses,' Pete says. I stick my middle finger up at him.

'It was the way he taught me to play the guitar. His hands – he was so patient with me. I could see something in him that no one else did. Maybe he thought I might become a better musician if he didn't lose his temper with me.'

'So how did you know he liked you?' Jason says, his voice croaky. I hope he's not coming down with a cold.

'It was over a year until our first kiss. I had to take a chance – we were friends first – I thought it might spoil everything.'

'What if you hadn't kissed him?' Jason asks.

'We would have exploded eventually –'

'It was obvious,' Pete says. 'He never said anything but you two were always together.'

'What about you, Ash?' Emma asks. 'Who was the first person you fell in love with?'

Ash looks cornered. He glances at me, appealing for help.

'Are we playing truth or dare now?' Jason asks, all wide-eyed innocence. But I know he remembers what Ash said to me in his Devon railway carriage.

'I thought you all knew.' Ash turns to me. 'I never stood a chance.'

'I know you've been seeing each other,' Jason says. 'I don't mind.'

'No we haven't,' I protest.

'Even when you were dead, I waited for you –' Ash says.

The awning unzips, and Ben bursts in, followed by a young blonde girl and Sam. They look triumphant.

'It's all ready,' Ben says. 'Tina's Café Mark Two.'

'We grabbed most of your gear out of the portacabin,'

495

Sam says, handing Jason his guitar case. 'You can just turn up and start playing.'

'What?' I gasp.

'I should have told you they were planning it but I never thought it would happen,' Jason says, gulping his wine. 'I thought you'd say no, anyway.'

'We've rigged up a stage – where Tina's Cafe used to be,' Ben says. 'We've been going round telling everyone Mission Control are on in half an hour.'

'It's a shame we're not playing,' Ash sighs. 'Kaz probably thinks we'll all die in an earthquake or something.'

'But people are really excited,' the blonde girl says.

I stand up.

'We'll play.' I look round at the others. 'You're up for it, aren't you?'

'We've already set up your drums, Pete,' Sam says. 'I hope you don't mind.'

'They might need a bit of extra TLC after being in a tornado, but thanks, yeah.' Pete gives him a bear hug.

'Sorry, I had no idea what to do with your stuff, or even if it's still working,' Sam tells Ash.

'Don't worry, I'll cobble something together,' Ash says. He spins me round, holding me tightly around my waist. 'Come on, Kaz, that dress should have dried off a bit by now.'

I've never seen Jason with such a big grin on his face.

'Now it's our time,' he says.

Jason

We walk purposefully together, our wellies sloshing through the mud. The low buzz gets louder – the thump of the dance tent, mixed with old ska music from the reggae café. We pass the bar tent – a band is playing an acoustic set, with people singing along. The festival is still alive. I feel a glow in my chest; part excitement, part pride.

'This way,' Sam says. We stumble after him, towards a

long, low tent, lit by a dim glow, where Tina's Café used to be. Old punk music is coming from speakers inside. Loads of people are packed inside the tent, and more are standing around outside. As we get closer, festival-goers part to let us pass, nodding and smiling.

'I can't believe we get to see Mission Control again,' I hear someone say.

'He does look like Daz Lightning,' a woman comments.

'Well, of course he does.'

I smile and keep my head up, until we reach the tent. The edge of it flops down so low I have to bend down and make sure my guitar case doesn't get stuck. It looks like we're under a giant multi-coloured parachute, propped up by flagpoles.

'Cassi's dad put it together for us,' Ben says. 'We all helped.'

'There's no way out now. We've got to play.'

The crowd starts chanting 'Mission Control', clapping in time. A man, older than Mum, unzips his cagoule to reveal a faded Mission Control t-shirt with the *Calling Earth* artwork stretched tightly over his beer belly. Mum smiles and shakes his hand.

As we get closer to the stage, a bloke bares his arm and gives Mum a marker pen.

'If you sign it and draw the Mission Control logo, I'll get it tattooed on.'

'That's a lot of responsibility.' Mum does it anyway.

It's the same stage me and Ben played on yesterday. Ash's keyboard stand takes up most of the room at the back, so Pete's drum kit has been set up next to it on a sheet of hardboard balanced on beer crates.

Pete starts tuning his drums, using the special key he always keeps on a chain around his neck. The PA system is balanced on beer crates too – one speaker on either side of the stage, with the microphones already set up.

Ash's equipment is in a pile on the edge of the stage.

'We carried it over for you – I think it's everything,' Ben says.

'Thanks, guys.' Ash starts setting up his gear, patching cables into sockets, deep in concentration.

I take my Marlin out of its case and plug it in. I tuned it earlier, but I fiddle with the machine heads to make sure it's perfect. I wonder what Daz would have thought about all this.

Mum stops drawing on people and straps on her bass. She's wearing her new dress again, but with her beaten-up old jacket over the top. Her hair is messed up and her make up is smudged, but she looks great. The audience stares at her in wonder but she keeps her head down, tuning up, checking the monitors.

Sam sits down at a small mixing desk at the side of the stage, balanced on one of the café tables.

Tina fights her way through the crowd and steps onto the stage. She's got dressed up again, too, with a long red velvet cloak and a painted-on beard and moustache.

'I can't believe how excited I am about what's going to happen here tonight. From a total disaster, we've united and, literally, cobbled a stage together faster than I would have thought possible. Bear with them while they do their soundcheck, but for the first time in fifteen years, I give you, Mission Control!'

The crowd cheers and claps. I try not to look at them. I can feel my pulse coursing through me, fast and strong, as I finish setting up my stuff, sorting out my effects pedal and turning up the distortion.

I take my wellies off and stand on the stage in my socks. I'm streaked with mud, wearing my fleece, with my fringe sticking up at odd angles, but tonight I don't care. I glance at Mum. She nods to tell me she's ready too, a half-smile on her face. Pete gives us the thumbs-up.

'I think everything's working,' Ash says. 'Let's give it a go.'

Mum turns round and kisses him, in front of the whole crowd. By the time she faces the audience again, Ash looks confused, but overjoyed.

'This isn't going to be the slick comeback show we've

been rehearsing for,' Mum announces into the microphone. 'We've been through hell this evening and we've had a few drinks since then. I think I can say the same for most of you too.'

The audience laugh, holding up cans, bottles and boxes of booze. I spot Rachel in the middle of the crowd with her mates, well away from Ben, who sticks both thumbs up and grins at me.

'This is a gig for the survivors. I'd like to introduce my son, Jason Knight, the newest member of Mission Control. He's responsible for getting the band back together.'

Hundreds of curious eyes are on me. I feel my cheeks glowing red but I look back at them, all whooping and cheering. I can't help smiling.

'One, two, three, four!' Mum shrieks into the microphone.

We launch into 'Rootless in Babylon', just the way we rehearsed it.

I concentrate on playing at first, eyes fixed on my fretboard but, as the chorus starts, I feel more confident and look around. Everyone is singing along, jumping around, filling the tent with triumphant noise.

At the side of the tent, I see a purple waterproof jacket and a sweep of long brown hair, a girl with her arm in a sling. Tracey gives me a massive grin and I smile back, bouncing up and down on the stage with pure happiness.

Hello! More about Anne Grange

A lot has changed since I published *Outside Inside* and got stuck into writing *Distortion*.

Some of you probably think that I've taken a long time to write this novel but sometimes real life takes over: buying a house (not with the proceeds of my first novel unfortunately) and a change of career.

After finishing my MA in Writing, I launched my freelance writing business, Wild Rosemary Writing Services, so I've spent a lot of time helping other people to write their books: something I'm very proud of.

I get quite immersed in writing my novels. I started learning the bass but now I've picked up my trusty Telecaster for the first time in years and have started playing in an all-women punk band!

I decided that my character Jason should be obsessed by the Manic Street Preachers. I bought a few of their CDs second-hand and then got stuck in a terrible traffic jam with their first album on repeat, turning it up louder and louder. When I finally got home, I was a firm convert! I've now seen them several times and I now have a 'Libraries Gave us Power' tattoo – very apt in these dark days of public libraries under threat.

My offer still stands. If you spot a mistake in Distortion, I'll buy you a pint of cider and I'll credit you in the next edition of the book!

Printed in Great Britain
by Amazon